GIANT BONES

～ BY ～

PETER S. BEAGLE

A ROC BOOK

ROC
Published by the Penguin Group
Penguin Books USA Inc., 375 Hudson Street,
New York, New York 10014, U.S.A.
Penguin Books Ltd, 27 Wrights Lane,
London W8 5TZ, England
Penguin Books Australia Ltd, Ringwood,
Victoria, Australia
Penguin Books Canada Ltd, 10 Alcorn Avenue,
Toronto, Ontario, Canada M4V 3B2
Penguin Books (N.Z.) Ltd, 182–190 Wairau Road,
Auckland 10, New Zealand

Penguin Books Ltd, Registered Offices:
Harmondsworth, Middlesex, England

First published by Roc, an imprint of Dutton Signet,
a division of Penguin Books USA Inc.

First Printing, August, 1997
10 9 8 7 6 5 4 3 2 1

Art by Tony DiTerlizza Illustration.

 REGISTERED TRADEMARK—MARCA REGISTRADA

LIBRARY OF CONGRESS CATALOGING-IN-PUBLICATION DATA:
Beagle, Peter S.
Giant bones / by Peter S. Beagle.
    p.   cm.
ISBN 0-451-45651-3
1. Fantastic fiction, American.   I. Title.
PS3552.E13G53   1997
813'.54—dc21   96-29872
                                                CIP

Printed in the United States of America

BOOKS ARE AVAILABLE AT QUANTITY DISCOUNTS WHEN USED TO PROMOTE
PRODUCTS OR SERVICES. FOR INFORMATION PLEASE WRITE TO PREMIUM
MARKETING DIVISION, PENGUIN BOOKS USA INC., 375 HUDSON STREET,
NEW YORK, NEW YORK 10014.

For Julie Fallowfield,
agent,
fellow connoisseur of truly dreadful poetry,
cherished friend,
with love.

CONTENTS

—⁓—

FOREWORD

—ᚐᚐ—

I don't write sequels.

Dearly as I loved Judy-Lynn del Rey, who invented the term, I don't do *prequels* either. I never slip back to the scene of the crime, not through any window.

Most particularly, I don't create epic trilogies culminating with elves, dwarves, wizards, and men standing at Armageddon and waving magic swords and assorted enchanted jewelry in hopeless defiance of this or that Dark (or anyway Grubby) Lord. Mind you, I have admired J.R.R. Tolkien, since I came across his work in the Carnegie Library of Pittsburgh in 1958, but he was one of a kind, as was his universe, fifty years in the building. The maps, the charts, the genealogies, the overnight histories, the unrelated snippets of half-invented languages—none of that adds up to Middle-earth. As many writers as I've worshipped and shamelessly imitated in my time, from Thorne Smith to T. H. White to Lord Dunsany, James Stephens to James Thurber to James Branch Cabell, Jessamyn West to my wife, Padma Hejmadi, it honestly never occurred to me to ape Tolkien. There didn't seem to be much point to it.

From the first, *A Fine and Private Place,* I wanted my novels to be as different from one another as I could make them, within the limitations of my skill and imagination. Setting more than one in the same world seemed to make that impossible—for me, anyway. I've always loved best stories that leave shadowy places, unplayed notes, stories that one can sense going on after one closes the book: never for a moment did I feel the least interest in exploring how

Mr. Rebeck and Mrs. Klapper got on together once he left his refuge in the Yorkchester Cemetery, nor in what became of Molly Grue and Schmendrick the Magician, or whether Joe Farrell ever caught up again with the old goddess known in one California town as Sia. They all have their own lives and I have mine. If they drop a tacky picture postcard in the mail once in a while, that'll be nice.

But that was before *The Innkeeper's Song*.

My friend Edgar Pangborn took a long time to realize that many of his stories were taking place in the same post-nuclear-holocaust world in which he had set his novel *Davy*. In the same way, I was never aware of creating a world with *The Innkeeper's Song*, except as every artist creates a certain kind of continuum—an energy field, if you like—in which the story or the dance or the painting or the four-minute song works the magic it needs to work. The world of *The Innkeeper's Song* was meant to exist only so long as its characters needed it to adventure in. My Lal, my Nyateneri, Lukassa, Rosseth, Tikat, the fox, the old wizard; my dear fat, surly, stubborn Karsh, whose voice was the first I heard in my head: these people whom I had never met, blooming and singing inside me one after another, all so intent on telling their fragments of a long story that I even began having their dreams—those voices, not their landscape, were what truly inhabited me. As long as the world of *The Innkeeper's Song* gave them ground under their feet and a varyingly shared folklore and natural history to refer to, I couldn't have cared less whether it even had a name, never mind a geography. I made it as convincing, as substantial, as I could, because that's my job; but it was never supposed to be more than a backdrop, a stage set. It wasn't intended to last.

But it wanted to last. The voices that filled my head for two years arose from a real place, one that they knew intimately, if I didn't. And at the last, with the book done and pruned and tidied and gone, I found myself missing their world as deeply as I missed them. I'd built it like a slapdash tree house, filled it with imaginary friends, each with a story to tell, and now it was gone—or I was gone from it—and I was curiously lonely for it. And that had never happened to me before.

Hence these stories. Five of them have nothing at all to do with *The Innkeeper's Song:* they happened in different corners of my nameless world, and might as easily have taken place before that other tale as afterward. It's worth mentioning that the central character of "The Last Song of Sirit Byar" is based, freely and with old love, on a great French singer-songwriter named Georges Brassens; and, perhaps, that the entire plot of "Giant Bones" itself showed up one morning in the shower. I'm good in the shower.

"The Tragical Historie of the Jiril's Players" isn't really a fantasy at all, as any theatrical manager can tell you. As for "Lal and Soukyan," the one story involving characters from *The Innkeeper's Song*, re-encountering each other long after the events described in the novel—well, I was very glad to see those two, that's all. I'd missed them especially, and wondered about them, and I was happy to be on the road with them once more, and to savor their prickly partnership, their irritable tenderness for each other. And I miss them more acutely now, because this time I know I'll never see them again.

Because I really don't do sequels. I'll certainly set more tales in the world of *The Innkeeper's Song* (that's all I know to call it; Edgar Pangborn never named his anything but "Davy's world"), but there will be other folk telling them, other shards of its history and legendry coming to light. I'm as much this figment's archaeologist as its bard—maybe more so. Hard to tell, just at present.

Then again, maybe it'll yet turn out, even this late in the game, that I actually do sequels. What do I know? Forty years spent in arriving at an appreciation of Chaucer's line, *"The lyf so short, the craft so long to lerne,"* and here I am, still surprising myself on a regular basis, still sneaking up behind myself and waggling derisive donkey-ear fingers behind my own head. And still assuring myself that some day, when I'm a bit older, I'll really, *really* know what I'm doing. I hope I'm wrong.

—Peter S. Beagle
Davis, California
9 December 1996

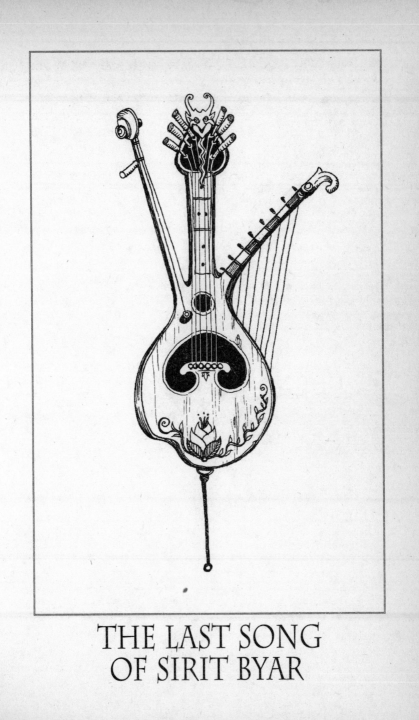

THE LAST SONG
OF SIRIT BYAR

How much? *How* much to set down one miserable tale that will cost your chicken wrist an hour's effort at very most? Well, by the stinking armpits of all the gods, if I'd known there was that much profit in sitting in the marketplace scribbling other people's lives and feelings on bits of hide, I'd have spent some rainy afternoon learning to read and write myself. Twelve copper, we'll call it. *Twelve,* and I'll throw in a sweetener, because I'm a civilized woman under the grease and the hair. I promise not to break your nose, though it's a great temptation to teach you not to take advantage of strangers, even when they look like what I look like and speak your crackjaw tongue so outlandishly that you'd mimic me to my hog face if you dared. But no, no, sit back down, fair's fair, a bargain's a bargain. No broken nose. *Sit.*

Now. I want you to write this story, not for my benefit—am I likely to forget the only bloody man who ever meant more than a curse and a fart to me?—but for your own, and for those who yet sing the songs of Sirit Byar. Ah, *that* caught your ear, didn't it? Yes, yes, Sirit Byar, that one, the same who sang a king to ruin with a single mocking tune, and then charmed his way out of prison by singing ballads of brave lovers to the hangman's deaf-mute daughter. Sirit Byar, "the white *sheknath,*" as they called him out of his hearing—the big, limping, white-haired man who could get four voices going on that antiquated eighteen-course *kiit* other men could hardly lift, let alone get so much as a jangle out of it. Sirit Byar. Sirit Byar, who could turn arrows with his music, call rock-*targs* to carry him over mountain rivers, make whiskery old generals dance like children. All trash, that, all marsh-goat shit, like every single other story they tell about him. Write this down. Are you writing?

Thirty years, more, he's been gone, and you'd think it a hundred listening to the shit wits who get his songs all wrong and pass them on to fools who never heard the man play. The *tales*, the things he's supposed to have said, the gods and heroes they tell you he sang for—believe it, he'd piss himself with laughing to hear such solemn dribble. And then he'd look at me and maybe I'd just catch the twitch at the right corner of his mouth, under the wine-stained white mustache, and he'd say in that barbarous south-coast accent he never lost, "What am I always telling you, big girl? Never bet on anything except human stupidity." And he'd have limped on.

I knew Sirit Byar from when I was eleven years old to his death, when I was just past seventeen. No, he didn't die in my arms—what are you, a bloody bard as well as a mincing scribbler? Yes, I *know* no one ever learned what became of him—I'll get to that part when I bloody well get to it. Don't gape at me like that or I'll pull your poxy ears off and send them to your mother, whatever kennel she's in. *Write*— we'll be all day at this if you keep on stopping to gape. Gods, what a town—back-country cousin-marriers, the lot of them. Just like home.

My name is Mircha Del. I was born around Davlo, that's maybe a hundred miles southwest of Fors na'Shachim. My father was a mountain farmer, clawing a little life from stone and sand, like everybody in this midden-heap. My mother had the good sense to run off as soon as she could after I was born. Never met her, don't even know if she's alive or dead. My father used to say she was beautiful, but all you have to do is look at me for the facts of that. Probably the only woman he could get to live with him up there in those starvation hills, and even she couldn't stand it for long. No need to put all that in—this isn't about her, or about him either. Now he *did* die in my arms, by the way, if that interests you. Only time I can remember holding him.

At the age of eleven, I had my full growth, and I looked just as hulking as I do now. My father once said I was meant for a man, which may be so, though I'd not have been any less ugly with balls and a beard. That's as may be, leave that out too. What matters is that I already had a man's strength, or near enough—enough anyway to get a crop in our scabby ground and to break a team of Karakosk horses—you know, those big ones? The ones they raise on meat broth?—to do our ploughing. And when our neighbor's idiot son—yes, a real idiot, who else would have been my playmate even when I was little?—got himself pinned under a fallen tree, they sent for me to lift it off him. He died anyway, mind you, but people took to calling me "the Davlo *sheknath*" for a while. I told Sirit Byar about that once, the likeness in our nicknames, and he just snorted. He said, "You hated it." I nodded. Sirit Byar said, "Me, too, always have," so maybe there was our real likeness. It made me feel better, anyway.

Well, so. There used to be a tavern just outside Davlo, called the Miller's Joy. It's long gone now, but back then it was as lively a pothouse as you could find, with gaming most nights, and usually a proper brawl after, and every kind of entertainment from gamecocks to *shukri*-fighting, to real Leishai dancers, and sometimes even one of those rock-munching strongmen from down south. My father spent most of his evenings there, and many of his mornings as he got older, so I grew in the habit of walking down to Davlo to fetch him home—carry him, more times than not. And all that's the long way of telling you how I met Sirit Byar.

It happened that I tramped into the Miller's Joy one night to find my father—purely raging I was, too, because our lone miserable *rishu* was due to calve, and he'd sworn to be home this one night anyway. I delivered the calf myself, no trouble, but there could have been, and now I meant to scorch him for it before all his tavern mates. I could hear their racket a street away, and him bellowing and laughing in the middle of it. Wouldn't have been the first time I snatched him off a table and out the door for the cold walk home. Grateful he was for it most times, I think—it told him that someone yet cared where he was, and maybe it passed for love, how should I know? He was lonely with my mother gone, and too poor for drink and the whores both, so he made do with me yelling at him.

But that night there was another sound coming from the old den, and it stopped me in the street. First the fierce thump of a *kiit* strung with more and heavier courses than the usual, and then the voice, that voice—that harsh, hoarse, tender southern voice, always a breath behind the beat, that voice singing that first song, the first one I ever heard:

> *"Face it,*
> *if you'd known what you know today,*
> *you'd have done the same stupid fucking thing*
> *anyway. . . ."*

Yes, you know it, don't you, even in my croak? Me, I didn't even know what I was hearing—I'd never heard anything like that music before, never heard a bard in my life. Bards don't come to Davlo. There's nothing for even a carnival jingler in Davlo, never mind someone like Sirit Byar. But there he was.

He looked up when I pushed the door open. There was a whole sprawl of drunken dirt farmers between us—a few listening to him where he sat crosslegged on a table with the *kiit* in his lap; most guzzling red ale and bawling their own personal songs—but Sirit Byar saw me. He looked straight across them to where I stood in the doorway: eleven years old, the size of a haywagon and twice as ugly, and mucky as the floor of that taproom besides. He didn't smile or nod or anything, but just for a moment, playing a quick twirl on the *kiit* between verses, he said through the noise, "There you are, big girl." As though he'd been waiting. And then he went back to his song.

> *"Face it,*
> *if she'd been fool enough to stay,*
> *you'd be the same mean, stupid bastard*
> *anyway...."*

There was one man crying, doubled over his table, thumping his head on it and wailing louder than Sirit Byar was singing. And there was a miner from Grebak, just sitting silent, hands clasped together, pulling and squeezing at the big scabby knuckles. As for my father and the rest, it was drinking and fighting and puking all over their friends, like any other night at the Miller's Joy. The landlord was half-drunk himself, and he kept trying to throw out little Desh Jakani, the farrier, only he wouldn't go. The three barmaids were all making their own arrangements with anyone who could still stand up and looked likely to have two coppers left in his purse at closing time. But Sirit Byar kept looking at me through the noise and the stink and the flickering haze, and he sang:

> *"Face it,*
> *if we all woke up gods one day,*
> *we'd still treat each other like garbage*
> *anyway...."*

What did he look like? Well, the size of him was what I mostly saw that first night. Really big men are rare still in those Davlo hills—the diet doesn't breed them, not enough meat, and the country just hammers them low—and Sirit Byar was the biggest man I'd seen in my life. But I'm not talking about high or wide—get *this* down now—I'm talking about size. There was a color to him, even with his white hair and faded fisherman's tunic and trews; there was a purpose about him as he sat there singing that made everything and everyone in that roaring tavern small and dim and faraway, that's what I remember. And all he was, really, was a shaggy, rough-voiced old man—fifty anyway, surely—who sang dirty songs and called me "big girl." In a way, that's all he ever was.

The songs weren't *all* dirty, and they weren't all sad and mean, like that "Face It" one. That first night he sang "Grandmother's Ghost," which is just silly and funny, and he sang "The Sand Castles"—you know it?—and "The Ballad of Sailor Lal," which got even those drunken farmers thumping the tables and yelling out the chorus. And there was a song about a man who married the Fox in the Moon—that's still my favorite, though he never sang it much. I forgot about my father, I even forgot to sit down. I just stood in the doorway with my mouth hanging open while Sirit Byar sang to me.

He really could set four voices against each other on that battered old *kiit*, that's no legend. Mostly for show, that was, for a finish—what I liked best was when he'd sing a line in one rhythm and the *kiit* would answer him back in another, and you couldn't believe they'd come out together at the end, even when you knew they would. Six years traveling with him, and I never got tired of hearing him do that thing with the rhythms.

The trouble started with "The Good Folk." It always did, I learned that in a hurry. That bloody song can stir things up even today, insulting everybody from great lords to shopkeepers, priests to bailiffs to the Queen's police; but back then, when it was new, back then you couldn't get halfway through it without starting a riot. I don't *think* Sirit Byar yet understood that, all those years ago in the Miller's Joy. Maybe he did. It'd have been just like him.

Anyway, he didn't get anything like halfway through "The Good Folk," not that night. As I recall it, he'd just sailed into the third stanza—no, no, it would have been the second, the one about the priests and what they do on the altars when everyone's gone home—when the man who'd been crying so loudly stood up, wiped his eyes, and knocked Sirit Byar clean off the table. Never saw the blow coming, no chance to ward it off—even so, he curled himself around the *kiit* as he fell, to keep it safe. The crying man went right at him, fists and feet, and he couldn't do much fighting back, not and protect the *kiit*. Then Kluj what's-his-name got into it—he'd jump anybody when he was down, that one—and then my bloody father, if you'll believe it, too blind drunk to know what was going on, just that it looked like fun. He and the crying man tripped each other up and rolled over Sirit Byar and right into the legs of the big miner's table, brought the whole thing down on themselves. Well, the miner, he started kicking at them with his lumpy boots, and *that* got Mouli Dja, my father's old drinking partner, "Drooly Mouli," people used to call him—anyway, that got *him* jumping in, yelling and swearing and chewing on the miner's knees. After that, it's not worth talking about, take my word for it. A little bleeding, a lot of snot, the rest plain mess. Tavern fights.

I told you I had near to my grown strength at eleven. I walked forward and yanked my father away from the crying man with one hand, while I peeled Mouli Dja off the miner with the other. Today I'd crack their idiot heads together and not think twice about it, but I was just a girl then, so I only dropped them in a corner on top of each other. Then I went back and started pulling people off Sirit Byar and stacking them somewhere else. Once I got them so they'd stay put, it went easier.

He wasn't much hurt. He'd been here before; he knew how to guard his head and his balls as well as the *kiit*. Anyway, that many people piling on, nothing serious ever gets done. Some blood in the white mustache, one eye closing and blackening. He looked up at me with the other one and said for the second time, "There you are, big girl." I held out my hand, but he got up without taking it.

Close to, he had a wild smell—furry, but like live fur, while it's still on the *shukri* or the *jarilao*. He was built straight up and down: wide shoulders, thick waist, thick short legs and neck. A heavy face, but not soft, not sagging—cheekbones you could have built a fence, a house with. Big eyes, set wide apart, half-hidden in the shadows of those cheekbones. Very quiet eyes, almost black, looking black because of the white hair. He never smiled much, but he usually looked about to.

"Time to go," he said, calm as you please, standing there in the ruins of a table and paying no mind to the people yelling and bleeding and falling over each other all around us. Sirit Byar said, "I was going to spend the night here, but it's too noisy. We'll find a shed or a fold somewhere."

And me? I just said, "I have to get my father home. You go on down the Fors road until you come to the little Azdak shrine, it'll be on the right. I'll meet you there." Sirit Byar nodded and turned away to dig his one sea-bag out from under Dordun the horse-coper, who was being strangled by some total stranger in a yellow hat. Funny, the things you remember. I can still see that hat, and it's been thirty years, more.

I did carry my father back to our farm—nothing out of the way in that, as I said. But then I had to sit him down on a barrel, bracing him so he wouldn't go all the way over, and tell him that I was leaving with Sirit Byar. And that was hard—first, because he was too drunk and knocked about to remember who any of us were; and second, because I couldn't have given him any sort of decent reason for becoming the second woman to leave him. He'd never been cruel to me, never used me the way half the farmers we knew used their daughters and laughed about it in the Miller's Joy. He'd never done me any harm except to sire me in that high, cold, lonely, miserable end of the world. And here I was, running away to follow a bard four, five times my age, a man I'd never seen or even heard of before that night. Oh, they'd be baiting him about it forever, Mouli Dja and the rest of his friends.

I don't think I tried to explain anything, finally. I just told him I'd not be helping him with the farming anymore, but that he wouldn't need to worry about feeding me either. He said nothing at all, but only kept blinking and blinking, trying to make his eyes focus on me. I never knew if he understood a word. I never knew what he felt when he woke up the next day and found me gone.

There wasn't much worth taking along. My knife, my tinder box, my good cloak. I had to go back for my lucky foreign coin—see here, this one that's never yet bought me a drink anywhere I've ever been. My father was already asleep, slumped on the barrel with his head against the wall. I put a blanket over him—he could have them both now—and I left a second time.

The Fors na'Shachim road runs straight the last mile or so to the Azdak shrine, and I could see Sirit Byar in the moonlight from a long way off. He wasn't looking around impatiently for me, but was kneeling before that ugly little heap of stones with the snaggletoothed Azdak face scratched into the top one. "Azdak" just means *stranger* in the tongue I grew up speaking. None of us ever knew the god's real name, or what he was good for, or who set up that shrine when my father was a boy. But we left it where it was, because it's bad luck not to, and some of us even worshipped it, because why not? Our own hill gods weren't worth shit, that was obvious, or they wouldn't have been scrabbling to survive in those hills like the rest of us. There was always the chance that a god who had journeyed this far might actually know something.

But Sirit Byar wasn't merely offering Azdak a quick nod and a marketing list. He was on his knees, as I said, with his big white head on a level with the god's, looking him in the eyes. His lips were moving, though I couldn't make out any words. As I reached him, he rose silently, picked up the *kiit* and his sea-bag, and started off on down the Fors road. I ran after him, calling, "My name is Mircha. Where are we going?"

Sirit Byar didn't even look at me. I asked him, "Why were you praying like that to Azdak? Is he your people's god?"

We tramped on a long way before Sirit Byar answered

me. He said, "We know each other. His name is not Azdak, and I was not praying. We were talking."

"It'll rain before morning," I said. "I can smell it. Where are we going?"

He just grunted, "Lesser Tichni or a hayloft, whichever comes first," and that was all he said until we were bedded down between two old donkeys in an old shed on very old straw. I was burrowing up to one of the beasts, trying to get warm, when Sirit Byar suddenly turned toward me and said, "You will carry the *kiit*. You can do that." And he was sound asleep, that fast. Me, I lay awake the rest of that night, partly because of the cold, but mostly because what I'd done was finally—*finally*, mind you—beginning to sink in. Here I was, already farther from home than ever I'd been, lying in moldy straw, listening to a strange man snoring beside me. Tell you how ignorant a lump I was back then, I thought snoring was just something my father did, nobody else. I wasn't frightened—I've never been frightened in my life, which is a great pity, by the way—but I was certainly confused, I'll say that. Nothing for it but to lie there and wait for morning, wondering how heavy the *kiit* would be to shoulder all day. It never once occurred to me that I could go home.

The *kiit* turned out to be bloody heavy, strong as I was, and bulky as a plough, which was worse. Those eighteen double courses made it impossible to get a proper grip on the thing—there was no comfortable way to handle it, except to keep shifting it around: now on my back, now hugged into my chest with both arms, now swinging loose in my hand, banging against everything it could reach. I was limping like Sirit Byar himself at the end of our first full day on the road.

So it began. We stopped at the first inn after sunset, and Sirit Byar played and sang for men dirtier and even more ugly-drunk than ever I'd seen in the Miller's Joy. That was a lesson to me, for that lot paid no attention at all to "The Ballad of Sailor Lal," but whooped and cheered wildly for "The Good Folk," and made him sing it twice over so they could learn it themselves. You never know what they'll like or what they'll do, that's the only lesson there is.

Two nights and a ride on a tinker's cart later, we dined and slept in Fors na'Shachim—yes, at the black castle itself, with the Queen's ladies pouring our tea, and the chamber that Sirit Byar always slept in already made up for him. Four of the ladies were ordered to bathe me and find me something suitable to wear while the Queen had to look at me. I put up with the bath, but when they wanted to burn my clothes on the spot I threw one of the ladies across the room, so that took care of that. It quieted the giggling, besides. So I've had royalty concerning itself with what nightgown I should wear to bed, which is more than *you've* ever known, for all your reading and writing. They'd probably have bathed you, too.

And two days after that, we were on our way again, me back in the rags I'd practically been born in (they probably burned that borrowed dress and the nightgown), and Sirit Byar wearing what he always wore—they didn't sweeten *him* up to sing for the Queen, I can tell you. But he had gold coins in his pocket, thirty-six new strings on the *kiit*, a silk kerchief Herself had tied around his neck with her own fair hands, and he was limping off to sing his songs in every crossroads town between Fors and Chun for no more than our wretched meals and *dai*-beetle–ridden lodging. I was a silent creature myself in those days, but I had to ask him about that. I said, "She wanted you to stay. They did."

Sirit Byar just grunted. I went on, "You'd be a royal bard—you could have that palace room forever, the rest of your life. All you'd ever have to do is make up songs and sing them for the Queen now and then."

"I do that," Sirit Byar said. "Now and then. Don't dangle the *kiit* that way, it's scraping the road." He watched me as I struggled to balance the filthy thing on my shoulder, and for the first time since we'd met I saw him smile a very little.

"The singing is what matters, big girl," he said. "Not for whom." We walked a way without speaking, and then he continued. "To do what I do, I have to walk the roads. I can't ride. If I ride, the songs don't come. That's the way it is."

"And if you sleep in a bed?" I asked him. "And if you sing for people who aren't drunk and stupid and miserable?" I was eleven, and my feet hurt, and I could surely have done with a few more days in that black castle.

Sirit Byar said, "Give me that," and I handed him the *kiit*, glad to have it off my shoulder for a few minutes. I thought he was going to show me a better way of carrying it, but instead he retuned a few of the new strings—they won't hold their pitch the first day or two, drive you mad—and began to play as we walked. He played a song called "The Juggler."

No, you don't know that one. I've never yet met anyone who did. He hardly ever played it—maybe three times in the six years we were together, but I had it by heart the first time, as I always did with his songs. It's about a boy from a place about as wretched as Davlo, who teaches himself to juggle just because he's bored and lonely. And it turns out that he's good at it, a natural. He juggles everything around him—stones, food, tools, bottles, furniture, whatever's handy. People love him; they come miles to see him juggle, and by and by the King hears about it and wants him to live at the palace and be his personal juggler. But in the song the boy turns him down. He tells the King that once he starts juggling crowns and golden dishes and princesses, he'll never be able to juggle anything else again. He'll forget how it's done, he'll forget why he ever wanted to do it in the first place. So thank you, most honored, most grateful, but no. And it has the same last line at the end of every verse: "*Kings need jugglers, jugglers don't need kings. . . .*" I can't sing it right, but that's how it went.

He sang it to me, right there, just the two of us walking along the road, and it's likely the most I ever learned about him at one time. Never any need to explain himself, not to me or anyone. I asked him that day if it bothered him when people didn't like his songs. Sirit Byar just shrugged his shoulders as though my question were a fly and he a horse trying to get rid of it. He said, "That's not my business. The Queen likes them; your father didn't. No business of mine either way."

He really didn't care. Set this down plain, if you botch all the rest, because it's what matters about him. As long as he could make his songs and get along singing them, he simply did not care where he slept, or what he ate, or whom he sang to. I can't tell you how much didn't matter to that man. When he had money he bought our meals with it, or more strings—that old *kiit* went through them like my father through red ale and black wine—or once in a while a night at an inn, for us to clean ourselves up a bit. When there was no money, there'd be food and lodging just the same, most often no worse. For a man who could go all day saying no more than half a dozen words, he had friends in places where I'd not have thought you could even find an enemy. The beggar woman in Rivni: we always stayed with her, just as regular as we stayed at the black castle, in the abandoned henroost that was her home. The wind-witch in Leishai, where it's a respectable profession, because of the sailors. The two weavers near Sarn—brothers, they were, and part-time body-snatchers besides. That bloody bandit in Cheth na'Deka—though that one always kept him up singing most of the night, demanding first this song, then that. The shipchandler's wife of Arakli.

I'll always wonder about her, the chandler's wife. Her husband had a warehouse down near the river, and she used to let us sleep in it as long as we were careful to leave no least sign that we'd ever been there. She was a plain woman—dark, small, a bit plump, that's all I remember. Nice voice. And what there was between her and Sirit Byar I never knew, except that I got up to piss the one night and heard them outside. *Talking* they were, fool—talking they were, too softly for me to make out a word, sitting by the water, not even touching, with the moon's reflection flowing over their faces and the moon in Sirit Byar's white hair. And I pissed behind the warehouse, and I went back to sleep, and that's all.

We had a sort of regular route, if you want to call it that. Say Fors na'Shachim as a starting point—from there we'd work toward the coast through the Dungaurie Pass, strike Grannach Harbor and begin working north, with Sirit Byar singing in taverns, kitchens, great halls, and marketplaces in all the port towns as far as Leishai. Ah, the ports—the smell, salt and spice and tar, miles before you could even see the towns. The food waiting for us there in the stalls, on the barrows—fresh, fresh *courel*, *jeniak*, *boreen* soup with lots of catwort. Strings of little crackly *jai*-fish, two to a mouthful. And the light on the water, and children splashing in the shadows of the rotting pilings, and folk yelling welcome to their "white *sheknath*" in half a dozen tongues. The feeling that everything was possible, that you could go anywhere in the world from here, except back to Davlo. That was the best, better than the food, better than the smells. That feeling.

No, you'd think so, but he hardly ever sang sea-songs in the port towns. One, two, maybe, like "Captain Shallop and the Merrow" or "Dark Water Down"—otherwise he saved those for inland, where folk dream of far white isles and don't know what a merrow can do to you. In the ports he sang—oh, "Tarquentil's Hat," "The Old Priest and the Old God," "My One Sorrow," "The Ballad of the Captain's Mercy." "The Good Folk." Now *they* always loved "The Good Folk," the ports did, so there you are.

From Bitava we usually headed inland, still angling north, but no farther than Karakosk, ever. I've been told that he sang often in Corcorua; maybe, but not while I was with him. He'd no mind at all to limp across the Barrens, and he disliked most of the high northland anyway for its thin wine and its fat, stingy burghers. So I never saw anything loftier than the Durli Hills in those days, which suited me well enough—I've never been homesick for mountains a day in my life. We'd skirt the Durlis, begin bearing back south around Suk'kai, and fetch up in Fors again by Thieves' Day. A bath and a warm bed then—a few days of singing for the Queen and being made over by her ladies—and start all over again. So it was we lived for six years.

Duties? What were my *duties*? How daintily you do put it, to be sure, chicken-wrist. Well, I carried the *kiit*, and I brewed the tea and cooked our meals, when we had something to cook. A few times, mostly in Leishai, I ran off pickpockets he hadn't seen sliding alongside, and one night I broke the shoulder of a hatchet-swinging Bitava barber who'd taken a real dislike to "The Sand Castles." For the rest, I kept him mostly silent company, talked when he wanted talk, went round with the hat after he sang, and kept an eye out at all times for that wicked west-country liqueur they call Blue Death. Terrible shit, peel your gums right back, but he loved it, and it's hard to find much east of Fors. He drank it like water, whenever he could get it, but I can't remember seeing him drunk. Or maybe I did, maybe I saw him drunk a lot and didn't know it. There were things you never could tell about with Sirit Byar.

Once I asked him, "What would you do if you weren't a bard? If you just suddenly couldn't make up songs anymore?"

I thought I knew him well enough to ask, but he stopped in the road and gaped at me as though he'd never seen me before. That was the only time I ever saw him looking amazed, startled about anything. He mumbled, "You don't know."

I stared right back at him. I said, "Well, of course I don't know. I didn't know a bloody thing about being a bard, not how it *is*, you won't ever talk about that. All I know is what you like to eat, where you like to sit when you sing. Maybe you think that's all a hill girl from Davlo can understand. Maybe it is. You'll never know that either."

Sirit Byar smiled a real smile then, not the almost-smile he wore for everyone always. "Listen to the songs, big girl. It's all in the songs, everything I could tell you." We walked along a way after that, and by and by he said, "A bard always hoards one last song against the day when all the others go. It happens to every one of us, sooner or later—you wake up one morning and it's over, they've left you, they don't need you anymore. No warning. No warning when they flew into you, no warning when they fly away. That's why you always save that last song."

He cleared his throat, spat into the road, rubbed his nose, looked sideways at me. "But you have to be very careful, because a bard's last song has power. You never tell that song; you never sing it anywhere; you keep it for that day when it's the only song left to you. Because a last song is always *answered*." And after that he hardly talked at all for the rest of the day.

He taught me a little about playing the *kiit*, you know. I'm sure he did it just because he'd never found anyone besides him who could even handle the thing. I'm no musician—I can't do what he could do, but I know how he did it. Someday I'd like to show someone how he played, just so it won't die with me. Not that he'd have given one tiny damn, but I do.

Every so often we'd strike a song competition, a battle of bards, especially in the southwest—it's a tradition in that country to set poets a subject and start them outrhyming one another. Sirit Byar hated those things. He'd avoid even a town where we usually did well if he heard there was a contest going on there. Because once he was recognized, he never had a choice—they'd cancel the whole event if he didn't enter. He always won, but he was always cranky for days afterward. Me, I liked the song tourneys—we ate well those days, and drank better, and some of the townsfolk's celebration of Sirit Byar was for me, too, or anyway it felt so. I was proud as any of the Queen's ladies to walk beside him in the street, holding the *kiit* so people could see the flowers woven in and out between its strings. And whenever Sirit Byar looked down through all the fuss and winked at me, bard to bard almost—well, you imagine how it was, chicken-wrist. You imagine this big freak's insides then.

No. Oh, no. Get *that* out of your head before it ever gets

in, if you know what's good for you. I was eleven, lugging that *kiit*, for Sirit Byar, and then twelve and thirteen and fourteen, sleeping close for warmth in fields, barns, sheds, whores' cribs, and never in all that time. *Never*. Not once. It wouldn't have occurred to him.

It occurred to me, I'll tell you that. Yes, you can gape now, that's right, I'd be disappointed if you didn't. Listen to me now—I've had three, four times as many men as you've had women, for what that's worth. You think men care about soft skin, perfect teeth, adorable little noses? Not where I've been—not in the mines, not on the flatboats, the canal scows, not in the traders' caravans slinking through the Northern Barrens. Out there, I even get to say, "no, not now, piss off"—can you imagine *that* at least, chicken-wrist? Try.

I had my first while I was yet on the road with Sirit Byar. Not yet fourteen, me, and sneaking up on myself in every stockpond, every shiny pot, just on the off-hope that something might have changed since the last time. If I'd had a mother . . . aye, well, and what could the most loving mother have told me that the bottom of any kettle couldn't? What could Sirit Byar have said, who never looked in a glass from year's-end to year's-end? I truly doubt he remembered the color of his own eyes. Now me, I couldn't remember not knowing I was ugly enough to turn milk, curdle beer, and mark babies, but it hadn't mattered much at all until that boy at Limsatty Fair.

Ah, gods, that boy at the fair. I can still see him, thirty years gone, when I can't remember who pleased me last week. Pretty as you like, with lavender eyes, skin like brown cambric, bones in his face like kite-ribs. He was selling salt meat, if you'll believe it, and when Sirit Byar and I wandered by he looked at me for a moment, and looked politely away, so as not to stare. That's when I learned that I had a heart, chicken-wrist, because I felt such a pain in it that I couldn't believe I was still walking along and not falling dead on the spot. We were to make our camp in a field a mile from the fair, and I think I walked backward all the way. Sirit Byar had to grip me by the back of my smock and tow me like a bloody barge.

There was a little creek, and I was supposed to scoop some fish out of it for our dinner. Any hill child can do that, but instead I lay there on my stomach and cried as I've never cried in my life, before or since. I didn't think it was ever going to stop. Leave that out. No. No, keep it in. What do I care?

Sirit Byar had probably been sitting by me for a long time before I felt his hand on my neck. He never touched me, you know, except to help me on the road, or to remind me about holding the damn *kiit* just so. Once, when I was sick with the white-mouth fever, he carried me and the *kiit* both for miles until we found a mad old woman who knew what to do. This was different, this was—I don't know, leave it, just leave it. He said, "Here."

He took off the Queen's silken kerchief he always wore around his neck and handed it to me so I could dry my eyes. Then he said, "Give me the *kiit*." I just stared at him, and he had to tell me again. "Give it to me, big girl."

He tuned it so carefully, you'd have thought he was getting ready to play at the black palace once again. Then he set his back against a tree, and began to sing. It wasn't a song I'd ever heard, and it didn't sound like one of his. The rhythm wasn't any I knew, the music was jags and slides and tangles, the words didn't make any sense. I told you, I had all his songs by heart the moment I heard them, but not that song. I do have a bit of it, like this:

> *"If you hear not, hear me never—*
> *if you burn not, freeze forever—*
> *if you hunger not, starve in hell—*
> *if you will not, then you never shall. . . ."*

That line kept coming round and round again—"*If you will not, then you never shall.*" It was a long song, and there was a thing about it made my skin fit all wrong on me. I lay where I was, sniffling away, while Sirit Byar kept singing, and the sun wandered down into twilight, slow as that song. At last I sat up and wiped my face with the Queen's kerchief, and remembered about our fish. I was moving myself back over to the creek when the music stopped, sudden as a doorslam, and I turned and saw the salt-meat boy from the fair.

He was still so beautiful that it hurt to look at him, but something in his face was changed. Some kind of vague, puzzled anger, like someone who hasn't been blind long enough to get used to it. But he walked straight to me, and he took my hands and drew me to my feet, and we stood staring at each other for however long. When he began to lead me away, I turned to look back, but Sirit Byar was gone. I don't know what he had for dinner that night, nor where he slept.

Me, I slept warm on a cold hillside, as they say in the old ballads, and I woke just a minute or two before I should have. The salt-meat boy was up and scurrying into his clothes, and looking down at me with such bewilderment and such contempt—not for me, but for himself—as even I haven't seen again in my life. Then he fled, carrying his boots, and I lay there for a while longer, to give him time. I didn't cry.

Sirit Byar was at the creek, breakfasting on dry bread and cheese and the last of our sour Cape Dylee wine. There was enough laid out for two. Neither of us spoke a word until we were on our way again, bound for Derridow, I think. Finally I said, "The song brought him."

Sirit Byar grunted, looked away, mumbled something. I stopped right there on the road—he actually walked along a few steps before he realized I wasn't with him. I said, "Tell me why you sang that song. Tell me now."

He was a long time answering. We stood there and looked at each other almost the way I'd stood with that salt-meat boy, years and years ago it seemed. Finally Sirit Byar rubbed his hand across his mouth and muttered, "You're my big girl, and you were so sad."

And that was how I knew he liked me, you see. Two,

almost three full years carrying his instrument, cooking his meals, grubbing up coins from tavern floors, and he'd never said. He turned right around then and started walking on, as fast as his limp would let him, and I hurried after him with the *kiit* banging the side of my knee. He wouldn't talk for a long time, not until a rainshower came up and we were huddled in the lee of a hayrick, waiting it out. I asked him, "How does it happen? The song making someone come to you."

Sirit Byar said, "Where I come from, there are songs for bringing game to the hunter—fish, birds. I just changed one a little for you."

I started to say, "Please, don't ever do that anymore," but I changed my mind halfway through. Whatever came of it, he gave me what I'd wanted most in all my life till then, and no blame to him if I woke from the dream too soon. So instead I asked, "Can you make other things happen with your songs?"

"Little things," Sirit Byar said. "The great ones who walked the roads before me—Sarani Elsu, K'lanikh-yara"—no, I never heard of them either, chicken-wrist—"*they* could sing changes, *they* could call rivers to them, they could call gods, lightning, the dead, not silly lovers." He patted my shoulder clumsily, I remember. He said, "All songs are magic, big girl. Some are more powerful than others, but all songs are always magic, always. You've seen me start our cooking fires in the rain—you remember the time I cured the farmer's dog that had eaten poison. My songs make little magics, that's all. They'll do for me."

Write that down, remember that he said just that. Remember it the next time you hear someone jabbering about Sirit Byar's great powers. *Little magics.* He never claimed anything more than that for himself. He never needed to.

Where was I? The rain let up, and we set out again, and presently Sirit Byar began singing a new song, one he hadn't yet finished, scrawling it in the air with one huge hand as we walked, the way he did. It ran so:

"Long ago,
before there were landlords—
long ago,
before there were kings,
there lived a lady
made all out of flowers,
made of honey and sunlight
and such sweet things. . . ."

Yes, of course you know it, that one got around everywhere—I've heard it as far north as Trodai, just last year. He sang it through for me the first time, the two of us shivering there in the rain, and when the sun came out, we walked on. Neither of us ever said another word about the salt-meat boy, as often as we came again to Limsatty Fair.

After that, something was a bit different between us. Closer, I don't know—maybe just easier. We talked more, anyway. I told Sirit Byar about the little scrap of a farm where I'd lived, and about how I'd chanced into the Miller's Joy that night, and that I was worried about my father—we hadn't been back to Davlo in three years. I asked after him whenever we met someone who'd passed through there, but for all I knew he might have died the day I left. I'd go days at a time without thinking of him at all, but I dreamed about him more and more.

Sirit Byar spoke sometimes of his south-coast town—not much bigger than Davlo, it sounded—and of his older sister, who raised him after their parents' deaths. Even now I can't imagine Sirit Byar having a family, having a sister. She set his leg herself when it got crushed between two skiffs and there wasn't even a witchwife for miles. She married there, and was killed in the Fishermen's Rebellion, and he never went back. Did you ever hear anyone sing that song of his, "Thou"? Most people think that song's about one god or another, but it's not; it's for his sister. He told me that.

Bedded down one night in the straw of a byre, with an

old *rishu* and her calf for company, I asked him why he'd said that in the Miller's Joy when he first saw me—"*There you are, big girl.*" How he knew that I was supposed to go with him and help him and do what he told me—how *I* knew. Sirit Byar was sitting up across from me, fussing over a harmony on the *kiit* that never did satisfy him. He answered without looking up, "He told me. The one your folk call Azdak." I didn't understand him. Sirit Byar said, "When I came to Davlo. I saw him by the road, and we talked. He told me to watch for you."

"Azdak," I said. "Azdak. What would Azdak care about me?"

"He is the god of wanderers," Sirit Byar said. "He knows his own." The *kiit* wouldn't do a thing he wanted that evening, and he finally set it down gently in an empty manger. He went on, "Your Azdak told me you and I had a journey to make together. I didn't know what he meant then."

"Aye, and so we had, sure enough," I said. "Where was the mystery in that?"

Sirit Byar laughed. He said, "I don't think Azdak was talking about walking the roads, big girl. Gods likely don't bother much with such things."

"Well, they bloody should," I said, for he'd been limping worse than usual lately, and I'd had a stone bruise on my heel days on end. "He's no more use than our regular gods, if that's all he could tell you."

Sirit Byar shrugged. "I know only what he didn't mean, not what he did. That's how it is with gods." He stretched out on the far side of the *rishu*, wriggling himself down into the straw till all you could see of him was a big nose and a white mustache. He said, "Our real journey is yet to come," and was asleep.

Now whether it was the words or the way he said them that took hold of me, I couldn't tell you, but it was nightmare on nightmare after that—every time the damn *rishu* snuffled in her sleep, another monster turned up in mine. The last one must have been a pure beauty, because I woke up on Sirit Byar's chest, holding him tighter than ever I had the salt-meat boy. That wild, deep-woods smell of his was the most comforting thing in the wide world just then.

Well, there's comfort and comfort. I'll get this part over with quickly—no need to embarrass us both for twelve coppers. He held me for a while, petting my hair as though it might turn in his hand and bite him any minute. Then he started to put me by, gently as he could, but I wouldn't let him. I was saying, "It's dark, it's dark, you won't even see me, just this one time. Please." Like that.

Poor Sirit Byar, hey? The poor man, trying to get this whimpering hulk off him without hurting her brutish feelings. Ah, *that* one you can imagine, I can see it in your little pink eyes. Yes, well, I pushed him back down every time he sat up, and when he said, "Big girl, don't, no, you're too young," I kept on kissing him, saying, "I don't care, I won't tell anybody, please, I won't ever tell." Ah, poor, poor Sirit Byar.

He did the only thing he could do. He shoved me away, hard—big as he was, I was the stronger, but it's amazing what you can do when you're desperate, isn't it?—and jumped to his feet, panting as though we really had been doing it. For a moment he couldn't speak. He was backed into a far corner of the stall; he'd have to bolt past me to get out. I wasn't crying or laughing, or coming at him or anything, just standing there.

"Mircha," he said, and that was the only time but one he ever called me by my name. "Mircha, I can't. There's a lady."

A lady, mind you. Not a plain woman, a lady. "The bloody *hell* there is," I said. I don't think I screamed it, but who remembers? "Three years, almost, never out of each other's sight for ten minutes together, what bloody *lady*?"

"A long time," Sirit Byar said very softly. "A long, long time, big girl." The words were coming out of him one by one, two by two. He said, "I've not seen her since before you were born."

Never mind what I said to him then. If there's little

enough in my life that warms me to remember, there's less that truly shames me, except for what I said to Sirit Byar in the next few moments. Just set it down that I asked him what he thought his great love was doing while he was wandering the land being forever faithful to her. Just set that much down—so—and let it alone.

Sirit Byar bore it all, big hands hanging open at his sides, and waited for me to run out of words and wind. Then he said, sounding very tired, "Her name is Jailly Doura. She is mad."

I sat down in the straw. Sirit Byar said, "Jailly Doura. There was a child. Her family married her to a man who took the child gladly, but it died." He swung his head left and right, the way he did sometimes, like an animal that can't find its old way out of a place. "It died," he said, "our child. She has been mad ever since, fifteen years it is. Jailly Doura."

Two *l*s in the name, are you getting it? I said, "Credevek. That place where the rich people live. We always walk wide of Credevek—you won't pass the city gates, let alone sing there."

"Once," Sirit Byar whispered. Slumped against the wall, gray as our old stone Azdak under the road-brown weathering, he looked like no one I'd ever seen. He said, "I sang once for her in Credevek."

"Once in fifteen years," I said. "We do better than that in Davlo. Well, maybe faithfulness is easier if you don't have to see the person. I wouldn't know." There was a calmness on me, just as new and strange as all those tears I'd shed over the salt-meat boy. I felt very old. I patted the straw beside me and said, "Come and sit. I won't attack you, I promise. Come *on*, then."

Fourteen, and ordering Sirit Byar about like a plough horse. But he came, and we sat close against each other, because the night had turned wickedly cold. Sirit Byar even laid his arm across my shoulders, and it was all right. Whatever happened, whatever it was took me for a little time, it never happened again. Not with him, not with anybody. I asked, "Did you know there was a baby?"

Sirit Byar nodded. After a while he said, "What could I have done? Her parents would have locked her away forever, rather than have her walking the roads with a moneyless, mannerless south-coast street singer. And here's a wealthy man waiting to marry her and take her to live in Credevek, and what's a street singer to do for a gently bred girl and a child?" He shivered suddenly, hard, I could feel it. He said, "I went away."

"What became of her?" He blinked at me. "I mean, after—afterward? Where is she now, who takes care of her?" In Davlo we had Mother Choy. She took in all our strays—animals, children, and the moontouched alike—and if the lot of them lived in rags, on scraps, and under rotting thatch, well, they were glad enough to get it. Sirit Byar said, "Jailly Doura's husband is a good man. Another would have sent her away, but she lives with him still, in a house just north of Credevek, and he looks after her himself. I have been to that house."

"Once," I said. Sirit Byar's hand tightened on my shoulder, hard, and his face clenched in the same way. I couldn't tell you which hurt me more. He said, "She would not come into the room. I sang all night for a dark doorway, and I could smell her, feel the air move against me when she moved, but she would not let me see her. I could not bear that. I could not bear to come back again."

I knew there was more. I knew him that well, anyway. Nothing to do but sit there in the stall, with the *rishu* snoring and her calf looking sleepily at us, and the air growing lighter and colder, both. And sure enough, in a year or two, Sirit Byar said, "I thought I could make her well. I was so sure."

He wasn't talking to me. I said, "All songs are magic, always. You told me that."

"So they are," Sirit Byar answered. "But my songs are for farmers' dogs, I told you that also. I learned that before you were born, in that house in Credevek." He turned to look at me, and his eyes were as old and weary as any I ever saw. He said, "The great ones, they could have healed her. Sarani Elsu could have brought her back. *I*—" and he just stopped, and his head went down.

I knew there wouldn't be another word this time, no matter how long I waited for it. So after a while I said, "So you tried to sing her madness away, and it didn't work. And you never tried again. Fifteen years."

"Her husband told me not to come back," Sirit Byar mumbled. "I left her worse off than before, what could I say to him? He is a good man, what could I say?" He looked at me for an answer, but I didn't have one. In a bit his head sagged forward again. I wriggled around until I could get comfortable with his head resting on my arm, and then I just sat like that until long into morning, while the old man slept and slept, and I just sat.

And the next day, and the days after that, you'd think none of it had ever happened. We walked the roads as usual, talking a bit more, as I've said, but we never once talked about our night in the byre, and there was never another bloody word about his Jailly Doura. Oh, I might have asked, and he might have answered, but I didn't think I wanted to know a thing more about her and him and their child than I already knew, thank you very much. No, I wasn't *jealous*—please, do me a favor—but I was fourteen and he was mine, that's all, whatever that means when you're fourteen. He wasn't my father or my lover, he was just mine. And if I *was* jealous, I had a bloody right to be, only I wasn't. Just big and ugly, the same as always.

One thing different, though. At night, usually when he thought I was asleep, he practiced a new song over and over. Or maybe it was an old one, for all I could tell—he kept his voice so low and his south-coast accent would get so thick that I couldn't make out one word in ten. Even when I really was asleep, the slidey, whispery music always filled my dreams full of faces I'd never seen, animals I didn't recognize. It sounded like a lullaby people might sing in some other country; like my lucky coin that's worth something somewhere, I've no doubt. Never had dreams like that again.

We did get to Davlo that spring—Sirit Byar went out of his usual way to make sure of it. There was nothing for him there—he didn't bother with even a single night at the Miller's Joy, but stayed with a farmer while I went on alone. I found Desh Jakani at his smithy, and he told me that my father hadn't been into the Miller's Joy for more than a month now, and that he'd been thinking seriously of going by our farm any day to look in on him. "Never the same man after you ran away," he told me. "The spirit just went out of him, everybody says so." My father hadn't had much spirit in him to begin with, and Desh Jakani was a liar born, but all the same I scrambled up that mountain track as though a rock-*targ* were after me, really thankful that I'd come home when I had, and wishing with all my heart that I were anywhere, anywhere else in the world.

The way had disappeared completely. I'd always kept things cut back at least a little, but everything—the path, the pasture, our few poor fields—everything was smothered in foxweed, ice-berry brambles and *drumak*. I looked for our *rishu* and the two Karakosk horses, but they were gone. The door of the house hung on one hinge. My father squatted naked in the doorway.

He wasn't mad, like Sirit Byar's Jailly Doura, or even very drunk. He knew me right away, but he didn't care. I picked him up—all cold bones, he was—and carried him into the house. No point in going into what it looked like; it was just the house of a man who'd given up long ago. When I left? Like enough. Likely Desh Jakani was right about that, after all.

My father never spoke a single word during the two days I stayed with him. I put him to bed, and I made soup for him—I'm no cook, and proud of it, but I can make decent soup—and managed to get some of it down his throat, while I told him all about my travels with Sirit Byar, the things I'd seen with him, the people I'd met, the songs I'd learned. I think I sang him every song I knew of Sirit Byar's during those two days, including "The Good Folk," the one that started the brawl in the Miller's Joy so long ago. He listened. I don't know what he heard, because his eyes never changed, but he was listening, I know that much. I swear he was listening.

I even told him about the salt-meat boy. That was on the morning of the third day, when I was holding him steady on the chamber pot. That's when he died, trust my father. Not a sound, not a whimper, not the tiniest fart—he was just dead in my arms, just like that. I buried him at the doorstep, because that's the way we do in Davlo, and left the door open for the animals and the creeping vines, and walked down into town one last time to join Sirit Byar.

What? What? You should see the look on your little face—you can't wait to know if we ever went to Credevek together, ever tried a second time to sing Jailly Doura back from wherever her poor ragged mind had been roaming all this long time. Well, let me tell you, for the next two years, Sirit Byar saw to it that we didn't go anywhere near Suk'hai, let alone Credevek. He'd have us veering back south as early as Chun, never mind who expected him where, or what bounty he might be passing up. When I asked, he only grunted that he was getting too old to trudge that far uphill, and anyway, those folk were all too tightfisted to make the extra miles worthwhile. Wasn't my place to argue with him, even if I'd been of a mind to. I wasn't.

Those were good years, those last two we had together. My strength had caught up with my size, and I could have carried the *kiit* all day by a couple of fingers. We tramped every road between Cape Dylee and Karakosk, between Grannach Harbor and Derridow, him writing his new songs in the air as we went, and me eyeing every pretty boy in every town square as boldly as though I were some great wild beauty who'd been the one to do the choosing all her life. There wasn't one of them as beautiful as my salt-meat boy, and they didn't all come bleating after me by night—no fear about that—but I'll tell you one thing, Sirit Byar never had to sing anybody to my bed again, no bloody fear about *that*, either. You're almost sweet when you blush, chicken-wrist, do you know that? Almost.

Yes. Yes, yes, we did go to Credevek together.

It was my doing, if you want to know. I won't say he'd never have gone without me; all I *will* say is that he hadn't been back there for—what's that make it?—seventeen years, so you figure it out. What put it into my head, that's another story. I wanted to see her, I know that. It started as a notion, just a casual wondering what she looked like, but then I couldn't get it out of my head; it kept growing stronger and stronger. And maybe I wanted to see him, too, see him with her, just to know. Just to find out what it was I wanted to know. Maybe that was it, who remembers?

So that last morning, after we'd been to Chun—I remember it was Chun, because that was one place where Sirit Byar did sing "The Juggler" in public—and came once more to the Fors na'Shachim crossroads, I said to him, as casually as I could, "That peddler yesterday, the man we traded with for the new kettle? He spoke of trouble on the Fors road. I meant to tell you."

Sirit Byar shrugged. "Bandits." One fairy tale's true, anyway—there wasn't a high-toby in the country would have laid a hand on Sirit Byar or lifted a single copper from him. They used to come out of the woods sometimes, bashful as marsh-goats, and travel along with us a little way, hanging back to encourage him to try over a new song as though they weren't there. They couldn't make him out, you see. I think they felt he was somehow one of them, but they couldn't have said why. That's what I think.

"Plague," I told him. "Fire-plague, broken out all down the Fors road between here and Dushant. He said the only safe route south was the Snowhawk's Highway. It's a good road—we can follow it as far as Cheth na'Vaudry and then cut west to Fors. We could do that."

Sirit Byar looked at me for a long time. Did he know I was lying? I've no more idea than you have. What *I* knew was that fire-plague hits the south coast, his country, at least once every ten years; people die in hundreds, thousands sometimes. He said at last, "We would have to pass through Credevek."

I didn't answer him. We stood silent at the crossroads, listening to insects, birds, the wind in the dry leaves. Then Sirit Byar said, "Azdak." Not another word. He took the *kiit* from my hand and set off toward Credevek without looking back. Limp or no limp, I had to trot to catch up with him.

So there's how we came to Credevek, which is a strange place, all grand lawns, high stone houses, cobblestone streets, servants coming and going on their masters' errands. No beggars. No tinkers, no peddlers. A few farm carts, a few children. *Quiet*. The quiet sticks to your skin in that town.

Sirit Byar marched straight down the main street of Credevek, with me trailing after him, not knowing what to do or even how to walk if I wasn't carrying the *kiit*. People came to their windows to stare at us, but no one recognized Sirit Byar, and he never looked this way or that. Straight through the town until the paved streets and the stone houses fell away, nothing much after but meadowland gone to seed, a few pastures, and the brown Durli Hills in the distance. And one big wooden house snugged down into the shadows between two foothills—you could miss it if you didn't look sharp. Sirit Byar said, "If we travel by night, we will reach the Snowhawk's Highway before noon tomorrow."

I said, "That's where they live, isn't it? That's where Jailly Doura lives."

Sirit Byar nodded. "If she lives still." He turned to look at me, and suddenly he reached out to put his hand on the side of my neck, right here. My hair, the roots of my hair, just went cold with it. He said, "Between that house and where we stand, there's our journey. That's what the god of wanderers was saying to me. Whatever happens in that house, this is why we met, you and I. I would never be here, but for you. Thank you, Mircha."

I didn't know what to say. I just said, "Well, I wanted to get out of Davlo, that's all." I tried to take the *kiit* back—I mean, it was my *job*, carrying it, from the first day—but he wouldn't let me. He swung it to his shoulder and we started on our journey.

And it was a longer journey than it looked, I can tell you. By noon, which is when we should have reached the house in the foothills, it hardly seemed any closer than when we'd first seen it. Barely this side of sunset, it was, before we'd done with trudging through empty, stony defiles and turned up a last steep road that ran between two huge boulders. There was a man waiting there. He was short and old, and the little that was left of his hair was as white as Sirit Byar's, and if he wasn't exactly fat, he looked soft as porridge, and about that color. But he faced us proudly, blocking our way like one of those boulders himself. He said, "Sirit Byar. I thought it would be today."

Now. I have to tell the rest slowly. I have to be careful, remember it right, so you can set it down exactly the way it was. Sirit Byar said, "Aung Jatt," and nothing more. He just stood looking down at the other man, the way the high, shadowed house looked down on us three. Aung Jatt didn't take any notice of me, which is difficult. He said to Sirit Byar, "You cannot see her. I will not allow it."

"It has been fifteen years," Sirit Byar began, but Aung Jatt interrupted him. "And if it had been fifty, she'd still not be healed of you, healed of your music. I told you never to return here, Sirit Byar." You know how, when you grip something too tightly, it starts shivering and slipping in your hand? Aung Jatt's voice was like that.

Sirit Byar said only, "I must sing for her once more."

"Oh, aye, once more," the old man answered him. "And when you have sung your songs of love and ghosts, dragons and sailors, and gone your way again, who will stay behind to piece what's left of her into some kind of human shape *once more*?" He mimicked Sirit Byar's deep, hoarse voice so bitterly that I giggled. I couldn't help it. Aung Jatt never took his eyes off Sirit Byar.

"She did not know me for three years after you were here," he whispered. "Three years. What possessed me to let her listen to you? What made me imagine that the music of the father might keep her from trying to follow the child? For three years, she wept in the dark and ate what I pushed under her door—for two years more, she said no word but the child's name, over and over and over. For five years after that—" He made himself stop; you could hear his throat clicking and grinding. Sirit Byar waited, blinking in the setting sun.

"Fifteen years," Aung Jatt said presently. "There are times even now when she takes me for you, do you know that?" He grinned like a dead man. "You might think that would hurt me, and in a way it does, because then she sometimes tries to kill me. I must always be watchful."

Sirit Byar closed his eyes, shook his head, and started to move around Aung Jatt, up the road toward the house beyond. Aung Jatt stopped him with a palm gently against his chest. He said, "But she has stopped calling for the child. Most often she sleeps through the night, and it has been some while since I had to feed her. And she hates you far more than I do, Sirit Byar."

You couldn't be sure, because the sunlight was slanting off the windows, but I thought I saw someone moving in the house, just for a moment, the way you can see a feeling flicker across someone's eyes and gone again. Aung Jatt went on, "She hates you because she knows—she *knows*— that the child would still be alive if you had defied her parents and stayed with her. I know better, but there." He chuckled and patted Sirit Byar's chest with his fingertips. He said, "Did I tell you when you were here before that it was a boy? I'm growing old, I forget things."

Sirit Byar said, without looking at me, "Come on, big girl," and put Aung Jatt out of his way with one arm. Aung Jatt made no protest this time. He was still smiling a little as he watched us step past him—I say *us*, but he never saw me, not for a minute. He didn't follow, and he didn't speak again until we were on the stone steps that led to the front door. Then he called after us, "Beware, Sirit Byar! The second floor is her domain—when you are there with her, you are in the moon. The servants will not ever climb the stair, and should she come down, they scuttle away into corners like beetles until she passes. Beware of her, Sirit Byar!"

I heard Sirit Byar's scornful grunt next to me—after six years, there wasn't a grunt or a snort of his I couldn't translate. But I wasn't scornful, I'll tell you that much. I said I've never been frightened, and it's true, but madmen— madwomen—make me uneasy, if you like. Madwomen in the dark make me very uneasy. Sirit Byar pushed the door open. Just before we went inside, I looked back at Aung Jatt. He was standing exactly where we had left him, and he was laughing without making a sound.

It was a fine, proud house, certainly—and remember, I've slept in a palace. Felt bigger inside than outside somehow, and it felt *soft*, too—lots of thick Tahi'rak rugs and drapes and those buttery cushions they sew in Fors out of traders' old saddle-blankets. Hardly an inch of floor or wall showing: the whole place was made like a cradle, like a special box you keep something precious and breakable in. Servants slipped past us without a word, or anyway their shadows did, for I couldn't hear their footsteps, nor our own, come to that. I couldn't hear the front door swing shut, or any sound from the outside once it had. What I did hear was someone breathing. It wasn't Sirit Byar, and it wasn't me—I don't think either of us had breathed since we came through that door. Sirit Byar touched my shoulder and nodded me left, toward the stair. You'd expect a house like this to have a grand spiral stairway, but this was just a narrow little one, not room enough for the two of us to go abreast. Sirit Byar had to hold the *kiit* tight against his side to keep it from hitting the railing. I followed him, not thinking too much, not feeling anything, because why not? Where else was I to go right then?

It was different on the second floor. Deepsea cold, it was, and thick with twilight, old stale, mushy twilight filling our eyes and ears and nostrils, like when you get smothered in the bedding when you're asleep, and then that's all you can dream. The breathing was all around us now, no louder, but quickening, eager. There wasn't another sound anywhere in the world. Sirit Byar stopped on the landing. Clearly, loudly even, he said, "Jailly Doura."

The breathing never faltered. Sirit Byar said again, "Jailly Doura. I am here."

No answer. Where we stood, I could make out a chair, a wall, another chair, a gray face floating in the air, the gray mouth of a corridor. Sirit Byar looked left and right, trying to guess where the breathing might be coming from. My eyes were growing used to the dimness now—I saw that the floating face was a painting hanging on the wall, and I saw other paintings, and lamps and braziers as tall as me, taller, all unlit, and a great dark chandelier swinging overhead. The corridor lay straight ahead of us, with high double doors on either hand. Sirit Byar said, "This way," and went forward like a man moving in his own house in full day. I hurried after him. I didn't want to be left behind, left alone in the moon.

He never looked at any of the doors, only strode along until the corridor bent right and opened out into a kind of—what?—well, like an indoor courtyard, I suppose. There must have been an opening to the sky somewhere, because the twilight was more watery here, but I still couldn't see as far as the walls of the place, and the little warm night wind I felt on my face now and then made me wonder if it *had* any walls. There were a couple of benches, and there were pale statues in alcoves—and, of all the bloody things, a tree, set right into the floor, right in the middle of the room. A *sesao*, I think, or it might have been a red *mouri*, what do I know about trees? I certainly don't know how Aung Jatt ever watered and nourished the thing, but its trunk disappeared in darkness, and its branches reached out almost as far as the bench where Sirit Byar had calmly sat down and begun tuning the *kiit*. I stood. I wanted my feet under me in that house, I knew that much.

The breathing still sounded so close I thought I could feel it sometimes, and yet I couldn't even be sure where it was coming from. Sirit Byar looked up into the tree branches and said, "Do you remember this song, Jailly Doura?" He touched the *kiit* with the heel of his hand, to get a sort of deep sigh out of all the strings, and began to sing.

I knew the song. So do you—if there's one song of Sirit Byar's that the wind carried everywhere, and that clung where it landed like a cocklebur, it was "Where's My Shoe?" Right, that funny, ridiculous song about a man who keeps losing things—his shoe, his wig, his spectacles, his false teeth, his balls, his wife—and that's the way people sing it in the taverns. But the melody's a sad one, if you whistle it over slowly, and people don't always sing the very last verses, because those are about misplacing your faith, your heart. Nobody ever sang it the way Sirit Byar sang it that night, quiet and gentle, with the *kiit* bouncing happily along, running circles all around the words. I can't listen to it now, never, not since that time.

He spoke to the tree again, saying, "Do you remember? You always liked that song—listen to this now." And his voice, that damn fisherman's growl of his, sounded like a boy's voice, and you'd have thought he'd never trusted anyone with his songs before.

He sang "The Woodcutter's Wife" next, that odd thing about an old woman who doesn't want to die without hearing someone, anyone, say, "You're my dear friend, and I love you." Anyway, she goes from her husband to her

children, then to her brothers and sisters, and finally hears
the words from a tired village whore, who'll say anything
for money. And yet, when she does say it for money,
somehow it comes out true, and the old woman dies happy.
Not a song I'd choose, was it me trying to woo a mad-
woman out of her tree, but he knew what he was doing.
About songs, he always knew what he was doing.

I think it was "The Good Folk" next, and then "The Old
Priest and the Old God." By then it had gotten so dark in
that strange courtyard that I couldn't see the tree, let alone
Sirit Byar. He took flint and steel out of one pocket, a candle
end from the other, and made a little sputtering light that
he stood up on the bench beside him. He sang the song
about the lady made out of flowers, and he sang "Thou,"
the one he wrote for his sister, and even my favorite, the
one about the man and the Fox in the Moon. Never moved
from where he sat in his tatter of candlelight, no more than
I did. I just stood very still and listened to him singing, old
song on new, one after another. I could hear Jailly Doura's
heart beating somewhere near, as well as her breathing,
both quick as a bird's—or a *shukri*'s—and one time I was
sure I could smell her, like faraway water. Twice Sirit Byar
asked, "Will you show yourself, Jailly Doura?" but no
chance of that. So he just sang on to someone he couldn't
see, making his magic, drawing her in through the dark, so
slowly, the way you can sometimes charm a dream into letting you remember it. That's magic, too.

Then he sang the lullaby. The one he'd been practicing
every night for two years. I remember a bit of it, just a little.

> "Don't fall asleep,
> don't close your eyes—
> everything happens at night.
> don't you sleep—
> as soon as you slumber,
> the sun starts to ripen,
> the flowers tell stories. . . ."

She made a sound. Not a moan, not a cry, not anything with a name or a shape. Just put down that she tried very hard not to make it. It came out of her anyway.

When she hit him, she knocked the *kiit* out of his hands. That time he couldn't save it—rugs or no rugs, I heard it crack and split, heard eighteen double courses yowl against stone. I just caught a lightning flash of her in the candle-light: matted gray hair flying, eyes like gashes in dead flesh, gaunt arms flailing out of control, beating her own head as much as Sirit Byar's. Something bright flickered in her hands against his throat. The candle fell over and went out.

The darkness was so heavy, I felt myself bending under it. I said, "Jailly Doura, don't hurt him. Please, don't hurt him." I could hear the *kiit* strings still thrashing and jangling faintly, but nothing more, not even the dread-ful *breathing*. Nothing more until Sirit Byar began to sing again.

> *"Don't you sleep—*
> *the marsh-goats are singing,*
> *the fish are all dancing,*
> *the river asks riddles. . . ."*

You couldn't have told that he was singing past a dagger, or a broken piece of glass, or whatever she had been saving for him all this long while. He sounded the way he always did—gruff and south coast, and a little slower than the beat, and not caring about anything in the world but the song. He might have been back in the Miller's Joy, sitting on a table, singing it to fighting, bawling sots; he might have been trying it over to himself as we trudged down some evening road looking for a place to sleep. He sounded like Sirit Byar.

He sang it through to the end, the lullaby, so I knew she hadn't killed him yet, but that was all I did know. I couldn't see anything, I couldn't hear anything, except the footsteps beginning to shuffle slowly toward me. They dragged a little, as though she'd somehow taken on Sirit Byar's limp. I'd have run—all bloody *right*, of course I'd have run, that's just good sense, that's different from fear—but in that crushing dark the steps were coming from everywhere, the way the breathing had been at first. My knees wouldn't hold me up. I sat down and waited.

Close to, she didn't smell like a distant river at all, but like any old hill woman, like my father. She smelled lifelong tired, lifelong dirty, she smelled of clothes sweated in and slept in until they've just *died*, you understand me? I know that smell; I was born and raised to it, and I'd smell just like that now if I hadn't run off with Sirit Byar. What chilled my bowels was the notion that a wealthy mad-woman, prowling a grand house among terrified servants, should smell like home.

When I felt her standing over me, with the stiff, cold ends of that hair trailing across the back of my neck, I said loudly, "I am Mircha Del, of Davlo. You should know that if you're going to kill me." Then I just sat there, feeling out with my skin for whatever she had in her hand.

Her breath on my cheek was raw and old and stagnant, a sick animal's breath. I closed my eyes, even in the darkness, the way you do when you're hoping the *sheknath* or the rock-*targ* will think you're dead. I was ready for her teeth, for her long, jagged nails, but the next thing I felt was her arms around me.

She rocked me, chicken-wrist. Jailly Doura held me in her sad, skinny arms and bumped me back and forth against her breast, pushing and tugging on me as though she were trying to loosen a tree stump in the ground. Likely she didn't remember at all how you rock somebody, but then I don't remember anybody ever rocking me in my life, except her, so I wouldn't ever have known the right way. I did have an idea that it was supposed to be more comfortable, but it wasn't bad. And the breath wasn't so awful, either, when you got used to it, nor that hair all down my face. What was bad was the little whimpering sound, so soft that I

didn't truly hear it but felt it in my body, the broken crooning that never quite became tears but just shivered and shivered on the edge. That was bad, but I kept my eyes closed
tight and helped her rock me, and Sirit Byar began to sing
again.

It doesn't matter what he sang. I know some of the songs
in my bones to this day—bloody well *should*, after all—and
there were others I'd never heard before and never will
again, no matter. What matters is that he sang all night
long, sitting by his shattered *kiit*, with a madwoman's
grieving for his only applause. Jailly Doura went on
rocking me in her arms, and Sirit Byar sang about merrows
and farmwives and wandering Narsai tinkers, and I'll be
damned if I didn't fall off to sleep—only a little, only for a
moment now and then—as though they were really my
parents putting me to bed, just the way they did every
night. And stone Azdak only knows what Aung Jatt
thought was going on upstairs.

Dawn came suddenly, or maybe I'd been dozing again. It
was like staring through rain, but I could see the courtyard
around us—there were walls, of course, and a few narrow
windows, and the tree wasn't *that* big—and I could see Sirit
Byar, looking a bit smaller than usual himself, and white as
his own hair in that rainy light. Jailly Doura was still
holding me, but not rocking anymore, and sometime in the
night she'd stopped making that terrible silent sound. If I
turned my head very slowly and carefully, I could see most
of one side of her face—a thin, lined, worn face it was, but
the nose was strong and the mouth wasn't a dead slash at
all, but full and tender. Her hair was a forsaken birds' nest,
thick with mess—well, about like mine, as you can see. Her
eyes were closed.

Sirit Byar stood up. His voice was a rag of itself, but he
spoke out loudly, not to Jailly Doura this time, nor to me,
but to *someone*. I couldn't tell where he was looking, what
he was seeing. He said, "This is my last song. Take it. I
make this bargain of my own will. I, Sirit Byar." He stood
silent for a moment, and then he nodded once, slowly, as

though he'd had his reply. Oh, chicken-wrist, I can still see him.

I'm not going to sing you the whole song, that last one. I could, but I'm not going to. This one dies with me, it's supposed to. But this is the ending:

> *"Merchant, street girl, beggar, yeoman,*
> *king or common, man or woman,*
> *only two things make us human—*
> *sorrow and love, sorrow and love. . . .*
>
> *Songs and fame are vain endeavor—*
> *only two things fail us never.*
> *only two things last forever—*
> *sorrow and love, sorrow and love. . . ."*

By the time he finished, it was light enough that I could see Aung Jatt standing in the courtyard entrance. Behind me Jailly Doura stirred and sighed, and as I turned my head she opened her eyes again. But they weren't the same eyes. They were gray and wide and full of surprise, curiosity, whatever you want—they were a young woman's eyes in a tired grown face. Maybe I had eyes like that when I was first traveling with Sirit Byar, but I doubt it. She said softly, just the way he'd said it to me, "There you are." And Sirit Byar answered her, "Here I am."

Careful now, both of us, chicken-wrist, you and me. Jailly Doura looked down at me in her arms and said—said *what*? She said, "Are you my daughter, little one?"

"No," I said. "No, no, I'm not. I wish I were." Then I was horribly afraid that I might have lost her again, saying that, driven her right back to where she'd been, but she only smiled and touched my lips and whispered, "Ah, I know. I was just hoping for a moment, one last, last time. Never mind. You have a sweet face."

I do not have a sweet face. There are ugly people who have sweet faces, much good may it do them in this world. I have the face I want, a dirty, mean wild animal's face that makes people leave me alone. Fine. Fine, I wouldn't have it different. But if ever I wanted in my life to have sweetness that somebody could see, it would have been then. I stood up, cramped and cranky, and helped Jailly Doura to rise.

She was small, really, a tiny gray barefoot person in a mucky ruin of a gown that must have cost someone a few gold *lotis* a long time ago, and that a beggar wouldn't have wiped his nose on now. She was as shaky on her feet as a newborn marsh-goat, but she wasn't mad. I looked over toward Aung Jatt, trying to beckon him over to her, but he was staring at Sirit Byar, who had stumbled down to one knee. Jailly Doura was by him before I was. She knelt before him and took his face between her hands. "Not so soon," she said. I remember that. She said, "Not so soon, I'll not have it. I will not, my dear, no. Do you hear me, Sirit Byar?"

You see, she knew better than I what he'd done. He had given up his last song to the gods, the Other Folk, whatever you people call them. And a bard's last song has power, a last song is always answered, as this one was—but what becomes of the bard when the song is over? Sirit Byar's face was a shrunken white mask, but his eyes were open and steady. He said, "Forgive me, Jailly Doura."

"Not if you leave us," she answered him. "Not if you dare leave now." But there was no anger in her voice, and no hope either. Sirit Byar made that half-grunt, half-snort sound that he always made when people were being a little too much for him. He said, "Well, forgive me or no, you are well, and I've done what was for me to do. Now I'm weary."

I wanted to touch him. I wanted to hold him the way Jailly Doura had held me all night, but I just stood with my fingers in my mouth, like a scared baby. Sirit Byar smiled his almost-smile at me and whispered, "I'm sorry the *kiit* broke, big girl. I wanted you to have it. Good-bye." And he was gone, so. Aung Jatt closed his eyes himself, and began to weep. I remember. Jailly Doura didn't, and I didn't, but old Aung Jatt cried and cried.

I buried him myself, and the shards of the *kiit* with him, under the threshold of the house, as I'd done with my father. The others wanted to help me, but I wouldn't let them. When I was finished, I scratched a picture of Azdak, god of wanderers, on the stone stair, and I walked away. So now you know where Sirit Byar lies.

There's no more worth the telling. Aung Jatt and Jailly Doura, wanted me to stay with them as long as I liked, forever, but I only passed a few days at the house with them. What I mostly remember is washing and washing Jailly Doura's long gray-black hair in her bath, as the Queen's ladies used to do with me, four of them at a time to hold me in the tub. I always hated it, and I've not put up with it since, but it's different when you're doing it for someone else. You don't wash fifteen, sixteen years of lunatic despair away in three days, but by the time I left, Jailly Doura could anyway peep in a mirror and start to recognize the handsome, dignified mistress of a great house, with servants underfoot like *dai*-beetles and a husband who looked at her like sunrise. I don't begrudge it—whatever was hers she'd paid double-dear price for it, and double again. But I'd have liked Sirit Byar to see her this way, even once.

When I left, she walked with me down to the two great stones where we'd first met Aung Jatt, a hundred years ago. She didn't bother with saying, "Come back and visit us," and I didn't bother promising. Instead she took both my hands and swung them, the way children do, and she just said, "I would have been proud if you had been my daughter."

I didn't know how to answer. I kissed her hands, which I've never done with anybody except the Queen, and you have to do that. Then I swung Sirit Byar's old sea-bag to my shoulder, and I started off alone. I didn't look back, but Jailly Doura called after me, "So would *he* have been proud. Remember, Mircha Del!"

And I have remembered, and that's why the fit took me to have someone set it all down, the only true tale of Sirit Byar you're ever likely to hear. No, I told you I don't want it; what good's your scribble to me? I can't read it—and besides, I was there. Keep it for yourself, keep it for anyone who wants to know a little of what he was. Bad enough they mess up his songs, let them get *something* the right way round, anyway. Farewell, my chicken-wrist—here's your twelve coppers, and another for the sweet way you blush. There's an ore barge tied up at Grebak, waiting for a good woman to handle the sweep, if I'm there by tomorrow eve.

THE MAGICIAN
OF KARAKOSK

What, what—is it my turn? No, I was not asleep—I would never be so unmannerly as to doze off when someone else was telling a story. I was thinking only, thinking about how long it has been since I sat like this with friends—oh, with anyone, really—listening to wonders and sillinesses and wonders again by firelight. I have lived an odd sort of life, and I am afraid that it has left me with little to tell that would not bore the young ones here and antagonize the old; and I would not do either tonight for worlds. You must indulge me—I promise to keep the tale short, and leave plenty of evening for Gri and Chashi and Mistress Kydra here. I am as eager as anyone else to be done with my rambling mumbles.

Well, then. Once, a very long time ago, in the land I come from, there was a magician who was too good at magic. Ah, you stare, you look at each other, you snicker, but it's so—it is quite possible to be too good at anything, and especially magic. Consider—if you only need a gentle shower to restore your thirsty fields, what good is a wizard who can bring nothing but storms that will wash them away? If you ask for a little kitchen charm to keep your man faithful, what's the use of a spell that will have him underfoot and at your heel every hour of every day, until you could scream for a single moment to yourself? No, no, when it comes to magic give me a humble mediocrity, always. Believe me, I know what I am saying.

Now the magician of whom I speak was a humble man in every way. He was of low birth, the son of a *rishu*-herder, and although he gave evidence of his abilities quite young, as most wizards do, there was never any possibility of his receiving the proper training in its use. Even if he could have had access to the teaching scrolls of Am-Nemil or Kirisinja, such as are preserved in the great thaumaturgic library at Cheth na'Bata, I much doubt that he could even have read them. He was a peasant with a gift, nothing more. His name was Lanak.

What did he look like? Well, if your notion of a magician is someone tall, lean, and commanding, swirling a black cape around his shoulders, you would have been greatly disappointed in Lanak. He was short and thickset, like all the men of his family, with their tendency to early baldness, I am afraid. But he had nice eyes, or so I have heard, and quite good manners, and large, friendly brown hands.

I repeat, because it is important: this Lanak was a humble man with no high dreams at all—most unusual in a wizard of any origin. He lived in Karakosk, a town notable only for its workhorses and its black beer, which suited our Lanak down to the ground, as you might say, for he understood both of those good creatures in his bones. In fact, the first spell he ever attempted successfully was one to strengthen his father's rather watery home brew, and the second was to calm a stallion maddened by the pain of a sand-spider bite. Left to himself, he'd likely never have asked to do anything grander than that with his magical gift. Spending his life as a town conjuror, no different from the town baker or cobbler—aye, that would have suited him right down to the ground.

But magic has a way of not leaving you to yourself, by its own nature. Magic has an ambition to be used, even if you don't. Our Lanak went along happily for many years, liked and respected by all who knew him—he even married a Karakosk woman, and I can count on the fingers of one hand those wizards who have ever wed. They simply do *not*; wizards live immensely alone, and there it is. But Lanak never really thought of himself as a wizard, you see. Lanak thought of himself as a Karakosk man, nothing more.

And if his talent had been as modest as he, likely enough he would have spent his life in perfect tranquility, casting his backyard spells over fields, gardens, ovens, finding strayed children and livestock impartially, blessing marriage beds and melon beds alike—and yes, why not? bringing a bit of rain now and then. But it was not to be.

He was simply too good. Do you begin to understand me now? The colicky old horses he put his hands on and whispered to did not merely recover—they became twice the workers they had been in their prime, as the orchards he enchanted bore so much fruit that the small farmers of Karakosk found themselves exporting to cities like Bitava, Leishai, even Fors na'Shachim, for the first time in the town's history. There was a hard winter, I remember, when Lanak cast a spell meant only to ease the snowfall, just for the children, so their shoes would last longer—and what was the result? Spring came to Karakosk a good two months before a single green shoot stuck up its head anywhere else in the entire land. This is the sort of thing that gets itself noticed.

And noticed it was, first by the local warlord—I forget his name, it will come to me in a moment—who swept down on Karakosk one day with his scabby troop at his heels. You know the sort, you doubtless have a Night Visitor or a Protector of your own, am I right in that? Aye, well, then you've an idea what it was like for Karakosk when their particular bravo and his gang came swaggering into the market square months before their yearly tribute was due. There were close on forty of them: all loud, stupid and brutal, except for their commander, who was not stupid, but made up for it by being twice as brutal as the rest. His name was Bourjic, I remember now.

Well, this Bourjic demanded to see the great wizard folk had been telling him about; and when the townspeople appeared reluctant to fetch their Lanak on a bandit's whim, he promptly snatched the headman's little son up to his saddle and threatened to cut his throat on the spot if someone didn't produce a wizard in the next five minutes. There was nothing for it—Bourjic had made similar threats in the past, and carried them all through—so the headman himself ran to the very edge of town to find Lanak in his barn, where he was once more redesigning his firework display for the Thieves' Day festival. Lanak's fireworks were the pride of the region for twenty miles around, but he was forever certain that he could improve them with just a little effort.

When he understood the danger to the headman's son, he flushed red as a *taiya*-bush with outrage. Rather pink-faced as he was by nature, no one had ever seen him turn just that shade of redness before. He put his arm around the headman's shoulders, spoke three words—and there they were in the market square, face-to-face with a startled Bourjic trying to control his even more startled horse. Bourjic said, "Hey!" and the horse said, "*Wheee!*" and Lanak said the little boy's name and one other word. The boy vanished from Bourjic's saddle and reappeared in his father's arms, none the worse for the experience, and the spoiled envy of all his schoolmates for the next six months. Lanak set his hands on his hips and waited for Bourjic's horse to calm down.

I've told you that Bourjic's men were all as stupid as gateposts? Yes, well, one of them cranked up his crossbow and let a quarrel fly straight for Lanak's left eye, as he was bending over the boy to make certain that he was un-harmed. Lanak snatched the bolt out of the air without looking up, kissed it—of all things to do—and hurled it back at Bourjic's man, where it whipped around his neck like a noose and clung very tight indeed. Not tight enough to strangle, but enough so that he fell off his horse and lay there on the ground kicking and croaking. Bourjic looked down at him once, and not again.

"The very fellow I wanted to see," says he with a wide,

white smile. Bourjic was a gentleman born, after all, and had a bit of manners when it suited him. He said now, "I've grand news for you, young Lanak. You're to come straightway to the castle and work for me."

Lanak answered him, "I'm not young, and your castle is a tumbledown hogpen, and I work for the folk of Karakosk and no one beside. Leave us now."

Bourjic reached for his sword hilt, but checked himself, keeping that smile strapped onto his face. "Let us talk," he said. "It seems to me that if *I* were offered a choice between life as a nobleman's personal wizard and seeing my town, my fields, my friends all burned to blowing ashes—well, I must say I might be a bit more inclined toward seeing reason. Of course, that's just me."

Lanak nodded toward the man writhing in the dirt. Bourjic laughed down at him. "Ah, but that has just made me want you more, you see. And I simply must have what I want, that's why I am what I am. So float up here behind me, or magic yourself up a horse, whichever you choose, and let's be on our way."

Lanak shook his head and turned away. Bourjic said nothing more, but there came a sound behind him that made Lanak wheel round instantly. It was the sound of forty men striking flint against steel at once and setting light to tallow-stiff torches they'd had ready at their saddles. The townsfolk looking on gasped and wailed; a few bravely, hopelessly, picked up clods to throw. But Lanak fixed his mild, washed-out-looking blue eyes on Bourjic and said only, "I told you to leave us."

"And so indeed I shall," the warlord answered him cheerfully. "With you or without you. The decision is yours for another ten seconds."

Lanak stood fast. Bourjic sighed ostentatiously and said, "So be it, then." He turned in the saddle to signal his men.

"Get back," Lanak said to the folk of Karakosk. They scrambled to obey him, as Bourjic's grinning soldiers raised their torches. Lanak folded his arms, bowed deeply—to the earth itself, as it seemed—and began to sing what sounded like no more than a nonsensical nursery rhyme. Bourjic, suddenly alarmed, shouted to his men, "Burn! Now!"

But even as he uttered those two words, the ground before him began to heave and stretch itself and grumble, like an old man finally deciding to throw off his quilt and get out of bed. Where it stretched, it split, and some bits fell in and down and deep out of sight, and other bits swelled right up to the height of storm waves heading for shore. Bourjic's horse reared and danced back from the chasm that had just opened between him and Lanak, while all his men fought to control their own terrified beasts, and the folk of Karakosk clung to their children, to each other, to anything that seemed at all solid. The earth went on splitting, left and right, as though it were shedding its skin: raw red canyons were opening everywhere, and you could see fire crawling away and away in their depths. Shops and houses all around the square were toppling, bursting apart, and the angry, juddering, groaning sound kept getting louder, louder. Lanak himself covered his ears.

Bourjic and his lot crumbled like dry cheese. They yanked their horses' heads round and were gone, a good bit faster than they'd come, and it was hard to say who was doing the more screaming, man or mount. The ground began to quiet, by little and little, as soon as they were out of sight, and the townsfolk were amazed to see the fearful wounds in the earth silently closing before their eyes, the scars healing without a trace, the buildings somehow floating back together, and the Karakosk market square demurely returning to the dusty, homely patch of ground it had always been. And there stood Lanak in the middle of it, stamping out a few smoldering torches, wiping his forehead, blowing his nose.

"There," he said. "There. Nothing but an illusion, as you see, but one that should keep friend Bourjic well clear of us for some while. Glad to be of help, I'll be off home now." He started away; then glanced around at his dumbstruck neighbors and repeated, "An illusion, that's all. No more. The fireworks, now, those are real."

But the citizens of Karakosk had all seen one of Bourjic's soldiers—the one with the crossbow quarrel wrapped so snugly around his neck—plummet straight down into a bottomless crevasse that opened where he lay, and that closed over him a moment later. And if *that* was an illusion, you could never have proved it by that man.

As I'm sure you can well imagine, the whole business made things even more difficult for poor Lanak. Bourjic was probably as interested as he in keeping the story from getting around; but get around it did, and it was heard in towns and cities a long way from black-beer Karakosk. Sirit Byar made a song out of it, I think. Lissi Jair did, I know that much—a good song, too. There were others.

And the Queen, in her black castle in Fors na'Shachim, heard them all.

None of you know much about the Queens in Fors, do you? No, I thought not, and no reason why you should. Well, there is always a Queen, which really means little more than the hereditary ruler of Fors na'Shachim itself and a scatter of surrounding provinces and towns—including Karakosk—and even particular manors. Most of the Queens have proved harmless enough over the years; one or two have been surprisingly benign and visionary, and a very few have turned out plain wicked. The one I speak of, unfortunately, was one of those last.

Which does not mean that she was a stupid woman. On the contrary, she was easily the cleverest Queen Fors na'Shachim has ever had, and it is quite an old city. She listened to new songs as intently as she did to the words of her ministers and her spies; and it is told that she walked often among her subjects in various guises, and so learned many things that many would have kept from her. And when she had heard enough ballads about the wizard Lanak of little Karakosk, she said to her greatest captain, the Lord Durgh, "That one. Get him for me."

Well now, this Durgh was no fool himself, and he had heard the songs, too. He'd no mind at all to have as many people laughing and singing about *his* humiliation by some bumpkin trickster as were still laughing at Bourjic. So when he went down to Karakosk, he went unarmed, with only two of his most closemouthed lieutenants for company. He asked politely to be directed to the home of a gentleman named Lanak, and rode there slowly enough to let the rumors of his arrival and destination reach the house before he did. He'd been born in the country himself, Lord Durgh had.

And when he was at last facing Lanak in the wizard's front garden, he got off his horse and bowed formally to him, and made his men do so, too. He said, "Sir, I am come to you from the Queen on a mission of grave urgency for the realm. Will it please you attend on her?"

Yes, of course, it was a trick, and all of us here would doubtless have seen through it instantly. But no high personage had ever spoken to Lanak in such a humble manner before. He asked only, "May I be told Her Majesty's need?" to which Lord Durgh replied, "I am not privileged to know such things," which was certainly true. Then Lanak bowed in his turn, and went into his house to tell Dwyla, his wife, that he had been summoned to the Queen's aid and would return in plenty of time for the Priests' Moon, which is when the folk around Karakosk do their spring sowing. Dwyla packed the few garments he requested and kissed him farewell, making him promise to bring their little daughter something pretty from Fors.

There's been a new road cut long since, but it is still three hard-riding days from the market square at Karakosk to the black castle. Durgh made a diffident half-suggestion that the wizard might like to call up a wind to whisk them there instantly, but Lanak said it would frighten the horses. He rode pillion behind Lord Durgh, and enjoyed the journey immensely, however the others felt about it. You must remember, Lanak had never been five miles from Karakosk in his life.

Trotting over his first real cobblestones in the streets of

Fors na'Shachim, he almost disjointed his neck turning it in every direction, this gawking peasant who could chase away winter and make the earth rend itself under bandits' feet. He was so busy memorizing everything he saw for Dwyla's benefit—the marketplace as big as his entire town; the legendary Glass Orchard; divisions of the Queen's household guard in their silver livery wheeling right about and saluting as the Lord Durgh cantered by—that the black castle was looming over him before he realized that they had arrived. He did, however, notice Lord Durgh's poorly concealed sigh of relief as they dismounted and gave their horses over to the grooms.

Does anyone here know Fors at all, by any chance? Ah, your father did, Mistress Kydra? Well, I'm sure it hadn't changed much from Lanak's time when your father saw it, nor would it be greatly different today. Fors na'Shachim never really changes. For all its color, for all the bustle, the musicians and tumblers and dancers on every corner, the sharpers and the alley girls, the street barrows where you can buy anything from *namph* still wet from the fields to steaming lamprey pies—those *are* good—for all that, as I say, one never truly escapes the taste of iron underneath, of dutiful abandon working overtime to mask the cold face of power. And even if that power casts no shadow beyond the city gates, I can assure you that it is real enough in Fors na'Shachim. I have been there often enough to know.

But Lanak had never been to Fors, and he was thrilled enough for any dozen bumpkins to be marching up those obsidian stairs with Lord Durgh's hand closed gently enough just above his left elbow, and all those silver-clad men-at-arms falling in behind them. He was not taken directly to see the Queen—no one ever is. Indeed, that's rather the whole point of being Queen, as you might say. There have been those who forced their way into the presence, mind you; but these were a different sort of people from our modest Lanak. Most of them ended quite differently, too.

Lanak was perfectly content to be shown to his quarters

in what used to be called the Hill Tower because you can just make out the haze over the Ghost Range from the upper windows. They call it the Wizard's Tower now. There was food and drink and hot water waiting, and he used the time to wash, change from his grimy traveling clothes into something more suitable for meeting the Queen, and then to begin a long letter to Dwyla at home. He was still hard at it that evening when Lord Durgh came to fetch him.

What is the black castle really like? Well, it is as grand as you imagine, Hramath, but perhaps not exactly in the *way* you imagine it. It began as a fortress, you know, in the old times when Fors was nothing more than a military outpost; which is why it is black, being mostly built of dressed *almuri* stone from the quarries near Chun. Every queen for the last five hundred years has tried in turn to make the castle a bit more luxurious for herself, if no less forbidding to her subjects: so there are a great many windows and rich carpets, and countless chandeliers, even in places where you would never expect more than a rush-light. There is always music, and always sounding just at your shoulder, even if the players are a dozen galleries distant—that's a trick of *almuri*, no other stone does that. And of course the walls of every room and every corridor are hung with real paintings, not merely the usual rusty shields and pieces of armor—and the paintings are done on real cloth and canvas, not bark or raw wood, as we do here. The food and wine served to the Queen's guests is the best to be had south of the Durli Hills; the ladies of her court have Stimezst silk for their everyday wear; the beds are almost too comfortable for comfort, if you understand me. Oh, you would want for nothing you know how to dream of in the black castle at Fors, Hramath.

Even so, just like the city itself, it is always the stone fortress it always was, with the Silver Guard never more than a room away, and Lanak was not bumpkin enough to miss that for long. Not that he was especially on his guard when Lord Durgh bowed him into the Queen's presence—

perhaps what I mean is that he was attempting from the first to see his marvelous adventure through his wife's eyes, and Dwyla was a shrewd countrywoman who missed very little. Wizard or no, he did well to marry her, Lanak did.

Yes, yes, yes, the Queen. She received Lanak in her most private chambers, with no one in attendance but Lord Durgh himself, and she packed *him* off on some errand or other before Lanak had finished bowing. I am told that she was quite a small woman, daintily made, with a great deal of dark hair, a sweetly curved mouth, skin as smooth as water, and eyes as shiny and cold as the gleaming black walls of her castle. She seemed no older than Lanak himself, but of course you never know with queens.

Well, then. She greeted Lanak most royally and courteously, even saying to him with an appealing air of shyness, "Sir, I have never received a great wizard in these rooms before. You must pardon me if I hardly know how to behave."

Those were her very words, as I was told them, and of course she could have said nothing more calculated to reach the heart of Lanak, who really *was* shy. He swallowed hard several times, finally managing to reply, "Majesty, I am no great wizard, but only a journeyman from a town of journeymen. As honored as I am, I cannot imagine why you have summoned me, who have your pick of masters."

And he meant it, and the Queen could see that he meant it, and she smiled the way a cat smiles in its sleep. She said, "Indeed, I must confess that I have made some small study of wizards. I know very well who the masters in this realm are, and who the journeymen—every one—and which lay claim to mastery who would be hard put to turn cream into butter. And nowhere have I heard tales to equal the word I have of you, good Lanak. Without even stirring from your dear little town whose name I keep forgetting, you have become the envy of magicians whose names I am sure you cannot know. What have you to say of that, I wonder?"

Lanak did not know at all what to say. He looked at his hands, stared away at the pale-rose canopy over the

Queen's bed, and finally mumbled, "I think it is no good thing to be envied. If what you tell me is true, it distresses me greatly, but I cannot believe it is so. How could a Rhyssa, a K'Shas, a Tombry Dar envy Lanak of Karakosk? You are mistaken, Majesty, surely."

"Queens are never mistaken," the Queen answered him, "as even great wizards must remember." But she went on smiling kindly and thoughtfully at Lanak. "Well, I will test your skill then, though for your reassurance, not my own. The water of my domain is not of the best, as you know."

Lanak did know. As you here cannot, even the oldest among us. In the time of which I tell you, the water of Fors na'Shachim and the country round about was renowned for its bitterness. It was not vile enough to be undrinkable, nor foul enough to cause sickness or plague, but it tasted like copper coins and harness polish, with a slight touch of candle wax. Clothes washed in any stream turned a pale, splotchy yellow which came quickly to identify their owners to amused outsiders; indeed, citizens of Fors were often referred to as "pissbreeches" in those days. The term is still used now and then, even today, though no one in the city could tell you why.

The Queen said, "I have requested several wizards to improve the water of Fors na'Shachim. I will not embarrass such an unassuming man by revealing their names. Suffice it to say that not one succeeded, though all proved most wondrously gifted at vanishing when I showed my displeasure." She leaned forward and touched Lanak's rough brown hand. "I am confident that it will be quite otherwise with you."

Lanak answered helplessly, "I will do my best, Majesty. But I fear sorely that I will disappoint you, like my colleagues."

"Then I hope you are at least their equal at disappearing," the Queen replied. She laughed, to show him that this was meant humorously, and stood up to indicate that the interview was at an end. As Lanak was backing out of the room (Dwyla had read somewhere about the proper way to take leave of royalty), she added, "Sleep well, good friend. For myself, I will certainly be awake all night, imagining my subjects' surprise and pleasure when they brew their afternoon tea tomorrow."

But Lanak never even lay down in the grand, soft bed which had been prepared for him. He paced his room in the moonlight, trying as hard as he could to imagine which magicians had already tried their skills on Fors's water, and which charms they might have attempted. For there is a common language of magic, you know, just as there is in music: it is the one particular singer, the one particular *chayad*-player, the one particular wizard who makes the difference in the song or the spell. Lanak walked in circles, muttering to himself, that whole night, and at last he stood very still, staring blankly out of the window at the dark courtyard below. And when morning came, he ate the handsome breakfast that the Queen's own butler had brought to him, washed it down with the eyewash that still passes for ale in Fors, then belched comfortably, leaned back in his chair, and turned the water of the realm sweeter than any to be found without crossing an ocean. And so it remains to this day, though apparently he could do nothing with the ale.

The Queen was mightily pleased. She brought Lanak out on a high balcony and embarrassed him immensely by showing him to her folk as the wonder-worker who had done for them what the mightiest sorcerers in all the land had incessantly promised and failed to do. They cheered him deliriously, celebrated him all that day and the next, and were generally useless as subjects until the Silver Guard harried them back to work. Most of that last was done out of Lanak's sight, but not all.

"There," said the Queen. "Have you not satisfied yourself now that you are wizard enough to serve me?"

But Lanak said, "Majesty, it was merely my good fortune that I understand water. Water, in its nature, does not like to feel itself foul; it recoils from its own taste as much as you do. All I needed to do was to *become* the water of Fors na'Shachim, to feel my way down into the source of its old bitterness and become that too. Your other wizards cannot have been country people, or they would have known this, too. In the country, spells and glamours are the very least of magic—understanding, becoming what you understand, that is all of it, truly. My Queen, you need a wizard who will understand the world of queens, ministers, captains, campaigns. Forgive me, I am not that man."

"Do not speak to me of my needs," the Queen answered him, and her tone was hard for the first time. "Speak of my desires, as I bid you." But she quickly hid her impatience and patted Lanak's hand again. She said, "Very well, then, very well, let me set you one last unnecessary test. It is known to be beyond any doubt that three high officers of my incorruptible Silver Guard are in the pay of a foreign lord whose name does not matter. I cannot prove this, but *that* would not matter"—and she showed just the tips of her teeth—"if I but knew who they were. Find these traitors out for me, simple country Lanak, and be assured forever of my favor."

Now even in Karakosk, Lanak had resisted all efforts to make him, with his magical talents, a sheriff, a constable, a thief-taker. He wanted no part of the Queen's request, but even he could see that there was no courteous way to decline without offending her hospitality. So he said at last, "So be it, but give me the night once again to take counsel with my spirits." And this being just the sort of talk the Queen wanted to hear, and not any prattle of understanding and becoming, she smiled her warmest smile and left Lanak to himself. But she also left two trusted men-at-arms clanking back and forth outside his door that night, and another under his window, because you never know with wizards either.

And there went another night's sleep for our poor Lanak, who had been so peacefully accustomed to snuggling close to Dwyla, with his arm over her and her cold feet tucked in between his. As before, he brooded and pondered, proposing courses of action aloud to himself and each time breaking in to deride himself for an incompetent fool. But somewhere between deep midnight and dawn, as before, he grew very still, as only a wizard can be still; and by and by, he began to draw odd lines and shapes in the dust on the windowsill, and then he began to say words. They made no more sense than the dust trails he was tracing; nor was there anything grandly ominous in the sound of them. By and by, he stopped speaking and just leaned his head against the window like a child on a rainy day, gazing silently down at the courtyard. I think he even slept a little, with his eyes half-open, for he was quite weary.

And presently what do you suppose?—here came the sound of quick hoofbeats on stone, and a horseman in the glinting livery of the Silver Guard clattered across the courtyard, past the inner gatehouse without so much as a glance for the drowsy sentry, and away for the portcullis at full gallop. Nothing stirred within the black castle, least of all the wizard Lanak.

An hour, maybe less, and by all the seagoing gods of the terrible Goro folk, here's another rider heading away from Fors as fast as he can go. Panting on his heels comes another, and what Lanak can see of his face in the icy moonlight is taut with fear, wooden with fear. No more after them, but Lanak leans at that window all the rest of that night, maybe sleeping, maybe not.

In the morning he went to the Queen in her throne room and told her to turn out the Silver Guard for review. Since she was used to doing this no more than once a week, she looked at Lanak in some surprise, but she did what he said. And when she noticed that three of her highest-ranking officers were notable for not being there, nor anywhere she sent to find them, she turned on Lanak and raged in his face, "You warned them! You helped them escape me!"

"I did no such thing," Lanak answered calmly. Even a wide-eyed countryman can take the measure of royalty, give him time enough, and he had the Queen's by now. "Seeking to learn who your turncoats might be, I sent a spell of fear over your entire garrison, a spell of guilt and unreasoning terror of discovery. Those three panicked and fled in the night, and can do you no more harm."

"I wanted them," the Queen said. Her own face was very pale now, and her voice was gentle as gentle. "I wanted to see them with their bones broken and their skin stripped off, hanging from my balcony, still a little alive, blackening in the sun. I am very disappointed, Lanak."

"Well," Lanak murmured apologetically, "I did tell you I was not the right sort of wizard for a queen." He kept his face and his manner downcast, even somber, trying hard to keep his jubilation from spilling over. The Queen would be bound to dismiss him from her service on the spot, and on his own, unburdened by mounted companions, he could be home in Karakosk for lunch, bouncing his daughter on his knee and telling Dwyla what it was like to dine in the black castle with musicians playing for you. But the Queen confounded him.

"No, you are not," she said, and there was no expression at all in her voice. "None of you are, not a preening, posturing one of you. But I realized that long ago, as I realized what I would have to do to attain my desire." She was staring at him from far behind her dark, shiny eyes; and Lanak, who—without ever thinking about it, feared very little—looked back at her and was afraid.

"You will teach me," the Queen said. "You will teach me your magic—all of it, all of it, every spell, every gesture, every rune, every rhyme of power. Do you understand me?"

Lanak tried to speak, but she waved him silent, showing him the tips of her teeth again. She said, "Do you understand? You will not leave this place until I know everything you know. Everything."

"It will take your lifetime," Lanak whispered. "It is not a business of learning one spell or learning a dozen. One is always becoming a wizard, always—"

"*Becoming* again," the Queen snapped contemptuously. "I did not order you to teach me the philosophy of magic—it is your magic itself I desire, and I will have it, be very sure of that." Now she softened her tone, speaking in soothing counterfeit of the way in which she had first greeted him. "It will not take nearly as long as all that, good Lanak. You will find me quite a good pupil—I learn swiftly when the matter is of interest to me. We will begin tomorrow, and I promise to surprise you by the end of the very first day. And Lanak"—and here her voice turned flat and hard once again—"please do not let even the shadow of a thought of taking wizard's leave of me cross your mind. Your wife and child in quaint little Karakosk would not thank you for it."

Lanak, who had been within two short phrases and one stamp of his foot of taking that very course, felt himself turning to stone where he stood. His voice sounded far away in his own ears, empty as her voice, saying, "If you have harmed them, I will have every stone of this castle down to make your funeral barrow. I can do this."

"I should hope you can," the Queen answered him. "Why would I want to study with a wizard who could do any less? And yes, you could have your dear family safe in your arms days before I could get any word to the men who have been keeping friendly watch over them since you left home. And you could destroy those same men with a wave of your hand if they and a thousand like them came against you, and another thousand after those—I know all that, believe me, I do." Her sleeping-cat smile was growing wider and warmer as she spoke.

"But for how long, Lanak? For how long could you keep them safe, do you think? Never mind the legions, I am not such a fool as to put my faith in lances and armor against such a man. I am speaking of the knife in the marketplace, the runaway coach in the crowded street, the twilight arrow in the kitchen garden. Is your magic—no, is your *attention* powerful enough to protect those you love every minute of the rest of their lives? Because it had better be, Lanak. I have my failings, queen or no queen, but no one has ever said of me that I was not patient. I will not grow weary of waiting for my opportunity, and I will not forget. Think very well on this, wizard, before you bid me farewell."

Lanak did not answer her for a long time. They stood facing one another, alone in the great cold throne room, hung with the ceremonial shields and banners of a hundred queens before this Queen, and what passed between their eyes I cannot tell you. But Lanak said at last, "So be it. I will teach you what I know."

"I am grateful and most honored," replied the Queen, and there was almost no mockery in her tone. "When you have completed your task, you may go in peace, laden to exasperation with a queen's gifts to your family. Until tomorrow, then." And she inclined her head graciously for Lanak to bow himself out of the room.

If no one would mind, I'll pass quickly over what Lanak thought that night, and over what he felt and did in solitude—even over whether he slept or not, which I certainly hope he did. I doubt very much that any of you could have slept, or I myself, but magicians are very different people from you and me. It was the Queen's misfortune that, clever as she was, she could not imagine just how different magicians are.

In any case, she appeared in Lanak's quarters early the next morning, just like any other eager student hoping to make a good impression on her teacher. And the truth is that she did exactly that. She had not been boasting when she called herself a quick learner: by afternoon he had already taken her through the First Principles of magic, which are at once as simple as a nursery rhyme and as slippery as buttered ice. Many's the wizard who will tell you that nothing afterward in his training was ever as difficult as comprehending First Principles. Kirisinja herself took eight months—so the tale has it, anyway.

And the Queen did indeed surprise Lanak greatly that day when, illustrating the Sixth Principle, he made a winter-apple fade out of existence, and she promptly reversed his gesture and called the apple into being again.

Elementary, certainly; but since the Sixth Principle involves bringing back, not the vanished object itself, but the last actual moment when the object existed, it is easy to understand why Lanak was a good deal more than surprised. A great many people have at least a small gift for magic, but most die without ever realizing this. The Queen knew.

Now I will tell you, the appalling thing for Lanak was that he found himself enjoying teaching her; even rather looking forward to their lessons. He had never taught his art before, nor had he ever had much opportunity to discuss it with other wizards. Dwyla was as knowledgeable as one could wish about the daily practicalities of living with magic, but as indifferent as the Queen to the larger reality behind the chalked circles and pentacles that she scrubbed off the floor many mornings. But the Queen at least was hungry to know every factor that might possibly affect the casting or the success of even the smallest spell. Lanak felt distinctly guilty at times to be enjoying his work with her as much as he was.

Because he had no illusions at all regarding what she proposed to do with the skills she was acquiring from him. She said it herself, more than once: "This whole realm south of the Durlis should be a true kingdom, an empire—and what is it? Nothing but a rusty clutter of overgrown family estates, with not even energy enough for a decent war. Well, when I am a wizard, we will see about *that*. Believe me, we will."

"Majesty, you will never be a wizard," Lanak would answer her plainly. "When we are done, you may have a wizard's abilities, yes. It is not at all the same thing."

The Queen would laugh then: a child's spluttering giggle that never quite concealed the iron delight beneath. "It will serve me just as well, my dear Lanak. Everything will serve me, soon enough."

And *soon enough* would arrive altogether too soon, Lanak realized, if the Queen kept up her astonishing pace of study. She was not so much learning as devouring, annexing the enchantments he taught her, as she planned to annex every one of the little city-states, provinces, and principalities she derided. He had no doubt that she could do it: any competent wizard could have done so straightforward a thing long before, if wizards were at all concerned with that sort of power, which they are not. Even the most evil wizard has no real interest in land or riches or great glory in the mortal world. That is a game for kings, and for queens—what those others covet is a tale I will not tell here.

This tale, now—it might have had a very different ending if Lanak had not been a married man. As I have said, magicians almost never take wives or husbands; when they lie sleepless, it is because they are brooding mightily over the ethics of conjuration, the logical basis of illusion, the influence of the stars on shape-shifting. But Lanak's nights were haunted by his constant worry about Dwyla and the little one, and about Dwyla's worry about him (he had not dared attempt to communicate with her for weeks, even by magical means, for fear of provoking her watchers), and the deep-growing anger of a mild man. And this last is very much to be wary of, whether your man is a wizard or no. But the Queen had never had to consider such things. No more than had Lanak, when you come to think about it.

So. So the Queen came to know more spells than anyone but a wizard ever has known; and, also, that she learned them far faster than a true apprentice wizard ever would have done. She walked through the walls of her castle, utterly terrifying her servants and soldiers, who took her for her own ghost; she caused the dishes being prepared for her in the great kitchens to rise and float solemnly through the halls to her dining table; at times she left a smiling, regal shadow to debate with ministers and counselors, and herself slipped away unnoticed to gaze from her highest tower far over the lands she intended to rule. There is a legend—no more than that—that as she grew even more accomplished, she took to prowling the midnight alleys of the city in the lean, man-faced form of a *lourijakh*, straight out of the

Barrens. Further, it is told that she did not go hungry in that form, but that I do not believe. Lanak would never have allowed it, of that much I am sure.

Finally Lanak said to her, "I have kept our agreement, Majesty. You now know what I know—every spell, every gesture, every rune, every rhyme. Except, perhaps—" and he suddenly coughed and looked away, so plainly trying to swallow back the betraying word. But it was too late.

"*Except*," repeated the Queen. Her voice was light, her tone no more than respectfully curious, but her eyes were bright stone. "Except what, my master?" When Lanak did not answer, she spoke once again, and all she said was, "Lanak."

Lanak sighed, still not looking at her. "Sendings," he mumbled. "I did not teach you about sendings, because I do not use them myself. I would never employ a sending, for any reason. Never."

The Queen said, "But you know how it is done."

"Yes, yes," Lanak answered her. He rubbed his hands hard together and shivered, though it was a hot day for the time of year. He said, "A sending is death. That is its only purpose—whether it ever touches its victim or not, its presence kills. It may appear as an ordinary man or woman, as any animal from a snake to a *shukri* to a rock-*targ*—but it is in truth born of the very essence of the magician who controls it. And yet it is *not* the magician, not at all." His voice grew more urgent, and he did look straight at the Queen now. "Majesty, magic is neither good nor bad in itself, but a sending is evil in its nature, always. How you will use what I have taught is your own affair—but ask me no more about sendings. I implore you, ask me no more."

"Oh, but I must," replied the Queen prettily. "I simply must ask, since you have so aroused my curiosity. And you must tell me, good Lanak." They stared at each other, and I think there was something in Lanak's eyes that made the Queen add, "Of course, I have no intention of ever using such a thing. You are my master, after all, and I take your words most seriously. That is why I would hear all of them. All of them, Lanak."

So Lanak taught her about sendings.

It took him more than two weeks: still far less time than it should have, when you consider the memorizing alone, never mind the embarrassing rituals, the herbs that have to be gathered and cooked into stinking brews, the merciless disciplining of your mind—and all that for a single sending! But the Queen took it in as though it were no more than another lesson in predicting the sex of a child or the best month for planting. Truly, she was a remarkable woman, that one, and no mistake.

At the end, she said, "Well, Lanak, you have indeed kept your word, and I will keep mine. You may depart for home and hearth this very moment, if you desire, though I would be truly honored if you chose to dine with me this one last night. I do not imagine that we will meet again, and I would do you tribute if I may. Because I may have mocked you somewhat at times, but never when I call you *master*." And she looked so young when she said this, and so earnest and so anxious, that Lanak could do nothing in the world but nod.

That night the Queen served Lanak a dinner such as he never had again in his life, and he lived to be very old and more celebrated than he liked. They drank a great deal of wine together—yes, you are quite right, Chashi, the vineyards of this province have always supplied the black castle—and both of them laughed more than you might think; and Lanak even sang a few bars of an old song that the folk of Karakosk sing about their rulers in Fors na'Shachim, which made the Queen laugh until she spilled her drink. Nevertheless, when Lanak went off to his quarters, he was dreadfully, freezingly sober, and he knew that the Queen was, too. He turned in the doorway and said to her, "Above all, remember the very last word of the spell. It is a sure safeguard, should anything go ill."

"I have it perfectly," answered the Queen. "Not that I would ever need it."

"And remember this, too," Lanak said. "Sendings call no one *master*. No one."

"Yes," said the Queen. "Yes. Good night, Lanak."

Lanak did not go to bed that night. By candlelight he carefully folded the clothes that Dwyla had packed for him—how long ago!—and put them back into his traveling bag, along with the gifts and little keepsakes that he had bought for her and their daughter, or been given for them by the Queen. When he had finished, the moon was low in the east, and he could hear a new shift of guards tramping to their posts on the castle walls. But he did not lie down.

If you had been there, you would have watched in wonder as he wrapped his arms around his own shoulders, just as precisely as he had packed his bag; and even if you missed the words he murmured, you would have seen him stand up on his toes—a little too high, you might have thought—and then begin to spin around in a curious way, faster and faster, until he rose into the air and floated up toward the arched ceiling, vanishing into a corner where the candlelight did not go. And how he remained there, and for how long, I cannot say.

By and by, when all the candles save one had burned out, and every other sound in the black castle had long been swallowed by other high, cold corners, there came the faint scratching of claws on stone in the corridor just outside his door. There was no rattling of the knob, no trying of the lock—which Lanak had left unturned—there was simply a thing in the room. The shadows by the door concealed it at first, but you would have known it was there, whether you could see it or not.

It took a step forward, halfway into the shivering light. It stood on two legs, but looked as though it might drop back down onto four at any moment. The legs were too long, and they bent in the wrong places, while the arms—or front legs, whichever they were—were thick and jointless, and the claws made them look too short. There were rust-green scales glinting, and there was a heavy swag to belly and breast—like a *sheknath*, yes, Gri, but there was a sick softness to it as well, such as no one ever saw on a living *sheknath*. It was not dead, and not alive, and it smelled like wet, rotting leaves.

Then it took another step, and the candlelight twitched across its face. It was the face of the Queen.

Not altogether her face, no, for the delicate features had blurred, as though under layers of old cobwebs, and the rusty skin of it seemed to be running away from her eyes, like water crawling under a little wind. But there were tears on it, a few, golden where the light caught them.

In the darkness, Lanak spoke very quietly. "I have done a terrible thing." The Queen, or what remained of the Queen, turned ponderously toward his voice, her blank black eyes searching for him. Lanak said, "But I saw no other way."

The creature lifted its ruinous head toward the sound, so that Lanak could see for the first time just what had happened to -the Queen's hair. The mouth was squirming dreadfully, showing splintery brown teeth, and the eyes had grown suddenly wide and deadly bright at the sound of his voice.

"A terrible thing," Lanak said again. "There was no need for me to mention sendings, knowing you as I do. I knew very well that you would command that I teach you to summon them, and that you would set about it as soon as I was out of your sight. For whom this first one was meant, I have no idea. Perhaps for the Council in Suk'kai, over the hills—perhaps for the Jiril of Derridow—perhaps even for me, why not? Sendings call no one *master*, after all, and you might easily feel that it might be safer to silence me. Was that the way of it, Majesty?"

The Queen-thing made a sound. It might have melted your bones and mine with terror, or broken our hearts, who can say? Lanak went on. "The last word of the summoning. I did not lie to you, not exactly. It is indeed a ward against the sending—but not for the sender. Rather, it balks and nullifies the entire enchantment by protecting the target itself against the malice of the enemy. Thus you set your arrow to the string, and let it fly, and struck it aside, all in the same spell. My doing." His voice was slow and weary, I should imagine.

"But sendings call no one *master*. I did warn you. Finding itself thwarted from its very birth, it turned back in fury toward its source and its one home—you. And when it could not unmake itself, could not reunite with the soul from which it was spun, then it chose to merge with your body, as best it might. And so. So."

Somewhere in the town a cock crowed, though there was no sign of morning in the sky. The Queen-thing lumbered this way and that, looking up at Lanak in raging supplication. He said heavily, "Oh, this is all bad, there is no good in it anywhere. I do not think I will ever be able to tell Dwyla about this. Majesty, I have no love for you, but I cannot hate you, seeing you so. I cannot undo what you and I have done together, but what I can I will do now." He spoke several harsh words, pronouncing them with great care. If there were gestures to accompany them, of course these could not be seen.

The Queen-thing began to glow. It blazed up brighter and brighter, first around its edges and then inward, until Lanak himself had to shut his eyes. Even then the image clung pitilessly to the inside of his lids, like the sticky burning the Dariki tribesmen make in their caves south of Grannach Harbor. He saw the outlines of the Queen and her sending, separate and together at once: her in her pride and beauty and cunning, and the other—*that other*—embracing her in fire. Then it was gone, but I think that Lanak never really stopped seeing it ever again. I could be wrong.

The room was indeed growing a bit light now, and the cook outside was joined by the wail of a Nounouri at his dawn prayers. There are a lot of Nounos in Fors, or there used to be. Into the silence that was not emptiness, Lanak said, "No one else will ever see you. I cannot end your suffering, but you need not endure it in the view of all men. And if a greater than I can do more, I will send him here. Forgive me, Majesty, and farewell."

Well, that is all of it, and longer than I meant, for which I ask pardon in my turn. Lanak went home to Karakosk, to Dwyla and his daughter, and to his fields, his black beer, and his fireworks; and he did the very best he could to vanish from all other tales and remembrances. He was not wholly successful—but there, that's what happens when you are too good at something for your own ambitions. But I will say nothing more about him, which would have made him happy to know.

As for the Queen. When I was last in Fors na'Shachim, not too long ago, there were still a few street vendors offering charms to anyone bound as a guest to the black castle. They are supposed to protect you from the sad and vengeful spirit that wanders those halls even now. Highly illegal they are, by the way—you can lose a hand for buying and a head for selling. I myself have spent nights at the castle without such protection, and no harm has ever come to me. Unless you count my dreams, of course.

THE TRAGICAL HISTORIE
OF THE JIRIL'S PLAYERS

To this day Lisonje will tell you that what happened in Derridow could have been avoided if I had only shown a little foresight and a little resolve. This from a woman whose incessant complaint for thirty years has been that I am perversely obsessed, if you please, with controlling every aspect of my company's existence, from the permitted degree of offstage contact with local citizens to exactly how many times a week we will rehearse *The Blind King* or *The Comedy of the Three Priests*. Now if I draw certain lessons from a lifetime spent, as often as not, in teetering on two planks set on two muddy trestles in a barnyard, yelling out poetry, and attempt to apply them as seems wisest and most professional to me, how does that make me a fussy, finicking, carping, domineering old scold of a tyrant? Ask Lisonje.

And yet she sees no contradiction at all in proclaiming that I should have been more decisive twenty years ago in Derridow! There's no reasoning with a woman like that, nor any chance of winning if there were; and the gods know there would be no living or working with her if she weren't—when properly cast and in the right humor—very nearly as good as she thinks she is. One has to keep one's temper firmly in hand and remember that you still won't see a soul—not such of Leishai, at any rate—whose Lady Vigga or Sul'yarak comes anywhere near hers. No, I'll go further, if I must, and whisper that even at her age she can give you a flawless, flawless Mistress Haja four times out of five. *That* I'll never tell her, not on my deathbed; but you're a showman yourself, you know this life. Children, the best of them. Especially the best of them.

You do know my company? Ah. Ah, well, I don't know yours either. Sad, really reprehensible when you think about it—here we are, two troupers, experienced managers both, two battle-tried veterans of hauling wagonloads of gifted hysterics from one place to another, of having endlessly to coax and cozen the most common civilities out of them, let alone anything like a performance. And yet we've never crossed paths, nor even heard of one another before this evening. Sad, sad, too few like us these days. Your health, colleague.

No, no, I'm ashamed to admit we don't perform the classic repertoire as much as we'd choose. Not but what we *could*—you'll find no one in my company, down to the lowest apprentice, who doesn't have his Jurai or her Shaska by heart, scene for scene, role for role. I won't have it otherwise, and they know it. We may have come down somewhat in the world, if you will; we may spend season after dusty season touring the same unspeakably dreary, benighted, plague-ridden provincial towns, but our standards are only the higher for it, I can assure you. We could play *The Horseman's Tragedy* tonight, on ten minutes notice, even Lisonje would say so. Yes, she would.

But no one will ask us for *The Horseman's Tragedy*, or any such masterwork, not in this filthy wilderness. Oh, yes—on occasion we may still find ourselves engaged by some guild or other, some city council, even some minor lordling, to put on *The Fishermen's Rebellion* or *The Marriage of the Wicked Lord Hassidanya*; for the rest, we plod along, staging our country farces of priests and adulterers, our stupendously inaccurate histories, our monumentally absurd sagas of heroes who never existed. Lisonje and I, in fact—well, and Trygvalin, our overage juvenile, and Nususir, who plays all our old wives, nurses, and sibyls, because Lisonje won't touch those—by now we four are the only ones left in the company who remember another sort of existence. I don't fault the others for falling away, mind you, not at all, don't misunderstand me. One lives as one can; who knows that better than I? Loyalty, friendship, a certain sense of community—should such things stand in the way of a chance to play blind King Bel'ryak or the wizard Khyr, on something a bit grander than a few tables pushed together? Who am I to judge? all I can say is that I am humbly thankful *I* wasn't raised to abandon comrades, fellow artists, at the first inconvenience, the first temptation. But there, never mind, I wish them all success, and may they enjoy it in good conscience. The lot of them.

Derridow, Derridow. You wouldn't be familiar with the place, of course. . . . No, no reason why you should, not these days. And you with your own theatre in the Old Keep right here in Fors na'Shachim itself, only touring when you choose, imagine. Well, Derridow's a handsome city still— all those archways and gardens, they won't have changed anyway—but I wonder whether one would still feel that certain tingle, coming in along the Queen's Road, that certain sense that anything was possible, that one's life could change quite surprisingly at any moment. Not that it's ever been a place of real consequence, like Fors, or a wild, wide-open stew like Bitava—even so, you wouldn't have mistaken it for any other town, nor wished to be somewhere else while you were there. Dear, dear Derridow. Certainly would be nice to be able to go back.

Well. As you likely won't know, twenty-odd years ago things in Derridow were a good deal different from what they are today. The old Jiril was still alive, for one thing, and still well able to keep his four quarrelsome sons from tearing one another to pieces, and the town with them. A decent man, *I* always thought him, the Jiril—killed people only when he thought it really necessary, and never tortured them, didn't believe in it. Hard to imagine what more you can ask from the nobility. And a true lover of the theatre with it, an open hand to any troupe passing through Derridow. Acrobats, tragedians, Leishai dancers, knockabout clowns, they all played for the Jiril's pleasure and applause, and dined magnificently with us afterward—his cook Deh'kai was the best I've ever known—in his great hall at the high table. A real enthusiast, bless his bad teeth and dyed black beard. I don't blame him in the least for what happened in Derridow.

"Dined with us?" Did I say that? Ah, forgive me—I thought I'd schooled myself out of all such foolish nostalgia. But yes, it's quite true. We were the Jiril's personal resident company—a full six years, the Jiril's Players, we had a charter—and consequently we were always on display at his banquets in honor of any show folk passing through town. We performed for him on command, of course, but our principal concern for those six seasons was mounting plays to which the Jiril might enjoy bringing his family. His wife, the Jirelle, invariably fell asleep at anything but the loudest and bawdiest of farces; but strangely enough, all four of those strutting, swaggering, brawling boys of his were as devoted to the theatre as their father. If I had known—no, no, you'll have to forgive me again, I'm sounding like the Prologue to some melodrama or other, and I never could abide Prologues. I didn't know, and I couldn't have known, and I did the best I *did* know at the time, and this is what happened. Mmm—yes, thank you, why not? Your health.

Dramatis personae. The Jiril you know about, but his sons take some describing. The oldest was called Gol—smallest of the lot, oddly—meaning no bigger than a bull *rishu.* Liked revenge tragedies, the bloodier the better—oh, *The Conspirators, Tumurak's Return,* that sort of thing. A second lead's conventional good looks, rather spoiled by a comedian's small, pale, calculating eyes. Quite clever: one of those types who make a prompter unneccessary, because he'll shout out your next line at the top of his voice if you should go dry for an instant. Lisonje put something really awful in his beer once.

The second son was Javeri—or was he the third? No, definitely Number Two, he was, and not happy about it for a minute. Huge and red and bullying, already losing his hair—the last man you'd imagine would waste an evening on the philosophical comedies of K'daro-daraf. I'm quite fond of them myself, but they're an acquired taste, quite wasted on all but the most sophisticated audience. Nevertheless, loutish Javeri never missed a performance, even if it meant passing up a dinner or a woman. If you'll believe it, he was forever hectoring me to put on *The Shoemaker's Search for True Wisdom*. Gods, even *I* don't understand that one, and I'm not sure K'daro-daraf herself did, let alone Javeri. A stupid man, but not quite as stupid as he looked. It was hard to keep that in mind, but you always had to.

Number Three Son now, Torleg. Ah, *there* was a jewel, if you like, *there* was a darling. He was the pet of the house, having Javeri's size, Gol's sharpness—not to mention being far handsomer than both of them together—his father's kindly manner, and a soul of ice and ashes. Aye, Torleg frightened me, for all his charm; he had only to catch my eye during a performance, and I'd instantly start sweating and mumbling, and changing my blocking so as not to have to look at him. He frightened Lisonje, too, which isn't easily done. Yet he was the one for romantic comedies: everything from *The Shepherd's Folly* to *Love or No Love*. That was his favorite, by far—I can't tell you how many times he had us substitute it, without the least notice, for whatever we might be playing at the moment. At times, he even insisted on taking a small part: usually it was Numi, the wise and witty clown who gets most of the best lines—delivered quite well for an amateur, I will say. The old poet Chanir, which is my role, has no scenes with Numi. I was always grateful for that.

Now enter Davao. Davao, the baby, who clearly never stopped being the baby. An utterly unprepossessing stripling with a high, whining voice, a perpetually wet nose, and an entirely justified feeling that no one in the whole world liked him. Yet even he had his hangers-on, by virtue of his noble birth and his unquestioning acceptance of the most transparent flattery. Like his mother, he favored the noisy farces: whenever we had reached a perfect peak of closet doors slamming, lovers whisking under beds, clowns popping up to bellow ribald nonsense verses—at such moments, Davao's ecstatic gobble of laughter could be heard, I have been advised, by boats passing on the river. Trygvalin used to swear that he often left his seat wet, but that's probably not true. Trygvalin will say anything.

You're clear on the major roles, then? Remember that each of them, by all accounts, had hated the others since childhood, no doubt for excellent reasons. The Jiril himself had a grim joke to the effect that his true security against a revolt led by any of his sons lay in the fact that the other three would betray the rebel the moment they got wind of the plot. Cooperation in any matter was completely beyond them; it was all they could do to keep from disemboweling one another with the butter knives at teatime. Their father thrashed them and imprisoned them on a regular basis, solely to remind them that he was still the Jiril of Derridow. He had as yet named none of them as his heir, remarking often that to do so would make his will his suicide note. Which was surely true, and a mistake even so.

We were three-quarters through our sixth season in Derridow, with every reason to assume that we had found a permanent home in the huge old tannery the Jiril had so graciously refurbished for us. The smell was all but gone, and we could easily seat seven hundred at a time without having yawning, spitting nobles asprawl all over the stage. Superb lighting, sconces anywhere you might need them— I could weep, just thinking about it—a gallery for as many musicians as I cared to hire, and space enough backstage to store an entire repertoire's worth of scenery and still have room for the horses we used in the last act of *The Defenders of Bitava*. I wouldn't say a word against the Old Keep, but if you've never played Derridow and that tannery, you simply don't *know*. Gods, I could weep.

Lisonje still insists that it was my notion to revive Surjk's *The Tragedy of King Vilnanash the Accursed*, which we had staged only twice, very long before. It may indeed have been my decision, loosely speaking, but the actual suggestion came from the Jiril himself. No, it wasn't a command, but what would you have done? The Jiril was better pleased with us than he ever had been with a company, and we were far more than pleased with him and our wonderful theatre. Deny his request and chance troubling this tranquil harmony, so rarely found in our profession? I never even considered the possibility. It was worth any compromise, any concession, that stage of ours.

Besides, what harm was there in faded old *King Vilnanash*? I must say, I never understood why the Jiril wanted to see it: neither a bad play nor a particularly good one, it demands too large a cast, too long a rehearsal period, and far too many effects to be worth the cost of mounting for most companies. There are some rolling, rumblesome speeches in it—typical Surjk, Trygvalin would love those—and a handful of scenes between the doomed king and his pathetically loyal queen that Lisonje and I could likely wring tears from an outhouse wall with. Beyond that, it was going to be a tedious and unrewarding production to put on; but, as I told the Jiril, his enjoyment was reward enough for his players. Call me hypocrite.

By the by, if I have been making Lisonje sound like nothing but a grumbling shrew, let me do her better justice. In truth, she's as knowledgeable an assistant as a manager could ask for, no gainsaying that. She will work all day with a carpenter or a seamstress, coach a frightened apprentice for hours on end; then turn around and box the ears of a lead who may be getting above himself. She has no hesitation about serving as dresser or prompter, even when she is performing herself; and her ardor, her—what shall I say?—her *gaiety*, will pick up and drive a company through the exhaustion and boredom of preparing a new production with a certain flair, if you will, that I myself cannot always achieve. Oh, she knows her business, Lisonje, none better, never doubt it. I only wish that she could refrain now and then from teaching me mine.

Whatever she says today, Lisonje thought reviving *The Tragedy of King Vilnanash* a splendid idea *then*, and set about the practicalities of the matter immediately. It wasn't one of the forty-some-odd plays all of us carry in our heads (nearly sixty in my case, though I can testify that the great K'sharik, from whom I inherited this company, was master of fully ninety-three roles, I'll swear to it); so a mildewed copy had to be exhumed from my trunk, more copies made by the Jiril's scribes, parts allotted, and everyone set at once to memorizing. To make matters more difficult, *King Vilnanash* requires nearly twice the cast I normally carry, even doubling and tripling the smaller roles. That always means begging players from other companies, should any be within call, at bloodsucking rates. As it happened, there chanced to be a strolling troupe—such as we are now—in town, not for any engagement, but to cadge used costumes and pieces of scenery from the local pawnbrokers and warehousers. We arrived at a bargain. I was quite proud of it at the time.

In exchange for a load-lightening assortment of rags and remnants from plays we performed even more rarely than *King Vilnanash*, we acquired eleven miscellaneous actors on two months' loan, with the Jiril agreeing to feed and house them as handsomely as he did us. Which showed his generous nature, I might add, since of the eleven only two might have deserved better than the haylofts, horse-boxes, dubious scraps, and sour ale to which they'd been long accustomed. To which we ourselves, alas, have been even longer accustomed now, but who could have known? I assigned them their diverse roles, passed out their pages, acquainted them with everything they needed to know about the theatre itself, and instructed them in the deportment expected from all members of the Jiril's Players, even temporary ones. Then, at last, we set to rehearsal in earnest.

I've said that *King Vilnanash* is a mediocre play, not at all worth the time and effort it requires, but not especially dreadful either. That is a showman's reasoned judgment, if I may say so, founded on a lifetime spent largely in making similar judgments. Twenty years ago, however, I'd have told you within a week of commencing work that I had been afflicted with the most stupefyingly overblown, overwrought, overplotted, and underentertaining jumble of claptrap since the very first man to kill a *sheknath* acted his triumph out for his tribe. It was the poetry, you see. We do very little Surjk, and I had completely forgotten that, though most of his plays are written in fairly straight-forward, if rather uninspired prose, in this one the grand speeches are all in verse, and such verse, *such* verse! For instance, take the king's monologue on discovering that he has incurred the condemnation of the gods by unwittingly killing his own natural son in battle. I'm afraid I remember quite a lot of it.

> *"What? Slain? Him slain?*
> *Him slain and me to blame?*
> *No! No! No, no, no, no, no, no, no, no!*
> *It cannot be! It would not dare be so!*
> *Ah, woe!*
> *It is—and yet it cannot, cannot be!*
> *And sayest thou the gods are wroth with me? . . ."*

Enough? Crying mercy so soon? There's a good deal more in that vein. Lisonje, as Queen Noura, had an oration over Vilnanash's body which I may be compelled to recite in full unless you buy the next round. Ah, thank you. As I've said, it really isn't all as bad as that, but when you're in rehearsal and hearing those lines over and over dozens of times a day, in the toneless voices of bored, bewildered journeymen—well, after a while it all *sounds* even worse than that. It was a difficult time.

Nevertheless. Nevertheless, we could have succeeded, we could so easily have triumphed over that wretched play the Jiril's whim had lumbered us with. Our undoing, dear colleague, was not in the work itself, nor in the production or the preparation—two weeks before our opening we were at performance pitch, absolutely, and that includes our bor-rowed ragbag contingent. No, the trouble began with Gol, the Jiril's eldest son. Began, and went on from there.

Gol sauntered up to me one morning, while the company was assembling for rehearsal, and asked brightly, "Well there, Dardis, my friend, and how are we coming along, then?" He was twirling a flower between two fingers, and hardly looked at me as he spoke, being far more absorbed in ogling Lisonje and the two ingenues who played King Vilnanash's daughters. "Ready to go right now, are we?"

I particularly dislike being called "friend" by people who are not my friends. Answering him as coldly and distantly as though I were playing the evil minister Glaum in *The Horseman's Tragedy*, I said, "The company is somewhat ahead of our ideal schedule, that is true. I am trying to keep them from reaching their precise artistic peak too soon. If you will excuse me." Minister Glaum is one of my best roles.

Gol put a hand on my shoulder as I turned away. He had a heavy, damp touch—they all did in that family, even the old Jiril. He said, "Walk with me a moment. Your mummers are still painting their cheeks, and I have a matter to discuss." He put his arm through mine and drew me outside.

The tannery stands on the bank of the Tomelly River—really just an oily little stream that slips quickly through Derridow as though hoping not to be noticed. Gol guided me down to the water with a politely paralyzing grip on my forearm, chatting of inconsequential theatre gossip as we went, yet turning often to look around him, rather like the river itself. When he was certain that we were unobserved, he stopped walking, abruptly whirled me to face him, and said, "Dardis. This play needs a little something, don't you agree?"

I must confess that I simply blinked at him. Whatever I may have expected from his manner, dramatic criticism was not it. Undoubtedly seeing this, Gol released my arm, patted it, and smiled his most pleasant smile. In a burst of apparent candor, he said, "Dardis, you of all people know how I am when I see a play that could so easily be made perfect. I ask your pardon most humbly for intruding on your craft, but you yourself must see that it would take so little to turn poor old Vilnanash the Accursed into an experience my father would never forget. One additional scene would do it—one single speech, perhaps. You know exactly where the weak spot is, of course."

"No, I cannot say I do," I replied. "And you must know yourself, my lord Gol, how profoundly opposed I am to tampering with the original text of a classic play. I am aware that this is done more and more frequently, to suit this actor's limitations, that ruler's fears and fancies—" I stopped myself hurriedly, as some notion of what Gol might have in mind began to dawn, and ended rather lamely, "But I do not approve. Whatever the case."

Gol's smile never flickered. He said, "Dear Dardis, I've always admired your devotion to your artistic principles. As does my esteemed father, who unfortunately cannot be with us forever, which will come as a great surprise to him. Be assured, I have every intention of keeping your little troupe on here in Derridow when the tragic time comes; but if we are to begin our association with so basic a disagreement—well, one of my own principles has to do with loyalty. You do understand me, Dardis, surely?"

I thought he might be testing me. The nobility always need to do that—you've noticed?—and Gol in particular was forever prodding, probing to find out at what point the animal would snap, the woman slap him, the follower refuse to go one step further. An entertainer's living, if not his life, so often depends on knowing when—and *what*—his employer wants to play. I said, "One speech, you think?"

"Eighteen lines, and not a word more," Gol answered. "Here, I have it with me," and he pressed a folded sheet of foolscap into my hand. "You'll see, it will fit perfectly in the last scene between Vilnanash and his ministers. And you'll do wonders with it; it was written for you." I started to protest—feebly, yes, certainly feebly, how else should the feeble protest?—but Gol thumped my shoulder, said, "Gods, but I envy an artist!" and was striding away up the bank as I gaped after him. He knew how to make an exit, that one. I've used it since, as a matter of fact.

Lisonje had the rehearsal in full swing when I returned to the theatre. I had no chance to look at the speech until the midday meal, which I usually took by myself in those days, to assess the morning's work in solitude. This time, in honesty, I didn't want to be alone even with Gol's hand-writing, never mind his poetry. I sat down with Lisonje and one of our borrowed actors, a clown-named Chachak, with whom she was flirting at the time. A fine step-dancer, but incapable of any but the most vulgar humor. Without pre-amble I said, "Gol gave me this," and spread the paper on the table between us.

Lisonje is a quick study. Chachak was still moving his lips and scratching his head when she looked up at me and demanded, "He wants us to interpolate this trash? Where, at the end?"

I nodded. "It would work," I said. "The moment never quite plays as it should, you've said so yourself. Done right, this ought to make it at least a little more dramatic. I'm rather impressed, actually."

Lisonje favored me with a look she generally saves for a juvenile who has begun to fancy his own ad-libs. She said, her voice dangerously level, "This impresses you?" and read aloud, as best I remember:

> *"My lords, my noble friends, my subjects all,*
> *My grievous fault I freely here confess.*
> *The curse that on this land so heavy falls*
> *Falls on my shoulders, mine and mine alone.*
> *For I have ruled too long, past all deserving,*
> *Past strength, past wisdom, past favor of the gods,*
> *And here and now I do renounce my crown.*
> *Let those take up the burden of the state*
> *Who have the youth and vision that's requir'd,*
> *Whilst I do fare me forth into the wild. . . ."*

She looked up at me, curling her lip in that way of hers, as though drawing it out of range of the fire to follow. "Dardis, this is worse than the original, and I never imag-ined I'd hear myself saying that. You can't have Vilnanash abdicate; it kills the whole ending—"

"Which is better than the ending killing *us*," I broke in. "Think what you like, but I am not disposed to make an enemy of Gol. The abdication was always implicit in the scene, and if all he wants is for us to make it clearer, more explicit—"

"More crude, more heavyhanded, more ponderous," Lisonje interrupted me; but Chachak interrupted *her*—not with one of his usual bawdy jokes, but with his face wrinkling like an infant's as he puzzled out what he meant to say. "That isn't all Gol wants," he finally blurted. We stared at him. Chachak said, "That's meant for the Jiril. It's a warning."

"Chachak, dear," Lisonje said. "Go dance. There's no comparison between the Jiril and poor old King Vilnanash. Nobody would ever make the connection." But I raised my hand to silence her and read out the last bit myself.

> *"And I admonish all who hear me now,*
> *If I, or any other senile king,*
> *Recant this just retirement, this farewell,*
> *Do you without compunction him remove*
> *To whatsoever fate his treachery*
> *Shall have requited. . . ."*

Chachak was pale under his brown southern skin. He said, "I was born around here. My ancestors knew the Jiril's ancestors. That speech is a demand for his abdication—and if I know that, everyone will know. The Jiril will know. You cannot put those lines into the play."

Lisonje, as is her way, reversed her field and took his side without the least concern for consistency. "Dardis, he is absolutely right. I don't care what you promised Gol—"

"I promised him nothing," I snapped at her. "He did all the promising. He made it very clear that if we don't do as he wishes, we won't have a theatre once the Jiril's gone—"

"You won't have a cast if you do," Chachak burst out. "We may only be a gang of fourth-rate bumpkins—oh, we know what you think of us, Dardis!—but we aren't stupid. *We've* no theatre to lose, just our lives. The moment they learn who wrote that speech—"

"But they won't," I said. "Will they, Chachak?"

Well, there's no point going into ignoble detail here. For a rapacious consideration, Chachak eventually swore on the unmarked graves of his unwashed grandparents never to reveal to his fellows the authorship of King Vilnanash's new climactic oration. I counted less on that than on my threat to make certain that he never worked again for any reputable company this side of the Barrens if he betrayed me. I could promise such things with authority, in those days.

Lisonje said afterward that she didn't know which of us she was more ashamed of. I paid her no heed then, and I wouldn't today, even knowing what I know. For people like you and me, artistic principle is not what people like Gol think it is. For us, the first principle of art is to feed your company, then to keep your company as safe and as whole as possible, to find them work and get them to it. And always, always to make sure they are adequately rehearsed. The rest—honor, courage, vision, taste—that's all luxury. That comes after.

The speech went in. It was mine to deliver, after all, and you well know how little attention actors pay to speeches that aren't theirs. I had only to change two or three lines in the scene to accommodate it; within a few days you couldn't have told the difference. No real harm done to the ending, no curiosity about the origins of the new passage. Chachak kept his mouth shut, as he had pledged, though I felt sourly certain that I had overpaid him for his silence. The company surely never would have panicked at the thought of Gol opaquely suggesting that his father abdicate. They knew the Jiril, and they knew his blowhard sons—more than likely they'd simply have laughed the whole idea away and gone on practicing their entrances and costume changes. I rather expected Lisonje to change course again and deride me for having let a clod like Chachak swindle me, but she never said a word. I should have taken *that* for an omen, if nothing else.

Then Javeri paid us a visit.

A week or ten days after Gol, I think it was—maybe less. He turned up at the start of a morning rehearsal, as his brother had done; but instead of waylaying me directly, he planted himself in one of the grand chairs always reserved for the Jiril's family and sat expressionlessly through the entire runthrough, looking like nothing so much as a swollen, royally inflamed carbuncle. I found this disturbing—not his appearance, which was normal, but his patience, which was not. Javeri had no manners that the Jiril had not beaten into him, and those few were hardly to be squandered on his inferiors. Nevertheless, he waited until the players were dispersing before he approached me. He even attempted civility, growling that he'd seen worse companies than ours, before he dragged me into a corner and pulled the ball of crumpled pages from his pocket.

"Not my sort of play, this, you understand," he grunted. "Old-fangled, no delicacy of wit in it, no true philosophy, no precise balancing of humors choleric and melancholic, such as one finds in K'daro-daraf." Try to imagine a *nishoru*, one of those flightless eight-foot-high man-eating birds they have up north—as I say, try to imagine a *nishoru* reciting classical poetry, and you may have some idea of Javeri's presence. He went on, "But since the old brute insists on your staging the thing, here's a bit to fix up the big scene with Vilnanash's bastard. No, no, don't thank me. Least, very least a person who cares about theatre could do."

Unlike Gol, he read it to me on the spot. The scene is the one in which the king's beloved son Sakha breaks with his father over the issue of granting freedom and independence to a beleaguered enclave of runaway slaves who have taken refuge in the marshes. Vilnanash refuses, and Sakha spits in his face and goes to live with the fugitives and, eventually, to share their fate. It's quite the best scene in the play, and Trygvalin and I did it well, underplaying as we built up to the point of Sakha's sudden shocking revolt. Even now you have to watch Trygvalin every minute, or he'll turn elocutionist on you; but I had him properly—if temporarily—disciplined just then, and the very last thing he needed was to have some new melodramatic tirade shoved into his hands. But there was nothing more for it than there had been with Gol. I sat down where I was and listened.

"What, say you so? And that's your final word?
Why, then, I name you no king but a beast.
No father but a cruel degenerate,
A heartless, ruthless, vile, vengeful villain,
Whom all are honor-bound to overthrow,
To drag his putrid, stinking reign to ruin,
To celebrate the fall of such a fiend
And quench our swords in his inglorious blood! . . ."

There was a good deal more along those lines, but you get the general tone. All I could manage to say, having finished, was, "I thought spitting in his father's face expressed his emotions rather concisely." Javeri loomed over me, making unpleasant sounds to himself. I went on, "It lacks a certain balancing of humors, wouldn't you say?"

"So does the whole bloody play, I told you," Javeri growled. "But just you put that speech in as it stands, and you'll see the groundlings on their feet, I promise you. That's what we want, after all, isn't it?" When I was slow to reply, he squinted down his great pimply fist of a nose at me, as though he were taking aim, and repeated, "Isn't it, Dardis?"

For all his size and aggressiveness, Javeri generally intimidated people less than Gol, and decidedly less than Torleg. I would never have dared speak to either of them as I answered him. "Javeri, I thank you most humbly for your efforts on behalf of our company, but the speech will not do. It is completely unnecessary to the scene, and clumsily written besides." I'm quite sure I actually added that last, and fairly sure that I then bowed and turned to walk away. Hard to remember one's blocking from so long ago.

Javeri spluttered, as one could have predicted. He seized my shoulder and whirled me around, thundering, "Imbecile, that speech is perfect for that scene!" He had a tendency to spit when he talked himself, now I think of it. I pried vainly at his fingers, all the while telling him, "For one thing, it is utterly redundant, overstated. Excessive."

"It is *not!*" Javeri roared back. "It's lean and economical, and well you know it! It makes that stupid, boring scene *move*, for a change!"

"Move? It would stop the play in its tracks!" Considering that he had me completely off the ground at that point, I do think I was remarkably firm and composed.

Javeri was turning an interesting sunset color: mottled mauve, with a green underlay. "And so it bloody well should stop it! If you want the truth, Dardis, that speech is too good for that miserable relic of a play!"

"And if *you* want the truth, it's the worst speech I have ever heard in my life!" Which is actually untrue, to be fair. I'd been a showman for a very long time, even then.

Javeri dropped me. His voice was very quiet when he spoke again: frightening, that can be, when you're used to a bully's empty bellow. He said, "It's mine."

We looked at each other. Javeri said, still in the same soft, unnaturally precise voice, "It is mine, Dardis. You *will* put my speech in the scene, and you *will* see it performed exactly as I've written it. Exactly. Because I am who I am, and you are who you are, and that is how things are. Do you understand me?"

I didn't say anything. I bowed. Javeri glowered at me a moment longer, and then shoved the pages at me again, whipped his cloak around with a swirling flourish that ended by hitting himself in the eye with the heavy hem, and lurched away. And I? I had just time for a cup of hot *boreen*, to calm myself down a bit, before calling the company back to work. When I introduced the new speech, Lisonje looked up sharply, but she neither protested then, nor said anything at all for the rest of the day. I found this distinctly unnerving. As for Trygvalin, *he* looked as though he had been left a fortune by a total stranger. More lines. Nothing, then or now, has ever made Trygvalin happier than having more lines.

Lisonje came to see me that evening. (I should mention that, although the rest of the Jiril's Players were housed together, as manager I had my own cottage down at the end of a tiny flowering alley just off the main square.) It was not unusual for her or any other of the senior players to call on me there, but it *was* surprising that she had not come to berate me for knuckling under to Javeri as I had to Gol. She appeared subdued, pensive, even anxious—none of which is natural to Lisonje—but she came directly to the point, which is. Straightaway she asked me, "What do you plan to do when Torleg hands you the speech *he* wants in the play?"

"What makes you think he will?" It was a stupid question, and I knew it, and Lisonje surely heard it in my voice. She said, "Torleg next, then Davao—not because he's the youngest, but because it will take him that long to get the idea. Dardis, each of those four idiots has his followers, and all *those* idiots are waiting for a signal to rise against the Jiril, and that's what those speeches are. We're rehearsing rallying cries, Dardis, calls to arms. That's the truth."

"We don't know that," I answered lamely. "I am not about to chance angering any of them on your suspicion that one or another might be planning some half-baked revolt. True or not, it's no business of ours. We are entertainers, Lisonje. We entertain."

" 'We entertain,' " Lisonje mimicked me—she has a brutal gift that way. "Dardis, I've known you too long to expect you to understand. I just want you to remember what I say now. *We* are going to be the ones caught in the middle when whatever is to happen happens—*we* are going to be the ones blamed for whatever happens, half-baked or not. But we could still avoid this, if you had the courage to cut every single word of theirs out of the play. You don't even have to tell them—let them find out when we open." She gripped my shoulders hard, and I was startled to feel her fingers trembling. "I promise you, if you do this, you will be so grateful to me that you'll make an impossible nuisance of yourself thanking me every ten minutes. I promise you, Dardis."

Oh, yes, yes, it's easy enough to say now that I should have taken her advice unquestioningly. But I still cannot honestly say that things would have been any better if I had. I quite liked the Jiril, but I feared his children: unlike their father, they all knew how to hold grudges very tenderly, as one might hold a baby bird. He would most likely have forgotten my supposed courage in a week; they never would. Call me coward.

So I did nothing. Javeri's speech was added to the scene, and though this time I needed to do a good bit of trimming and shifting to make it look as though it belonged there, the stitches showed hardly at all, if I say so myself. Indeed, the cast generally seemed to prefer the altered version. Trygvalin devoured his new lines in a single gulp, neither questioning nor comprehending them. Chachak looked horrified, but never said a word; and even the Jiril himself, when he threw us into hysterical disarray by appearing unannounced at a rehearsal, seemed hardly to notice the two additions at all. I think he commented on Gol's speech for King Vilnanash, saying something like, "Completely forgot the man abdicates, been such a time since I saw the thing. Very moving, very moving." When he left I sighed an immense, grateful sigh and smiled triumphantly at Lisonje. She pretended not to have seen me.

Then came Torleg.

Your pardon, but I need another drink. No, it is my turn, it must be. I was never a stingy man—no, nor a sponge. The worst anyone can say of me is that a certain professional vanity sometimes leads me to assume that because I know much, I know all. Sometimes. Yes. But that was not my failing in this instance, whatever Lisonje says. It was not pride that undid me, but fear; and not even that so much as a sense of responsibility that has too often been my ruin. Perhaps you have something of the same problem? Yes, I thought you might.

Where was I? Right. Torleg made *his* appearance, not at the theatre, but in a hot, grimy warehouse by the river, where I had gone alone to rummage for a particular bolt of russet stuff for King Vilnanash's first-act costume. It was not a place where anyone would expect to encounter the Jiril's cleverest, best-beloved, and most dangerous son; and in candor, when I turned a corner on my way out, collided with Torleg's broad chest, and peered over my roll of cloth to see that terrifyingly beautiful face smiling down at me, those coldly merry blue eyes twinkling away—very well, I came as close as you like to wetting myself. I told you Torleg had that effect on me.

"Well met, Dardis," he purred—he was the only one of that lot who could really purr, if you understand me. Gol could do it, after a fashion, but it was never more than a shadow of that treacherously warm rumble of his brother's. He repeated, "Well, met indeed, how truly fortuitous. Here you are, a man seeking ways to trick out a drab antique play, all for my father's amusement, and here am I, entirely at your service. Do but tell me what scene you wish enhanced, what speech spiced, what verse revivified—I'll have it for you tomorrow, and thank you for the opportunity besides." He threw an arm around my shoulders, leaning toward me like a lover. "Now speak to me, Dardis, say how I may help you. Are we not both lowly servants of the Jiril?"

Have I drawn him at all for you? I am an actor—have I shown you something of his beguiling power? It was laced through with humor, you see, always—he was also the only member of his family who had even a touch of that; though Gol, again, could feign it for a little. As deeply as he had always frightened me, in less time than I care to confess, I had let slip to him that both of his older brothers had already made the same offer, though I still think I managed to avoid any mention of their interpolated passages without ever directly lying to him. Perhaps I deceive myself, but it hardly matters—Torleg was far too wily to believe for a moment that Gol and Javeri had sought me out for any reason but his own, or to imagine that I could have denied them with impunity. His arm never left my shoulders, tightening the more cozily as he assured me that he had no speeches to force into my hands—and my play—but only waited to be told how he might make himself useful to me.

Yes, well, get it over with, Dardis. In no bloody time at

all, I found myself asking him—*asking*, mind you!—to tidy a troublesome second-act scene in which a drunken sorceress predicts to King Vilnanash that he will soon be overthrown by a despised alliance of small merchants and apprentice boys, because the gods have abandoned him. Nususir could handle the drama of the role, no one better; but there's comedy to it as well, and dear Nususir simply cannot play comedy—that's Lisonje's job. I told Torleg that I wished someone could rearrange the scene, shifting the humorous elements from Nususir's shoulders and leaving her free to do what she does best, which is pronounce doom. There, it is confessed. I was neither bullied nor coerced nor blackmailed, but simply seduced into conniving at my own downfall. I saw what was happening, understood it perfectly, and still could do nothing about it. There it is.

As he had promised, Torleg met me next day with the altered scene, handing it to me with the anxiously delighted air of any youth who dreams of running away with the players. He had quite daringly given the sorceress's comedy lines to a mocking, disbelieving Vilnanash, where they fit as though they had always belonged there. Ironically, I completely missed the three lines of his own that he had given her, as though by way of compensation. Lisonje it was who pointed them out.

"And it is writ your foes shall muster this new moon by wash-maids' humble pool, where once a despot fell, to share their weapons out and ready them th'attack. . . ."

The reference meant nothing to either of us, but it did to Trygvalin, oddly enough. He'd had a rendezvous with some local girl a few days before, and she had met him at a little stony hollow beyond the city gates, long dry and so overgrown with scraggly weeds that Trygvalin would never have seen it if not for the girl. A generation past, she told him, it had been a deep, spring-fed pond where all of Derridow's laundresses gathered to chatter and work. Then the spring failed, and the washerwomen moved down to the river, and the pool's existence was forgotten by all but a few. One of those, apparently, was Torleg.

"Well, there's three," Lisonje said with a tired sigh. "I wonder where Davao will want *his* revolutionaries to assemble. Probably in the Jiril's kitchen—it's hungry work, overthrowing tyrants." She had long since given up expostulating with me, and seemed if anything resigned to our situation, whatever it was. I add that because I myself had no real notion of how much trouble we were in, nor had Lisonje, let her say what she likes. What did it mean, after all, that three of the Jiril's sons were planting messages to their devotees in our harmless old play? They might all try to stage a rebellion at the same time, or they might just as easily go off and get drunk together. Derridow was a famously peaceful town in those days, always had been; you can have no idea how absurd it seemed to imagine a violent end to that bumbling placidity. Ah, well, we know better now, don't we? Mmm, yes, why not, thank you? Your health. Everybody's health.

No. No, Davao wasn't the next to seek me out. The girl was next.

I didn't? Oh, I ask your pardon, but there you are. Even now I invariably forget Firial, the Jiril's only daughter. Older than Davao by a year or two, she was—quiet girl, a pleasant creature; and in that family there was no surer way to oblivion than being quiet and pleasant. The Jiril himself quite forgot on occasion that he even had a daughter, and her mother always seemed vaguely irritated with Firial, as though on principle. Likely that was why she so rarely attended the theatre—which may give me some slight justification for not recognizing her when she spoke to me on the street. I was walking to clear my head after one of those nightmare rehearsals you invariably get when everyone knows his part altogether too well, and is deathly bored with it. That's one thing, anyway, about playing the provinces out of a couple of wagons—whatever else, we're all long, long past that particular stage. We're bored with everything we do, but we know in the marrow of our bones how it's done. Perhaps that's actually preferable to what we had in Derridow. I doubt it.

In any case. As I say, when Firial approached me as I was turning from the town square down my charming little alley, it took me a moment to recognize her. She was nice-looking enough, don't misunderstand me: long, straight hair—blondish, I *think*—intelligent, slightly weak brown eyes, rather a round face, decent sort of figure, not too thin, not too plump. Not too anything, in fact, and there you have it. The poor child had been born into a family who were all too *everything*; what was there left for her but mild-ness, gentility, good manners? No, her hair was brown, brown it was, I'm almost sure of it.

"Dardis," says she, coming right to the issue—very unusual, she was ever a diffident, dithering girl—"Dardis, I need a favor."

"There's a change," I answered her fairly shortly. I had put in a maddening day, as I've said; otherwise I'd not have dreamed of speaking in that tone to one of her rank. "Your brothers never *need* anything from me, it's always what they want. In truth, I am very tired of your brothers, my lady Firial."

Firial smiled then. She did have a very nice smile, I remember that. "I often am myself," she said. "May I walk with you, Dardis, to your house?" I bowed, and she put her arm through mine.

So we walked together, and townsfolk saluted Firial as we passed always recognizing her a little too late for more than a hasty scramble of a bow. After a few polite questions about the rehearsals (she hardly ever came to the theatre, and never with her family), she told me straight out, blushing only a little, "Dardis, I am to be married."

"I wish you joy," I replied. There had been two or three lordlings from the northern provinces hanging about the Jiril's court that summer; apparently, he had concluded negotiations with this one or that. "If you should desire my company to perform at your wedding, I can assure you that we would be greatly honored. We have a wide repertory of suitable scenes, songs, poetry, selected monologues—"

She cut me off with a single shake of her head. "Thank you, but this wedding may as like as not be held in a barn, performed by a drunken peasant priest, with gaping shepherds for witness. My choice of a husband will greatly displease my father."

"Ah, ah—an elopement," I said. I hate elopements. You don't just lose the ingenue who runs off in the night; most often she takes a perfectly good musician or comedian with her. I asked, very cautiously, "Your pardon, my lady, but it must take a rare man to so offend the Jiril that he would forbid you to wed him. May I know the name of this remarkable gentleman?"

Firial again gave me that smile that transformed her ordinary little face. "But you know it well already, good friend," she replied. "He is Deh'kai, my father's head cook. We have loved one another since he was a potboy getting beaten for stealing bits of cake for me. We are promised, and I will have no other."

I understood her situation altogether too well. Young as he was, Deh'kai was already a master cook: not only could he play superb variations on the most common regional dishes—what they call *soudrilak* these days and ask half the earth for is no more than Deh'kai's version of a stew every local farmwife knew—he had also invented recipes of his own that were just beginning to become famous beyond the borders of Derridow. Believe me, the Jiril would have parted far more willingly with any of his children than with that boy. At the same time, he was certainly not about to let his daughter live in Derridow as the wife of even such a cook as Deh'kai. I felt quite sorry for her. I was younger then.

We had reached my cottage. Hoping to avoid asking her in, which would mean hurriedly preparing a suitable meal when all I wanted in the world was to down my usual glass of black wine and take a nap, I cautiously asked what favor I could do for her. The words were hardly out of my mouth before Firial pounced on them, and on me as well, dragging me inside as I unlocked the door and slamming it behind us. "We have planned our escape on the first night of your play. My father has insisted that I attend, along with the rest of my family, but he will pay no attention to me once the performance begins. I *must* let Deh'kai know where we are to meet, the moment the play is over—but I have so few moments with him, and I dare not write, and I thought that perhaps you might ..." She let her voice trail off, very affectingly, and looked away.

"That I might add a speech with a meaning for him alone," I said. Firial looked up, her eyes shining. "Dardis, if only you would! It is our one chance, we will never have another like it. My father suspects us, I know he does, and he will be sure to keep us apart forever and make me wed some stupid, hateful baron, unless you help us. Oh, please, *please*, Dardis!"

A born blackmailer, you see, like her brothers. Only the leverage employed was at all different. At least she had the finesse and the subtlety not to weep, there's that. I said wearily, "Lady, I will do what I can. Doubtless you have your speech with you?"

She had it indeed, a few barely legible lines scrawled in the margins of a book of etiquette. I don't remember them at all—thank the gods for *something*—but they went well enough into a scene in the last act in which King Vilnanash's dying son tells his dearest friend where he wishes to be buried. A Fors boy named Brij—easily the slowest study I have ever known—played the friend, and I dreaded the thought of having to teach him new lines at this stage of things. But I told Firial all the same that she could count on me, and she left in a state of such grateful bliss as would nauseate a rock-*targ*. I drank more than one glass of black wine that afternoon, and napped not at all.

So that's everyone except Davao, isn't it? He showed up himself a day or two later, an anticlimax as always. I actually pitied Davao, I must say, at long intervals, for his position in his family wasn't one I'd have wished even on certain theatre managers of my acquaintance. He burst in on me in my dressing room—gods, just to say it, *dressing room*, brings back a time, a world, a life I have spent so many years trying to forget, for my own sake. And yet, perhaps it is as well to whisper the words aloud once in a while—"dressing room, dressing room, yes, I had my own dressing room once, all to myself, and not on wheels. It had a real mirror, and a special shelf for my makeup kit."

Anyway. Davao found me trying on a new face for King Vilnanash, a more stylized one, something like the shaded black-and-white faces that actors in the west coastal provinces give their legendary royal personages. I was just at the point of deciding that the old look was best when Davao slammed into the room without bothering to knock. His skin was misbehaving again—I wonder whether it ever cleared up—and his thin yellowish hair looked like the old urine-damp straw my company beds down in most nights. But the quality of his rage was as new minted and feverish as though he hadn't been devotedly cosseting it since the day he was born.

"Dardis!" he shouted, making my name sound insult enough to demand a duel. "Dardis, what's this I hear about all three of my bloody brothers sneaking around to see you? What did they want, hey? What did you promise them?"

He was trying to sound like the Jiril, you see, as they all did in one way or another. But he never got it right, poor boy—even Firial did a much better imitation than he. I said, "Nothing at all, my lord. They came only to catch a glimpse of the production, and to wish us luck. Nothing more, I do assure you."

Davao glowered suspiciously at me, but he did it so poorly that I was able to beam back at him, my own face full of benign and humble innocence. I could never have gotten away with it with Torleg. Davao finally muttered, "That's as may be, but I *do* want something from you, and I'm not to be trifled with. You understand that, Dardis? No trifling."

And what was to be *his* contribution to *The Tragedy of King Vilnanash the Accursed*? Not a line of verse, not so much as a stage direction: no, our Davao wished to interpolate exactly one word—the name *Riath*, to be exact. He laboriously explained to me that it was the name of a martyred patriot, who also happened to be the distant ancestor of one of his dearest friends. Now, by sheerest coincidence, our first performance would fall on the eve of his dear friend's birthday. "I want you to put his ancestor's name into that speech where Vilnanash starts talking about all the great and famous men who have died for his country. It's to be his birthday present, he'll like that, that's what I want. Do it."

Well, assuming you could swallow the notion of Davao *having* a dearest friend, let alone his actually giving anybody anything, the request itself was by far the easiest one to comply with. Lisonje, being the person to whom I spoke the lines, caught the new name in the list immediately, but did nothing beyond raising a weary plucked eyebrow. When I explained afterward, she only shrugged, saying, "Why not, why on earth not, how much more trouble can we be in? I just want to remind you, Dardis—when they are coming for us, and we have ten minutes to pack and get out, the good makeup towels are *mine*." She would have fitted quite neatly in with the Jiril's family, Lisonje, in some ways.

So there you have it, if you're still paying attention and haven't fallen asleep behind those politely open eyes. Five interpolations, none really damaging in themselves—oh, a couple perhaps showing a few seams, nothing embarrassing—but each one a signal to *somebody*, and all of those somebodies being alerted through our mouths. If I was still taking it all too lightly, by Lisonje's standards—and yes, yes, as matters did turn out, yes, I suppose I was—my defense must be that I had a role to perfect myself, a huge cast to teach and direct, musicians to supervise—musicians to *find*, that was most of it—and the Jiril's resident lighting experts to wheedle and cozen and cajole into giving a scene something resembling the mood I asked for. A poor excuse, doubtless, but the very best a poor player can afford.

So, then. The eve of our first performance came at last. I had a horrendous case of nerves all that day, but I always do—like you, I'm quite sure. It's a simple question of knowing, in a way that no mere actor can ever know, exactly how much can go wrong, how rich and vital with appalling possibilities is the disaster waiting hungrily for you. Nususir remained as placid as only the truly unimaginative can be; but Trygvalin was like a horse who smells fire somewhere near, and Lisonje—Lisonje was calm without being in the least tranquil. She had spent most of the day packing all her props, costumes, and makeup for abrupt departure; and as often as I told her that she was wasting her time, just that often she rolled her eyes scornfully without bothering to answer. Someone is going to strangle her one day, when she does that with her eyes. I can wait.

As for the rest of the troupe, they went about the usual business of any company just before its opening: vomiting, sweating, shaking, card playing; fits of screaming laughter alternating with a kind of hysterical silence I have known nowhere but in the theatre. Chachak the clown spent the day drinking, deliberately—I am certain of it—reducing himself to a state where he couldn't even stand up to be sick, let alone to dance or sing. We had no Second Clown, so I was forced to parcel out his lines between several other actors, and delete his jigs and clogs altogether. No great loss in this play, but disconcerting to the cast, who were nervy enough already. I busied myself, as is my custom, with the most ordinary tasks I could find, making certain that costume changes would be ready, that the musicians in the gallery knew every one of their cues, that the fresh torches were set into the proper sconces, and the smoke and thunder and lightning machines also just where they should be. Lisonje jokes with frightened actors before a performance, teasing and comforting them. This is what *I* do.

From time to time, one or another of the younger ones would slip forward to peep from behind a flat at the spectators, which is always a mistake. Each time they came back dazed and terrified all over again by the commotion that seven hundred people can make shuffling into a theatre, quarrelling over places, calling out to friends, bawling for the vendors of fruit and sweets and ale, while those in turn bawl their wares until our flimsy backdrops billow with it. I've breathed that noise in and out for so long that it becomes difficult to remember right just how frightening it was when I was sure they were all howling for my blood. But I do remember, yes, I do still.

The Jiril and his small entourage arrived just as late as they should have, and not a moment later, and took their seats in the row reserved for them, while their subjects cheered exactly as lustily as was expected. His four sons filed in one at a time, each nodding briefly to clumps of louts wearing their well-known colors—the Jiril appeared to be taking no notice of these—and Firial trailed behind, eyes dutifully lowered, nothing in her bearing to suggest that she had every intention of absconding with her father's cherished cook that same night. The said cook, Deh'kai, I saw high in the servants' gallery—a handsome lad, rather slim for a cook—craning constantly forward to stare down, never once taking his eyes from her. I recall thinking, *ah, you'll learn, you'll learn.*

I waited until all of the Jiril's people were seated, and then I stepped out in my role as the Chorus (the actor playing King Vilnanash *always* doubles as the Chorus, not that it's at all necessary. I don't know who started it. You never do know) to welcome the audience and assure them that they were in for a rare treat:

> "... *a tale of woe greater than words can tell,*
> *Of pride, power, vain ambition, all cast down,*
> *A house supreme dispersed to such blind dust*
> *As all we come to, howsogreat our might—*
> *As all we come to, sitting here tonight. ..."*

I don't care for Prologues or Choruses, as I've said, but there are worse, if you have to have them. And the first act, showing King Vilnanash at the height of his reign, is the only one in the play that really holds together—as an act, I mean, not as an assortment of loosely related scenes. We sailed through it, with Lisonje stealing every scene she was in—every gesture, every smile, every sideways intonation, every turn of her body on the stage, every shifting rhythm of her speech, all workman's tools in her shameless seduction of the audience. And I not only let her get away with it, I helped her—I played her foil for that first act as though the entire play were about Queen Noura, not her pitiful accursed consort. Tomorrow night I would tread on her gown, if I had to, to keep her from upstaging me . . .

. . . but then, tomorrow night the worst would surely be over and perhaps nothing at all be changed. Perhaps none of the Jiril's sons' followers would turn out to be as ready for a revolution as they thought they were; the old man might well have bought them all off himself, as he once subverted the priests of an invading barbarian army so that they predicted utter disaster if the attack were not indefinitely postponed. But what I was truly betting on, as I always do, was inertia: the fact that most of the time, in any human situation, nothing much actually *happens*. You're a man of some experience, you know where to put your money when it matters. Tell me I am wrong.

Yes, well, I was wrong that time. Right in principle, but wrong in result, the old story. The oration into which Davao had desired me to insert the name of Riath occurs in the first act, and the moment I spoke it, shrill, if thin, cheering broke out in various corners of the house. I grew tense at first, and then had to struggle manfully to keep myself from breaking into laughter. If that lot represented the sum of Davao's cohorts, the Jiril had more to worry about from colic and hoof-rot in his stables. So much for *those* rebels, anyway.

And so much for the first act and on into the second with a fine rhythm building, the spectators already gripped (those who were actually there to see the play) by the ruin looming ahead for King Vilnanash, and I myself drawn so much deeper into that proud, doomed imbecile than I had expected—you know how that oldest magic happens—that I completely forgot about the three new lines Torleg had written in for the sorceress. When Nususir delivered it, in her best prophetic style, a hungry roar went up all around the theatre that was as shockingly different—in kind, not merely in volume—from the yelping of Davao's gang as a puppy's whimper for milk is from the hunting howl of a rock-*targ*. Nususir froze where she stood and had to be prompted to recall her next words. Not I, never; but I lost poor Vilnanash for the rest of that night. From then on, of course, it was nothing but lines and gestures and crossings, playing with one eye on the audience and one ear desperately alert for the next interpolation. Probably one of the worst performances I ever gave, not that it matters.

They never fully quieted down again, Torleg's folk, once having acknowledged their leader; nor did Davao's, though you couldn't always hear that lot. And in Act Three, when Trygvalin brayed his defiance of his father in Javeri's inflammatory rant—why, then here came a new faction altogether, reared up on their stamping feet and blaring their support till the solid old walls of our former tannery shook with it. After that it was pure chaos, with only occasional interludes of simple, wholesome bedlam. We on the stage could barely hear one another, and then only because we abandoned any notion of projecting over that uproar and spoke *under* it, as one can do. And even so, there were long stretches where for the canniest of us—let alone our utterly panicked apprentices and journeymen—we'd no choice but to mouth the words, if terror hadn't ridden them out of our heads, tread our practiced measures from entrance to exit without colliding, and pray that we were all still somehow in the same scene of the same act of the same play. And mind you, mind you, that was yet early on.

Backstage, the tumult was hardly less. I cut the intervals between the third, fourth and fifth acts down almost to nothing, because that howling out front, regardless of content, was raw madness, whether you actually feared it or no, and would swiftly make every one of us mad. If Lisonje was white about the mouth, bumping into the set and dropping her props, you can imagine what the rest of them were like. I wished to give them no time for the terror to take real hold; nor those others time to measure and savor their strength. Once I peeped out myself and saw the Jiril sitting calmly in his grand chair, looking around him with interest as his sons' partisans chanted their slogans, each side mocking and threatening all the others. The sons themselves had not yet dared to stir from under the Jiril's eye, not one of them. His wife was looking as annoyed as though Firial had disappointed her again; while as for that demure minx, she barely raised her eyes from some rather gaudy beadwork she had brought along with her. Even in the last act, when the dying Sakha gasped out the words which (if he could hear them—Trygvalin couldn't) would enlighten her lover as to their meeting place, she appeared to be paying no attention to anything but her domestic task. Gods, there are times when I wonder why I bother dragging men along in my company. Men always think acting is playing, pretending; you never can really teach even the best of them otherwise. Women know it's life.

Gol's bit came last, the abdication speech that I had managed to work into the scene just before King Vilnanash's long-overdue suicide. Amazingly, the house quieted somewhat for that one moment, and I was able to deliver the lines with some attempt at interpretation, at nuance. They were actually listening, if you'll believe it; they were so still that I was able to hear Lisonje's urgent whisper behind the backdrop, "Dardis—die as close to the wings as you can! I'll drag you off, and we'll make a run for it. Fall toward the wings, Dardis!"

It was quite sweet of her, but really—King Vilnanash the Accursed to die up left? Not possible, not remotely possible, not even in such extraordinary circumstances. My ministers filed offstage, sniveling and honking in an attempt to portray loyal grief, and I spoke my last rhymed couplet (its moral: don't irritate the gods, even if you don't know you're doing it), drew forth my bejewelled royal dagger with its collapsible blade, smote myself fatally, and died center stage, sprawled across the apron—center stage, where I bloody well belonged. And the house went wild.

If I choose to believe—quietly, only quietly, to myself—that some little scrap of that mad roaring and cheering was actually in tribute to my performance . . . well, well, what of it? It harms no one, comforts me, and makes no difference at all to the tale. Granted, the body of the roar was composed of assorted war cries and screams for vengeance, as half the audience fell upon the other half—no, the fractions were more complex, more like thirds and fourths and eighths, and all going murderously at one another with whatever weapons they had smuggled in under their cloaks. Cudgels it was, mostly, but I saw dirks—yes, and bungstarters, hayforks and butchers' cleavers too, if you can credit it. Something for everyone, you might say.

Of course, any sort of bow was definitely out of the question. I leaped to my feet and shouted, "Mudbaths all around!" which is still our particular cant for *abandon ship, head for the hills*. To the rest of my troupe the rioting must have looked insanely random—assault for the blind joy of assault—but Lisonje and I at least knew better. I also knew much better than to linger onstage, but I did anyway, watching the last of Davao's weedy crew being run over and kicked aside, mostly by spectators making for the doors, while his brother's gangs hurtled together almost under my nose, yelling their squalid slogans, smashing the seats with one another's head, trampling panicky innocents, and generally doing the berserk best they could to reduce our poor theatre to matchwood. I could hear both Gol and Javeri above the bedlam, bellowing furiously at their minions to stop murdering each other and concentrate on the Jiril's retinue. They might as well have been pleading with walk-ons not to fatten their roles by strutting and jigging and inventing their own lines. I know the feeling.

Torleg, on the other hand, had his forces under absolute control. I would have expected no less; still, it was undeniably chilling to see those bullies in his neat maroon livery moving through such chaos with such dispassionate brutality. They never lost sight of their goal, which was to isolate the Jiril, and that they achieved easily, since the old man had obviously no intention of offering any resistance. He himself had hardly stirred since the outbreak began, watching placidly under puffy eyelids as Torleg's men steadily hammered their way toward him. The Jirelle was seriously put out with her sons, and was letting them know it above the commotion; but Firial, ignored as always, just went on with her beadwork. I thought she must be frozen with panic, not to take advantage of the tumult around her to escape with Deh'kai; but then she looked up and saw me across a welter of sprawled bodies and shattered sweets carts. She winked. I will be swearing after my burial that she winked.

Lisonje was hauling at my arm, trying to drag me off the stage, as she will do when she thinks I am letting my curtain speech ramble. I was yielding, touched by her obvious concern, and realizing also that she might well have snatched the good makeup towels after all, when Torleg shouted a command and his followers halted instantly, with the Jiril and his group completely surrounded. Torleg came forward, smiling. He said, "Well, Father."

"Well, boy," the Jiril answered. Have I mentioned that his voice had a distinct hoarse whistle to it, and a twangy hill accent that he took great care never to lose? It added greatly to a general bumpkinish air, which was dangerously deceptive. "You've been busy children, all of you. Not a bad job."

"Praise from such a father is praise indeed." Torleg's words were notably muffled by the creamy richness of his self-satisfaction. You can go mad trying to break overpraised actors of just that sound. He spread his hands graciously now, saying, "I hope you won't take any of this as a reflection on your rule in Derridow, Father. It's just that my friends and I rather think it's come time for you and Mother to start taking life a bit easier. Enjoying yourselves."

"I was enjoying myself very nicely as I was," the Jiril said, gruffly imperturbable as ever. "Almost as much as you and your brothers will soon be enjoying my prison. I think I might mew you all up in the same cell, and take a few bets on who survives the first night. My money's on you, boy, I'll tell you that right now."

Torleg laughed outright and shook his head. "I think not, sir. My beloved sibs, yes, quite possibly, but my parents—oh, and, of course, sweet, retiring Firial—will be given safe conduct and first class transportation as far as Leishai, where they will choose to take ship for the gracious isle of Lang-y-fydyss, there to spend their declining years in simple peace and beauty. I promise faithfully to visit once a year. At least."

Those who could flee, on both sides of the proscenium, had done so long since: our devastated theatre—chairs and benches in bloodstained splinters, carpeting torn up, hangings torn down, torches trodden underfoot, nothing but the stage itself ironically untouched—was empty of all but assorted clumps of battered insurgents, outnumbered and efficiently surrounded by Torleg's men. Gol, Javeri, and Davao themselves were already in chains, their faces bleeding. Lisonje had left off tugging at me, and was standing as helplessly ensorcelled as I by a performance so surpassing our own. No, perhaps not quite as spellbound—I must grudgingly admit that it was her sharp elbow that called to my notice the utterly unremarkable men in nobody's livery drifting blandly through the ruins, looking like nothing so much as a rather bemused cleanup squad. Indeed, a few of them carried pails and brooms, as I recall. Torleg might have recognized them as the Jiril's legendary Nameless Ones—word has it that their crest reads *never seen, always near*—but he was too busy trying to astound his father with his cleverness. Aye, I know that feeling, too.

He was still keeping up his air of lightly mocking triumph, but the Jiril's plain indifference had by now provoked him to proclaim, "Actually, the whole plan was just a slight modification of your own insurrection, all those years ago. I was a bit fearful you might notice the resemblance."

"Insurrection?" the Jiril rasped. "What bloody insurrection? I was acclaimed rightful Jiril the first day I set foot in this city, and well you and your wretched brothers know it.

And I am Jiril here still, boy, as you're a moment or two from finding out." There was that in his voice would have told me, even without seeing the Nameless Ones moving in, that this was no bluff, no playacting; but Torleg hadn't my expertise in such matters. The difference between journeyman and gifted amateur, I suppose, when all's said.

Torleg went on obliviously preening and prattling— things like, "At a certain point, a man has to put family considerations aside and act for the greater good"—right up to the moment when two of those ordinary-looking men pinioned his arms, and a third touched a dagger very gently to a place just below his left ear. I don't know what became of the buckets.

The Jiril said, "Go on, son. You have all my attention." Torleg never lost control, not for a moment. There was an instant when his eyes widened slightly as he stared at the three men; then he laughed a different sort of laugh and said, "I could have sworn you lot were with us."

"We took your money, lord," the man with the dagger replied gravely. "It seemed the courteous thing."

"Indeed," Torleg said. "Well. If you will permit me to salute my father." The men holding his arms slacked their grip briefly, and he bowed gracefully to the Jiril, saying, "Farewell for now, sir. We are always underestimating you, are we not?"

"Every time," the Jiril grunted. "Good-bye."

Torleg nodded once to his mother and sister as he went with the Nameless Ones. I looked around to see that his rebels—triumphant only a little before, dazed and meek now—were themselves being hustled away, who knows where? In the silence, the Jirelle asked wearily, "How long will you keep them in prison this time?"

"A year," the Jiril said. "A year anyway, by the gods' arseholes, this time a full year." He caught sight of Lisonje and me then, and called out, "Dardis, my apologies for the damage. It will be made good."

"We never doubted it, lord," Lisonje answered him brightly, just as though she didn't have everything she owned packed for flight backstage. The Jiril turned abruptly and snapped at Firial, "Girl, is there nothing in the world you can do but that bloody broidering? Your brothers have all four just sought to overthrow me, and are under hatches for it, and you sit there with your eyes on those idiot beads, not a word, not even so much as looking up when Torleg says we're being sent into exile. Are you weak in the head besides being plain as two sticks?" There was more, but let it be. He had an ugly anger at times, the Jiril.

Firial did look up then, and whatever there was in her pleasant brown eyes shut the Jiril's mouth with a click Lisonje and I heard where we stood. She put away the beadwork and rose swiftly to her feet, standing very straight. At my shoulder Lisonje whispered, "Ah, Barduinn, let me do it! Let me change places with her for two minutes, two minutes only!" Barduinn is supposed to be our god, the special deity of all actors, but I must say I never got any decent use out of him—perhaps you've had better luck, yes? As always, he paid Lisonje no heed: she was to be compelled to watch yet another amateur play out a scene that she knew she could have handled with vastly more panache. I felt for her, I must say that. But then Firial spoke, and everything changed.

Firial said, "That will do, Father." The Jiril's head snapped around—as did ours—plainly not at the words themselves, but at the way she read the line. Tone and timing, it's everything, I've always said that. Lisonje couldn't have done better, and a side glance told me she knew it. Firial gave it just the right pause, just the right turn of the shoulders, and then the absolutely perfect small smile as she said clearly, "Because my husband will be very annoyed if he hears you speak to me so."

Well, there may have been a jaw somewhere in the theatre that didn't drop, but I never saw it. I certainly never saw Lisonje so flabbergasted, before or since. The Jiril turned any number of colors, spluttering like an unprimed pump, while his wife stood up, her eyes all abulge, and said, "Hussy, I don't believe it, how *could* you?" and sat

down again. There was any amount of gasping and gobbling from the entourage; and I remember one bedizened
bolster who must have been Firial's old nurse trying to coax
her back to her chair and her beadwork. But Firial put her
firmly aside, calling, "Deh'kai, my lord, I am here." I have
rarely heard such serene invitation as was in her voice, and
never quite such triumph.

Nor have I ever in my life seen such astonishment as
undid every muscle in the Jiril's face and turned it the color
of a Cape Dylee fog against that dyed beard when he saw
his men—his very own incorruptible, utterly loyal Nameless Ones—turning to greet his very own cook as their
master. For it was indeed young Deh'kai who came saun-
tering toward them now, the most nonchalant, least preten-
tious conqueror you ever saw, calmly greeting his turncoats
by name and bowing with great respect to the Jiril and his
wife before he embraced Firial. "Your pardon and your
love, my parents," he said, cool as Torleg. "I think I am as
well entitled to one as to the other."

"You're entitled to have children kicking your head up
and down the street!" the Jiril howled at him. "Get your
greasy hands off my daughter, or I'll have them off with
your own draw-knife—aye, and a few other things with
them, you jumped-up potboy! You ash-pit, you scullery
beetle, I refused six horses for you—six horses and a
breeding pair of hunting *shukris*—and you do this to me!
Rape my daughter, seduce my Guard—gods' balls, is there
anything in the world you won't—?"

Firial stepped between them and slapped the Jiril hard
across his wet mouth. She would have done it again, but
Deh'kai stopped her, gripping her wrists gently, smiling all
the while. "Dearest heart, dearest," he soothed her, "no one
raises a hand to my father-in-law, I'll not have it. I promise
you he will come to treasure me in time, as I do you. He
means none of these words, none—do you and Mother take
him sweetly home, while we tidy somewhat here." So he
cozened her, and the Jirelle as well, as Lisonje and I gaped;
until he actually had the two of them on the Jiril's arms—

like the men who had seized Torleg—and easing him away, carefully, the way you move an unwieldy wardrobe, turning it this way on this leg, this way on that. The old man was in such shock that they almost had him out of the theatre before he lunged free and came at Deh'kai. His eyes were mad, and there was a little ceremonial dagger in his hand.

Men moved in fast from all sides, but Deh'kai waved them back and waited for him, his own eyes as friendly as could be. The Jiril halted before him, glaring like a trapped *shukri* himself, demanding, "What did you give them? My sons, others, other people, dozens, they've tried and tried to bribe my Nameless Ones—never, they never could, not for anything. What did you give them? What did you *do*?" He dropped the dagger and collapsed weeping at Deh'kai's feet, and the former kitchener stooped quickly and respectfully to raise him.

"Why, I gave them nothing, sir," he answered the Jiril. "As you so rightly say, there's nothing in the world could buy the fidelity of such men." Oh, he *was* good, that one— I'd have given a deal to have had the training of him. A year, six months even, and he'd have been playing the wizard Khyr, or even Lord Crocius in *The Horseman's Tragedy*. He said, "They were always very fond of my cooking, your Nameless Ones. I used to save the leftover dishes from your high table for them, whenever I could." The Jiril stared at him. Deh'kai went on, "By and by, they thought perhaps they might like to eat such meals every night, just as you do. We came to an understanding."

"Dinner," the Jiril said. "They betrayed me for dinner." He looked vaguely at the dagger still clenched in his fist and dropped it on the ground. "But I fed them," he whispered. "If I fed no one else, I always fed the Nameless Ones."

For the first time Deh'kai looked just a bit smug, just a trifle too pleased with himself for my taste. He said, still pointedly humble, "Well, sir—Father—there's feeding, and then there's food, if you see what I mean. It's rather a different thing."

The Jiril gave him one last despairing glance, and then

turned silently away and wandered back to the arms of his captors. I never heard him speak word again, though I'm sure he must have done. As I remember, he died either just before or just after Deh'kai was installed as the new Jiril of Derridow. The Jirelle—or ex-Jirelle, Dowager Jirelle, whatever the exact term is—spent her remaining days, which were many, as the honored, ignored guest of her daughter, son-in-law, and grandchildren, while her four sons were sent into four very separate exiles, from which none are reported to have returned. All epilogue, this, all anticlimax, and it's gotten dreadfully late, I do apologize. At least you and your lot can sleep in—*we'd* better be long past Lis by the time you're at breakfast, if we're to play in Goliak tomorrow night. Miserable town, Goliak. My deepest thanks for your courtesy to a babbling old colleague.

What? Oh, of course, they'd been married by some hedge-priest or other before Firial ever came to see me. Just shows you, doesn't it? As for the why and how of our leaving Derridow forever—well, Lisonje never did unpack, for all Deh'kai's apparent friendliness, and she was right, as she may one day tire of reminding me. Because Deh'kai called us to the great hall, together with Trygvalin, Nususir, and one or two more, not long after his installation. I can tell you his exact words this moment, as I'm sure those others could.

"I greatly admire you all," is what he said, "and it causes me no end of rue to tell you that you must be gone by tomorrow's sunset and never return." He still maintained a modest, amiable air, Jiril or no, but he was already putting on a bit of weight and beginning to show a fondness for uniforms. Putting his fingertips together, he continued, "To be quite candid, you know rather too much about how I came to be sitting where I am. There are those near who would much prefer that none of you ever left this hall."

At the time I assumed that he was referring to this minister or that, or to the Nameless Ones, but today I wonder. Could he have meant Firial herself, do you suppose? There was far more happening behind that round, mild face than any but Deh'kai ever learned. He said, "Myself, I see no need to begin so—what price the tales of a ragbag gang of mummers against the Jiril of Derridow? You may go freely, therefore, and if it is any consolation to you, the tannery stage will stand empty from this day. As I have reason to know, even the most domesticated theatre has in it too much potential for disturbance and uncertainty to run loose here while I rule. Pass the word, of your kindness, to any troupe you encounter—Derridow has no more welcome for players, move along. Yet be assured"—and yes, he studied us all, but those smiling eyes rested longest on *me*—"that my wife and I will remember you with affection, and with a certain real gratitude. Farewell."

So there you are, there's how we lost our beautiful theatre. We took to the road next day, and we have been on it ever since, more than twenty years now. Deh'kai is still Jiril of Derridow—governs indifferent well, too, from what I hear—bar the odd crackdown, lockup, banishment or vanishing—but you won't find so much as a juggler or a rope-dancer crossing his border even today, and his folk are said to live with this comfortably enough. What they think about it, what they feel—aye, well, that's what theatre's for, isn't it? To discover just such things about ourselves, all of us together? He was quite right, you know, Deh'kai.

I sometimes ponder whether they remember us in Derridow, if only when they pass that twice-abandoned tannery on the Tomelly shore. We gave them some proper shows there, in the old times. Anyway, good night to you, and good luck to your season here in the Keep—full houses, sober stage managers, industrious apprentices who can speak lines if they have to, leads who can at least *remember* their lines, tolerable clowns, and the blessing of divine Barduinn over all. For what that's worth. None of them *really* like players, the gods, none of them, not really.

LAL AND SOUKYAN

B eyond the whitewashed one-room hut there is only desert. The old black woman saw him coming a long way and a very long time off, and knew him before the girl could even discern movement on the milky horizon. She set her long, still-youthful hands on her hips, cocked her head and shook it slowly from side to side without saying a word.

Skin bag in one hand, crude rush basket in the other, the little girl watched intently, mimicking the old woman's silence as she copied everything else about her. There was no one else in the hut, and nothing to be seen within its walls but a few dishes, a firepit, and two sleeping mats away in a corner. In a startlingly deep whisper the girl finally asked, "Shall I go, *inbarati*?"

"Of course not," the old woman said. "Set the water down in the shade, you know where. And bring the basket here. I'm hungry." She was a small woman, completely white-haired, with a cat's triangular face and smoky golden eyes; and her own voice had a distinct up-and-down lilt to it, different from the child's husky singsong. She remained in the doorway, watching the distant figure making its way toward them.

The little girl set the basket at her feet and crouched there herself, bright-eyed with curiosity but patiently immobile. Presently the old woman sighed, muttered something the girl could not make out, and dropped down easily on her own heels beside her. Lifting the lid of the basket, she brought out several broad, thick yellow leaves, setting them on the ground one after another. Most of them were folded over strips of dried meat, but a few contained small, stubby vegetables, and there was even an overripe melon, purple and sticky. The old woman divided the food carefully between herself and the girl, giving her most of the melon. "I can't taste sweet anymore," she explained dispassionately. "Never waste sweet things on someone who cannot taste them. Tell me a story now, while I have my breakfast."

The girl took a long, slow breath, closed her eyes, and began to recite a tale involving a mighty lord, his wicked minister, a peasant and her daughter, a clever thief, and a singing fish. Her hands shaped them all in the air, and her voice took on a droning, chantlike quality. The old woman ate without looking at her, grunting now and then at a particular turn in the story, though whether with pleasure or disapproval the child could never tell. The tale and the meal came to an end at the same moment, but the old woman said nothing for some time. She stood up and went to lean in the doorway again, squinting against the newrisen sun. Staring across the desert made the little girl's eyes swim and sting: she could not see that the tiny figure was any nearer, nor whether it was man or woman, old or young, or even mounted or afoot. She waited, alert as a lizard, ready for anything, thinking of nothing.

"You must tell that story this way," the old woman said. Her bare feet made no sound on the hard mud floor as she came back, walking with a slight seagoing roll, to squat in front of the little girl. Looking directly into her face now, she began to repeat the entire story from the beginning. She told it in almost the same words that the girl had used, but in a voice like muffled drums and like sails snapping in the wind. Now playful, now resonant with action, now shivering with pity or wonder or rage, now briefly flowering into song, her voice built and kept a hypnotic rhythm that held the girl absolutely still even after the tale was over. She never moved until the old woman passed a hand back and forth before her eyes, saying in an ordinary voice, "There, that is how I learned to tell it. That's how it is done."

"Another," the little girl whispered. "Please, *inbarati*."

The old woman smiled for the first time. Her teeth were small and remarkably white against her plum-dark skin. "First you will tell me the tale of the thief and the singing fish once again. Then you will bring in some firewood while I sweep out the hut, and then we will have our nap. *Then*"—and she tugged gently on one coarse black braid—"*then* you will hear of Zivinaki, who was the greatest liar in the whole world. It is most important for you to know about Zivinaki if you wish to be an *inbarati*."

The girl looked down forlornly at her own tiny brown feet. "By then your—guest—will be here, and you will send me away."

"My guest?" The old woman laughed outright: an odd, throaty crackle that always retained a quality of surprise, as though amusement were constantly catching her unaware. "Child, whatever else that one may be, he will never be my guest. Besides, he is ancient, doddering, practically senile, like me—I assure you, it will take him all the rest of the day to reach this house. Now. Tell me a story."

The sun was halfway down the sky, and the little girl was sound asleep on a straw mat by the time the old woman walked out to meet her visitor. They met by the one tree in the vicinity, a stunted, charred-looking object like a clenched fist. The old woman was the first to speak. She said, "You are thinner than you were."

"Only a whittling away of the inessential," he answered her gravely. "Nothing needed is lost." He was a tall old man, all knobby bone and gristle and weathered brown hide not many shades lighter than the old woman's skin. He wore little more than light trousers, a leather vest, and a pair of bald, splitting boots. A bow nearly as long as himself was slung over his right shoulder. The bowstring pulled the vest open, revealing several thin white scars up and down his ribs, and one great jagged cicatrice just above the waist that ran halfway around his body. When he smiled, his eyes, which were of a nameless, impermanent twilight shade, warmed to a color that was almost lavender. "Look at you," he said, "Greetings, Lal."

"Hello, Soukyan," the old woman said. "What do you want?"

"A cup of tea would be nice," the old man replied. "A cup of tea, a night's lodging, and a kind word—I cannot imagine desiring anything more in the world, just at present." He put his hands lightly on the old woman's shoulders. "Look at you," he said again. "Look at you."

"Not for years, thank you." The old woman pulled away from him. "There are no mirrors in my house, and no portraits either. There is no Lal in my house, Soukyan, no more."

The old man's smile widened slightly. "No? Then who is that waiting for us there?" She turned swiftly to see the little girl standing at the door of the hut, rubbing her eyes as she peered out toward them. Soukyan said, "Lal, surely."

"*No.*" The answer came quietly and savagely. "Her name is Choushi-wai. After I had been in this place awhile, and the people had grown used to my presence, they sent her to me. 'She lies all the time,' they said, 'but she is strong, and she can cook. Use her as you will.' So she is my housekeeper now, and my apprentice as well, the only one I ever had. But she is not me, Soukyan, not me, never." The long fingers dug hard into his upper right arm. "Thank all the imbecile gods who made me what I am—what I was—she will never, never have to be Lal."

The big old man put his hand on hers. "Ah. Now it seems to *me* that there are many worse things in this world than being Lalkhamsin-khamsolal."

"Not for Lal," she said. "Soukyan, you may have the tea and the lodging, but tomorrow I want you gone. Whatever you want of me, the answer is no. You came seeking Sailor Lal, Swordcane Lal, Lal-Alone, and you have found a folktale crone, withered and forbidding, living out her time by telling stories to a barbaric desert tribe which is not her own but will do well enough. I am at last what I was always meant to be—all the rest, all of it, that was a dream, one of my old bad dreams. You remember my dreams."

"As many of them as I held you through?" They were walking slowly toward the hut now, blinking against the setting sun. The old man said, "As you will. I'll drink my tea and be grateful for the night's lodging, and be off where I'm bound in the morning. But in the hours between may we not speak of Lal, even a little? I did have a message for her, that much is true. Perhaps you will see that it reaches her."

The old woman did not reply. When they reached the door, Choushi-wai bowed to the ground three times to greet the guest, as was the custom of her tribe; but when Soukyan solemnly knelt before her to kiss her hand, then her courage failed and she fled wailing into the hut. Coaxed back, she quickly grew shyly flirtatious: she would not say a word to the old man, but by the end of dinner, she was leaning against his shoulder, alternately eating from his dish and offering him bites from her own. Lal ignored this until the girl had left for her mother's house, where she still spent every night. Then she said irritably to Soukyan, "Now she will be useless to me for days. Instead of learning the immortal chronicles and praise-songs and ballads she must know, she will fill her mind with a dozen soap-bubble fancies that have you in them—and herself, of course. Can you never come into my life and leave things the way you found them?"

"And have you never made up such foolish tales, but only retold those same immortal old ones, over and over?" Neither question expected an answer. They sat silent, looking at each other across two small, smoky oil lamps in the darkening hut. Lal said in time, "These people are some way related to my own folk. The language is much the same, and they know what an *inbarati* is, though they have never had one among them. Now they do. I am well content here, Soukyan."

"Contentment becomes you. Truly, I am not mocking."

The old man stretched out his long legs and arms, smiling wryly as joints crackled like pine knots in a fire. "Where has the swordcane gone, then?"

Lal nodded toward a slim rosewood stick leaning against the far wall. "Enough dust on it for a king's library. I do use it once in a while, to knock down fruit, to draw pictures on the ground for Choushi-wai. She has no notion of what it contains, and presently neither will I. That will suit me."

"Well, well, and so it should." Soukyan's tone was drowsily tranquil, and his strange eyes were half-closed. "But does it suit the swordcane? there's the question." He chuckled very softly. "Now I myself owe my life three times over to that dainty weapon, so I have reason to be concerned for its peace of mind. You understand how such a thing might be?"

"I understand you," Lal said flatly. "Which is what matters. I never knew anyone more devious who wasn't a wizard. Understand me once for all—the swordcane and I are both where we belong, and there's an end of it. Here, you can sleep on the child's mat. She would be thrilled to idiocy if she knew."

Straightening and brushing the worn straw, she added over her shoulder, "As for myself, that bow of yours kept me alive three times, at very least, so we're long quits, as you well know. There, so, there we are. Now we have dined, and we have talked together, and now we will sleep, and in the morning say our farewells one more time." She turned to face him fully then, and the long golden eyes were at last permitted some emotion. She said, "How many of those have we said, do you suppose? I lost count somewhere around Arakli."

"And well you might have," the old man answered her, "since that's where I lost you. In a marketplace full of drunken soldiers, it was, with half the stalls on fire, and you crouched over that poor crazy street-girl like a mother *sheknath*." He stood up, his own eyes gone dark and distant. "I knew you were dead, Lal. For three years I *knew*. The sun rises, the stars move, the breeze is pleasant today, the beer is miserable in Chun, Lal is gone."

"I searched for you," she said hotly. "You know how I searched, how I left word everywhere you might possibly seek me. And it was no whit worse than Bitava, when I watched you off on the Queen's Road—you *would* ride that way, never mind any warnings—knowing where you were bound, not knowing if I would ever see you alive again. How different was that? How different was the parting at Cheth na'Bata? at Rhyak? Soukyan, I think we were never meant to be friends, comrades, companions, whatever word you will. Neither of us ever can be certain of what we are entitled to ask of the other, so we wear each other out, and enough good-byes are enough after forty years. We do not want the same things from what's left of our lives, you and I. Sleep well, and go away."

"And my message for Lal?" Gray and gaunt and inexorable, he stood too close to her, smelling of roads through woods long cut down, of stories forgotten, of towns and people long since left behind. "Will she never receive it, after all?"

"You'd do as well to put it in a bottle," the old woman said, "and drop it in the sea off Cape Dylee." They stared at each other in an instant of almost unbearable familiarity, memories measuring themselves fiercely against memories. At length, Lal shrugged very slightly; anyone but the old man would have missed it. She said, "Bloody hell. I'm not going to get *any* sleep tonight, am I?"

"Ah, that depends." Soukyan let his legs fold under him, lowering himself onto the sleeping mat with no more than the slightest grunt. "Where's yours? Drag it over here and let's talk. The way we used to talk at night, once you'd found exactly the right twig to clean your teeth with. That tiny chip of a boat, on the Susathi—do you remember?"

"The very best thing about being old," Lal said, "is the privilege of remembering exactly what you choose to remember, and no more." But she smiled then, the lean, three-cornered face momentarily as soft as Choushi-wai's, and as wondering. She brought her mat from the corner, saying as she did so, "Very well, we will talk of times past. Anything you like, but nothing—*nothing*—beyond tomorrow. This is agreed?"

"Agreed, and welcome." The old man waited patiently for her to settle on the mat, where she arranged herself with care, curling her own surprisingly long legs just so, propping her chin on a hard-knuckled fist. He asked, "Just because I think about such matters—did you ever go home?"

"No," she said fiercely. "No, never. Home to where I was stolen and sold, and sold again—home to where no one cared enough to follow and find me? Soukyan, if anyone in the world knows better—" She broke off and looked away from him; when she spoke again, her tone was carefully flat. "We will not talk about that either."

"No, we will not." The old man leaned forward; he seemed about to touch her face, but did not. "Rather, let us remember a place where we were together, very long ago. Let us consider Surijat."

"Surijat." Lal blinked at him. "Surijat. That pretty little place up in the Durli Hills, where we were escorting the caravan. Surijat, I remember."

"No, you remember Toshtiyk. This was before Toshtiyk—you were just back from sea, I think, and we met on the wharf—"

"Kulpai," Lal said. "Kulpai, and it wasn't the wharf, it was in the cells." She laughed a sudden broken bark of a laugh. "I told Choushi-wai you were as senile as I am, and you really must be, to have forgotten the lockup at Kulpai. I'd gotten swept up with a gang of smugglers—I never did know what you were in for."

Soukyan grinned, lips flattening over stained teeth. "Just as well. Much too embarrassing to go into, even now. Kulpai, then—what matters is that you and I found ourselves together there, and what really matters is that we escaped on the second night. You do remember that much?"

"Better than you do," the old woman replied tartly. "It was the third night, and *I'd* never have had the cheek to call it an escape. The guard"—she halted for only an instant—"the guard fell asleep, that was it. And you hooked the keys out of his belt and unlocked all the cells. There, ask me if I remember Kulpai."

Soukyan leaned closer, not smiling at all now. She noticed an unfamiliar scar, half-hidden in the white stubble along his jawline. "No. No, that is not what happened. You told the guard a story."

Lal sat up, the golden eyes round and indignant. "Oh, you *are* starting to unravel. That was never in Kulpai."

"Yes, it was," the old man said. "You told him a tale of a lord who could turn himself into a rock-*targ* when he chose, and of a lady who fell in love with him even knowing what he was. And she had a friend who was only a seamstress, but who wanted very much to help her. You told that story, and he came closer and closer to the bars and listened as that little girl of yours would listen. I was standing beside you, and he never saw me move—he never saw me at all until I had my hands on his throat. Now? It comes back?" His voice was harsh with intensity, and the brown skin had gone strangely pale.

Lal did not speak for a long time. The old man watched her, studying her face as he might have studied himself in a mirror. She said finally, "There was a boy. I can see him, but I can't recall. . . . A small boy."

"The guard's son." Soukyan spoke now utterly without inflection. "Yes, he was there—asleep in the scullery, he must have been. And he woke up just after we took his father prisoner, and he came charging to the rescue, swinging a slop bucket or some such at my legs. But you stopped him."

"I did not hurt him." Lal's voice had risen sharply. "That I know, Soukyan."

"No, no, of course not," the other agreed. "We only hurt his father. And he saw."

Lal was on her feet in a single motion far too fluid for her age. "What are you talking about? All we wanted from that fool was silence and the key, and those we had of him in an instant. There was no question of hurting him."

"This is how it was." Soukyan's flat tone did not change. "It was late summer, and very hot in the cells, and the food was dreadful—worst I've ever had in anyone's prison. Also we two both had serious business elsewhere, which was making us irritable. Perhaps then we had some little excuse for what we did."

"What we did? What did we do?" Anger continued to strip years from her movements as she paced the mud floor of the hut, her great stooped shadow lurching to keep up. "We never harmed him—do you think I'd forget if we had? He was a slow, thick sort—I remember that much—and he spoke that toothy lowlander dialect and affected to understand nothing we said. He was a guard, like all guards, he did what they all do. What of it? Why are we talking about him?"

"Because we humiliated him in front of his son," the old man said. Lal came to a halt and simply stared. Soukyan was standing too, pointing first at her and then to himself. "Both of us. Half-strangled, he was still struggling to keep hold of the keys. You had to drag his belt off, Lal, and when you did his trews fell right down his flabby white legs. Yet he kept flailing out as well as he could—he caught you in the eye, do you remember that?" Lal shook her head. "It was all more trouble than we expected, and it made us angry. I pinned his arms behind him against the bars, holding him with one hand hard under his chin, so that he looked like a bird stretched for slaughter, fluttering and squawking. It was you who took the keys and opened the other cell doors—I had my hands full with a sweaty, smelly, half-naked dolt who simply didn't know when to give up. He even bit my wrist."

In the complete blackness outside, a small wind was

making the sand whisper. A pair of *mardriu* lizards quarrelled piercingly over a mate; a *tharakki* scuttled by, tiptoeing on two long-clawed feet, taking advantage of the night hunters' preoccupation. Soukyan said, "This is what happened. As they were freed, every one of those other prisoners ran past where I held that guard and spat in his face. There were quite a few of them." His voice was very low, but very clear. "The boy saw it all."

She shrugged. "Well? I never knew a prison guard I'd not have done the same to, and glad of the chance. You are forgetting whom we were then, Soukyan, and where we have been."

"No," he said. "No, I forget nothing. And I remember that he was decent to us, that one, anyway as decent as he could be. It wasn't his fault that the food was so bad, and that there wasn't enough water. He spoke politely to us. He actually tried to be kind. I have no idea why."

"And I still have no idea why you are going on so about him. It was long ago, and whatever was done to him, it was surely his due. There are no innocent guards."

"True enough, doubtless." Soukyan dropped heavily back onto the mat, looking at his big clasped hands. After a moment, he said, "But the boy was innocent."

Lal snorted without answering him. Soukyan continued, as though to himself, "And what was between them, him and his father, that was innocence." He looked up at her, his face suddenly as young as Choushi-wai's with confusion. "It plagues me, Lal."

The old woman was plainly about to say something derisive, but she checked herself almost audibly and only stood looking silently back at him. He repeated, "All these years, and yet it plagues me—I am the one troubled by dreams now. The gray spittle running all down that fat, bewildered face, the look in that boy's eyes. I never used to dream about it before."

Still without speaking, Lal sat crosslegged facing him, reaching forward to put a hand on his ankle. In a little, Soukyan's knuckly brown hand joined hers. She said quietly, "There is a song to chase away such dreams. It is quite a long and boring song, but it does work. Believe me, I would know."

"But I do not want the dream gone!" he cried out. Anger and desperation were mingled equally in his voice. "I need it, I need to remember." He paused, rubbing a hand fiercely across his forehead. He said slowly, "I need to go back there. Kulpai. To apologize."

"To do *what*?"

The next ten minutes were entirely Lal's, although Soukyan began to laugh during the last four or five. When she ran out of breath, he said, "There, I knew it. For all the talk of having closed your circle, having found your way home to true serenity, I knew my old Lal was here somewhere. Go on, don't let me stop you—you cannot imagine what a comfort it is to have you berating my stupidity again. Oh, you are absolutely right—we were never supposed to have anything to do with each other, but who cares? Hello, dear Lal."

"Be quiet," the old woman said. "I am not speaking to you." She stood up again and crossed the hut to a battered wood-and-leather sea chest hidden in the darkest corner. From it she withdrew a gray earthenware wine bottle, the seal on its neck so old that the edges were already falling to powder as she held it up. Behind her Soukyan laughed again, this time in amazement. "Dragon's Daughter, I don't believe it. Here?"

Without answering, Lal knocked the rest of the seal off with the hilt of a table knife and took a quick swig. She frowned, studying the bottle. "Probably all right. It's hard to tell with this swill." She handed the wine bottle to Soukyan.

"Dragon's Daughter," he said again. "The inn near Corcorua. It's too much nostalgia for a man of my age." He drank, wiped his mouth, and grimaced contentedly. "Dreadful as ever, thank the gods. So. Are you coming with me?"

Lal wheeled on the instant and pointed a swordcane

finger at the bottle. "Keep at it. I opened that, after all these years, not out of sentiment, but to get you drunk enough that there would be no more babble about Kulpai this one night at least. Just keep drinking."

The old man smiled bitterly. "A waste. I could have told you." Nevertheless, he tilted the gray bottle again as she watched. When he lowered it, they looked at each other for a long while, until she said at last, "Kulpai will be a waste. I can tell you that."

Soukyan nodded judiciously over the bottle. "Most likely."

"Most likely. Yes, well, he will most likely be dead, the guard. And the boy, who knows? If he is even in Kulpai, he will most likely have forgotten the whole business by now. Like everyone else."

"Everyone else but one ancient mercenary with a cramp in his conscience." He offered the bottle, but she shook her head impatiently. "No," he said, "no, the boy will not have forgotten. You've never had children, Lal, or you would understand."

"And you never *were* a child, not for ten minutes together. And you never had a conscience—only loyalties." She stopped herself abruptly, actually putting a hand over her mouth. The old man said nothing. Presently she lowered her hand and said, her voice determinedly clear and even, "Very well. We always did know one another's unhealed places. I still think that it would be foolish and useless for you to make your pilgrimage all the way to Kulpai to say *I am sorry*. There will be no one to say it to, except yourself, and no forgiveness but your own. There never is."

Soukyan set the bottle down and reached both hands toward her. After a moment she came and knelt by him, putting her long fingers between his. He said, "Dear Lal, I know that. And you are probably right about my having nothing but my odd, meaningless loyalties in place of a conscience. But one of those loyalties is to my idea of myself. It was hard come by, and a weary time in the coming, as you know well, and now it is truly all I have. Is it different for you, at the last?"

Lal did not withdraw her hands—if anything, she pressed them closer into his—but she did not answer him. They sat so for a very long time in the flickering lamplight, while their shadows shivered on the walls.

Choushi-wai arrived with the false dawn, as she always did. The hut was empty, and the little girl's quick eyes took in the fact that the few cooking pots and the swordcane were gone even before she saw the message scratched into the dark underside of one of the leaves that had wrapped yesterday's meal. She mouthed the words over to herself several times—reading was recent, and Lal had not quite finished the job—and then went to stand in the doorway, unconsciously imitating the old woman's posture as she stared out at the two sets of tracks leading away across the white desert.

She was a tracker born, like all her people, and it was not even a matter of conscious thought for her to realize that one of the trails was some hours fresher than the other. If asked, she could have predicted the exact place and moment when Lal must catch up with the big old man who had shared bites of food with her last night. But there was no one to ask her. After a time, she turned away, found the broom in its accustomed place, and began to sweep the floor. She would sleep here tonight, and all the nights until Lal returned.

They walked on side by side for a good while before either of them spoke. The old man said in time, "We'll need horses. It is a very long journey to Kulpai."

"I am still not speaking to you." Lal's feet made as little sound on the sand as they had on the floor of her hut. "I am not speaking to myself, for the matter of that—not until I can provide myself with one halfway adequate reason for my being here." Despite the heat, she was clad all in rough, faded leather, from worn low boots to leggings and shirt, to the curious arrangement of black bands that covered her

head. The swordcane hung down her back, between the jutting shoulderblades. Her sailor's gait matched Soukyan's
pace easily, but she never looked at him as they plodded
toward the thin dark-green ribbon that fluttered where the
horizon should have been.

Soukyan said, "Unfortunately, there will be no horses to
be found between here and Jahmanyar, at best—nothing
but *churfas* in this country. Have you ever ridden a *churfa*,
Lal?"

When she did not reply, he went on cheerfully, "You'll
hate them. They're evil-tempered, utterly untrustworthy,
they stink, and the worst of it is they're a pure bloody nuisance to steal. Do you recall the nightmare it was lifting
those horses out of Stro Gandry's stables when we went to
Kashak? Aye, well, that will be a fond memory after we've
had a midnight hurrah with a couple of *churfas*. No choice,
I'm afraid. Any luck yet in finding a reason to talk to me?"

But Lal kept her resolve and did not speak at all until late
in the afternoon. They were resting at the bottom of a dry
creek bed, taking advantage of the little shade offered by
the crumbling walls. Allowing herself very small sips from
her waterskin, she announced brusquely, "I have decided
that I am traveling with you precisely in order to prove to
myself that this is not my life anymore. You were right last
night—every rare now and then I am troubled a little by
thoughts of far places we saw together, strange folk I
hardly believe we knew, happenings that I could never
make tales of or talk about with anyone but bloody you.
Plainly, the best way to be rid of this excess baggage would
be to put myself through one last such journey—the most
absurd, most pointless, most exhausting expedition a
decrepit old fool might hope to survive." She closed the
waterskin carefully and smiled for the first time that day.
"There. I do like to understand these things."

Soukyan was using the halt to restring his bow. Without
looking up, he asked, "Which decrepit old fool are we
talking about?"

"Oh, as you please," Lal said serenely. Soukyan bent the

great bow, fitted the new string with only the slightest grunt of effort, and rose almost in the same motion. "There's a waterhole to reach before nightfall." He seemed unwearied by the distance they had traveled, but his cheekbones and the bones of his forehead were more prominent than she remembered them, the skin grown oddly taut with age rather than sagging. She took the hand he extended and pulled herself to her feet, feeling the familiar spark of pain in her left knee. *Thirty, thirty-five years since that fight in the winecellar with what's-his-name, and it's never been right since.* She slung the swordcane over her shoulders again, and straightened her spine to cradle it.

For the most part, they journeyed by night. The green ribbon seemed no nearer each dawn, except for the occasional shooting-star flurry of mirages, when they would be accosted by momentary rivers, assaulted by fleeting oases, lured along by shards of gardens, slivers of jungle waterfalls. At such times, they scooped hollows in the sand for themselves and dozed out the day, keeping their heads covered, moistening their lips and tongues every few hours to mumble a bit of dried meat or dried fruit. They hardly spoke after the first day; not until one late evening when the breeze brought at least a memory of coolness and the smell of what might almost have been a cooking fire. Soukyan said, "That will be Doule. A small place, but big enough to stable a few *churfas*. Tomorrow this time, if we keep this pace, we'll be riding on our way like gentry."

Lal was massaging swollen feet, and did not look up as she spoke. "You may as well know that I haven't ridden a horse since that business in Kashak. Let alone stealing one. You'll have a very old greenhorn on your hands when the big moment comes."

"It wouldn't make any difference if you had," Soukyan replied. "Absolutely nothing that works with horses works with *churfas*, anyone will tell you that." He beamed and waggled a forefinger at her. "Fortunately, I do know a trick that comes as near to working with the revolting beasts as anything ever will. What you must do with a *churfa*, old companion, is stick your arm in its mouth."

Lal did look at him then, for quite a long time. She said finally, in a remarkably amiable voice, "I stick my arm in its mouth. I see. Which arm is that?"

"Oh, as you please," he mimicked her impatiently. "What's important is to shove the whole arm between its jaws as quickly as you can. All the way back, mind, where there aren't any grinders. No matter how angry they are—and they're always angry—something about having a nice arm to chew on always calms them down straightaway. Sweet memories of infancy, *I* think, or possibly of eating their young. It's hard to say."

"But boundlessly cheering to know. Whatever am I supposed to do with the other arm?"

"Ah. I'm glad you asked." Soukyan was up and pacing now, not quite meeting her eyes. "The thing is to keep them from screaming. Forget the teeth, forget the smell, never mind rousing the watch—believe me, you do not want to hear a *churfa* scream if you can avoid it. So. As you force your arm into its mouth, you must at the same time cover the beast's nostrils with your free hand. Squeeze tightly, *tightly*, and it will fall to its knees so that you can mount. And don't ask me why this should succeed, Lal, because I simply don't know. But it always does, practically."

"Practically. Yes." Lal forced her feet back into her boots and stood up. "Well. I am too eager to wait any longer to meet such wondrous creatures. If you're ready."

When the sun rose the next morning, they were near enough to Doule to hear Nounouri devotees at their prayers, and to smell fresh *rishu*-dung in the streets. Grown too populous to be called a village, yet never a real town, Doule remained a thorn-walled enclave of dirty white huts, differentiated from the desert only by a whimsical rainy season and an increasingly put-upon underground spring. The huts were thatch-roofed and squat, with a scattering of larger dwellings set apart in fenced-off compounds. These had wooden or tiled roofs, hesitant flower gardens, proper windows, and their own stables, from which the early breeze brought a smell like burning urine and the sounds of heavy claws scraping on wood.

Lal and Soukyan entered Doule through a side gate in the barricade, barely noticed by the porter, who was busy coercing a bribe out of a group of indignant spice merchants. The two of them moved wearily among the brown-skinned, caftan-clad farmers and shopkeepers without attracting attention, except for the occasional side-glance at the tall old man with the great bow. Lal pointed out the common stable in the center of town, but Soukyan shook his head. "Much too public. Too many beasts, too much noise, we can't risk it. We want one of those," and he nodded toward the wealthier-looking homes. "And right now we want a bed, a bath, and a decent meal. There's a hard night waiting up ahead for us." He put a hand on her shoulder. "I am glad of your company. Like the oldest old times, isn't it?"

"Yes," Lal said. They walked on, lifting their feet high to keep from stepping in steaming piles and puddles. She said, "I think I really disliked the old times. I'm trying to remember."

The inn looked a decided step down from the public stable, but neither of them was of a mind to be finicky. They washed in tin buckets smelling of stale grain, dined on bread, weak ale, and the pottage of fermented milk and cheese that is the main dish of the region, and then slept until close on midnight in a bed apparently stuffed with knees and elbows. Soukyan woke first. He sat up slowly and leaned back against the wall, studying Lal's sleep. She woke within a minute, and had her hand on the swordcane before she recognized him. "I hate that," she said. "You know I hate being watched like that."

"I know," the old man answered. "I'm sorry. But it has always been my only chance to spy on your childhood, and I've never once been able to resist it. Forgive me."

Lal was already off the bed and peering out of the room's

murky horn-paned window. "Can't see a bloody thing," she muttered. "Dark enough, anyway." She turned back to face him. "What do I look like, then?"

"Trustful," Soukyan said. Lal made a wordless disrespectful sound. She ran both hands vigorously through her short white hair, shook herself once, and said, "I thought we were going to steal a couple of mounts, not sit here chatting all night. Your *churfas* can't be any fiercer than the bugs in that bed."

They slipped out of the silent inn without waking even the two Tazri watchbirds stationed at the back door to greet just such fly-by-night guests. The desert night was cool, almost cold, and tasted sour as they stood letting their eyes adjust to the blackness. There was no light to be seen anywhere, except for the half-moon overhead. Soukyan muttered, "We could have done without that, but at least it will quiet the *churfas*. They're impossible in full dark."

"Better and better," Lal said. Soukyan, having gotten his bearings, started off down an alleyway behind the inn. He was invisible in two strides, but the old woman followed without faltering. Soukyan took a jagged route that dodged the town center, but then doubled back along its farthest edge, skirted a scummy stockpond, and finally scurried up a low rise toward the back of one of the private stables. Lal knew it by the smell, and by the guttural breathing that sounded like flames.

Soukyan halted abruptly, cocking his head. "Two. Only two, bless every one of the blessed gods for that." He turned and gripped Lal lightly by her upper arms. "It has to happen very fast. Do you remember all I told you about *churfas*?" Lal's response was quiet, precise and profoundly obscene, and Soukyan grinned happily in the hard silver light. "There's my old Lal, ready for anything. All right, then. All right."

There were two locks, heavy as anchors. Soukyan had them open so quickly and daintily that the breathing within never changed. He looked over his shoulder, whispering, "The one in the far left-hand stall. Don't bother with saddle or bridle—just get the bloody beast out and gone. All right. Now."

Lal had braced herself for the howl of the hinges when they dragged the stable door open, but in fact her own panting was louder in her ears than any other sound, until the *churfas* sprang to their clawed feet. They were little taller than horses, but far more massive, with thick coats of sticky-looking fur, tufted round ears and heads so disproportionately broad and blunt as to look truncated. Their lips were grotesquely soft, almost pendulous, which made the tusks protruding from their lower jaws appear longer and sharper than they were. Lal had no chance to take in anything more, because the *churfas* were raising their heads and opening their immense mouths to scream.

Out of the corner of her eye she saw Soukyan come off the floor, one hand over the nostrils of a *churfa*, the other arm shoved crosswise as far into the slobbering mouth as the old man could force it. His legs were already grappling for a grip on the beast's flanks. Smaller than he, and long out of practice at such things, she lunged up at the great reeking head swinging above her, catching hold at neck and nose, but not before the *churfa* had let out the first half of a freezing, shattering cry that seemed to set every bone in her body at lunatic war with her skin. But it did thump down onto its foreknees then, as Soukyan had said it would, and she scrambled high onto the burly neck and reached forward to push her arm between its jaws, feeling the rake of every yellow tooth as she worked the arm all the way back to gummy safety. The *churfa* fell shockingly silent on the instant, but still threshed its head this way and that, wild to be rid of her. Lal held on, methodically cursing Soukyan, a prison guard, the guard's son, and the entire population of Doule in three languages.

On her left, wooden planks splintered under frantic claws, and Soukyan's *churfa* exploded past her through the stable door. Her own beast surged to follow, and she had barely time to flatten herself into its harsh mane to keep from being dashed against the doorframe. Then they were outside in the dark, and Soukyan was leading them, not back the way they had come, but directly past the main house of the compound. Torches were showing in one window after another, and she could hear the voices of running men.

She had no idea of how to control the *churfa*, but fortunately she had no need. The creature kept close enough on the heels of its stablemate that the other turned and bit viciously at it several times. How Soukyan conducted them back down through the town without raising any alarm, and how he discovered the unattended gap in the thorn barrier, she never knew nor cared. She clung to the neck of her mount—astonishingly tractable now, even after she risked easing her numb arm out of its mouth—and she thought only, *I am infinitely too old to be doing this*, over and over.

The *churfas* were natural pacers, both legs on either side moving at once. Soukyan kept them traveling hard south and west, with the half-moon behind them, until dawn. Lal nodded in and out of dreams, wakened only by her mount's hiccupy gait, and by the throbbing of bruises that Sailor Lal would never have deigned to notice. She sensed water near, off to their right, and could tell that the ground was rising and softening slowly under the *churfas'* taloned feet. Despite the animals' inescapably vile stench, she frequently caught the sharp woodsmoke scent of purple *calocali*, which grows in hill country everywhere. Twice, to her drowsy delight, she heard a female *desidro* calling softly to tell her mate and cubs that she had made a kill. *Desidri* are rare and beautiful, and are almost never seen below the timberline. Soukyan turned and smiled. In the moonlight he looked like a young man, a stranger.

They were not followed from Doule. Soukyan had doubted they would be; yet he rode wide arcs across their backtrail for the next two nights, to be certain. Even so, he hardly eased their pace, but drove the *churfas* steadily on through foothills that kept climbing, yet never quite became real mountains, being in their green hearts too soft and good-natured for the job. They were steep enough, in places, and their nights were chill enough that Lal and Soukyan often slept curled together, warming one another's backs by turns ("Now this is something like—this is the past come again, say if it's not!" "Old man, keep those feet to yourself, if you hope to wake tomorrow!"); and there were high-country birds and animals in plenty, like the *desidri*, and trees like the scarlet *hajyll*, whose dusty seed-pods can cure half a dozen afflictions, and the mist-silver *cromni*, which cures nothing at all but gives joy to see. But for all that, they remained gentle, buttocky hills, with their bones well-covered by shrub and scrub and down, and Lal and Soukyan were thankful. The *churfas* appeared thankful too, though it was difficult to be sure.

In a life whose length had surprised her more than any of its events, Lal had never before encountered creatures remotely like the *churfas*. Close to, in daylight, their astonishing ugliness became almost endearing: there was a certain uncompromising grandeur even to the burnt-piss aroma, of which all she and Soukyan owned was long since redolent. Their manners, however, showed absolutely no promise of future charm, being far worse than Soukyan had had time to forewarn her. They shied and balked for deeply personal reasons, or for none, bit where the chance presented itself, screamed hideously at private demons on moonless nights, and shat in great semiliquid splatters of orangey-brown malice with an exquisite sense of placement and timing. They also ate everything from poisonous *royak*-bush to tree bark to entire rotten branches, and galumphed along tirelessly all day on wide padded feet with the blunt claws halfway retracted. Riding bareback, Lal nevertheless grew comfortable with her mount's gait in time, learned in time to govern its direction by knee pressure, and gradually became at least accustomed to the stink; as for the biting, she cured it, to a degree, by biting the *churfa*'s vulnerable tufted ears in immediate retaliation. The night shrieks, however, remained a problem.

Since the first few days, they had spoken very little of

Kulpai. The long ride on such strange beasts through half-strange country made most of their talk: both Lal and Soukyan found themselves falling easily into past ways of speaking and moving, as well as taking on, with no discussion, the camp tasks each had assumed so long ago, time out of memory. Lal fought this backsliding at first, with considerable irritation; for all that, it was yet more than she could tolerate to allow Soukyan to fish for their dinner when they came to a brook or a river, or to build the cooking fire. Her legs remembered, even this late, the slow-swinging pace of the purposeful wanderer; her senses sharpened themselves gleefully against each other, so that she kept the old fierce watch for warning signs or sounds, while at the same time marveling like Choushi-wai at the morning song of small gray birds. *Aye, I'm too old to be doing any of this, surely—but as that great fool said, who cares?*

For his part, Soukyan placidly occupied himself in hunting with his bow, tending the *churfas*, and scouting the trail before and behind them every night. But for his grayness and the new scars, Lal would have seen no difference in him from twenty years before. He had always been a slow-moving man, slow enough that when he did move swiftly, the eye was not prepared for him; he had always chosen deliberately to mute his natural color, preferring to go as much unnoticed as possible, which was difficult work for a big, shambling person with remarkable eyes. Lal had known him to fade in and out of any background—wood or palace or town square—as it suited him; there, too, he was unchanged. He cooked what they killed quickly and inventively, talked too much or not at all, and complained as ever about the long, tuneless epic ballads of her own people, which she habitually chanted to herself as they rode. Yet it was he who noticed that the *churfas* seemed to find them soothing, especially in the dark. "Who am I to claim that I have finer taste than a *churfa*? Besides, anything is better than hearing them screaming. Sing. Please."

All hills in the south country are bandit country; but they had met only three other persons since fleeing Doule: a

woodcutter, an anchoress who made spectacularly appalling brandy in the tranquility of her cave, and a herdboy,
whose gloomily bellowing *rishus* frightened their beasts
into a serious attempt at tree climbing. Despite the quiet,
Lal and Soukyan continued to take their regular turns at
night guard, and to study the trail constantly for hoofprints,
droppings, or a carelessly buried campfire. Once or twice,
for the briefest moment, the wind did carry voices to their
ears, distant as remembered dreams. Lal said, "There," and
Soukyan said, "Maybe. Maybe."

The weather was slanting gracefully into autumn as the
way began its descent toward the flatlands, now visible
occasionally around the shoulder of an escarpment or
through a gap between the hills. Soukyan said, "It is all
farmers from here, and nothing even the size of Doule until
we strike the Churush road and turn toward the coast.
From there it will be easy sailing to Jahmanyar and
Kulpai."

"Kulpai," Lal said sourly. "I had almost forgotten
Kulpai."

Soukyan touched her shoulder. "To tell the truth, so had
I. I don't look forward to Kulpai, Lal. As long ago as it all
was, there's never any joy to be had in confronting one's
own cruelty, nor any way to wake up from it, to make it not
have happened. Nevertheless, this is what I have to do."

"Stupid," the old woman muttered. "I never could abide
stupidity." But she did not shrug away from his hand, and
Soukyan smiled.

"A further confession. If you had utterly refused to
accompany me on this undoubtedly ridiculous journey, I
am not sure that I would have gone any farther than that
white desert hut of yours. Oh, yes"—as she began to
speak—"yes, you did say *no*, and I did leave alone. But I
knew you would follow, because I know you. As you know
me—as no one living knows either of us." He touched her
cheek quickly, and surprisingly shyly. "So I am even glad
of Kulpai, in a way, because we would never have had this

time together otherwise. Whatever happens there will have been worth it. As all the rest was, all those years."

Lal did not answer him for some while. An upland breeze brought the sudden faint scent of new-harvested *kohi* grass, making the *churfas* growl like the loping stomachs they were. The tall, supple hill trees were beginning to give way to the ubiquitous *harishi* of the south, that are really only great thick shrubs, but yield a fine wood and a bitterly delicious yellow berry. The brook that had accompanied them sedately on the right almost all the way from Doule now broke into the open, raucously greedy for the sea, barely able to wait for the river waiting below. Lal heard the unmistakable *let-me-be, let-me-be* crying of a grasshawk, which subsists on small creatures turned out of their dens by the plow. She said, "We should try not to lose each other this time," and nothing more.

It was getting on toward evening of that same day when they heard the breathing—first, before they heard the voices. The breathing was coming up the path toward them, rasping with a sound that comes only when the lungs are too weary to take in air. The *churfas* shied violently from it and Soukyan was almost thrown. The bow was already in his hand as he regained his balance, and the swordcane was off Lal's shoulder, both of them fearing a wounded animal. When the boy dragged himself out of a thicket, they thought him indeed a beast for a moment, for he was going on all fours, and barely moving at that. As they gaped and the *churfas* pitched and yawped, he managed to stand precariously erect, gripping a tree branch for support, staring back at them out of a dead man's eyes. He wore the dirty, patched half-smock and breeks of a southern farmer. His face was bloody, and his nose was obviously broken, and he could not have been more than seventeen.

The voices were coming up fast, and there were hounds. The boy started to labor on, but he fell down as soon as he let go of the branch. Lal and Soukyan looked at each other, and the boy looked at them: hopeless, fearless. Soukyan spoke to him in two languages, but he made no reply. Lal tried a third, gesturing for him to take shelter behind the *churfas*. He moved so slowly that he had not quite reached them when his pursuers came crashing out of the woods. The hounds were in the lead: three shaggy red Metzari dogs with sea-green eyes. Behind them, half a dozen men, all but two clad much as the boy was. The other pair carried double-edged shortswords, wore studded leather and grand long boots, and carried themselves with the insolent vigor of the backland lords they plainly were, for all their own grime and slovenliness. They had thick black beards and thick red faces.

The lead hound sighted the boy and sprang, its deep baying splitting shrilly in its throat. It would have flanked Soukyan's mount to get at him, but Soukyan did something with one heel that Lal could not see, and the *churfa* erupted instantly into a spitting, bucking mass of indignation. It caught the red dog mightily with one clawed hind foot and hurled it twenty feet, end over end, into a "hello-friend" thornbush, from which the squalling victim seemed in no immediate hurry to emerge. The second dog charged in its turn, abruptly reconsidered and sat down, looking around for instructions. The boy clung to Lal's boot.

The larger of the two armed men, first to take in the situation, strode forward and planted himself, gauntleted hands on his hips, facing Lal and Soukyan. His grin revealed yellow-and-black corncob teeth. Speaking in the second of the languages that Soukyan had tried on the boy, he said, "Give you good day, Grandmother, Grandfather."

"Sunlight on your road," Soukyan said politely. "I'd not stand too near, if I were you." The *churfa*'s head shot out, the man leaped away with a curse and a ragged leather sleeve, and Soukyan slapped his mount's neck and said, "Naughty."

The second man wasted no time on civilities. Ignoring the riders completely, and moving faster than expected, he lunged between the *churfas* and actually had his hands on the boy before a long, thin blade nuzzled coldly at the back of his neck. He whirled and saw the white-haired black woman smiling thoughtfully at him. She said, "Gently, I think? He's quite young."

The man swatted the swordcane's point away, free to deny its reality because of the age of the hands that held it. "Young, is it, hag? Aye, well, he was old enough to say *no* to his appointed master—he was old enough to come between his betters and their lawful desires. Old enough to defy those whom the gods have set over you is old enough to die, by my count. On your way, ancient ones—don't trouble your venerable heads on his base account. My lord takes care of his own."

Soukyan never moved. He said, almost absently, "This is quite interesting. I must tell you that *no* is very nearly my favorite word. I believe it to be my companion's favorite word as well, unless I am wrong?" He slanted a bristly gray eyebrow at Lal.

The old woman pondered, as the armed men and their servants rumbled and shifted and laughed among themselves, as the boy waited empty-faced for life or death, as the Metzari hound still whined in the thornbush. She said slowly, "Of course, *maybe* is good, too—*maybe* is an excellent word. But at the last, when you come down to it, there is really nothing like *no*."

Soukyan nodded, unsmiling. "I am glad you think so." He glanced directly at the boy for the first time since Lal had offered him refuge. "What do they call you?"

It took the boy three tries to shape words with his cracked and bloody mouth. "Riaan. Cajli's Riaan."

"Cajli's Riaan," Soukyan repeated. "Ah, Cajli would be your father, then. I was called Jamurak's Soukyan myself, long ago."

The man, whose sleeve Soukyan's *churfa* was still champing desultorily, now guffawed and swaggered toward them again, keeping a careful eye on the animal. "I am Cajli, Grandfather. This filth is *my* Riaan, and it is my right to dispose of him as I will. Doubtless you come from a civilized land, and will understand such things."

"Yes," Lal said. "Quite well." She spoke so quietly that only Soukyan heard her. Cajli went on. "Not to offend respectable antiques like yourselves, but I'd long planned to throw this worthless tup of mine in with friend Boudrigal's little yellow-haired nanny"—he thumped the other armed man's shoulder—"and see what comes of it. And what happens? What do you think happens? He'll not have it, if you please! *She*'s primed and willing—*he*'s the one just wilts and walks away, can't be bothered, thank you very much. As though he had a bloody say in the matter. A bloody say!"

The boy's voice was clearer when he spoke again. "She was not willing. And if she had been, I'd still not have touched her. The gods made us your servants, not your beasts."

At that the man Cajli lost speech entirely along with anything resembling prudence, and started for Riaan, spittle flying and his shortsword out and up. Lal nudged her *churfa* slightly with one knee, and Cajli ran full-tilt into the animal's flank and bounced. Sitting on the ground, he gobbled commands that set Boudrigal and the four bondmen moving grimly forward. Boudrigal waved Lal and Soukyan aside; when they remained where they were, he bared his teeth briefly and kept coming.

Soukyan turned his head unhurriedly to look straight at Lal. He said, "I had forgotten about this country. I am sorry."

"Mind the one on your left," the old woman said. "You were always slower on that side."

"True," Soukyan said; and if Lal had not been expecting it, she would never have seen the bow come off his shoulder, nor the arrow melt to the string. The first shot, deliberately wide, made Boudrigal laugh outright, and he was still grinning when the second took his right leg from under him. Blood welled, but did not fountain, *ah, he can still miss the artery when he wants to.* The four churls froze where they stood, but Cajli sprang forward to clutch savagely at Lal, grunting, "Come down here to us, Grand-mother. Come down, old bitch, come *down*."

Once she could have kicked him off; now she landed tumbling, and was on her feet before he was, with the swordcane trained on his heart. "Let be," she told him des-perately, "let be," but he roared and charged again, the shortsword that would have shattered her own blade swinging like a brush-cutter. Lal backed and backed, con-stantly warning, "Let be, do not trifle with old people. Old people are dangerous; old people don't *care*." Cajli paid no heed. She glimpsed Riaan's broken face out of the corner of one eye, felt her *churfa*'s foul breath on her neck, and struck. *The body remembers—slide, stamp, lunge, and away to the next before he knows he'd dead. . . .* But she could not pull the swordcane out of his chest, and Cajli took it from her as he fell. Two of the bondmen were on her then, equally weaponless, clumsily battering her with their raw weight and momentum. She ducked, sidestepped, let herself go down and rolled, fumbling for the tiny dagger tucked ever inside her right boot. Boudrigal was bawling louder than the *churfas* in fury and pain; from shouts behind her she could tell that Soukyan was keeping the other two men at bay with his drawn bow and waiting, deadly patient as ever, for a clear shot at her attackers. *Don't kill them, Soukyan, not these, don't kill them.*

A stone flashed past her ear and cracked against the grubby temple of the man ineptly attempting to strangle her. He fell back, half-stunned, and she heard Riann's shrill, hoarse cry, distorted by his broken nose, "Groy, stop it! Chash, Stenyi, what are you doing? Leave the old ones alone—they've never harmed you, I've never harmed you, and those two have hurt you all your lives! Why are you fighting for them?"

The bondman still blundering against Lal faltered in obvious bewilderment. He rubbed a hand over his face, blinked at her, at the boy and Boudrigal, and Cajli's motion-less body, and half turned to help his groggy companion.

The two besieging Soukyan also looked doubtful and confused, and for a single moment Lal thought all might yet be well. But Boudrigal, scrabbling to one knee, hysterical with rage and pain, shrieked, "Kill him, you miserable vermin! Kill them all, or I'll burn your homes—I swear I will! Kill them now!"

"There are four of you, and he is alone!" Riaan shouted wildly. "Change your lives! Must you always be slaves?"

The four churls' hesitation was brief: they consulted without words, weighing their entire histories and their bitter and precise understanding of the world against the ravings of a mad boy and the lives of two old strangers. Then they came resignedly on, by two and two, the red hounds yapping behind them, as though they had been set to clear land or plow it. Lal's pair were slogging at her again, crowding her against her *churfa*, while Soukyan's assailants kept shuffling in half-circles, feinting crudely to get in under the great bow. It was plain to them that the old brown man was reluctant to shoot, and they were accustomed to taking every small advantage they could get, without pondering.

Boudrigal had collapsed, increasingly delirious, but still yelling frenzied orders and threats. Riaan was firing stones from a herder's sling so fast that two were often in the air at once—which was a good thing, since he was likely to hit one of his defenders at least half the time. Soukyan wheeled threateningly on him in a moment of exasperation, and was promptly rushed on his vulnerable left side. His *churfa* squalled and reared, and the bow flew from Soukyan's hand as he hit the ground. Awkward as they were, the bondmen were on him before he could rise.

Standing considerably aside from herself, Lal watched in distant fascination as a lean old woman she almost recognized kicked one of her attackers in the groin, simultaneously catching the other in the throat with a bony elbow, bent to her boot in the same sleek motion and came up throwing. The daggerlet flickered in the dusk like a bright insect, and one of the ungainly men astride Soukyan cried out before he fell, the jeweled hilt humming in his right eye. His companion stared dumbly at him, then shrieked much louder and longer and fled away weeping into the woods. The old woman stooped swiftly to retrieve her dagger, wiped it on her leg, and walked over to free the swordcane from Cajli's chest. She was humming absently to herself.

Boudrigal had fainted, and the boy Riaan looked ready to do the same. The two remaining bondmen were climbing to their feet, looking very tired. Glancing constantly sideways at Lal and Soukyan, they trudged to their fallen masters: one of them timorously closed Cajli's eyes, while the second knelt by Boudrigal, trying vainly to tug the arrow out of his thigh and staunch the bleeding. Soukyan put him aside gently enough, snapped off the feathered end of the arrow and forced it on through the leg. Boudrigal woke, drew breath to scream, tried to spit, could do neither, and lost consciousness again.

Lal shook her head once, violently, as though waking herself from a clinging dream, and came to squat on her heels beside Soukyan. She cleaned Boudrigal's wound as well as she could, ordering a dazed, silent Riaan to tear strips from his master's shirt for a bandage. "We will bury your dead, if you like," she said bluntly to the bondmen as she worked. "We are old, but we still clean up after ourselves."

But the men shook their heads, answering that there were rites due Cajli that none but his high family could perform; that they themselves might only report his death and chance punishment for doing even that. The dead churl could not be buried at all, having failed his lord, but must be left for the birds and insects to devour. Only Boudrigal, injured, were the two survivors permitted to carry home; and he would need to be extensively purified of their touch when he recovered. They bore him up between them now and trotted away, showing neither sorrow nor fear, anger nor regret on their dirty, worn faces. They never looked back at Riaan.

Slow, buzzing shadows had already settled over the two

bodies. Soukyan and Lal looked at each other, and Riaan saw that the old man was trembling, and that the black woman had her arms wrapped tightly around herself, as though trying to contain something on the verge of breaking free. Soukyan said quietly, "We always seem to be digging graves by moonlight, don't we?"

"We have to bury the one I killed," she answered. "I don't care about *him*, but that one anyway. We have to."

"They'll just come back and dig him up," Riaan blurted. "They will, I've seen them do it." Soukyan nodded silently. Lal said, "Let them."

It was full night by the time the three of them had gouged a shallow trench out of the ground and heaped it high with stones. Lal whispered something in her own language, and Soukyan said formally, "We had no wish to kill you. We forgive you for making us killers." He stepped aside and looked at Riaan.

For a moment the boy stared blankly; then he knelt by the cairn, threw back his head and spoke to it. "Stenyi, you were a fool, and you died for nothing, nothing, as you always have and always will. I loved you. Good-bye." He stood up slowly, his eyes dry and fiercely miserable under the moon.

"Your nose," Soukyan said. He gripped the back of Riaan's neck firmly with one hand, the broken nose with the other. Riaan yelped once, briefly. Soukyan said, "There, that is the best I can do. It will heal." He turned to Lal. "Are you all right?"

"I hurt all bloody over," she said petulantly. She was rubbing her left arm hard, and wincing slightly with each breath. "Gods, did I always bruise this easily? I had no idea I'd softened up so. Two minutes' pushing and shoving with a couple of unarmed yokels, and I'm absolutely pulp. Disgusting."

Soukyan smiled as well as he could through split, puffed lips. He had lost a side tooth, one eye was all but closed, and he grunted himself as he bent to pick up his bow. "My fault. We could have avoided this."

"No," Lal said. They both turned toward Riaan, who flushed under their regard, looking even younger than he was. "I am sorry you suffered hurt in saving my life," he said with surprising dignity, "but you need not concern yourselves with me any further. I will take care of myself now. Good-bye. I am grateful."

They watched him start on the way they had come, even attempting to hum jauntily as he walked, as Lal had done. He managed perhaps ten yards and crumpled down in slow sections. Soukyan limped over to raise him easily in his arms and regard Lal wryly. "I'm afraid this one is ours, after all."

"Put him up with me, in front," she said. "I can hold him on."

"*Churfas* will not carry double. They will not, Lal."

"Butterfly will."

Soukyan almost dropped the boy. *"Butterfly?"*

"I named her," Lal said calmly. "Or him, whichever. And if she won't carry us both, I'll walk. I most certainly need the exercise."

The *churfa* did, after much vivid and well-phrased outrage, consent to carry two, and they went on until moonset, for fear of pursuit. Riaan slept through everything, whimpering now and then, but never waking, not even when he was lifted down, set carefully on dry grass in a weed-choked clearing and covered with Soukyan's ragged spare cloak. Lal and Soukyan lay nearby, talking drowsily.

"My fault, my fault, all of it. If I had even half my old sense left, I would have remembered what the folk of this bloody country are like. Boudrigal—if only I had not shot him, it could have been different. . . ."

"You think so?" The black woman's voice was hard and cool. "If he had killed you, as Cajli meant to kill me—yes, I suppose that would have been different. I must say, I like this better."

"Unarmed yokels," Soukyan said bitterly. "That's all they were, even those two. Pitiful. Pitiful. To think of the places we have been, we two, to think of the things that have happened to us, the things we have seen and done, and had to do, the strange friends we knew, and the enemies—the terrible, honorable enemies—and to end so, butchers of peasants on a country road. I am sick ashamed, Lal. I wish I had never lived to see this dawn."

"I'm sure Boudrigal feels the same way," she answered. "I have less pride than you. To me death is death; it is all equal, and honor doesn't come into it. I wish I had not had to kill those men, yes, but it's done. On to Kulpai."

"Kulpai," Soukyan said. "Kulpai. What possessed me? why was it so important that I must drag you along with me on such an idiot journey? Forgive me, Lal. Go home—just leave me with this other idiot and go back to that wise, hard-bought life I could not leave the way I found it. I will not trouble you again."

Lal was silent for such a while that Soukyan thought she had fallen asleep. He had almost drifted off himself, when he heard her voice: quiet and distant, but very clear. "I had my reasons for following you. Worrying about a mad old man was only one of them." Then she did sleep, and so did he, and the sun was well past midday when they woke again.

Riaan had built a small fire, and was already cooking three small fish over it on peeled *harshi*-bush skewers. He had filled the waterskins from wherever he had found the fish, coaxed the *churfas* to a patch of the blue brambles they preferred, and was now sitting close by the fire, arms around his knees. His nose was still badly swollen, and a good half of his face was blotched purple with bruises. Nevertheless, he was a pleasant-looking boy, gray-eyed and black-haired, and he seemed content to be where he was, staring into the fire, waiting for them to wake. Lal had seen Choushi-wai just so, many a morning.

"I have never been this far from home," he said quietly to them. "I have never seen people like you. Except for pilgrims and peddlers, I have never seen anyone I have not known all my life. And you can't ever have met anyone as ignorant as I am." His uncertain half-smile made him appear even younger than seventeen.

"I killed two just yesterday," Lal said. The boy swallowed hard. Soukyan said, "We are bound for Kulpai. You may travel with us that far, or part company with us at Jahmanyar, as you decide. I think your masters will not follow."

"No," Riaan whispered, "no, they will not. They are ignorant too—they would think words like *Kulpai* and *Jahmanyar* were curses, or things to eat. I know they mean towns, cities, but I do not know what a town *is*, nor even another village. The moment I saw you, the two of you looking at me, I understood that I do not know anything, *anything*, not even what I do not know. I will be no use to you on your road, no company even, but only a stupid burden. Forget about me. Thank you, and forget me."

Soukyan sat down by the fire without answering. He pulled one of the fish from its skewer and devoured it in three bites. "Good," he said. "Very nice." Lal patted Riaan's shoulder lightly and took her own fish. She said only, "You have courage, and you can cook. Eat your breakfast, and then I will introduce you properly to Butterfly."

Even down in open country, most nights had turned frosty, and there was not always dry wood enough to keep a fire alive until morning. The old people—by now thoroughly inured to the stench—slept closer and closer to the *churfas* for warmth. The boy made no complaint; but after watching him spend all one night walking up and down, beating his arms across his body, Soukyan disappeared early that day and caught up with them only after sunset, the thick-haired hide of a lowland *guangsu*, wild cousin to a *rishu*, bundled across his shoulders. "I gave the meat to the villagers who helped me with the curing," he told them, grunting away Riaan's gratitude. "They have a trick of tanning a skin quite quickly in this country—matter of hours, once the scraping's done. Rough, sloppy way to do the job, but it will serve." And Riaan slept warmer than they that night, as Lal pointed out several times.

It was indeed all farmland, once they were out of the hills. The pastures came first, the richest fields teeming with fat *rishus* and cloud-fluffy *jejebhais*; the poorest able to support only a few scrawny bipedal *drushindis*, worthless for anything but their droppings, which made both fuel and good fertilizer. Soukyan and Lal had met few enough people since Doule; now they could ride for a day or more without seeing another human. The sky was high and pale and constantly hazy, making distances almost impossible to estimate. It was all as fascinating to the boy as anything else would have been, but Lal found it dull, even depressing, and Soukyan pushed their mounts along briskly, hardly looking to left or right. "We can still reach Kulpai well before the snows, if we travel from first light to last. And if we don't have to stop and bury anyone else."

The orchards were better. The ground turned rolling again—though never swelling back into real hills—and the white sky broke up into thousands of tiny polished clouds. The leaves of the *ki*-trees were already as deep-golden as their wrinkly, fist-sized fruit, which were everywhere being gathered by swarms of yelping children with latticed nets on the ends of poles longer than they were tall. There were late-ripening *maradis* on the vine, as well, and there were even winter-apples, though Soukyan said they were used strictly as fodder this far south. Lal snatched a few as she rode under the sagging boughs, and taught Riaan how to eat them. He spat out the first, sampled another warily, and then ate all of hers.

He was easier with her than with Soukyan, despite the *guangsu* hide. Mostly silent during the day, at night when they had bedded down in some thicket or coldly fragrant grove, he plagued her with ceaseless questions about the world beyond, and beyond that, and their lives in it. That much Lal had expected; what surprised her was how many of the questions had to do with her family, and Soukyan's as well. When she said, "Riaan, I don't really know," or

"Riaan, we don't talk about certain things very much, he and I," he seemed genuinely shocked, and she began slowly to understand.

"*Churfas*," she said to Soukyan as they rode together. "They breed them like that, like animals." She spoke in an old language they shared, while the boy dozed against her back. "He knows who his mother is, but that is all. He thinks he has half-brothers, half-sisters, but he can't be sure. It's a miracle to him that you and I actually know our families—it's all he can do to imagine such a thing." Her voice was completely without expression, as it became when she was very angry in a particular way.

"He might be better off," the old man answered. "And yes, I do mean it, and I do know what I am saying. Perhaps they are wiser than we thought in that miserable hill country."

"I know about your sister," Lal said. "You know about—about what happened to me when I was stolen. This is different."

"Is it, then? Is what happened to my sister—being sold by our parents to the vicious fool who killed her—is that any different from what has been done to Riaan all his life? At least he has never learned to love anyone who was to be snatched away from him forever—forever—between one minute and the next. Teach him to consider his blessings and be grateful." Soukyan spoke no further for the rest of that day.

Two nights later, they made camp at the edge of one more orchard, dining on *ki*-fruit, the last of their dried fish, and water from a nearby stream. Soukyan told them that they were a day's journey from the Churush road, and three from Jahmanyar. "Ten days at most, and we'll be smelling Kulpai. Tell me you don't remember the scent of Kulpai, Lal."

"Stagnant water," she said. "Spoiled vegetables. I never knew a coast town that smelled less like the sea." Soukyan slept quickly, but Riaan stayed wide-awake, which meant that Lal remained more or less awake herself. Riaan asked her for a story: never having heard more than the few sad fragments his mother could recall, he was as guilelessly greedy for tales as a child much younger. Lal told him Choushi-wai's favorite, which had to do with a magic tree, a queen's twin daughters, and a young monk on a dreadful quest, aided by the ghost of a poet. When she was done, Riaan sighed wistfully and said, "I wish that were true. I wish all stories were true."

Lal smiled in the darkness, though he could not see her. "All stories are lies, just because they *are* stories. But they are true even so, every one of them, and sometimes the biggest lies turn out the truest of all. And don't ask me why that is, Riaan, because I could never tell you. But it is so with stories."

The boy was silent long enough that Lal almost dozed off; but he roused her abruptly by saying, "So then ghosts are true. I'm glad. The ghost in the story, who was a friend—it would be good to meet a ghost like that. It could tell me about my father."

"Depends on the ghost," she mumbled. "They aren't all like that one, take my word." Then his last words penetrated, and she shook herself awake to demand, "Why should you care? Why should it matter which of those"— she struggled fruitlessly for a word in his language—"those bad people bred your mother?"

"Oh," he answered with surprising eagerness, "because I know that it was not Cajli. He wanted to, but he couldn't, I know that much anyway. And if not Cajli, then none of the other great lords . . ." His voice trailed away for a little, but then he went on. "My mother will never say, but I think my father is dead. And I think he was someone like us, someone like me. I think he—he *cared* for my mother. Maybe he could not protect her, maybe he could not be with me, but he did care about us. Sometimes I make it up in my head that he died trying to save us. I have to know, Lal, do you see? Do you see?"

"Yes," she said. "Yes, of course you do." She felt ponderous with memories, sticky and sluggish with time, and knew that there was no hope of sleeping now. She began to say, "Riaan, you might well be sadder for the learning, you have to know that, too," but he was sitting up, staring away, groping for her hand like any frightened child. "The lights," he said. "Lal, the lights, what are they doing? Over there, *look.*"

There were a dozen or more of them, tiny and fragile, bobbing slowly between the trees, circling like dancers. Now and then one dropped swiftly, almost to the ground, then shivered straight up again to the height of a human heart. Riaan's hand was cold in hers, but Lal said, "Night gleaners, nothing more. They come to pick up the windfalls, anything the pickers pass up or reject. Anything."

"We do that," Riaan said softly, "my mother and I. Not at night, not in orchards—in the cornfields, the berry fields. We do just the same." He stared at the little flames for a long while before he lay down again; and Lal stared up at the moon and told herself very old tales until morning.

The Churush road was a proper highway—at least, by comparison with the brambly wagon-roads and *rishu*-paths they had been traveling—and Riaan constantly slipped delightedly down from his usual perch behind Lal to investigate everything from unfamiliar flowers and animal tracks to the small fish of the murky ditches. Periodically he would sprint to catch up with the jogging *churfas*: his natural strength and resiliency had returned, and he often ran circles around them for the pure pleasure of it. Lal took the opportunity to relate their night conversation to Soukyan. The old brown man barely let her finish before snapping, "No! No, absolutely not!"

"No what?" she asked, genuinely startled. "What did I suggest that I don't know about?" But Riaan bounded back up behind her then, and they were unable to talk in privacy until evening, when they had made camp in a wild bare meadow and the boy had gone off gathering firewood. Soukyan, sitting on a stump to skin a plump, long-eared *sayao* was pointedly silent, leaving it to her to bring up the subject that was not yet a subject. She said at last, "He just wants to know who his father was. Even the gods couldn't find anything wrong in that."

Soukyan did not look up. "And his father is dead. Yes?"

"He thinks so. He's probably right."

"Probably." Soukyan spun around suddenly—*Damn the man, he's always moving faster than you think, even sitting down*—and leveled a forefinger at her exactly as though he were fitting it to a bowstring. "And *you* are nursing the truly insane notion of calling that dead peasant—no, no, worse off than a peasant, he was a plow, a shovel, a slop bucket—calling that wretched *thing* back from a rest more dearly earned than you or I could imagine, all because his wretched son has had a moment's curiosity about him! Don't even bother denying it—it's not worth the effort, not between us. Just no, put it out of your mind right now. No, Lal."

He had hardly raised his voice, but even through the cold, quick dusk she could see his eyes. She walked over and sat down beside him, reaching to take the carcass and the skinning knife. "Give me that. He's the one chopping wood, not you."

Soukyan indignantly snatched the mess away from her. "I was cleaning *sayaos* when you couldn't tell a ballad from a belch." But he smiled then, and she realized one more time how long and bitter a journey his face had made from its born gentleness. He said reflectively, "Of all the spells. The one bit of magic you and I ever managed to learn, for all the time we've spent around great wizards. If you remember, we also learned why even great wizards fear to summon the dead."

"Of course, I know that," she retorted. "Of course, I know it's no parlor trick. But they do it, all the same." They could hear Riaan singing in the distance: a cheerful, wordless attempt at one of Lal's *churfa*-calming airs. She said, "In a just cause, and with respect, where is the harm?"

"Harm? The harm is to the tissue of things, Lal—the things that exist beyond our desires. If we ever did learn anything from a magician, we learned that it is not a wall that keeps this world apart from ... from those others that we know some little of—not a wall, but a dam. Open the way, with the very best of intentions, for one perfectly harmless spirit, and neither of us can possibly guess what might come spilling through. But we both know very well what could." He flourished the gutted *sayao* at her dramatically. "They are not supposed to be here, never, the universe hates it. Lal, let it alone."

Riaan's singing was drawing nearer; they could just make out his log-laden silhouette through the darkness. She said, "You're right, I know it, I am not arguing. You're right."

Soukyan regarded her with distinctly heightened suspicion. "The last time you listened to me this meekly, we were in the worst trouble of our lives not ten minutes later." But the boy was there, proudly flinging down more than enough wood for the night and setting immediately to fire building. There was no chance to talk further until he had had his story and fallen asleep; and by that time Soukyan had drifted away, as he did every night, to prowl the meadow and the woods nearby until he knew their surroundings better than anything that lived there. Lal buried the remains of the meal and sat cosseting the fire, performing her own nighttime ritual of cleaning her teeth with a broken twig. Now and then, in a whisper, she practiced a word or two words in a language that sounded like the cracking and grinding of bones between great jaws. She tried the phrases over and over, changing the order and the accent, plainly never satisfied. The firelight turned her eyes and cheekbones red-gold as its own coals.

Beside her, Soukyan murmured gravely, "It's certainly a good thing you never could pronounce *g'reuilljk* correctly. Where might we not be otherwise?"

A lifetime of control—no more natural to her than hardness to Soukyan's mouth—kept Lal from even turning her head. She tossed her twig into the fire, spat after it, and said, "I speak the spell as well as you. It's the ingredients I can't remember."

"The ingredients are quite simple," Soukyan replied,

"and more available than I care to think about just now. Fortunately, the moon is not in the right quarter, nor is the Gardener"—he pointed up at the overcast sky—"in the ascendant. Therefore, you may at once abandon whatever is brewing under that elegant cap of white hair—which is very becoming, have I mentioned that? Utterly deceptive, but becoming." When Lal did not answer, he rested a hand gently on her shoulder. "This matters more than I thought," he said. "Why?"

"Because I am Riaan," the old woman said. Her face was stiff and taut, as though with great cold, and the golden eyes were very far away, gone further than Soukyan had ever seen them. "Because I know what has been done to him better than he does, and because I know what such a life can make of a child. As that prison guard and his boy still trouble you, so it would haunt me for all the time I have left not to do the little I can for him. Because I *know,* Soukyan."

They sat together in silence, staring into the darkness made all the more smothering by the firelight. Above them the wind miaowed thinly in the treetops, and even the sputter of the flames sounded like branches cracking under the weight of snow. A *korevu* cried plaintively somewhere too near, and Soukyan muttered, "Bloody things should be hibernating by now." He drew his bow closer and prodded the fire to make it flare.

"After Kulpai," Lal said.

"I don't know." Soukyan did not look at her. "You have a place to return to, a place where you are pleased to belong. My atonement, my apology to the man I hurt so—that has been all my destination for so long that I forgot it was not home. A sign of age, surely." He spread his hands to the fire, gazing down at their scarred, ridgy backs. "After Kulpai I don't know where I will go, Lal, or why. There will be something."

The *korevu's* moan came again and again, seemingly from every direction, as it always does. Soukyan spoke no further, but fitted an arrow, drew without appearing to aim, and loosed off into the night. There was no answering hiss of pain or alarm, but the deadly lament was not repeated that night, though they sat very still until dawn.

Unlike Doule, Jahmanyar is a real city, and a handsome one, near enough to the coast to have first choice of everything landed from the southern islands and the Strange Lands beyond. It has everything a true port could want, except the sea, and it makes up for that with a romping overabundance of all else. Riaan, seeing absolutely everything for the first time—from street dancers to public poets yowling their verses, from *jai*-fish barrowmen to slinking poison-mongers, to grand courtesans being borne to their assignations by liveried bearers—had to be physically threatened to keep him from sliding happily off the rear of Lal's *churfa* and vanishing forever through a hundred gilt-curtained doorways, or into the wondrously anonymous mystery of a hundred alleys. Only the warning that they would pass straight through Jahmanyar instead of staying even the one night had the slightest sobering effect.

They spent that night at an inn called the Golden Sea-drake. It was located on a side street; but from the fighting, screaming, and singing that went on below their window at all hours, they might as well have made camp in the market square. Lal immediately ordered their meal to be brought up to them, but Riaan begged so earnestly to have it served in a real taproom that she and Soukyan yielded, against misgivings, and went downstairs. On the way, Soukyan said to her out of the side of his mouth, "This is what it is to be grandparents. I hate it already."

"I think we must have had a nice daughter, though," Lal said softly. "I do think so."

The taproom was a proper chaos, which clearly suited Riaan perfectly. Coast city or not, the landlord's menu was limited to overdone chops and underdone green-eel pies, accompanied by wine that appeared to have begun life as a stockpond. Soukyan sized up the drunken men lurching into their table, stopped Lal from drawing on one who was about to urinate on her leg, and told Riaan to eat up quickly so that they could be gone within half an hour. When the boy asked why, Soukyan answered, "Because there are a dozen bargemen in tonight, and at least that many sailors off the coast freighters. Half an hour, likely less."

"There's a magician," Riaan said in wonder. And so there was: a short, irritated-looking man dressed in the black and gray of the lower ranks of his trade, standing on the bar and snapping his fingers to make fire leap from the tips. Riaan gasped, and Lal grumbled. "Always, the third-raters always start like that, that's how you tell." But his audience paid no mind, not until the magician stamped in a certain way, and something with hot yellow eyes, long yellow teeth, and bloodred wings flashed high across the taproom, shrieking like steel on stone. It circled the room, stooping viciously at terrified tosspots, then vanished up the chimney with a thunderous fart. Riaan cheered rapturously, and the magician bowed directly to him, causing Soukyan to snort like a peeved *churfa*, and Lal to whisper, "Don't spoil it for him. What does it matter?"

"Yes, Grandmother," Soukyan muttered back. The magician played directly to Riaan after that, the bargemen and sailors being already too reeling drunk to take any heed of anything but their old hatred of one another. The boy sat enchanted, forgetting to eat, while ale mugs, first juggled, then tossed in the air, floated down as flower petals; while small birds bloomed between the magician's empty hands; and beer better than any the Golden Seadrake had ever pumped fountained from the magician's ears, nose, the top of his head, even his coat pockets. That did get even the sailors' attention, briefly; even Soukyan laughed, and even Lal murmured, "Very well, then, *second*-rate . . ."

To finish, the magician called for silence, and did not get it, except from Riaan and his companions; the clientele was rapidly approaching a joyous boiling point. Someone bellowed and threw a chair at someone else. It missed, smashing against the bar. The magician's cross little face darkened, the gray cloak was flung back, and he nodded a brisk, private nod. He took a handful of red powder from one secret pocket, a bunch of scraggly herbs from another, hurled both down on the bar before him, spat on them three times, and spoke words that neither Lal nor Soukyan could make out above the turmoil, as the bone-white, maggot-white, hideously white figure began to take form in the middle of the smoky air. It grew just as a pearl grows, or a child, accumulating itself around a single fiery spark where its heart should have been. But it was dead; it had been dead for a very long time, and it had not died peacefully, or found any grace beyond the grave. Its robes were stiff and brown with blood, and its transparent, empty-eyed face was wrenched out of all human shape with furious envy of the living. It crouched in the air, hissed silently, lunging out in vain at the meanly unremarkable man who had summoned it. He balked it with a single word, smiling.

What that word was, there was still no way of hearing, since none but Lal, Soukyan, and Riaan were paying the least heed to the thing raging overhead. One sailor did throw a bottle at it, but that was most likely meant for a drunken bargeman who was holding two sailors off the floor with a hand around each throat while he laboriously explained some point of etiquette to them. The bottle passed through the apparition and caromed off the bald skull of the landlord, who, with the weary ease of long experience, snatched up a worn cudgel from behind the bar and began flailing away at any head within range. This included the bargeman with the dangling sailors: he promptly threw them at the landlord and followed them over the bar. Half a dozen sailors were right behind him.

"Out," Soukyan said, and he and Lal, warding away all combatants with bow and sheathed swordcane, whisked Riaan from the table a moment before it was kicked over by bargemen charging to their fellow's rescue. The boy made no protest, but he twisted around in the doorway to stare back at the magician. The little man was standing against a side wall, ignored as ever in peace or war, while his equally slighted specter stalked and gibbered impotently above the fray. He mopped his forehead and absently flicked a finger at the creature to banish it. Catching sight of the three of them then, he made a deep formal bow to Riaan, spun around on his toes in the usual manner of magicians, and disappeared into the same smoking hole in the air as the apparition. They left a smell of rotting flowers behind them.

"Out, out, out, *out*," Soukyan said. Lal, Riaan, and he spent the rest of that evening in their room, listening to the debate belowstairs going on well into the night. Riaan said almost nothing, asking only once, "That was a ghost, wasn't it? That was a real ghost."

"I told you they weren't all like the one in the story," Lal said. Riaan nodded. Soukyan, sleeping as warily indoors as out, woke fully several times, each time to see the boy lying still on his cot by the window, with the moonlight silvering his wide eyes.

He continued unusually quiet during the next few days on the Churush road. The country between Jahmanyar and Kulpai is boggy but lovely in its own dank way, rich with water birds' cries and the scent of winter-roses, the *luraveli*, whose instant of loveliest bloom is set off by the coming of the first cold. Sometimes a traveler's presence will startle a marsh-goat and its twiggy-legged kid from their bed in the rushes and send them off in great splashing leaps down water-lily alleys to find another. Ordinarily, Riaan would have been chattering like a bird himself, calling his companions' attention to even the most common flower or footprint; now it was his silence they found distracting. It was not a brooding, resentful silence, only thoughtful, and there was no penetrating it. Lal said privately to Soukyan, "Real grandparents would know what to say to him," to which the old man replied, "Real grandparents wouldn't have started him thinking about ghosts and calling his father back. This is your doing, never forget it. Kulpai will be a holiday, a carnival, compared to this."

Lal watched the boy carefully, never letting him quite out of her sight, even when he thought he was. Soukyan did the same. The levee roads through the marshland most often necessitated riding single-file; but three days from Kulpai she guided Butterfly alongside Soukyan's *churfa* to ask, "And when we get there—what then?" Riaan, mounted behind her, had been so especially lost that day in—fancy? memory? daydream?—that he might not have been there. Butterfly, who always complained loudly when he hauled himself up on her back, appeared not to feel his weight at all.

Soukyan hunched his shoulders. "I don't know. I suppose I will start at the cells, and if he is not there, then I will ask for his family, anyone who might have known him. After that . . ."

When he did not finish, she prodded him further. "After that? Find him or not, when is it over for you? *I* have no desire to winter in Kulpai."

"I never asked you to come with me," he said harshly. "I never asked that." He said nothing further for a little; then, quietly, "A day, Lal. One single day, no more. If there is anyone in Kulpai for me to speak to, to say what I must say, I will know by then. If not—so be it, then not. This or that, one day."

Lal nodded. She inclined her head slightly backward, indicating Riaan, who seemed to have heard none of their conversation. Soukyan gave a helpless shake of his own head, and looked away.

That night neither of them slept well. Soukyan found no comfortable way to arrange his big body on the damp ground; he heaved and struggled after slumber, never achieving more than a twitchy, short-lived doze. Lal, for her part, was visited by such dreams as had not found her in many years' hungry searching. *I thought surely you had forgotten where I lived,* but they were all over her like murderous children, taking her so by surprise that none of the old shifts and sidesteps she knew to slip them, even in her sleep, were of any avail. She woke violently, running from a man long dead, who laughed sweetly as he followed.

Soukyan roused instantly at her small cry, and came, out of old understanding, to hold her. He said only, "Who was it?"

"Shavak," she whispered. "Shavak. I didn't even kill him, and he is always the worst one. What are those lights?"

"What lights?" He turned his head and saw them as she had, bobbing and dancing far away, moving slowly closer; and as she had answered Riaan, he said, "Night gleaners again, poor souls. Nothing more."

She sat up straight, pushing him away. "What gleaners? In this country? *Where is the boy?*"

They had the answer a moment later: Riaan's voice, sounding more distant than it really was because of its anxious softness. Lal could not make out the words he was chanting, but Soukyan was on his feet with the first one. "Gods, he's doing it, he's *summoning!*" The lights were moving faster now.

Soukyan was already gone, taking long, lunging bounds, even in the darkness. Lal followed, calling, "He doesn't know the spell, he can't know it. I never spoke the words when he was by." She was running as frantically as in her dream, as though she had never wakened.

Soukyan answered in hoarse gasps, not turning his head. "The magician did. . . . *We* didn't hear . . . all the noise . . . but the boy heard—heard and remembered. . . ."

"But not the same spell! The moon is wrong—and the Gardener—"

"I made all that up . . . so you'd behave. . . . Many spells to call a ghost. . . ." He did look back then, his face gaunt and drawn and truly old now. "*Hurry*, Lal!"

Riaan's voice was closer, more confident, repeating the same few words over and over. Lal could distinguish his form in the darkness now, because the lights were joining, flowing eagerly into one another to become one scarred, splotchy brilliance, as though the moon were shining up through the silt and roots and decay of the marsh. A figure was taking form, growing out of the light, around the light, and the boy's voice leaped up in exultation, itself turning into light. Lal tripped over something she never saw, and fell flat, but Soukyan kept going, shouting back to her, "*Move*, Lal, *move!*" She heard Riaan's victory chant suddenly splinter into a cry of horror, and she was back on her feet and moving.

There was only one light now. The shape was all but complete; only the face was yet indistinct, but Riaan already knew who it was. So did Lal, by its heavy-shouldered swagger and the fine boots. It walked toward Riaan, reaching out for him with its powerful arms, smiling with its shining face.

"*Cajli*," Lal whispered at the same time that Riaan wailed the name. The light had faded notably, the creature being fully materialized now, but the face was beyond mistaking. No longer dull red, but a pulpy mushroom-white, its grin stretched too wide in the greasy black beard as it spoke. "Cajli's Riaan," it said, the jovial human menace in its tone far more dreadful than any sepulchral hollowness could have been. "Well met, well met, Cajli's Riaan."

Riaan made a tiny sound. Soukyan, still a good fifty yards away, shouted, "Cajli, *skay'vas*, Cajli!" He gestured with both hands as he ran, shouting that word and another. The ghost laughed at him. Even at a distance, the sound froze Lal as still as the boy: for a moment she could feel neither her skin, nor her thoughts, nor the feet on which she was trying to run. But she was not Riaan, and she had met ghosts before, and she was free of the chuckling cold and laboring doggedly on.

"Cajli's Riaan," the ghost said. "In your world or mine you belong to me, and nothing will ever change that. Not while you live, not after you die. Here to me, Cajli's Riaan."

The boy could not move, not even when Soukyan reached him and put his own arm tightly around his shoulders. "*Skay'vas*, Cajli! Hear me, dead man—*skay'vas, tuja!*" He brandished the great old bow like a wizard's wand.

The ghost of Cajli halted, focusing its barren stare on Soukyan. It said, "Grandfather, do not come between us, for peril of your soul. All that was mine before is mine now—stop your useless, dribbling mouth and totter no nearer." Soukyan could see the dainty wound in its chest where Lal's swordcane had gone home.

Then she was there: a very old woman who had run too long on old legs, stumbling between Riaan and the white figure to gasp defiantly, "Back from him! Back! I have no word of power to banish you to where you belong, but I sent you there once and I swear I will again!" The swordcane was out and glinting, and if the legs were shaky, the black hand was not. "Ghost or demon or walking heap of putrid meat, back from him or you die a second time!" Soukyan moved up beside her, arrow at the string.

The ghost's abrupt bay of laughter was chilling cousin to the sad crying of the *korevu*, and surrounded them in the same way. "Nay, stand clear of me, Grandmother. What you could do to me, you have done. Touch me now with that sacking-needle of yours and shrivel where you stand— come within my reach and learn how cold it is where I live now." It reached as though to ruffle Riaan's hair, but Soukyan pushed the unmoving boy away. The dreadful mirth redoubled. "Ah, have no fear, Grandfather—why would I harm my faithful servant? Did he not most slyly summon me home to this upper world, missing his lord as he should, pining for his dear servitude? Aye, freedom's wasted on his breed, and *he* knows it if you don't." It put out its thick, pale hands to Riaan once again. "To me, boy," it said. "Quickly, before I grow impatient. You know how I am."

Soukyan loosed his arrow. It passed through Cajli's body as the bottle had through the magician's taproom specter; but this time the arrow blazed up in a sickly yellow-green fire, which sprang back along its path straight to Soukyan's hands. He opened his mouth and fell, curling on his side almost at Riaan's feet.

Lal had started her strike as soon as the arrow took fire, and had no chance to turn the swordcane's point aside. She felt its contact with the ghost as an instant of agony so cold that her flesh barely had time to recognize it as pain before she was down, face hard against mucky grass, body flopping like a landed fish. Unable to rise, or even to raise her head, she yet managed to use the momentum of the fall to twist onto her back, where she lay gaping helplessly at smeared, distorted stars and a moon like a rotten fruit. The mushroom-face was grinning down at her, saying, "I did warn you, Grandmother. Lie there, so, lie there and ponder the evil day that you crossed my path. I have business with my servant."

Out of the side of her eye, she could see that Riaan had finally shaken free of his paralysis and was edging away, sliding one foot after the other only by force of will. The ghost followed, still unhurried; but the grimly benign chuckle had turned threatening. "Enough of this. We have far and further to go, and I'll not be kept waiting by such as you. You were born to serve me for eternity, Cajli's Riaan, and you will serve me better in that other world than ever you did in this, or have eternity to regret it. Take my hand." Riaan scrambled aside once more, and the ghost's voice lowered to a snarling whisper. *"Take my hand, boy!"*

In the water moonlight Riaan's face looked as white as that other face, and seemed on the edge of flying completely apart; it had gone almost as far beyond his controlling as Lal's body had beyond her own. For all that, when his answer came, it held a trembling pride unassailably high. "I was not calling you. I would die and be a hundred times more rotten than you before I would ever say your name again. I was calling for my father. I call him now."

Lal heard him shout the fierce, bone-grinding word at the same time that she began dazedly to regain herself. She rolled over, clawed air to rise to her knees, and saw Riaan fronting the ghost of Cajli, fearless as only a person dancing on the furthest edge of terror can be fearless. Soukyan was standing—Lal breathed a formal phrase of gratitude in her oldest language—but when Cajli lunged at the boy again, Soukyan stumbled forward, and immediately fell over with the effort. Riaan dodged away, crying the spell louder a second time, as Lal lurched to aid Soukyan.

Nothing happened. The stars and moon went on slinking through a sky as dank as the ground underfoot, and the ghost's laughter rose to a howl. "Why, there's your answer, boy, there's your father indeed. Son of nothing, child of no one, there's not even a ghost that knows your name. Ash, ember, vile little cinder, you've no one in any world to belong to, save only me. Welcome, then, welcome twice over, Cajli's Riaan." Lal saw the name slash across Riaan's shoulders, and fully expected blood to follow.

Later, two oceans from that place, she sometimes told it to herself, chanting it over like one of the tales she had trained little Choushi-wai to remember always, word for word. "Oh, but he never gave in, that Riaan, even then, never surrendered to what must have been a loneliness more fearful than I ever knew. No, he sang back at it, sang back clear as spring rain, 'I don't believe you! Alive or dead, I don't believe you!' And he called to his father yet once again, called with stolen words he did not understand to someone he did not know, someone so hopelessly far away in the endless dark. And yes, yes, yes, *yes*, someone came."

No lights this time, no playful brightnesses swarming together to puddle into a deathly shining. There was only a rather small, nondescript figure taking shape before them so slowly that it seemed to be trudging a black desert far wider than the sands Soukyan had crossed to Lal's door. Nor was there any sound, save for another yell of laughter suddenly cracking in Cajli's throat, and the sound of Riaan not breathing. Soukyan fumbled blindly for Lal's hand, already seeking his.

She never got as close a look at its face as she would have liked, but the body was as slender and deceptively sinewy as Riaan's, and the wary, determined carriage just the same, though the boy's lightness was long gone from that slouching form. Tired to death in life, it was nowhere near the end of its weariness; it had merely come one more journey to answer one more command. It said simply, in a flat country voice, "Well, here I am."

The ghost of Cajli hissed like an angry *shukri*, but said nothing. Riaan gave a curious little sigh that Lal remembered all her days. He whispered, "You. You, please. Is it you?"

It did not speak again for a very long time, or perhaps a little while. Lal never knew. Its eyes were as uninhabited as the eyes of that other ghost, and its presence far less charged with the mockery of life that animated Cajli. But it seemed to her then that something trembled down below the emptiness, something came near to flickering into a human light. So softly that Lal's heartbeat almost drowned the words, the ghost whispered, "Riaan?"

Riaan wept.

"I named you," the ghost said. It leaned a little toward him, its hanging arms coming forward, the palms open. It asked, "Is that crying? Why do you cry? Here I am." But Riaan dropped down on the ground and sobbed, not loudly, but as though he would never stop. Lal held on hard to Soukyan's hand.

And so they might well have stayed until dawn, but for the ghost of Cajli. It stalked to within inches of the newcomer, who looked back briefly without expression, neither cringing away nor straightening its bowed shoulders. Cajli said, "I remember you. A field hand, you were, a tiller, never saw you without a sack of shit on your back. Well, well, fancy, and here we are."

But the other's strange attention was bent all on Riaan. It yearned toward him as he wept with a kind of terrible clumsiness, never quite attempting to touch him, but staring with eyes much too wondering and sad for its dead face. It said, "Eliath. My name is Eliath."

Riaan managed to stop crying. He wiped his still-tender nose with the back of his wrist, winced, and snuffled, "Then I am Eliath's Riaan." The sound of the two words together brought a raw growl from Cajli, and at that Riaan smiled for the first time, and began to sing them over again and

again. "Eliath's Riaan, Eliath's Riaan. I am Eliath's Riaan."
And that too might have gone on till morning and long
past, but for Cajli's ghost.

"No," it said. "Oh, no. Garbage has no father, a sack of
shit leaves no heirs, a churl has no family but his mother's
master." He had come too close; a bloodless hand closed on
Riaan's forearm, and Riaan screamed. Cajli's ghost said,
"*Now.*"

Soukyan and Lal never agreed on what happened next.
They spoke of it once, just long enough to realize the depth
of the difference in their understandings, and avoided the
matter entirely after that. To Lal it seemed that the weary
little phantom that called itself Eliath instantly seized the
hand of Cajli's ghost, breaking its grip on Riaan in a motion
as swift and burning as a shooting star. So much she was
certain about: beyond that image, she retained only a stubborn memory of the two ghost hands, milkily transparent,
blurring and melting hugely together in a sudden blizzard
of white light. Somewhere very far away the *churfas* were
screaming horribly.

Soukyan remembered the light also, but what he had
seen moving against it were figures ripped from the night
itself: inhuman silhouettes, all but shapeless, all but joined,
swaying back and forth, dancers ringed by white fire. Both
of them were making a wordless roaring sound, such as
distant waterfalls make, or trees in a storm. There was no
distinguishing Eliath's ghost from Cajli's, nor any way of
knowing which would prevail, or what prevailing meant.
The savage milkiness was rising, at once brightening
unbearably and pulling apart, and the struggling figures
themselves were beginning to come undone with it, rad-
dling and unraveling like worn silk. He could not see Riaan
at all, but he heard the boy cry out again, not in pain this
time but in desperate fear, and not for himself.

"It was all *wrong*," he said to Lal that one time. "They
should never have been here, those two, I told you that, and
they should not have been fighting. The more they fought,
the more wrong it became, until the tension was too much

for—for someone, for *something*. You saw none of that, truly?"

"Only the hands," she answered. "The hands, no more."

But what she did see at the last, and what Soukyan never mentioned at all, was a third hand. Small and dim against the light, it yet preserved its outline, not dissolving into the others, but on the contrary appearing to seek out and grip one of the hands fiercely, beginning to tug it toward the edge of the circle. Only for a moment Lal glimpsed this; then the whiteness ate up the sky, and she heard—or forever after thought she had heard—a sound like the banging of the windblown door of a great empty house.

Until she heard the boy calling, "Lal! Lal, Soukyan, here is my father!" she did not realize that her eyes were tightly closed. She opened them very slowly to find that the night had returned to its usual business of being dark and still—though the moon was low, and there was a hint of false dawn back over the levee road—and that Riaan was standing before her with the ghost of a bondman glimmering shyly at his shoulder. Of Cajli's ghost there was no trace, no least echo, not even in the boy's eyes. Riaan said again, "Here is Eliath, my father."

Lal bowed awkwardly, saying, "You have a fine brave son, Master Eliath." The ghost inclined its head in return, but never stopped gazing at Riaan. Soukyan pushed abruptly past her, in his turn ignoring the ghost completely. "Let me see your hand," he demanded. "Why are you holding it like that? Show me."

Riaan had been keeping his right hand rigidly at his side, hidden slightly by his leg. Reluctantly, he put it forward now, and Lal caught her breath to see the four parallel marks on his palm, the exact color of the moonlight, and the single fat sear crossing the back, where a thumb would have clenched. Soukyan peered at the hand closely, swore in a whisper, and said, "Bloody thing's *frozen*—there and there and there. What have you *done* to it?"

"It doesn't hurt, not really," Riaan said quickly. "See, it's fine, I can use it," and he made the hand open and close, though his eyes closed for an instant as he did so. He said, "I had to get him away, I had to make Cajli let go. Otherwise—I don't know, I *had* to, otherwise—"

"Otherwise he would have been gone," Soukyan said. "Everything in this world tries to force a ghost back where it belongs—most cannot even keep a foothold here until dawn. Cajli might have lasted that long, but no longer."

"But he could have taken me with him," the boy challenged. Soukyan nodded. "And you and Lal could do nothing—it was my father who saved me." He burst out laughing with such rare, utterly unused joy that even the ghost of Eliath smiled. "And I saved *him*, only think of that. I, Eliath's Riaan, I saved my father from going where Cajli has gone." He broke into a shuffling, stamping jig of victory, spinning like a leaf in an eddy, wheeling suddenly to take Eliath's hands and draw him into the dance.

"Riaan, *no!*" Soukyan's voice sounded like a knife skidding on bone. "On your life, do not touch him again! Look at him—*he* knows."

The ghost had drawn sharply away, dodging Riaan as the boy had Cajli. Riaan stared back and forth defiantly before he lowered his head in a barely perceptible nod. He spread his right hand out before him—though by now he could not open it quite fully—studying the strange scars intently. "I'm glad I have these, anyway," he said in a small, quiet voice. "I am."

A faint breeze, bringing with it a rumor of the sea, brushed by Lal's cheek on its way to morning. She said, "There is little time. We will go apart and wait for you." Soukyan would have lingered in his fascination to observe the living son and long-dead father together, but Lal took his elbow and they moved away to stand on a muddy hummock in the damp loom of one of the enormous fern trees that grow only in the marshes north of Kulpai. Birds they could not see were waking in its frondy branches, and Lal could make out a few slim, slow clouds crossing the thinning stars. She realized absurdly that she was quite hungry.

"I told you," Soukyan said quietly. "Better as it was."

Lal shook her white head. "Never. Not for this one. This one has to *know*. Like you."

Soukyan grunted, rubbed the back of his neck and sighed. He said only, "Look at them," nodding toward Riaan and Eliath where they stood facing each other, not two feet apart. What they were saying could not be heard, but the yearning between them was plain even at that distance; for the night was ebbing swiftly now, leaving them naked to a watery sky. Riaan was still holding his right hand down and away from his body, moving it slightly as though he were quieting an animal.

"If I had never come to find you," Soukyan said. "If we had never been to Kulpai—or if we had sailed to Kulpai, as we did that other time. If that bloody boy had kept his mouth shut and bred whomever they put him to. If *we* had only kept our mouths shut—"

Lal put her hand on his arm to stop him. She said, "If we had at last somehow managed, after all these years, to disown our hearts. To sell them, to pawn them, to leave them in a ditch and walk away fast. As often as we've tried, you would think . . ." She did not finish.

"Oh, you would think," Soukyan agreed fervently. "You *would* think." The ghost of Eliath was becoming more tenuous and filmy by the moment; from a certain angle it could not be seen at all, and Riaan might have been talking earnestly to a patch of moss on a fallen tree. Lal edged around slightly to put her back to the east, having an absurd notion of keeping the rising sun's rays from touching Eliath for a few seconds more.

"He's gone," Soukyan said, but the ghost was not gone, not quite then. Lal could still discern even the thin whiplash scar down Eliath's right cheek, looking itself like the ghost of a tear. But it faded as she focused on it, and Eliath faded around it, until all that was left of him was Riaan—Riaan and a soft, raw gasp of bereavement that could have come from either of them, or from Lal herself. She was never sure.

Both Soukyan and she started down the slope toward

Riaan; then, without a word to one another, both of them turned quickly away. He came to them in his own time. His face was pale and dirty and very tired, but the rain-gray eyes were clear as the new morning, and he was smiling a little, in private, like a lover returning home.

"My father will come again if I have need," he said. "But I will not."

With its sour-smelling streets and its sullen folk in their narrow, lowering houses, Kulpai was exactly as unpleasant a place as Lal remembered. She found this remarkably comforting.

The inn that had offered the least dangerous beds and food was still standing, kept up by the widow of the old proprietor. Soukyan left Lal and Riaan asleep there on the morning following their arrival. She woke when the room door closed and stood at the window to watch the taut stride that had replaced his usual diffident amble taking him now toward the lockup under the city wall. When he passed from sight, she went back to bed and slept dream-lessly until midafternoon, and when she woke, Riaan was gone.

"Ah, no," she said aloud. "Not today, child. You are on your own today." She bathed and washed her hair in the questionable water provided, made a knowledgeable but vain attempt at cleaning her journeying clothes, then went downstairs and menaced the inn's cook into producing something that came quite close to being a meal. After that, and after asking a number of questions of the landlady, she made her leisurely way down to the harbor.

Riaan was where she had thought to find him, sitting on a stanchion at the end of the wharf. An unseasonably warm sun was turning the water a sparkling, slippery purple, and the squat little coasters were already setting out for a stolen night's *tejadi* netting in the lee of the Unseen Islands. Three or four merchant ships lay at anchor just within the mole, tenders and lighters butting at their flanks like nursing marsh-goats, taking off cargo. A dozen fishermen, the crew of one of the deep-sea boats, had careened it on the beach, so that the leering demon face on the prow was half-buried in the sand. They began scraping a thick, stinking crop of scarlet *fa*-weed from its hull.

Lal dragged a coiled hawser up beside the stanchion and made herself comfortable, sitting crosslegged. She said, "You have been here all day."

Riaan nodded without turning his head. Lal said, "The first time they took me to the sea, I thought it was a great green animal. I tried to pet it. They used to tell me—" She stopped herself, then finished lamely, "I believe I almost drowned."

"I can swim in rivers and things," Riaan said. "My mother taught me." Now he looked at her, and she saw that his eyes were too wide, his face almost as transparent as his father's. "Lal, it is too much," he whispered. "Too much world beyond my village—too much sky—now *this*. It is too heavy for me. It crushes me even to think about it. I am so afraid, Lal."

"You?" she said. "You have more courage than Soukyan and me together." But Riaan would not be comforted. "What is to become of me? Where am I to go from Kulpai, Lal?"

"Where are any of us to go from Kulpai?" she asked gently. "Shall I return to telling stories in the desert? Is Soukyan to go on wandering like dust in the wind, with no more cause than seeing what happens next? He and I, we have never had a purpose in our lives beyond survival, beyond vengeance, or pride—yes, or atonement, why not? You'll do better than that, take my word." She reached up from where she sat and took light hold of his right hand, studying the unfading scars. "You know you can come along with us," she said, "with either one, as you will. But I would wait if I were you. I would wait right here for the sea to speak to me."

Riaan gave a short laugh that was too old for him and

looked away again. "You are Sailor Lal, born on the water—the sea will always speak to you. Why should it bother with someone who never saw it until this morning?"

"I never know the sea's reasons," she answered him. "Wait, Riaan. The sea is looking at you right now, making up its mind. If it chooses, it will speak soon enough. Sit still now and listen."

So they sat on the wharf for the rest of that day, as the coasters vanished in sparkling haze and small children chased the longlegged shore birds down the beach after the ebbing tide. They said very little, and no one said anything to them, though they drew glances from the women bringing buckets of red ale to the men scraping at the fishing boat. They watched the high, hooked dorsal fins of a pair of *panyaras* drifting lazily beyond the harbor mouth; and once Lal pointed out a great blue-gray bird endlessly quartering the sky. *"Kulishai,"* she told him. "They have no legs—they are born on the cliffs, and just roll into the air when their time comes. Scavengers they are, and always alone. People here believe that they never mate and never die." Riaan did not answer.

When the children on the beach had been called home at sunset, when the fishermen had finished cleaning their boat's bottom, and the merchant ships were riding high and light in the fire-flecked water because of their empty holds, and Soukyan had not returned, they walked silently back to the inn and had their dinner. The landlady had already retired for the night, and a pleasant-faced, middle-aged woman they had not seen before was serving in the taproom. Her red hair and bright throat scarf marked her as a Nounouri, and the handful of other diners called her Deshka.

The meal was long over, and the taproom empty except for Lal and Riaan, who could not yet bring themselves to go upstairs, when Soukyan came through the door. A breath of the cool, dry evening entered with him: even so, he looked as though he had been in the rain for a long time. He sat down at their table, saying no word, and Deshka brought him a cup of *tamtha*, the fierce, oily Kulpai brandy, without being asked. She had gone for a second drink when Soukyan finally said, "His name was Haruk. Haruk Butcher's-Son, people called him. Some few remembered him, and liked him well enough and were sorry when he died. That was twenty-three years ago."

"The boy," Lal said. "What about his own son?" But Soukyan was already shaking his head. "One old man thought he married a woman from Arakli and moved there, but someone else said that he went to sea. No other opinions or memories, no other relations in all of Kulpai. So you were right, Lal, of course, you were right. Not even a cold trail, but no trail at all."

"It was worth the doing, well worth it." To her surprise, she found herself savoring the defiant absurdity of defending a completely absurd and pointless mission to its originator. "The journey itself was your apology—you know that and the journey knows that, and what else matters?" Riaan gazed wondering from one to the other of them.

"I suppose so," Soukyan said wearily. "I suppose that's true." He said nothing further until Deshka was setting the second cup of *tamtha* before him. "The odd thing," he said then, "is that no one at all seemed to recall our escape. Now we emptied an entire prison—such as it was, admitted—and that cannot be something that happens very often in Kulpai. Yet in a day's searching, I couldn't find a soul to remember it. As long as that time has lived with me, and Haruk Butcher's-Son himself probably forgot to mention the whole wretched affair."

The barmaid Deshka, who had started away from their table, halted and turned. "That was your doing?" she demanded. "A black woman and a tall brown man—*you* were the ones?"

The three of them gawked at her until she began to smile. "No," she said, "no, I am no relation of Haruk's, though I knew him a little when I was a girl. But my great-uncle

Gauvarda was one of those you set free that day. He spoke of it often to me—as well he might have, who was an innocent man—"

"Weren't we all?" Lal murmured, looking at the ceiling. Riaan giggled, and Deshka looked sharply at Lal for a moment before she went on. "Among the Nounouri it is a great shame to be imprisoned, innocent or not. My great-uncle never forgot the two of you, and I know he would wish me to offer his gratitude, as I do now." She set the empty cups she was carrying down carefully, and sank into a deep reverence, touching her hands and her brow to Lal and Soukyan's knees, whispering a few words neither could catch, then rising swiftly to become her amiable, efficient self once more. "You'll want more *tamtha*," she said to Soukyan. "I can always tell."

Soukyan was beginning to laugh, sounding as young as Riaan. "Yes," he answered, "yes, I'm sure I will. Deshka, I came here from a far country, dragging these two good friends along with me, all to ask forgiveness of a man I dishonored half my life ago. I wanted to ask him, or his son, or a grandchild, 'What may I do for you, how may I help you, that I may help myself to find peace?' Now I learn that he is long gone from Kulpai, and his family gone as well, and the only person who halfway understands my idiot quest is the great-niece of—oh, let it go, let it go, just let it go." He kept on laughing helplessly, trying to empty his cup, but spilling more of the brandy than he got down.

Lal rose. "Riaan, help me get him upstairs. He never did have any head for this buckle polish."

But Deshka nodded in sympathy, saying, "Aye, atonement matters greatly to us, too. We all die unforgiven by someone, that can't be helped. But penance at least is in ourselves." She laughed herself, as a fancy plainly occurred to her. "Ah, too bad it wasn't my family you offended, Master Soukyan. What with my son married and gone, and my husband short a hand at the tiller and the nets, even a grandsir like yourself would have come in useful. Gods, even a child with a bad hand." She turned away abruptly, dismissing the notion. "Your pardon, my troubles are my troubles. I will be in the kitchen, should you require anything more."

Riaan looked after her, and Lal looked at Riaan, and Soukyan wiped his mouth and stared at both of them as Lal said an odd thing. She said, "I think perhaps the sea just made up its mind."

Riaan saw them off the next morning, coming out from behind the bar where he would be helping Deshka until her husband's fishing boat returned. It was a cold morning, with thin frost crunching underfoot and a few hard gray snowflakes spilling over from a low sky. The *churfas* were champing their tusked mouths and drooling on everyone. Their winter fur was rapidly growing in, darker than their usual coats, and even fouler smelling. Riaan said shakily, "I hate saying good-bye like this."

"There isn't any good way," Soukyan answered. "Lal and I would know by now if there were." Riaan kissed them both, solemnly and tenderly, as one kisses one's grandparents. He said, "You know that I will never be done thanking you."

Lal snorted like a *churfa* herself. "That sounds remarkably dull. If by chance you ever do get over that, send to us and we will come and see you then." She embraced Riaan quickly, squeezed Butterfly's nostrils to make the *churfa* kneel, and swung up onto the broad, furry back. Soukyan said over his shoulder as he mounted, "Be careful on that bloody boat, that's all. Boats try to kill you; things swing around and hit you on the head. Never trust a bloody boat."

Riaan cried out sadly, "But how will I know where you are?"

Lal and Soukyan looked at each other without answering. Lal said finally, "Ask the sailors. Some will always know. Farewell, Eliath's Riaan."

They were well clear of dreary Kulpai before Soukyan said quietly, "You could have told the boy you would be returning home to your desert, your little house, your stories. What harm in that?"

"Because I am not returning home," she said. Soukyan stared at her. Lal said, "No, not to that home. I am about to do something more lunatic even than your chase after an impossible forgiveness. Knowing so much better, I am going back to the place where I was born." Soukyan was astonished to see tears forming in the golden eyes and freezing instantly on her eyelashes. "It plagues me, Soukyan," she whispered. "That land I never think of, that language I never speak. There are ghosts and ghosts, I told Riaan that. It is time, long past time, for me to turn and face mine."

Soukyan reached out to grip her forearm tightly as they rode. "And if the same thing happens to you? If there is no one left to know you, no one to rejoice with, to remember with, no one there who still wonders whatever became of little Lal? What then?"

"Then?" Lal shrugged. "Then there are other places I always meant to see, and perhaps one or two more things that always meant to happen to me. So much forgotten, so much of myself laid by, until you beguiled me into this very foolish journey. I will take ship at Ilu; it's less than two days' ride—" She frowned as a practical matter crossed her mind. "Choushi-wai," she said. "I can't have her spending the rest of her life in that hut, waiting for me to return. She'll do it, too, that child. I forgot about Choushi-wai."

"Well," Soukyan said, and then nothing more for some time as the *churfas* tramped on through the stinging little flakes. "Well," he said in time, "I could go back and tell her."

Lal hauled Butterfly to a stop and gaped at him as blankly as Riaan ever had. Soukyan said, "I thought I might rest there, perhaps for rather a while. You have some roaming yet to do, after all, while I seem to be at last coming to a stop inside myself. I need stillness now, Lal."

She continued to stare until he slapped her shoulder, not lightly. "Come on, keep moving, it's too cold to stand here. Come *on*, bloody Butterfly."

They were not traveling on the levee road by which they

had entered Kulpai, but on a narrower path along the coast, though the sea was all but hidden by the mist and flying snow. Half a day ahead lay a tributary of the Queen's Road, at which they had separated once before. They went on in a silence broken only by the bitter complaining of the *churfas*, until Soukyan asked, "Do you think they would mind? In the village, I mean."

"No," she said, "no, I don't see why they would. You've tales of your own to tell them, and those would certainly be a change from my old warhorses." She laughed suddenly, the tone bright both with irony and a curious relief. "And Choushi-wai would be thrilled right down to her bootsoles, if she ever wore boots. She'll teach you everything you need to know, and feed you into the bargain until you look like a *jejebhai* being fattened for Thieves' Day. By all means, I think you should do that. A splendid idea."

"So, then. At the small end of our lives, we trade places?"

"Yes, why not? It does seem the most natural thing in the world. As you say."

"Then why are you so angry?" Even through the snow she could see that he was regarding her in a way she had always hated, because its piercing affection left her no privacy. When she did not reply, Soukyan said, "Old friend. My old impossible friend. I have a right to know this."

"I am angry because we will never see each other again," she burst out. "You know it, and I know it, and there's no help for it, and there it is. Forty years' worth of farewells is enough for anyone—I told you that when you came to me—and still I let myself in for one more." When he reached for her hand, she snatched it violently away. "I am angry at myself, just let it *be*, Soukyan."

They came near to missing the inland road, because of the weather; it was Lal who noticed the wagon ruts half-covered in snow. They halted the *churfas* and faced each other across the wind for a long time. The old man said finally, "You know, the boy may turn out to be no fisherman after all. We may yet have to go back there and rescue him again."

"Good-bye, Soukyan," the old woman said. "Go well. Help Choushi-wai with her reading." She tugged Butterfly's right ear, and the great creature dutifully began to turn back toward the coast road.

Behind her an outraged silence, and then a bellow, "And that is *it*? That is *all*? After forty years?"

Without turning her head, she called, "I told you—it's just one good-bye too many." Butterfly slogged on.

She kept a vow to herself not to look back; she had even begun to sing, as a distraction from sleet and confusion. Consequently, she almost fell off Butterfly when Soukyan appeared on foot in her path, gripping the *churfa*'s jaw, and shoving his free arm into its mouth to forestall a scream of alarm.

"Get down," he said flatly, the effect spoiled only somewhat by his being out of breath. She dug her knees into Butterfly's sides, but the *churfa* only growled and remained planted where she was. Soukyan said, "Lal." The snow that had muffled his running footsteps was in his hair, turning it as white as hers.

"Ah, *damn*," she said at last, and slid to the ground. She stumbled on a patch of ice as she landed, but he caught her. They held one another tightly for a long time, grumbling inaudibly into shoulders and noses and the sides of throats. The wind slackened a little, but the snow went on falling, and still they stood together. The second *churfa* joined them for company, making plaintively flatulent sounds.

"I feel like that boy," she said, "like Riaan. Finding his father, losing his father, seeing the ocean for the first time. It's too much for me, Soukyan. Let me go, please."

The old man stroked her wet hair. "We might yet fetch up in the same lockup one more time. You don't know."

She pulled back to look directly into the twilight eyes. "Yes, I do. This time I do know. Good-bye, Soukyan. Good-bye, good-bye." She kissed him with the innocent ferocity of a young girl, and then she was up on the *churfa* again, saying, "Sunlight on your road," over her shoulder, as though they had shared nothing more than a meal, a stretch of road, or a single night.

"And on yours." Butterfly was already lumbering toward the coast road. He raised his voice to call after her. "At least you know where to find me. If you should need me."

"Oh, I will always need you." A sudden gust of snow hid her from him almost instantly, but the wind blew her words back clearly. "There's the plain bloody aggravation of it."

He did not stare after her, having made his own private vow; though he did hold the *churfa* steady for a moment after he mounted, thinking that he could still hear her singing. "Sour the milk, it would," he said very loudly. "Only a *churfa* could ever love that music of hers." The beast belched at both ends, and he grimaced, and then grinned, stretching his cold face painfully. "Right. Move your stinking old self, then—it's a long way home for everybody. We ought to be seeing farmhouses in a few hours. Move, so." The *churfa* shambled forward, and the mists closed around them.

CHOUSHI-WAI'S STORY

Attend, attend! Remember to pray for the poor, beloved of the gods, and remember to pray for the gods, who have no friends but the poor. Attend to me, the *inbarati* Choushi-wai, daughter of the S'dif clan, attend the tale of Tai-sharm and the Singing Fish, as I had it from Lalkhamsin-khamsolal, who had it from Sulij herself, who had it in turn from the great Vaivolkar, and she from Ti'hadri. I, Choushi-wai, tell it to you now.

Well, and so. In the longest-ago, even in the time before the mountains fell down, when there were mighty lords ruling realms far greater than the handful of villages that we call a kingdom today, there reigned a king in Baraquil who was growing old with neither a wife to grow old at his side, nor child to care for them both. And this troubled him not at all, for he was a silent man, and much enjoyed his solitude. Yet his Chief Minister reminded him ever more constantly that to die with no heir was to invite chaos, and the King in time reluctantly agreed that this was so. Therefore he bade the Chief Minister to go forth in the land and choose him a wife, but not to make too much haste about it. "For I do this for the tranquility of my country only," he said, "and not through any lust or longing of my own."

And the Minister then said to him, "This is well understood, Gracious Majesty—but will you not say how you would prefer your queen to be? Will you have her merry or somber? wanton or coy? self-willed or tractable? maddeningly beautiful or comfortably plain? Shall she be of the high old blood? or of the later-come nobility? A king desirous of marriage must consider such matters carefully, my lord."

The King answered him shortly, saying, "I am not *desirous* of anything save being left in peace—yet, if it must be, then by all the gods' grubby necks find me a woman of some intelligence, able at least to carry on a human conversation at mealtimes. The rest is for you to judge; one's very like another, take or leave a bosom, or an ankle, or a trick of the light. One's like another. Go away now."

So the Chief Minister left him and began his search for the woman who was to be queen, and Queen Mother after. And it must be fairly told that the Minister sought a bride for his lord as zealously as though he were an honest man. Which he was not; for he said to himself, "Be she never so wise, never so subtle, never so learned, what shall it avail her against me? When *he* is gone, she and the little one will be under my hand, and through them may I not govern as I choose?" Whenever he encountered a woman he deemed would suit both himself and the King, he had her brought straightway to the palace, whether she would or no. And always the King had her to breakfast, and sometimes dinner, and so safely on her way home by suppertime, and everybody much relieved except the Chief Minister. Yet he went on combing the realm, moving among high and lowly alike, in dutiful pursuit of an intelligent queen.

Now in those times, in a high, cold, flat eastern corner of the kingdom, famed for nothing but cheese and wild honey, there lived a certain woman named Sharm and her daughter, who was called Tai-sharm, which is how girl children are named to this day in that country. A son will have a name of his own, but a daughter shares her mother's name, and Tai-sharm was well satisfied with this. Indeed she was proud of it, for she admired her mother greatly, and she had never known her father. She worked their shred of land side by side with Sharm every day, from the first moment they could see the earth they plowed until it grew too dark even to distinguish the weeds and stones they knelt to grub up. At the age of seventeen years, her small hands were as strong and worn as her mother's hands, with dirty, broken fingernails like hers, and her knees and elbows and her bare feet were as hard as *rishu-horn*. And Tai-sharm was proud of these things also.

Of her looks she knew nothing; and how should she have known? say we who live yet as Tai-sharm lived then. Like us, she had never seen her face reflected in anything but a thick brown puddle where her eyes and teeth appeared the same color as those of any other village child. She washed herself when she thought of it, and when there was water to spare from beasts and crops; and she always combed the dusty tangles out of her hair on every market day. When her one *badrique*—such as women there wear still—fell to tatters, her mother would weave another. So she worked and she slept, and she ate, and she worked, and she was Tai-sharm.

Yet to this Choushi-wai must add something more, something that Tai-sharm would never have told you. Tai-sharm believed in her soul that she was a stupid woman. "Stoneskull," "lackwit," "echohead"—those were some of the names she'd taken to herself since she was quite small. Who can say where she came by such a notion? never from old Sharm, who was her most adoring companion. Children demand impossible things of themselves in secret; only they know why. Sharm grieved and stormed, and gave over storming, and never understood.

She took a fierce, cunning care of her daughter, old Sharm did, understanding as bleakly as any what can become of a peasant girl unlucky enough to catch the eye of some little lordling. Yet she did not disfigure Tai-sharm, as many such mothers have done; but she did what she might to keep her grimy and ragged and hidden away from strangers. And at the first word of the Chief Minister's coming, she sent Tai-sharm into the hills to study with her uncle Rynn, who was a smith and a *navdal* as well, able to put his hands on an animal and listen to its illness. Truly, when the Minister finally found his way to their village, he never should have met Tai-sharm at all.

Yet when a thing is set and bound to be, how shall a peasant woman or a master wizard hold it back? It happened that Rynn himself fell ill, and was tossing in bed, all a-fevered and delirious, when Tai-sharm came there. Well-tended, he was, by his wife and his two sons; so what was for Tai-sharm to do but see those three properly fed, and then kiss her uncle's sweated forehead and trudge the miles home to her mother? And to arrive at one end of the lane leading to their tiny hut just as the Chief Minister and his retinue turned in at the other? Tell me now, how shall such determination be held back?

Well, and so. What did Tai-sharm see then, meeting the Minister at her mother's door? Choushi-wai tells you that she saw a tall, pale, heavy man with a soft mouth and bright little eyes like nailheads. The trailing hem of his yellow robe of office was spattered with mud, and worse, but for that the Chief Minister cared nothing, having seen Tai-sharm. What *he* observed was a small person with black, black hair and skin the shade that water turns at dusk; a person who looked at him out of eyes the size and shape and color of the *mardou* figs that grow in this very courtyard. She was not beautiful, that person, in any of the Twenty-seven Recognized Ways; but if the Minister was not an honest man, he was not a fool either, and he bowed as deeply to Tai-sharm as his rank and his belly would permit him. He said to her, "Good madame, my salutations. Your pardon, but it may well be that the gods have sent me here to meet you."

Now Tai-sharm had never been called *madame* in her life; nor for the matter of that, had she ever seen a Chief Minister, no more than anyone here. The only robe of office she recognized was the shabby scarlet feast-day vestment of the village's one priest. More, she disliked the soft, mealy look of the Minister's attendants. Pausing warily therefore on the threshold of her mother's house, she gathered her faded shawl around her shoulders and pertly answered the Chief Minister, "Sir, in that case the gods must have even less sense of direction than your venerable self. Surely they meant to guide you to a proper city like Cheth na'Bata, or perhaps Sarn, where there are ladies who will understand such talk. As for me, there's work and supper waiting," and she made to pass him and enter the hut.

But the Chief Minister filled the doorway, smiling, saying, "My child, tell me your name."

Tai-sharm was tired from her long tramp. She said irritably, "I am no child of yours but Tai-sharm, daughter of Sharm. Let me by, silly man."

"Ah, better and better." The Minister fondled his smooth round chin. "Tell me then, Tai-sharm, what is the name of this village?" For he had no more notion of that than we do, or than the Queen in Fors na'Shachim has of ours, and well for us, oh indeed, well for us.

"Name?" It is said that the sound of Tai-sharm's laughter was like the soft chiming of the first spring rains. "Now surely it has as many names as it has dwellers—we call it *here*, or we call it *this place*, or we call it *home*. Each of us calls it whatever suits him, but we all know where it is. How else should it be with us?"

Then the Minister smiled again, and he put another question to Tai-sharm. He asked her, "And who is the king of this realm?"

"The king?" Tai-sharm laughed at him a second time. "Old man, here there is no king but the wind, no king but the locust, no king but the dry well. How else should it be with us?"

"How else indeed?" murmured the Chief Minister, as though in deep converse with himself. "Tell me one thing more, Tai-sharm, who is no child. Tell a silly man your heart's truest desire."

"To see a fish," answers Tai-sharm, without a moment's hesitation. "Not an old dried fish, such as they sell in the market, but one alive and swimming and all different colors." It is told that she smiled so tenderly at the very thought that for one single moment the Chief Minister became an honest man. And who knows what ending there might have been to this tale, had not old Sharm heard the voices and come to investigate. She knew a yellow robe, if her daughter did not, and she scolded the girl roundly for her inhospitality. "Please to come in, lord," she said. "Your servants likewise." What she'd have done if they had, the gods in their mystery know, for the hut was crowded enough with her and Tai-sharm. But the Minister briefly bade his attendants wait in the street, then courteously bent his head to stoop through the door of Tai-sharm's home.

There they are, then, see them: dark, ragged Tai-sharm, her little mother—a true "born-bent," as the folk there call themselves—sitting with the King's Chief Minister at the table made from a broken cartwheel, with the Minister's knees nudging his chin and Sharm serving him mug on mug of spiced spidergrass tea, and pressing him to try yet another of her dry *quiqui* biscuits. He spoke hardly a word to Tai-sharm then, but bent all his cunning toward cozening her mother with accounts of his royal master's vast wealth and his noble heart, his goodness and loneliness. He was a wondrous fine talker, that Minister was.

Old Sharm was casting side-glances at Tai-sharm and prodding her foot under the table before he was halfway done. Tai-sharm took no notice, but only sat gazing at the Chief Minister's left shoulder, and what she thought was what she thought. And the Minister still paid her no seeming mind, but began to confide in Sharm the difficulty of gratifying the King's preference for intelligence in his bride. "For one sort of wit may reveal itself in the wild deeps of philosophy, look you; a very different sort through the slide and chime of words one on another; yet a third in the wisdom needed merely to survive one wretched day more." Old Sharm nodded morosely at this. The Minister said, "And there must be as many more varieties, I doubt not, as birds in the air, insects in the grass, sycophants at court. Good mother, of your own country wisdom say, what would you do in my place to determine the precise cast of thought most suitable to my master's whim? I will abide your judgment."

Now see old Sharm, see her rocking back on her rickety chair, lifting her hands to slap them down on her thighs, then leaning forward until she's knobby nose to high, thin nose with the Chief Minister, beginning to whisper loudly to him, "Well, my lord, there's no mother but knows her daughter a match for the highest, true? I don't mind saying that when it comes to plain sense—sense, aye, and true cleverness as well—your king could go a long way and fare worse than my girl—"

But here's Tai-sharm, on her feet like *that*, almost toppling the table, her face gone tight and patchy-pale and older than her mother's face. "No," she says. "No, no more of this! I know what I am, and I don't mock and I won't *be* mocked." With that she's out the door and down the lane, and there's the King's Chief Minister left gaping across a rocking cartwheel table at a gaping, stub-toothed peasant woman, and one of them as dumb as the other. See them so, just as Choushi-wai sees.

"Eigh, dear," old Sharm sighs at last. Shamefaced, she swipes the grimy back of her hand across her mouth, mumbles behind it what we already know—that Tai-sharm, from childhood, has always believed herself an imbecile. "Praise that quick, canny head," Sharm laments, "and she'll swear you're making game of her, always; call her so much as shrewd, never mind clever, and the girl's at your throat or running off to wail all night in the barn, as she'll do now." She rubs her mouth again, belches, apologizes. "Eigh, dear—well, there it is, there it is. You'll not be interested in her for your king now, I don't suppose?"

"Ah, mother, I fear not," says the Minister sadly. And he fends off another *quiqui* biscuit and takes his leave.

But that same night, hours after Tai-sharm had finally whimpered herself to sleep, snuggled against the warm flank of her mother's one *rishu*, the minions of the Chief Minister flowed into the barn as soundlessly as the cold mist through the gaps in the walls. Tai-sharm came awake already bound and swaddled, thrown into a saddle and bumping on her way to the king whose name she did not know. Old Sharm never missed her until milking time.

Now it was never the Chief Minister's custom to accompany a new bridal prospect to the palace. Leaving that to his servants, he would be off elsewhere in the land, doggedly seeking out yet one more likely consort for his master. This time alone he rode by Tai-sharm's side day and night, and whether she cursed him or demanded her freedom or refused to speak at all, he chatted blithely along, telling her of all the wonders of Baraquil, and of the King's great victories in battle, of his learning and his simple wisdom. Twice Tai-sharm slipped her bonds and bolted in the middle of his prattle, and twice she was quickly retaken. The Chief Minister merely waited for her to be brought back to him, and calmly went on praising his master's virtues. Truly, he was a patient man, Choushi-wai tells you this.

Often he said to Tai-sharm, "My servants and I have tried our best to treat you gently and honorably. If we have injured you in the least, it was unintended, and I hope most earnestly that you will not bear it against us when you are Queen."

And each time Tai-sharm would answer him coldly, "No fear of *that*, since I will never be anyone's queen. Your troubles will begin when the King realizes what a dolt I am. He sent you to find a clever woman to keep him company at his breakfast, and you have returned with a fool. He will not be pleased."

"Ah, child," the Chief Minister would purr then, "who knows what pleases a king for how long? By the time we arrive, he may well have decided to be enchanted with foolishness, and there you will be, only fancy." But once he looked hard into her eyes in a different way and asked sharply, "*I* think you are feigning this faith in your own stupidity. In four days' acquaintance I have seen nothing slow or unintelligent about you. However could you come to believe such nonsense about yourself?"

When Tai-sharm did not answer, he went on, "Come, your mother's at least as shrewd as half the courtiers in Baraquil. Why should you be any different from her, tell me that? I don't believe you *are* any different."

"Oh, if only that were true," says Tai-sharm then, so softly that the Chief Minister has to bend close to hear. "If only that could be true."

Something about the simple words, about her voice, made the Chief Minister uneasy in his yellow robe. He spoke no more to her for the day and night that remained to their journey, but rode ahead from then on, leaving her under the constant watch of three of his attendants. But Tai-sharm made no further attempts to escape—and just where should she have fled, after all, who'd never been farther from home than her uncle's house in the hills? She came along in silence, watching the ground.

It was well past moonrise when they reached the palace at last, so Tai-sharm was not taken to the King that night. She was met instead by his own royal servants, who greeted her kindly and escorted her to a high room carpeted with *sheknath* pelts and hung with portraits of fierce men. There, in a tub as wide as the stockpond behind her village, and deeper, she was firmly scrubbed until she protested that her skin was coming unraveled. She was then put into a bed so splendid and so soft that she felt she was drowning in down, being crushed in a winepress of fur and satin. Barely had the servants bidden her sleep well and closed the doors when Tai-sharm had scrambled down to the floor and scratched a bare place for herself on good hard wood, as she was used to sleep at home. Not that she slept so much as a minute, nono, would you? She lay very still in a corner, her back curled against two walls, but she paced constantly back and forth in her mind, just as we see our half-wild *hamadris* do in their pens each night—back and forth, round and round, with the moon on their horns. So Tai-sharm, inside, until dawn.

The servants found her in the big bed, waiting with her

eyes wide open. They drew back the curtains, fed her heartily, then bathed her again—*ai*, our poor Tai-sharm, who could count the baths she'd had in her life if she thought about it a bit. And after *that*, she was perfumed until she sneezed and had her black hair braided and twisted and piled a foot high on her head; she was dressed in clothes she could never imagine, even while she was wearing them, and she was taken to the King.

What, has Choushi-wai not described to you the marvels of the palace, and of Baraquil, as was promised by the Chief Minister? Bide, bide, Tai-sharm has yet seen no more of these prodigies than you have, weary and lost and frightened as she is. Oh, she has *observed* them, if you like—the old suits of armor, the great mirrors, tables, bureaus, the hangings covering entire walls—but they have not seen her, do you understand? there has been no Tai-sharm truly there for them to see. Bide, bide. You will know always what our Tai-sharm knows when she knows.

Well, and so. The servants withdraw. Tai-sharm hears a familiar voice speaking welcome, and finally looks up to see the Chief Minister, and with him a man as tall as himself, but much differently made. This man is shaped like a block of building stone, everything thick and wide and gray. Even his jewelled crown looks gray in the shadows of the throne room.

"Approach, Tai-sharm," says the King. It is an order, but his voice catches Tai-sharm's ear for its dark gentleness—sadness, even. *He is not all the one thing*, she thinks, and she finds courage and walks toward him. The Minister is still talking, but Tai-sharm pays him no heed.

Near to the King as I am to you, she halts and waits. The King says in that strange voice of his, "Girl, have you ever seen a king before?"

"And where should I have seen such a thing?" answers Tai-sharm to his face. She has no wish to be impudent, but she is old Sharm's daughter, and her mother never could stomach a foolish question. To her wonder, the King smiles a little.

"Where, indeed? Far easier for me to meet a peasant, yet have I? So we are one another's first, then, which gives us at least that much in common." He sits down on his throne and turns to the Chief Minister, who is rubbing his hands, cracking his knuckles, looking anxious one moment and the next as vain as a *jejebhai* with two tails. "Well," he says. "You may tell me about this one, Majak."

Tai-sharm's as surprised as you to realize that the Chief Minister has a name like anyone else. He shows the King every one of his teeth now, petting Tai-sharm as though she'd performed some remarkable trick standing there. Says he, "My lord, as to breeding, she was born, there's the best I can tell you. But she has spirit, she is strong enough to bear you many strong sons, and I must say I find her comely in a completely unauthorized way. And as you specifically requested, she seems quite intelligent. Un-schooled, mind you—you said nothing about schooling—but definitely intelligent." See now, see how eagerly he pushes Tai-sharm's hair back a little to show the King her forehead. She slaps his hand.

The King laughs at that. It is a sudden bark of a laugh, almost a cough, so painful it sounds. "Perhaps—" he begins, but Tai-sharm breaks in just as she interrupted her mother, crying, "No! No, Your Kingship"—Aye? and which of *you* knows the proper way to address royalty, then?—"it is not true! I'm nothing but a common country wench, and stupid as a doorknob to boot. Anyone at home will tell you, I've no wit, no grace, no conversation—my manners even embarrass my mother. Lord, if you are as wise and good as *he* keeps saying, have pity and send me home."

She tries to fall on her knees before him, but the gown his servants have laced her into is too tight for that, and oh! there's Tai-sharm stuck halfway down. The Minister quickly rights her, while the King keeps looking and looking at her, heavy chin propped on his fist. Abruptly, he says, "Majak. Go away." Like that.

Well, the Chief Minister! His little nailhead eyes pop *wide*—his nose rushes up to join his eyebrows, but they are already hiding in his hair. He wants to speak, but what comes out? Noises like a leaky teakettle, like eggs frying in too much grease. The King does a little flick with one finger, and the Minister gives Tai-sharm one stare to singe the razor feathers on a *nishoru*, and he's gone, so. And there they are, Tai-sharm and the King.

Neither one of them says anything for a while. Tai-sharm looks around the room, carefully, as though maybe it is not allowed, and the King watches her doing that. She begins to realize just how huge it is: any two huts of her village would be lost between these walls—aye, and throw in the common granary while you're about it. What Tai-sharm will always remember about that throne room is not the great tapestries picturing the King's triumphs, nor the battle trophies—there were skulls on pillars, set in gold and silver, like jewels—but the ancient shadows in the corners. Solid as stone, they are, but hairy and breathing too, like big animals. That's an old palace, that one in Baraquil, and many kings have dwelled there.

"Little Tai-sharm," the King says presently. "I like you."

"Oh, sir, you never would, not if you knew me," Tai-sharm answers him. With the Chief Minister gone, she feels curiously safe speaking to the King like that, almost as if he were a friend from home, someone she'd grown up with. She says, "Sir, I don't mean to be disrespectful, but you are much too old and splendid for me, and I'm far too stupid and ignorant for you, take my word. You want a real queen; you want to marry a lady who would fit this room, who would know how to sleep in a bed like the kind you have here—"

"I do not want any sort of a queen, Tai-sharm," the King interrupts her, "even you." He smiles at her, and she sees that he's a bit of a handsome man in his dour fashion. The King says, "Girl, I no more wish to wed than you do, but what *are* we to do, the pair of us? Majak says I must look to my heirs, and about this, anyway, he is quite right. I can yet father children, and if your blood is humble . . . well, so was mine once on a time, I've no doubt of it. And I've said I like you, which is the most I ever hoped for. Is it so impossible that you might come to like me in time, do you suppose?"

"I do," Tai-sharm stammers back. "Anyway, I think I do, only—only not—"

"Not in that way." The King nods. No, he's not angry; his smile grows more gentle, if it changes at all. "Very well then, that's understood. But you will still have to be my queen, Tai-sharm. I am sorry, but there it is."

"My mother's forever saying that," whispers Tai-sharm. *"There it is, there it is.* As though looking straight at a thing always meant you could bear it." And she bursts into tears.

"Don't," says the King, looking as uncomfortable as any ploughboy. "Ah, don't, please, Tai-sharm. I wouldn't expect you to be honored, marrying me, but it's not generally supposed to be the end of the world." But here's our Tai-sharm, far from home and flat up against her future, and she weeps and weeps, and nothing the King can say or offer will make her stop. Horses, hawks, servants and suites of her own, a brace of hunting *shukris*, dresses of finest Stimezst silk and a seamstress brought all the way from Fors na'Shachim to run them up—nothing works, nothing helps. At last, desperate and practically in tears himself, he shouts, "A year! A whole year, then, before the wedding will take place. Surely there's time enough to grow accustomed to a new life, to a strange place—even to a strange old man. I will give you that year, Tai-sharm, on one condition."

Well, at that Tai-sharm does stop crying, though much less from consolation than curiosity. The King says, "A year's grace, if you will only tell me what makes you believe yourself a stupid woman. Fair bargain?" And he puts a hand out toward her hand, as friends do to seal a pledge.

Tai-sharm does not take it. She does not speak for a long time, but stands there in all her foreign finery, looking now this way, now that, still searching the darkness for—what? Rescue, is it? or wise counsel? A little hope? Whatever they seek, Tai-sharm's eyes return to the King without finding it. They are tired eyes, hers, and older than they were when we saw them first.

"I think too much," she mumbles at last. "So. There *that* is."

"You think too much," the King repeats carefully. Slowly, he takes off his gray crown to scratch his royal head. "Tai-sharm," says he, "this is not a common thing with stupid people."

"Lord," Tai-sharm says, "I am the daughter of a hundred generations of peasants. There wasn't a one of them ever had a day's schooling; there wasn't a single one ever had a thought in his head, save what to put in the ground when. They lived miserably, all of them, and they all knew they were living miserably, but they were some way contented, too, so the children were fed. Only I, Tai-sharm, I seem to be the only one who ever looked up from digging or plowing or clearing a field to think about . . . about fish. About what the gods have for their breakfast. About such stupid things—about songs and lightning, about sailing ships, about whether the sky is the same color on the other side of the world. About air, just *air*, can you imagine it? I was never unhappy, truly, but I have never been content— not as they are, my folk, my family, not like them. Plainly, I am too stupid even to be a peasant, and just as plainly there is nothing else for me to be. You'd do better to wed with a stone or a tree, Your Kingship, for at least they know themselves and ask no questions. Tai-sharm is a waste of time and bathwater."

The King laughs again—a real laugh this time, with no rusty rawness to it—but he shakes his head and slaps the arm of his throne, for all the world as old Sharm would do in her own special chair. "A year," he says firmly. "One year, Tai-sharm, and be assured my Chief Minister himself could not have won so much from me." Perhaps his smile turns painful as he reaches out to tilt Tai-sharm's chin and make her look straight at him? Choushi-wai cannot say if this is so, but she knows that he said then, "Girl, it will not be so bad. A king's word on it. Go now."

The servants returned silently, without any summons from the King, and they took Tai-sharm back to her room, where the Chief Minister was waiting, sitting very straight with his hands gripping each other in his lap. He said to Tai-sharm, "If *he* told you anything that you were not to tell me, you may as well reveal it now. Because I will find out. I always do."

Tai-sharm answered him, "I am to stay for a year, and at the end of the year I am to wed with the King. There is nothing more."

Her voice was so quiet and forlorn that the Chief Minister was a little moved, and he said, like the King, "Well, and is that so ill, then? You are to be a queen after all, Tai-sharm from nowhere, as I foretold. My congratulations, and may they cheer you as you deserve. He is a good man, for a king, as you would know had you met as many as I have. You have much to be thankful for, and so do I. Let us part now and each consider our good fortune."

But he had seen Tai-sharm's glance stray over the high windows, and seen her strong young legs tense and flex without her knowledge, and he gave orders when he left her that no fewer than two of the servants were to be watching her at all times, no mind if she knew or not. For the King, on his part, had already decreed that Tai-sharm was to have the free run of the palace and all its grounds, great and wide as they were, and bounded only by walls built to keep enemies out, but never a bride in. The Chief Minister understood very well who would bear the blame if the girl ran away, as she clearly meant to do. Each time he thought about *that*, he changed his order—three servants now to follow Tai-sharm, then four, five—until it seemed as though every eye in the palace was fixed on her day and night. For the Minister respected Tai-sharm's will a good deal more than she did herself.

Yes, of course she knew—would any of you not notice it

if all shadows held a spy, all mirrors reflected someone besides yourself? But she discovered an odd thing as well, which Choushi-wai will tell you: when everyone is indeed watching what you do, it becomes as though no one at all were watching—as though you were in a way invisible. Tai-sharm, stolen from her home, a prisoner in that huge, hollow palace, went about from the first day like a free woman with no secrets and nothing to escape. She roamed where she chose over the grand lawns and through the rich royal parklands, and few were the inches of the King's private domain that she left unstudied; yet she never approached the outwalls even close enough to study them for handholds. She wheedled no servant to smuggle messages for her—aye, and come to tell it, she was likely the only person about the court who did not ever attempt to bribe the Palace Guard.

Well, didn't *this* alarm the Chief Minister? and didn't he command then that she should be left alone as little as possible, so to have not as much as a waking hour to her private devices? So here's our Tai-sharm suddenly surrounded by more faces and voices than she had known in all her hard, shy life, and these no muddy-tongued peasant farmers but the King's chosen courtiers, well practiced in every sort of elegant beguilement. The women dressed and undressed and clothed her again, like a favorite doll; they did their earnest best to teach her to dance and to paint herself, and to take the country out of her talk. As for the men, they danced and chatted determinedly with her, took her riding and hunting—oh, well guarded, no fear—taught her the new card games, and even flirted a bit with her, if you can call it flirting with one eye ever out for the King. Tai-sharm never knew the difference—what she did know was that she was yet captive, dancing or no.

Now it happened that in her straying Tai-sharm turned her attention one day to a messy quarrel of *targary* hedges on a hillside behind the palace. They were the stubby yellow breed that look ragged even when they've been properly trimmed, which these had not, not for a very long time. Spindly and straggly, thin as rain, they were, every one of them dying. Tai-sharm understood slowly that she was standing in a maze, or what was left of one after years of neglect. Not that she'd ever seen a maze, of course, but she'd heard of them from travelers, though never such a maze as this; for the original outline, as much as she could find one, seemed to be of a fish eating a fish, which had already eaten another fish. Truly, yes, and Tai-sharm thought she saw yet others devouring others. She pushed her way in a little further, snapping off dead *targary* twigs left and right, and it was then that she first heard the singing.

> *"Round and round and up and under—*
> *who will hear my song, I wonder?*
> *This way, that way, high and low—*
> *who comes seeking what I know?"*

It's an odd, slippery tune, if it's a tune at all. Tai-sharm cannot imagine who might be singing, for the voice has neither the deep edge of a man's voice, nor the suppleness of a woman's. There is something altogether not right about it, something lacking or something too extra. If a dead person began to sing, or a child not yet born, it might sound like that.

"Well," says Tai-sharm. "What on earth?" She moves slowly deeper into the maze, and suddenly, right at her feet, she spies—what? a puddle? no, a pool it is, all but stagnant, matted with rotting leaves. It is from this pool that the singing comes.

> *"Child of sunlight, child of rain,*
> *child of dirt and dreams and pain,*
> *captive to a king's design,*
> *hear my call, as I hear thine."*

A sudden swirl in the foul water—a yellowish snout pushing dead *targary* twigs aside—a single round eye in the center of the eddy—it's a fish, her first fish at last! It's a very ugly fish, what Tai-sharm can see of it, being of a splotchy red-and-yellow color, with a tail and ragged fins too small for its thick body. The one visible eye is barely brighter than the water; the other is hidden by the slimy tangle of water weeds that have wrapped themselves like a bard's garlands around the ugly fish. Tai-sharm stands there and gapes.

The fish speaks to her in that strange voice it has. It says, "Child, if you would be so kind."

"Oh," Tai-sharm whispers. "Oh, yes, surely." She drops to her knees and has the fish free in no time. It doesn't flash off and vanish, but lingers between her hands for a moment, letting her feel its cool reality. Then it slips gently away from her, and as it goes it sings again:

> *"Tai-sharm, a fish does not forget,*
> *not a wrong and not a debt.*
> *I am very old and very wise,*
> *and I saw this palace rise.*
> *You are prisoned, as was I—*
> *call, and I will heed your cry."*

"Well, in that case," Tai-sharm says, raising her voice so the fish can hear her, "I'd be most grateful if you could help me escape this place. I must go home, fish, please."

But the ugly fish calls back to her, "It is not yet time." And then it *is* gone, down into the deeps of the little pool and leaves Tai-sharm to wander sadly back to the palace with a silly song wandering in her head. But there, at least she's seen a fish, whatever may come of it. And that night Tai-sharm sleeps as sweetly on the floor of her grand and smothering bedchamber as though she were once again warm against her mother's snoring *rishu*.

Yes, of course she went back to the pool—not the next day, nor the next, not for a week or even ten days. Why be disappointed any sooner than you have to be? But when she chanced to notice a potboy from the King's kitchens trotting down toward the *targary* maze with a fishing-line in his grubby hands, she followed him without even thinking yes or no. And well that she did, for she found the ugly Singing Fish already on his hook and out of the water, flapping and gasping as the potboy yanked it triumphantly high over his head. Tai-sharm was on that boy like a snowhawk on a *starik*, sending him back to the palace much faster than he came, ears boxed, fishing-line wrapped around his neck and his rump smoking behind him. She had the hook out of the Singing Fish's mouth and him safe back in the pool before the potboy's yowling had died away.

"Well," she says, and not quite as shy this time, "that's twice I've done you a service, sir. Do you think you could help *me* now, as you said you might?"

But no, that old thing is off without so much as a thank-you, singing as it goes:

> "Tai-sharm, a fish does not forget,
> not a wrong and not a debt.
> Many's the king sought my advice,
> and I told them once what I tell you twice,
> bide your time and wish your wish—
> be as patient as a fish."

Tai-sharm did not go back to the pool again.

And the King himself, all this while? Tai-sharm most often went all the day without seeing him, busy and solitary as he was; but she had her breakfast with him each morning before dawn (for the King was as early a riser as Old Sharm herself), and she dined with him most nights, unless he was occupied with ministers or foreign ambassadors—he did not dance or hunt—or alone on the roof of the palace, watching the stars. That was his great pleasure, and though he often invited Tai-sharm to share it with him, she refused each time, though she could not have said why, for she also loved the night sky, and she did like the King. You will remember that she had small experience of men, and of those never a one had treated her as thought-fully as he. She was always polite to him, and respectful, and she enjoyed trying out her new manners and courtesies on him, but she kept back her true kindness and she could not say why. The King knew, and she knew he knew, and there *that* was.

Well, and so. When she had been at the court for a bit more than half a year—and yes, much of that time dragged on her like chains, but not all of it, not all—the King asked her one day, "Tai-sharm, how is it with you, then? Is it so terrible for you—this court life, this old man—or does it begin to feel even a bit like home?"

"Never like home," says Tai-sharm, honest as ever. "Not ever." She touches the King's arm very lightly. "But not ter-rible either, not really."

"Ah," says the King, and nothing after that. This is late of a spring afternoon, and he's come upon her walking, not in the grand flower gardens where the Chief Minister brings other kings' ministers to stroll and murmur, but in the kitchen garden near the royal stables. The *ardeet* melons, the little early *jashimus*, and the red *zizo* squashes, they're already three times as big and fragrant as any vegetables Tai-sharm's ever seen back home. Hand-polished, they look; not a speck of dust on any of them. She says at last, "It would be nice if you were younger, and not a king."

The King laughs that sudden bitter bark of his. "If that were so, you wouldn't glance at me twice. Nor would you have to, being a free woman in the muddy streets of your village, and not a captive promenading my gardens." He takes hold of her arm now, tucks it firmly through his own as they move on. There's a slight limp he has: you'd likely never have noticed it, but Tai-sharm can feel the tiny tug with each step. He's not wearing his crown.

"Look at this, taste this," he'll say to her, lifting a leaf to point out an almost-ripe *dolmiri*, or pushing a handful of sweet climbing ice-berries against her lips. Almost, he might be a common high-country farmer like herself, except that none of her folk would ever show off their tired, sun-wizened crops in that way. Now he stops again, turns swiftly to take her by the shoulders. His face is like old stone, the same as always, and his hands the same, but his eyes . . . oh, Choushi-wai tells you that if eyes could tremble, those would be the ones.

"Tai-sharm, Tai-sharm," he says, "why delay longer? You'll not change, neither will I, and neither will the snare that has us both by the leg. What help or harm is there if we wed now that will be any different in six months' time? Let us be done with what must be done—today, even." And he tightens his hands on her, not knowing.

Tai-sharm never flinches, never even feels the hurt. She shakes her head over and over without taking her eyes from him, until the King cries out, "Why not, you stubborn peasant, why not? What can you be waiting for?" He lets go of her shoulders, so suddenly that she stumbles forward, and he walks away fast, stumbling himself once on a ridgy row of the *jashimus*. He does not look back. Kings never do.

Yes, yes, any of us would surely recognize that a king was in love with us, who here doubts it? But for Tai-sharm love was a stranger place even than Baraquil, and besides she had other matters on her mind. Because she was indeed waiting—the King was quite right about that much. She was waiting for Sharm.

Never think that because old Sharm was an unlettered countrywoman, she was the sort to let her only child be stolen and nothing done about it. A bit short of teeth she may have been; short of wit and resource, never. Once having tracked the Chief Minister's horses beyond the village, she nodded grimly to herself and returned home to pack a wallet with some dried meat and ask a neighbor to see to her field and her *rishu* for a few days. Then she set forth on foot for the town of Fulicha.

No, Choushi-wai said this was all long before the mountains fell. There's no Fulicha at all now, nor has there been a Fulicha for years beyond our counting. But then there was, and it was as sleepy-seeming a place as anyone ever saw, and not a law-abiding soul to be found from one end to the other, if you searched for days. Not bandits, as in Cheth na'Deka—smugglers they were, most of them, moving this and that back and forth across here and there without paying a solitary coin in fees or taxes. And there were false-moneyers, certainly, and no lack of cutpurses, and it might be the odd high-toby or two, if you insist. The headman himself in those days was a highly respected poison-monger, and the best inn by far was run by a retired fire-raiser. A remarkable place altogether, Fulicha.

But what old Sharm was looking for was a thief.

Not just any thief neither, but one so well-regarded in his trade as to be called by no name but "the Thief," as though there were never another. Sharm knew only that he lived in Fulicha, when he lived anywhere; but she was as patient as her life could make her, and a good asker of questions, and by dawn on her fifth day out, she was squatting by the door of a hut no larger than her own, waiting silently for it to open in its good time.

By and by comes a dark, slight man to stand on the stone threshold, yawning in the sunlight. Bright, bright eyes, silver-gray in color, and the prettiest hands old Sharm's ever seen on a man. Almost too long for his slender wrists they look, and graceful as clouds as he opens and closes them.

Listen now to Sharm's bones crackling like a forest fire as she rises stiffly to her feet and asks straight out, "Are you the Thief?" The dark man never turns his head.

"In the words of that immortal poet, Dhaj'mul," he asks the sunrise, "who wants to know?"

"I'm Sharm," says she, "and a king has stolen my daughter away, and I need you to get her back for me." The Thief shows no surprise, but now Sharm can feel the south-west corner of his left eye taking her in.

"And if I do this, you will naturally give me any amount of money, and your girl's hand into the bargain?" He has a soft voice, with a pleasing lowland accent in it. She cackles at the notion, and her dry old laughter makes the Thief look straight at her, smiling just a bit himself. Sharm says, "Boy, one look at me and you knew I'd nothing but starving fleas to offer you, and yet you haven't slammed your door in my face. Something I've said pleases you—what can it be, do you suppose?" She approaches the Thief, grinning her shameless stumpy grin, her head canted *so* to one side.

"Ah," says the Thief, "I was just thinking—I don't believe anyone has ever hired me to steal from a king before."

"Nay, I'm not hiring you," Sharm protests quickly. "I'm asking you. It's not the same thing."

"No? A pity." The Thief is studying her entirely now, and his eyes are so quick and friendly and amused that Sharm realizes she can't read them the least bit. She says, "But there's more to steal in a palace than just my daughter, surely. And she is very pretty, and well brought-up, too."

The Thief regards her a few moments longer, saying nothing. Then, quick as a fly goes down a frog, he pops back into his house, returning just as swiftly with a platter of black bread and spiced cheese for them to share. They sit companionably on the Thief's doorstep, feeling the sun warming as it climbs, watching the sly folk who've been out all night doing the gods know what come sidling home. And presently, the Thief asks old Sharm, "Which king is this, by the way?"

"Now how should I be bothered remembering such things?" she retorts. "The one who rules in Baraquil it is, whatever he calls himself." She recites it all for him—the Chief Minister's visit, the tale of the King's wish for an intelligent bride, Tai-sharm's tearful flight from the kitchen, and lastly her vanishment out of the barn in the night. The Thief listens and nods and munches his bread and cheese, and says not a word until Sharm is done.

"So," he says then. "It won't be easy; it may well cost me my head, and you have nothing to pay me with. Have I left anything out?"

"Not a thing," Sharm answers him mournfully. "Except about her being pretty. You wouldn't have a little ale to go with this?"

"No, I wouldn't," says the Thief. "I don't usually steal

people, you know. It's mostly *things*—money, jewels, horses, secret papers—I even stole a whole treasure ship once, right out of the harbor at Leishai. Now if your girl had been robbed of something valuable, something rare, I could probably get that back for her."

"Her freedom?" old Sharm suggests. The Thief sighs. He rises and looks down at her gray head, his thumbs hooked into his belt. Choushi-wai thinks that his eyes are probably a little more reflective, his face maybe a bit more stern. But maybe not.

Says he finally, "You wicked, artful woman. You gamble that I was as well brought-up as your miserable daughter, and leave me precious little choice in the matter. Oh, I tell you, old woman, that child had better be at least as pretty as you." And he ruffles Sharm's matted hair and stalks back into his house. Sharm slaps her hands together once, grins at a couple of passing graverobbers, and trots after him.

Well, and so. It took the Thief some while to find Tai-sharm. Not that he didn't know where she was, or how to get there, but it was not in him to journey anywhere by the straight road. By the time he'd amassed all the lore of Baraquil that he thought might come in useful, and by the time he had angled out of Fulicha one misty dawn and then circled and doubled and tripled on his tracks to shake off those envious followers who always sought to hunt where he hunted—well, what with one thing and another, it took some little while, that's all. But then the Thief never was in a hurry.

Indeed, even when he loped into Baraquil aboard a shaggy, scabby mountain pony so small that children laughed to see his heels almost scraping the ground, he did no more than stable his beast at a respectable inn and spend the afternoon wandering aimlessly in the town. Oh, he might have drunk a bit of the local *yaru* in one or two of the lesser taprooms, and perhaps he bought a few gifts for relatives he said he had in Bitava, and he did ask a few questions in a flat Fors na'Shachim sort of voice. And when he was told of their King's coming wedding, and of the young foreign princess said to be even now hidden away up at the palace—*there, man! see it? that glitter just beyond the hill?*—he only nodded, feigning interest out of courtesy. Folk lost interest in *him* soon enough. They always did.

Come twilight, he sauntered through the streets, nodding to this one and that one, plain as you please, and so went whistling up toward the first outwall, which ran along a bare ridge above the town slaughterhouse. And that evening, and each evening or earliest dawn thereafter for the next fortnight, he passed pleasantly in compassing the palace right round, meaning forest and park, meadow and mere and pastureland, stony hillock and sudden splut- tering waterfall. Where the walls went, there went the Thief, never hurrying; and though there were sentinels everywhere sentinels should have been, he did not bother to be seen. And at the end of that time, he knew as much about the glittering palace beyond as anyone ever could have learned from the far side of those walls.

Which was the near side of nothing, and sourly well the Thief knew it. Close as the walls came to the palace in a few places, he'd not had more than one or two glimpses of the woman he was supposed to be stealing for her mother, and each time she was in company with a big gray man, and seemed perfectly content so. Never a chance for him to catch her attention, not once, nor any means of getting a message to her. There was plainly going to be nothing for it but finding a way into the palace.

Now you are to understand that the Thief was not a brave man. "When one does what I do," he often told his odd ragbag of friends, "courage is your worst enemy. Wit's what's needed if you're going to steal—wit and more wit, and a decent pair of hands. As for daring"—and here he'd shrug crookedly—"daring is well enough, in its place. Which is afterward, when you're telling the story." Among those like old Sharm who took an interest in such things, his thefts were legendary, but it was his cowardice that he paraded like a great golden prize. Choushi-wai tells you this so that you will see how seriously annoyed he was to find himself scrambling over the palace wall.

He chose the hour before sunrise for his visit, and for a starting place a windwillow grove on a hillside above the palace. The climb itself was uneventful: no smallest harroo from a guard, no harm done to his best working clothes. The Thief dropped to the dew-soft ground like a falling leaf, rolled into the shelter of the trees—for there were guards prowling within the walls as well as without—and came up staring into the sweet idiot eyes of a great blue *jalduk*, of all things. Yes, *we* know them as greedy, garden-ravaging nuisances, but the King made pets of them and let them roam freely about the palace grounds. The Thief shooed this one way, and moved very cautiously down the hill.

That day he remained a little time, no more, never coming even within the shadow of the palace. He saw Tai-sharm not at all, neither did he learn anything to aid him in coming to her. One curiosity only: as he began the climb a second time, it seemed to him that he heard someone singing not far away. For a moment he thought it might be her, but the voice was not a woman's voice—no, nor exactly a man's either, come to that. The Thief hesitated, poised on the outwall, trying hard to grasp the words. But the singing ended as suddenly as it had begun, and the Thief finally shrugged and slipped back to safety, unseen, untaken, and no whit the wiser for his early rising. And if he drank too much that night, being vexed, yet he was back slipping over the wall before daybreak the very next foreday, ringing head or no. He was as patient in his way as old Sharm, that Thief.

Very well, this time he hears the singing while he's still climbing, clear and close as his own heartbeat, for all that he's lighted down in a completely different place from yesterday's dawn. Here the slope's almost bare of trees, far too exposed to any sharp eyes looking out from the palace. The Thief spies the *targary* hedge and makes for it, caring nothing for its shape or nature. He's interested in nothing but a bit of swift shelter, and in the singing, so near now. But we know that song already:

> *"Round and round and up and under—*
> *who will hear my song, I wonder?*
> *This way, that way, high and low—*
> *who comes seeking what I know?"*

"My," says the Thief very softly. He eases forward, not even considering calling out. The song goes on:

> *"Mazes are for lovers' pleasure—*
> *who comes seeking loves but treasure.*
> *Who comes seeking loves not me—*
> *who can this aging scoundrel be?"*

"Well," says the Thief, "well," and he strides indignantly forward into the depths of the ruined maze, head whipping left and right to find out who it is rhymes on him so mockingly. But there's naught to be seen—only more half-dead *targary* hedges, brittle as breadcrust. This way, that way he blunders, till he's as bewildered as a maze could wish, and still not a mortal body to house that annoying singing. And there's the sun already, and the voices he hears now are the new shift of sentinels as they bawl their all's-wells along to each other. Nothing for the Thief to do but crawl toward the yelling, find the outwall once more, and be wearily gone from there with his shirt stuck all full of crumbly yellow *targary* leaves and his head full of jingly riddles. He'll sleep all that day, and wake in darkness, swearing furiously to be bound for home by moonset. And by moonset, there he'll be again, over the King's outwall once more in search of Sharm's daughter. Because he is the Thief. That's his name.

No singing, nothing but shuffling iron feet and birds mumbling that it isn't time to get up yet. The Thief is taking a risk born of plain irritation, moving in soundlessly so close to the palace that he can see flickering lights in the great kitchens, and the shadows of the cooks already preparing the morning meal. He can hear all manner of snoring behind the tall, narrow windows; and he can even see, when he stands very still, movement on the palace roof, dark against darkness, where the King spies on the stars, though the Thief can't know this. What he does know is that he cannot see anything that might mean Tai-sharm: the only feminine movement in the night is the sleepy ripple of a *deshi* tree's branch against a high balcony. Still no song. The Thief sighs deeply, squeezes his chin hard in one hand. "Wicked old woman," he mutters once again to Sharm far away, "I hate this. I hate you, too."

And with that he's up the *deshi* tree as though it had rungs, and pattering along that branch toward the balcony railing, not knowing whether he'll be spied from the ground, find himself facing a barred and bolted window, or just fall out of the tree. But thieves' luck is at his back: the window is locked, but not seriously, and he is inside before the branch has stopped swaying. He blinks around him in furry darkness, knowing immediately that this room is empty, because the Thief has to know things like that. Carefully, he finds his way to the door and peers out into dwindling torchlight. Many other doors, but no guards, nor any sound but the occasional serene snore. Tai-sharm's, one of them? Only one way to learn.

Along corridor after corridor the Thief sidles, keeping to doorways and alcoves, turning to ice at every noise, trying each door so graciously that it never knows it's being opened, no more than any sleeper stirs. What a lot of them there are, too: not merely the usual mix of young courtiers and older ministers, but running to pairs—mostly married, by the look of them. Single or coupled, none of the women fits old Sharm's picture of her daughter. The Thief glides on.

Twice a brace of guards comes tramping toward him, but both times they look straight at the Thief and never see him—perhaps because ice is transparent, do you suppose? The second pair are grumbling loudly about standing double watches on little sleep because of tomorrow—*today*, thinks the Thief—being the King's wedding day. Ah, well, one thing, there'll be ale and *yaru* enough to go around for once. A fine king, their master, wouldn't hear a word against him, but he doesn't drink enough, and he thinks everyone else drinks too much. And so on and so on, their voices carrying clearly well after they've turned the corner, and too frigging bad whom they rouse. If the King sleeps at all tonight, he's not the man they take him for.

"The wedding day," says the Thief quietly to the cold, sleek walls. "Nobody tells me anything."

But he knows that this is not true. He's heard the talk in the town—he's even overheard the sentinels at the wall joking coarsely about the King's coming marriage. But he's the Thief, you see, *the Thief*, and even time knows what that means. Time slows down just for the Thief, it always has. There are always stray minutes, hours, even an extra day now and then, lying tidy to hand for when he really needs them. Now time and careless vanity together have undone him; if he fails to bring Tai-sharm home to her mother, it will be as much his fault as the King's or the Chief Minister's. What the Thief says aloud to himself in that passage Choushi-wai cannot tell you, but if it went unheard, that was only by grace of so many pillows being pulled up over so many ears after the guards had passed.

But finally he shrugs and even smiles a little, and says, "Well, what's a fool to do but push on with his folly? I will yet find old Sharm's girl, and if I am caught, that will serve me no more than my due." And on he marches, stamping right down the middle of the corridor now, like a bloody hero come to call on a palace full of wedding guests, instead of easing along the wall in a proper professional manner. Choushi-wai can tell you that never in his long life did the Thief quite forgive himself for carrying on so. "I steal things," he used to say irritably, "I don't bring them back. There's a difference, and I knew it as well then as I do now. Disgraceful, the whole business."

And fortunate he is to turn a corner and see six men-at-arms—not mere guards, but real soldiers of the King—pacing sentry-go before one door that looked no different from any other. Fortunate, I say, because his madness departs from him on the instant, and he flattens himself against the first shadow handy, not even thinking, for fear of the noise. By accident and arrogance, if you like, the Thief has found Tai-sharm at last.

Now the Thief has never carried a weapon in his life, not so much as a poacher's *jiyak*, not even a little boot-knife. If Tai-sharm's depending on him to spring out upon her jailers and cut them down single-handed, she will be Sharm's age by the time the last man-at-arms dies in bed. The Thief is himself again, snug at home in darkness, coolly considering half a dozen diversions that might leave Tai-sharm's door unguarded for the half-minute he needs. There's screaming, of course—gibbering, wailing, moaning like the spirits of the foully slain that haunt every castle everywhere, never mind the kingdom or the time—and then there's doing voices, the ones that come softly from every corner of the air, mocking and haunting any man who ever dreamed what he shouldn't. The Thief is good at voices.

But there's no need for him to trot them out this night, as it befalls. The door opens a wee way and out slips a small old woman, shutting it again quickly on the candlelight behind her. How can we be so sure of her age, muffled as she is in the tentish *sals'yaan* that marks nurse, witch, and midwife alike in this land? Well, the stoop, for one thing, and the puppety gait that comes with it and, of course, all the white hair crowding the edges of the kirtle's hood. There are orangey-brown spots on the backs of her hands, and her eyes are streaked and rheumy.

"Overexcited, the child was," she snickers shrilly to the men-at-arms. "*Ai,* even a hag like me can remember such eagerness. I've given her one of my special possets, she'll sleep soundly till the time. Now if you handsome gentlemen will excuse me."

The men part to let her by. They do seem a bit startled at

her sudden appearance, but not suspicious. The old woman stumps through, grinning and mumbling, and so away down the hall and around the corner. Where a hand promptly covers her mouth, while the long arm it belongs to scoops her neatly into an alcove, and a soft voice tickles her ear. "Well met at last, Sharm's daughter. Your mother sends her greetings."

With which the Thief releases his hold. The old woman whirls to face him, the hood falling back around her shoulders. "Who are you? How do you know my mother?" She has forgotten to cackle, but she still keeps the sense to whisper her demands. "How do you know *me*?"

The Thief holds her at arm's-length, thoughtfully studying her. "Oh, the hair is very good," he says, almost to himself. "The hands, well, that would be plain *rishu*-tallow, thinned with red ale—good enough in this light, at this hour. And the eyes, that's cloudflower sap; use it myself. Stings mightily, doesn't it?" The woman glares red-eyed up at him without replying. "Plenty of cloudflowers on these fine grounds, anywhere you look," the Thief muses along. "But the hair, the hair—how *did* you manage that? I've tried *chena*-leaf stain, such as players employ, I've used vile messes out of backrooms all thieves know—aye, and I have even attempted my own concoction, mixing powdered bone with different ashes, and just a bit of egg white for the binding. But yours, your hair—no, I never could have come near to such disguising. Tell me, girl, I implore you—"

"I must find my friend," says Tai-sharm. She ducks under his arm and she's off down the corridor—no flat-footed hobble, but the stride of a country girl with some beast in bawling trouble. The Thief follows at his best pace, well content to let her take the lead. Listen—the palace is definitely astir now. The torches in the halls are spluttering out, though the shadows they leave behind are yet more black than gray, and there's no cockcrow to be heard. But the Thief hears voices behind many a door; he hears drowsy laughter, cursing, groaning, and the familiar music of more than one man vomiting into his chamberpot. What he hears as well is the shivering chime of silver dishes on silver trays—the help are already about their chores, bringing breakfast to this room, doubtless wedding clothes to that one. Nowhere to turn, no doubling back; at any moment Tai-sharm and he are bound to be seen and seized, and whatever becomes of her, the Thief has no illusions about his own fate. "Slowly!" he hisses after her. "Scamper like that and we are lost—walk, *walk*, as though you had some proper business about this bloody place. Idiot, *walk*!"

Tai-sharm pays him no heed, but speeds on ahead, whisking into a side passage at the first sound of approaching footsteps, racing through a vast empty ballroom where their own steps chatter evilly back at them, dodging easily down the half-hidden servants' tunnel that the Thief had overlooked. That brings them straight into the kitchens, where Tai-sharm does slow her pace, instantly becoming the old witch-woman again, eyes on her shuffling feet, expression about halfway between amiable and senile. The Thief, for his part, takes her elbow, bending solicitously over her, and so through the busy, rackety kitchen, no one with a moment free even to glance at them, save for a young pastry apprentice who humbly begs a blessing on his little cakes. He gets it, and another for his pretty eyes as well. Tai-sharm is enjoying herself altogether too much.

"Out of here, Sharm's daughter," snarls the Thief sweetly in her ear. "Out of here before I start to scream. You don't want me to scream, truly."

Tai-sharm glances quickly back at him, and a smile darts across the face of the old woman like a falling star. She cackles, "Bide, little one, all will be well," and then, lower, in her own voice, "Did my mother really send *you* to find me? What can she have been thinking?"

"Rescue," is the Thief's dry answer. "Imagine it, she came a long journey to ask if I would kindly rescue you." But he says it to Tai-sharm's back: she's tottering on unnoticed, crooning mindlessly to herself as ancients will. The Thief sidesteps a pair of sweating spit-turners, dances backward like a mad *zuli-gaji* priest to keep from being trampled by a huge cook with a steaming tureen balanced on each shoulder, and only catches up with Tai-sharm on the far side of the kitchen, as she disappears through a smoke-blackened door. There's a stair, so steep and narrow it might as well be a ladder. Tai-sharm is already a glimmer in the cold murk high above him. The Thief swarms up after her.

The end of the stairway is a tiny cloakroom, hardly more than a cupboard, where the royal cooks and bakers leave their good clothes and put on their aprons. Beyond is one more corridor, this one wider than the road to Tai-sharm's village—and beyond that, at last, the great postern doors of the palace. Closed and bolted and barred, they are, and no chance at all of Tai-sharm and the Thief possibly getting them open in the bit of time they have. The Thief, who can hear a watchman picking his teeth two houses away, can already hear the hunt nearing the kitchen. He is neither trembling nor sweating, but his lips are very cold.

Tai-sharm never hesitates: she flies straight to the farthest, lowest left-hand panel of the left-hand door and fumbles swiftly, knowingly over it, prodding this carving, twisting that projection, pushing hard on that odd little bump. But nothing happens. She tries it all again, turns her head to look at the Thief, crying, "It opens, it *opens*, there is a way, I saw a soldier do it once. Every night I copied what he did, on the wall, so my fingers would not forget. Now I cannot, I cannot—"

The Thief nudges her aside, and not as gently as he might, either. Without a word, he crouches before the panel, whistling softly through his teeth, head turned away, those long fingers splaying and scattering over the harsh woodwork. The pursuit has reached the foot of the stair—Tai-sharm can even make out the Chief Minister's desperate baying as she turns from side to side, frightened now for the first time. The Thief grunts once, down deep, and

Tai-sharm hears the panel pop open and there's the silver morning sunlight and the bright lawns. She is through the gap like a *shukri* down a hole, and the Thief is right behind her.

"That way!" he barks, pointing into the sun. "The wall is closest there!" But no, Tai-sharm veers away downslope toward that ruinous old *targary* maze, which is no place at all to go to ground. The Thief thinks she has gone mad with fear. He runs as hard as he can, shouting that there's no hope, the hedges aren't tall enough to hide even a small person like her from those who follow. Like the queen she refuses to be, Tai-sharm never looks back.

And since we speak of royalty, here's a cry from the palace roof, and the Thief wheels to see the King, surely the King, dark against the pale new sky, leaning over a parapet and pointing after Tai-sharm. The Thief can catch only two words, of all those the King is bellowing—" . . . the fish . . . the *fish*!" The men-at-arms are crowding through the little door now, too many at once, stumbling into each other, clowns in chain mail—but they see him! The Thief turns again and sprints hopelessly for the maze.

He cannot see Tai-sharm for a moment, nor anything else, for the maze still holds a bit of last night at its parched heart. Then there she is, kneeling by a tiny leaf-choked pool, her face almost touching the water, her lips moving. The Thief pays no mind to whatever she is saying—what he hears is that voice again, that not-man, not-woman voice singing that same not-quite-tune:

> "Deeper down than you may dream,
> down where morning sends no gleam,
> where sun and shadow never fall,
> yet I answer when you call. . . ."

A sluggish eddy—the heavy slap of a tail—and it *is* a fish, after all, and ugly as you like, to boot. The Singing Fish says to Tai-sharm, "Child, what will you have of me?"

And our Tai-sharm answers, calm as though they were alone and the King's men-at-arms weren't tramping and roaring just outside the maze, "Once I besought you to help me escape from this place. You said it was not yet time."

"So I did," agrees the Singing Fish, and the Thief shakes Tai-sharm's shoulder, growling, "Girl, get in the water— we'll break off reeds and breathe through them." Tai-sharm pays no more heed to him than she does to the racket of the King's men, almost as near as he.

"And in a while I asked your help again," says Tai-sharm, "and again you told me that the time was not right."

"So you did, and so I did," the Singing Fish replies. The Thief himself is speechless. He can see two or three helmeted heads above the dried-up *targary* hedges, and he wishes for the first time that he carried at least a little knife with him, if only to cut his own throat. Beside him, Tai-sharm goes on talking to the ugly fish, asking most politely, "I thought, perhaps now would be the right time, do you suppose?"

"I think so myself," says the Singing Fish.

And with those words, everything changes. Tai-sharm flashes out of the Thief's sight—there one minute, *swoosh* the next, as though some fisherman in another world had hooked her right away from him. Then—without any splash, mind you, without any sound—he's head-down in the mucky pool and not feeling it mucky at all, nor even wet. And he isn't drowning, strangling on water: no, no, *no*, believe Choushi-wai, she says that he feels himself truly flying, soaring into light as though he were a bird, and not a little fish of some kind, as he already knows he is. He can just see a bit of his own tail, pale-green as the newest spring grass, if he angles his eye and body rightly. Beside him, below him, another fish, the color of the sea in sunlight, nudges impudently at his flank, and he realizes that this is Tai-sharm.

There are voices now, a lot of them, but so far away. The Thief can't make the sounds into words, but he can feel them, a sort of muffled jarring inside himself, dreamily alarming. Then he does hear real words, in his mind he hears them, the calm voice of Tai-sharm's ugly fish friend, saying, "Dive down, dive down. The King is here."

Even in this new shape, the Thief's first, best trick is to hide. The fish-body obeys him, no thought, wonderfully quick, slanting straight down toward depths much darker than he ever imagined that dirty washtub of a pool could hold. But when he casts an eye back for Tai-sharm—think what it would be like to have your eyes on the *sides* of your head, hey?—she's not following, not to be seen at all. The Thief swears fishily and turns again.

She is trembling just below the surface, staring up as well as she can at the faces gaping back down through the dead leaves. Most of them are topped by steel or leather, but one only by a shock of stone-gray hair, and the Thief understands that this is the King at last. The King's eyes are as deep as the pool with loss as they meet the eyes of the small sea-colored fish. He puts his hand out slowly, as though to grab at her—and likely he could catch her, too, for plainly Tai-sharm cannot move. But the King draws his hand back and goes on looking at her.

"Tai-sharm," says the Thief, hearing his own voice bubble in his head. "Tai-sharm, your mother is waiting."

At that Tai-sharm spins right round and is out of sight with one flick of her tail. The Thief himself is drawn to take a last look at the King who had thought to wed her that very morning. The King's face shows no sorrow now, and the Thief cannot see his eyes at all. But he cannot turn away from the water. Again the Thief hears the voice of the Singing Fish. "Down. Dive down."

The Thief dives then, once more chasing the tiny glint of Tai-sharm. No bottom to this pool? No end to its darkness? He's not been a fish very long, and everything in him wants to swim back up toward light and sky and floating *targary* twigs. But behind him he can feel the Singing Fish, driving them both on, deeper still, deeper and farther. And even here, even here, that song.

"Fishes for a little while,
let a fish's realm beguile.
Strangers from a world afar—
oh, taste and savor what you are."

And sure enough, the Thief finds that yes, he's beginning to enjoy his new fishness. He moves in the water as none of us will ever move in air, they flow through each other, no border where he ends and it begins. Quick and alert he's always had to be, but this little green body does what he wants before he knows that's what he wants, and by the time he *does* know, it's already on to the next thing a fish's body has to be doing. Gills to sift air from water, funny barbel whiskers to tell him what's good to eat and what's nearby wanting to eat him, fins on his sides and back and below to shape his flight just so, tail so small, so powerful— indeed, how fine to be a fish! The Thief laughs for pure joy, and he feels Tai-sharm laughing, too, somewhere far ahead.

The barbels and the taste of the water—not tongue-taste, mind, more like a tingle in his gills—tell the Thief that they've actually left the pool and are racing along some sort of tunnel, some outlet draining into . . . into what? He cannot see the walls close around him, but his new skin says they are of stone and clay, and there are tree roots thrusting out from both sides, clutching at the water, at him. Ahead, Tai-sharm, small and shining; behind, that endless riddling song:

"Peasant child and sly lightfingers,
even fishes may be singers.
Weeds and beetles, worms and kings—
all that breathes and hungers sings."

How long they hurtle so, the Thief will never know— fishes don't bother about such things—but presently the taste-tingle is different, and the weight of the water tells his skin that they are again in a pool. This one is quiet, clear, shallow. Tai-sharm and the Thief rest gratefully here, turning to face the Singing Fish. It looms above them: small for a fish, perhaps, but huge to smaller ones, and ugly even to another fish, with its piss-yellow jowls and saggy red-slubbered body. It says, "You are safe here, for the moment. We are beyond the walls."

"Thank you," answers the Thief when he has caught his breath. "Now, if you will kindly return us to our proper forms, I will return to the inn, fetch my horse, and take this young person straightway home to her mother."

"I think perhaps not," says the Singing Fish. "The King's men-at-arms will be all over Baraquil tonight like ants on a dead fly. Canny as you are, good thief, you'd not get a mile out of town, not as a mounted man escorting a young girl. Now as a man on foot carrying a basket containing two fish, you might have some small chance."

"Two fish," the Thief says, quite carefully. "*Two* fish."

The Singing Fish chuckles, or whatever fish do; all Choushi-wai knows is that the Thief and Tai-sharm feel the jar of it in the marrow of their bones. The Singing Fish says, "And why not? Am I not also entitled to be taken where I would be? Before ever you return the King's intended to old Sharm—and there's a woman for you!—you will carry me to the sea and release me there. This is my fee for aiding you in your time of need."

Fish or no, the Thief is the Thief. He says, "Wait, wait just a bloody minute here. In the first place, Tai-sharm has twice saved your life, so she owes you nothing, as well you know. In the second place, you wouldn't last a day in the salt sea. What are you playing at, tell me now?" Fish or no, the Thief is very tired.

"I wish only to see the ocean," answers the Singing Fish. "To be the least part of the ocean's imagining, as I have for so long imagined it. Whether I survive a day or a minute there is my own affair and none of yours. If you hope ever to return to your homes, you will do as I tell you."

The Thief has a word or two to say to that, but Tai-sharm

is in before him. Pushing swiftly past him, she swims close to the Singing Fish to reply, "We will that, sir, and glad of the chance. Pay no heed to this one here—he was my mother's idea, and she's quite old."

Well, and so. There *that* was. The Thief protested mightily against abandoning his mountain pony, and much good it did him. Had you or you or Choushi-wai been strolling Baraquil, come that evening, we might have seen a small dark man wandering absently down a narrow alley which turns quietly into a back road in a while. In one hand he'd have been carrying the sort of square, tight-woven basket that the fisherfolk make to keep their catch fresh on the long way to market. In the other would have swung a smaller one, full of soft buzzing, scratching, and scuffling. Fish need to eat, and the Singing Fish was extremely particular.

So the Thief walked all the way from Baraquil to the sea with those two baskets in his clever hands. Some say that he invented a new curse on fishes with every step, but that is not true. He was already running short on the fourth day.

Just as the Singing Fish had warned, the King's men were seeking everywhere for Tai-sharm, and he was halted again and again by different companies and searched at sword-point each time. When they asked him what he was doing carrying two live fish *away* from market, he gaped as foolishly as he could and answered that he was taking them home with him to make lots of little ones, so he wouldn't have to stand all day in the cold water throwing a net over and over. Each time the soldiers looked at each other, laughed, cuffed his head for luck, and rode away. And the Thief walked on.

At night, curled in damp hollows or shallow caves, he had no choice but to hear the faraway voices of Tai-sharm and the Singing Fish talking together in the basket. The Singing Fish told tales of kings and princesses sporting in the maze when it was new, and of the time before there was any maze or any palace at all, but only him in his pool, wise and cold and alone, dreaming of the open sea. But Tai-sharm would speak of her village and her mother, their stony, stingy fields and their one old *rishu*, who worked just as hard as they did for a mouthful of dry grass and another of grain. And the Thief, weary as he was, lay awake and listened.

Once he heard Tai-sharm ask the Singing Fish, "But can even you tell me why I was made so? My head full of fancies and wonderings that never yet thatched a roof nor put a crop in the ground—what is such a stupid head doing on a peasant body in a no-name village? I think I belong nowhere, except in this basket with you. I think I should just be a fish."

The Singing Fish gave her no answer for such a while that the Thief almost fell asleep waiting. Then he heard it say, "And what sort of a fish is it chooses to give up its life for nothing but to leap and play an hour among the great waves? To see the krakens and the green seadrakes for even a moment before they eat me? What is that but absolute stupidity? Down where I swim *stupid* is only a word, like *madness* or *love*." And there, in the Thief's basket, it began to sing once more:

> *"Old I am, and far I see,*
> *and much there is to learn from me.*
> *But how we are to live and die—*
> *child, you are as wise as I."*

A week or so later, and there's the sea—no great port, mind, nor even a fishing village, nothing but an empty place where the land stops. Tide past the turn, but hardly a ripple breaking; no boats to be seen except for a sail or two, so far out only their pale topsails show against a paler sky. A bit of a stony slope for the Thief to scramble down, basket held over his head and sloshing fishy water on him to boot. He crouches on the shingle, opens the basket and says, "Well, here we are."

"I thank you," says the Singing Fish, most courteously. "Now you have only to take me up in your hands and put me in the sea. Your task is done."

Yet the Thief hesitates, asking, "Sir, are you sure of this?"

And in the basket Tai-sharm cries, "No, he isn't! Don't do it!" Her thrashing tail and fins slop more water in the Thief's face.

"Be still," the Singing Fish tells her. "This is my desire. Take me up, good thief—and you, Tai-sharm, my friend, I bid you, be as you were. Assume your proper form again."

"I will not," says Tai-sharm, and for this one time she sounds like the child she is. "I will not, I will stay a fish and swim out to sea with you. That is *my* desire."

The Singing Fish barely glances at her as the Thief gingerly cups his hands around it, lifts it into the air and hurries to set it down in the shallows. But when the Thief turns his head, there's Tai-sharm as ever, looking silly with both feet in a fish basket. She says nothing to him, but comes quickly to crouch beside him, staring down at the ugly red-and-yellow fish tasting the sea for the first time.

"Interesting," it says at last. "A little tart, a little tinglish, but very interesting." The waves are beginning to come in now: let us try to imagine then, we who have never seen a wave or a sail, or a cloud-colored *kulishai* drifting alone above a bustling, stinking harbor. Long, low, silky rollers, these must be, just a dainty flurry of white along their crests and a sort of marbly veining where they curl. They make even the shallow water stir, and the Singing Fish has to back and fill with his side fins to hold itself steady.

"Farewell," it says. "Farewell, good thief who kept his word. Farewell, Tai-sharm—remember my song when you forget kings and palaces and handsome courtiers, and even that you were a fish with me. Remember my song." Half a wriggle of its body, a push with its ragged tail, and it's off with the next wave, gone from sight like *that*, and only a last tuneless rhyme floating back to them, faint as the *kulishai*'s hungry cry:

> "Thief, beware of what you seize—
> it may yet bring you to your knees.
> Tai-sharm, rejoice that you possess
> such a precious foolishness.

    Strangers from a world afar,
    oh, taste and savor what you are."

Tai-sharm strains her eyes for a glimpse of it, slipping through the waves as surely as though it had been born to them, leaping over them as it dreamed of leaping, dancing out to sea. She stares after it for so long that the Thief finally says beside her, "It is gone, Tai-sharm."

"No," she answers him, fiercer than ever she answered the King, or the Minister, or her mother. "No, I can still see him!" And she watches a long time more, until they have to move back and back from the hissing, bellowing high tide, and there's nothing to see but water and stone. The Thief turns away, shaking sand out of his boots.

"Come," he says. "You'll need a deal of practice in having feet again before you put them under your mother's table. And you won't get the same satisfaction out of eating bugs—we'll have to find a farm or an inn by nightfall, or sleep hungry. Come."

He's just setting the fish basket afloat, as seems proper somehow, when Tai-sharm snatches it up to keep always. "I was happy there," she says quietly to no one. "It was quite nice being a fish, even in a basket."

"Yes, I know," says the Thief. He puts his arm around her shoulders. "Besides, think of the children's faces when they hear how their father carried their mother in a fish basket to save her from being made a queen. Let's hurry—I can hardly wait to tell them."

Tai-sharm does not push his arm away, but she looks at him for a long moment before she begins to smile. "I liked the Singing Fish better," she murmurs, and our Tai-sharm has never murmured in her life.

The Thief smiles back. "Well, of course you would. Being a fish yourself at the time. We'll speak of such things as we go. Besides, we can name one of the girls for it. Or the boy, as you choose. Leave it to your mother, that's what I say."

It grows late, and the shadows lengthen—can you see them walking away together, the one dark head not much higher than the other? Can you hear their voices, if you close your eyes and make no sound? Tai-sharm is asking, "But one day they will find they might have been princes and princesses, instead of the children of a thief and a peasant. What will you tell them then?"

Listen, listen, don't breathe, you can hear the Thief's laughter, soft as it is. "Why, I'll say to them, *at least you all have a proper trade. How many royal brats can say that?*"

No, now they really are gone, like the Singing Fish, and the sad King in his palace at Baraquil, like the Chief Minister with all his secrets and his servants, like old Sharm herself—gone back into the basket whose name is Choushi-wai. Pray for the poor, pray for the gods, and remember to bring Choushi-wai the red *ardeet* melons in the morning—the others are still too sour. Walk safely on the night paths home.

GIANT BONES

oy, call me in to you just once more, and you will regret it until you're very, very old. I'll not tell you again, the *jejebhai*'s due any hour now—twins, by the look of it—and if I'm not with her she's like as not to smother one while she's dropping the other, crazy as she is. So I haven't the bloody time to tell you tales, nor smooth your blanket, nor bring you water. If your mother were here, as she bloody should be, instead of being off in Chun nursing your aunt because the idiot woman didn't have sense enough to leave red *kalyars* alone in the wet season, then she could play games with you all night, for all of me. But if I climb up to this loft again tonight, it will be with a willow switch in my hand. Do you understand me?

What? *What* under your bed? Rock-*targs*? There's never been a single rock-*targ* in this flat-arse farmland, you know that as well as I do. They're mountain creatures; they won't come below the snowline to feast on a fat caravan, never mind squeezing themselves under one scrawny little boy's bed. There aren't any even in our high country, come to that. The giants ran them all out, they're still afraid of the giants, even now.

What? No, there aren't any giants under your bed, either. The giants are gone, too, long and long since. Haven't been any since your great-great-great-grandfather's time, I can tell you that for a fact. Go to sleep, if you know what's good for you.

Now what's he crying about? Because there aren't any giants? Is that it? Boy, there are times . . . *what*? Oh now, don't you start *that* again, do you hear me? You are *not* too small, I never said that, that was your Uncle Tavdal, and he's a fool. But a tall fool, just as you'll be, stop stewing over it. You're small for your age, yes, but so were your sisters Rii and Sardur, whatever they say now. So was Jadamak—he didn't even start getting his growth until he was well older than you, there's another fact for you. And I'll tell you something more—

What? Be quiet, I thought that was the *jejebhai* bleating. . . . No, I guess not. Not that it would mean much if it were—she's just like you, call and call and carry on, and when you get there, nothing but big eyes and feeling a bit lonesome. Wouldn't surprise me at all if she decided not to drop them till dawn, like last time. Spiteful animal, always was. Like your aunt.

How do I know you'll be tall? Well, let *me* ask a question for a change—have you ever seen a short one in our family? Think about it, name me one—uncles, cousins, second cousins, distant as you like. No? Hah? No, and you won't either, I don't care how far you look. Every one of us is big, man or woman, wise or brainless. It's how we are, the same as those Mundrakathis down by the canal, all with those pale, pale skins and the men with their extra little fingers. Only with us it's a bit different, there's a bit more to it. Ask your mother sometime, she'll tell you.

I said your *mother*. No. No, absolutely not, I'm going back down to the barn this minute. Besides, your mother's the one to ask about things like that. She's the one who tells stories, sings the old wisdom songs, passes things on when it's time. I'm just the one who takes care of the beasts. Fair enough—we both push the plow. I'm going now, that's all.

No, I said *no*! Give it up, boy, before you really rouse me. I can't afford to lose even one *jejebhai* kid, let alone two, not with the price of vegetables gone so low it's hardly worth hauling them to market. Good night, good-bye, and go to bloody sleep!

Because I *do* know, there's why! Because of your three-times-great-grandfather and the giants of Torgry Mountain, there's why! Nine years old, she should have told you by now, and I'll tell her so when she comes home, if she ever does. Instead of leaving it for me.

All right. All *right*, then—but one squall from the barn and your mother tells you the rest, is that a bargain? And you'll keep to it, like a grown man? No fussing, no sniveling? Mind, now.

Well. I've not told stories much—I don't know where you're supposed to start, or what's important to put in. So I'm just going to begin with your great-great-great-grandfather, only I can't keep calling him that all through, so I'll call him Grandfather Selsim. I think that was his name, or close enough to it. No one's really sure.

Now. Grandfather Selsim was the first of our lot to come into this country. He didn't mean to, not as far as I ever learned, being no farmer but a coppersmith by trade—aye, a tinker if you like, and horsedealer as well betimes, tell the truth. But he was living in the north, beyond the mountains, when times were hard and land was dear. And that was good for the tinker, you see, because folk were mending and making do in those days, not buying all new like your aunt in Chun and that fat maggot she married. But it wasn't such a fine thing for the horsedealer, no, nor for anyone with even a few dreams of settling somewhere and might be starting a family. I was up north myself one time, working, before we had this place, before you were born. Never liked it much.

So one morning Grandfather Selsim just up and says, "Well, that's it, I'm surely done here," and he jumped on that ugly-tempered, leg-biting *churfa* he always rode and headed straight south. No notion where he was bound, no friends or relations beyond Rhyak, everything he owned sold fast and cheap to feed him along the way. Just going south, traveling by the sun and the mountains dead ahead. And that was your great-great-great-grandfather Selsim.

Did you hear anything just then? Tell me if you did,

mind, because I'll know. There's a sound she makes when the kid . . . no, no, nothing yet. All right. I hate this. Where was I?

Right, so. Grandfather Selsim, he'd been here and there enough to know that mountains aren't ever as close as they look, but for all that he was near to being out of food by the time he reached the northern foothills. Oh, he did some tinkerwork along the way for a meal or two, and he likely even begged when it came to it. There's those in the family wouldn't ever admit to that, but I say you do what's to do. All we know, we mightn't be here tonight, you and I and them, too, if Grandfather Selsim had been ashamed to beg. And maybe he was thinking about us all, that far back, hey? Who knows?

Now you've never been anywhere near a mountain, so I suppose I'd better tell you about being in the mountains. It's cold, that's one thing—maybe not all the time, but most always. And the roads are bad, when there are any roads, and you spend hours just crawling, scrambling, scuttling along on all fours. And all the while you're doing that, the air's growing thin and thinner, till you feel too weak to scratch your head and breathing doesn't do you any good at all. And there are the rock-*targs*.

You don't even know what a rock-*targ* looks like do you? All that carrying on about them being under your bed, and you don't even know. . . . You remember when your cousin Baj killed that *lourijakh* that climbed on the roof, trying to get in? Well, those are a little like rock-*targs*, only not as big, of course, not nearly as big. And the rock-*targs'* faces look more human somehow, and they can almost talk—not really talk, but it makes it worse. You don't ever find many of them in one spot, but in those days they were still scattered over Torgry Mountain and that whole northern range. Because of the *kagi*, there used to be a lot of wild *kagi* up on the high crags. But it doesn't matter—they're always hungry, always hunting. And they'd rather eat people. Your *lourijakh* doesn't care, he'll eat anything, but a rock-*targ* can smell you a mile upwind, and he'll leave a fresh kill to come after you. No, I can't tell you why, how do I know? It's just the way they are.

Well, in those days your Grandfather Selsim didn't know much more about rock-*targs* than you do. No reason he should have—I told you, they don't come down into the low country, thank the gods for *something* anyway. And mountain folk don't usually see them either, unless it's too late. Oh, they stay out of sight, but they're there.

What? I'm scaring you now? Well, there's just no pleasing you, is there? First you're at me and at me to tell you all about giants and rock-*targs* and how I know you're going to be as tall as the rest of us—next minute, there you are, head under the blanket, just carrying on. Shall I leave off the story, then? I'd just as soon, it's a deal more work than I expected. Your mother does it all so easily, every night, I don't know how she does it. You go off to sleep then, and I'll bed down with the *jejebhai*. Sooner or later she's bound to give in and drop those . . . what? No. Well.

Your Grandfather Selsim, he didn't know how high the mountains were, nor what grew or moved in them, nor what was on the other side. Some of the foothill folk gave him work to do, and a little food for doing it, and when he asked them the best way across the range, everyone said there wasn't any pass but the one over Torgry Mountain. Not that it was a real pass, nothing even like a real pass, but I'll get to that. Now, today, you can flank the range, just go all the way around—it takes forever, but you can do it. But back then, no road, only that mountain track. And your Grandfather Selsim never was much for going around things, people always say that.

Yes, naturally, everyone warned him about the rock-*targs*. They all said he'd best wait for winter, when the beasts get a bit sluggish, and you can see them better against the snow, so you've some sort of a chance to escape. But you can't cross the bloody range in winter—not then, not today—so what difference? And all those people told your Grandfather Selsim first one thing and then another about what rock-*targs* look like and what they do, so by and by he understood that not a one of them knew one thing for certain. So he said to the *churfa* as he set off again, "Well, we'll just go carefully, you and I, mind our manners and keep our wits about us, and might be we'll jog along all right. Carried us this far, anyway, manners and wits."

But I think what he really put his faith in was the big old *dasko* knife he had from his father: the real South Island make, it was, double-edged and so long that it stuck out a bit at both ends of his blanket roll. I haven't seen one of those in years—what? No, we don't still have it. I'll tell you why in a minute. Do you interrupt your mother all the time, every night, when she's telling you a story? I don't know how she does it.

Right, right. Up went your Grandfather Selsim into the high country, with that mean little scribble of a road twitching and jiggling underfoot, until suddenly there wasn't any road, and it wasn't plain high country anymore, it was pure Torgry Mountain, and he had to dismount and lead the *churfa*, even with those clawed feet they have. And from there on your great-great-great probably learned a deal about mountains in a very short time. How you're always thirsty, doesn't matter how cold it is, because the thin air dries the water right out of you. How you can climb for hours, and then look down and you'd swear you're hardly any higher than when you started out, except that back down there the sun's so bright you can see the shadows on the ground, and where you are it's gray and windy as—as what?—as your Uncle Tavdal. And how there's nothing like mountain quiet, and how sounds and smells are all so clear they almost hurt, and how they seem so much closer than they really are. Which is not good if you're listening for monsters and winding their lairs. And you can't mistake the rock-*targ* scent, even if you've never seen one. Even if you don't know the bloody name of whatever smells like that, you know.

Oh, no. You'll just get frightened again if I tell you—I'm not going through that a second time, thanks ever so kindly. Besides, I've only sniffed a few places where they'd been long before, and that's nothing like what your Grand-father Selsim had in his throat. I'll tell you this much—just that shadow of a smell and I was pissing down my legs, each time. Oh, you like that, that's funny, is it? Well, then you can just laugh yourself sick thinking what the fresh stink probably did to Grandfather Selsim. All *I* know is that the *churfa* screamed like a demon in foal, the way they do, and it reared and threw him, right there, and ran off back the way they'd come. Never did see it again.

Well, what do you *think* he did? With the beast carrying everything he owned in the world? Of course, he went after it, and a good thing, too. Not that he caught up, but at least he did chance on the blanket roll—yes, yes, *dashko* knife and all—tangled in the brush that must have snatched it off the *churfa*'s back. So he'd sleep warm, whatever, and maybe having the big knife was some comfort to him. That first day or two, anyway.

Far as anyone knows, nothing at all worried him those two days, except for the little matter of something to eat. I'm sure lower down he dug up some of those *tanku* roots you can't stand, and then higher up he probably found some wild mountain radishes. They aren't real radishes, but you can eat them raw, so your Grandfather Selsim can't have gone too hungry on Torgry. Come nightfall, he must have slept in the open—had to have the sense not to go into a cave. Late spring, it could have been worse.

But by the third day he'd have climbed above the snowline.

Now I'm not saying that everything changes the moment you take the first step into the first snowdrift. The birds don't stop singing, and things still grow—although by now you're down mostly to shrubs and cloudberries and wizeny little *sulsawi*-trees—and you don't see skeletons lying around everywhere and rock-*targs* jumping out at you from every direction. It's not like that. It's just the quiet gets qui-eter—well, it just *does*—and it gets colder as you go higher, and the shadows move quicker over the snow. Sometimes you see a flock of *kagi* away off on a ridge, all blue and ripply horned and so pretty. Only, all the time you're watching them, you keep knowing what else is watching, too, and watching you, and choosing.

Rock-*targs* hunt by day. Get safely past sundown, you'll be all right until morning. Story has it they're afraid of the moon, but I couldn't say. Anyway, your Grandfather Selsim would have been moving right on up Torgry Mountain, nearing dusk of that first day, probably some pleased with himself for managing as well as he was doing, alone, on foot, all his provisions gone. He couldn't have known it, but another good day would have seen him to the summit, and an easy enough journey down from there. And if it had happened so, who knows where we'd all be? Or who? Hey?

Gods, that was her! Sorry, boy, but we made our bargain. Ask your mother . . . no, no, she's just belching. They do that a lot when it's near time. No, I *wasn't* teasing you, I really thought—all right, all right, I'm sorry, be quiet! You do want to hear the rest of the tale? Then not another word, hear me? Not one word!

All right, then. I don't know just where or when the rock-*targ* came across the snowfield at your grandfather. One thing I know, he never heard it coming, because you don't; they can move like smoke, no mind how big they are. Only reason he wasn't killed in that first rush, it seems he turned for some reason—a bird, maybe a cloud red-gold with the sun behind it—and the thing's charge ripped his left shoulder open, spun him, and knocked him twenty feet away, all over blood and next to unconscious, surely. He carried that scar the rest of his life, Grandfather Selsim, and the arm never worked right again. The eye, too. It caught his left eye, some way.

I told you, I've never seen a rock-*targ* close to, myself, and I don't expect you'll ever meet anyone who has. But one thing people do say, when they're over you, gobbling their almost-talk and ready to tear you apart, their faces slide right up and back, straight back, showing the whole skull beneath. Now I can't tell you how that could be, I can't imagine it, and it's likely not true. But that's what people say.

When the creature came at him again, your Grandfather Selsim had just strength and wit enough to drag out his *dasko* knife and hold it on his belly, point up. They always go for the belly first, that's a fact anyway. And the rock-*targ* snatched the knife away from him and bit it in half! Right in half. And I know this is true, because I've seen the two pieces—your Uncle Lenelosi has them now, you can see them when we visit next. What? Because he's older than I am, will you hush? Yes, I'm sure we'll get them when Uncle Lenelosi dies. Will you *hush*?

All *right*. I won't say your Grandfather Selsim gave himself up for lost, but I certainly don't know what else he could have done, what with that thing blotting out the sky, its triple row of fangs becoming another kind of sky. Their spit burns if it gets on you, did you know that? He carried a few of those scars to his grave, too, I've been told.

And then.

Then a pair of hands as big as—as big as, I don't know, big as two plows they must have looked to Grandfather Selsim—took hold of the rock-*targ*, one at the back of its human neck, one wrapped right around those hindquarters that were already curling off the ground to rip your grandfather's belly clean out of his body. For a moment he saw it hanging up there, looking little and foolish, too bewildered even to snap its jaws. The hands shook it once; they shook it the way your mother snaps a sheet still wet from the river before she hangs it out on the line. Your grandfather heard the creature's back break, just before he fainted. Or maybe he fainted just afterward, when the big hands reached down for him. It was very long ago, and I wasn't there.

Anyway, however it happened, your Grandfather Selsim didn't remember another thing until he was suddenly wide awake and hurting everywhere as he'd never hurt in his life. Somebody'd neatly bound up his shoulder with his own torn shirt, and he was lying in a heap of leaves, looking up with his one good eye into what he thought were trees, great ragged trees with dark moons floating in their branches. It took him a long, long while to understand that those weren't moons but huge bearded faces, not just bearded but swallowed up in mucky black hair that wasn't really like a beard at all. And the size of them . . . well, they weren't nearly as big as trees, but close enough, close enough. Nobody knows, not anymore, but from what I've been told I'd guess they'd have been between twelve and maybe fourteen feet tall. Now your Uncle Tavdal, *he* says they couldn't have been that tall, says bones wouldn't carry bodies that heavy. Your Uncle Tavdal is a fool.

They were talking to each other, the faces were. Grandfather Selsim could feel the words, not so much hear them, right through his body, thumping and thrumming in his bones. Because their voices were so deep, you see. At first he figured they were like rock-*targs* that way, just imitating the cries of the things they killed. But then he got to realizing that the words made sentences, and that they sounded a little like the same dialect the foothill folk used, only with strange grumbles and gurgles mixed in. And after another really long time, the sentences even started to make some sense. They were about him. The hairy faces were trying to decide what to do about him.

He couldn't tell them apart, of course, not then, not at all. What he *could* tell was that most of them were for getting rid of him, doing him in—what? Well, how should I know? Likely just by leaving him there to starve or freeze or bleed to death. Maybe by stepping on his head, all right? If you want to hear the rest of this story, not another question. I can't believe you ask your mother so many questions.

Why did the giants want to kill him? Well, I was getting to that, if you hadn't interrupted. Best your Grandfather Selsim could make out, they were afraid he would tell the other humans about them. It didn't matter whether he meant them any harm—once humans know about you, you come to harm, that's how it is. Well, *I'm* not saying that,

that's how those giants felt. And maybe it's so. I'm not saying.

They were the last ones, you see, the giants of Torgry Mountain, and they knew they were the last. "Giants know when giants go," that's something people always say your Grandfather Selsim always said. The odd thing, the funny thing, is that in those days it was the rock-*targs* that kept this lot of giants from being discovered. People were that afraid of the rock-*targs*, they wouldn't ever cross the mountain except in winter, and not many then. Now I don't know if the giants new that the rock-*targs* were protecting them, just by being there, being what they were. Wouldn't have made any difference, chances are.

But that all comes later. Meanwhile, your Grandfather Selsim was lying there, looking away high at those great dark shaggy faces, hoping even one giant would speak for keeping him, though he couldn't think why they should want to. For the babies to teethe on, maybe, the way you chewed that stuffed *sheknath* I made you to pieces. He just lay still and hurt, and hoped.

And one giant did speak for him. Right when he was giving himself up a second time, one giant did speak out.

Oh, you knew that would happen? There you are, then, the smartest child who ever interrupted his father's story one time too many. Then you'll know what the giant said, and what came of it, and I'll be off to the barn, good night to you. The *jejebhai*'s making that sound again.

No? Really? Well, there may be something to this storytelling business, after all. I'm holding you to that promise, don't think I'll forget. Get back in that bed and keep still.

The giant who put in a word for your Grandfather Selsim was the biggest and hairiest of them, and smelled the worst. Not but what they all stank like—what? Because they did, because they just smelled that way, that's all, worse than rock-*targs*, even. Yes, I'm sure they smelled all right to each other. What was it you just promised?

Anyway. Your grandfather felt that biggest giant saying

to the others, "I will keep this little one. It was I who killed the rock-*targ*, so this one belongs to me, and it is my choice to keep him. No more talk."

And there it stuck, though they kept at it until your grandfather had to roll himself up in a ball and cover his ears. Well, you think what a roomful of giants shouting and arguing would feel like if it was all booming around in *your* body. It went on a good long while, too.

But all the booming and bellowing didn't make any difference. That biggest giant seemed to be someone really grand among them, because the others couldn't shift him an inch, and they couldn't say no to him either. So at last they gave up, they wandered off one by one, rumbling away like thunderheads, and were gone into the trees like *that*. Took him the longest while to get used to it, your Grandfather Selsim, the way those great crashing things could just not be there, disappear without a sound when they wanted to. I've been told he got so he could do it himself, but I wouldn't swear to that.

Well, he figured he might as well stand up as not, so he grabbed on to a low-hanging branch and pulled himself up on his feet. He was a small-made man, your grandfather—now this is important, why do you think I'm telling you this bloody story?—and they say he stood about knee-high to that creature that looked down at him, not saying a thing with the others gone, watching him silently out of its shadowy black eyes. Your Grandfather Selsim got tired of that in a hurry, and he tilted his head back and bawled, "Can you hear me?"

No answer. He tries again, loud as he can—"*Do you understand me?*" Nothing more aggravating than someone staring at you and not speaking. I don't care who it is.

Then the giant laughed at him. They say your grandfather had to hang on hard to that branch to keep from falling, because the ground shivered under his feet, but maybe that's just talk. Maybe it's just he was so amazed at the notion of those faces even smiling, let alone laughing like that. The giant slapped his legs—must have sounded like trees snapping when it's so cold the sap freezes—and dropped down, squatting, leaning in close. Your Grandfather Selsim didn't back away. The giant said, keeping his voice as low as he could, "My name is Dudrilashashek"—or something like that, your grandfather wasn't ever really sure. "Do you have a name, little one?"

"Of course I have a name!" your grandfather yelled up into that face. "Why wouldn't I have a name?"

"No need to shout," the giant answered—he was almost whispering himself, but with every word he spoke your grandfather's hair blew straight back. "There are so many of you, and you swarm around so, squeaking and chittering. How are we to know if you all have proper names? If you think of yourselves as yourselves?" He talked like that, I'm not making it up. That's just how your Grandfather Selsim said he talked.

Well, your grandfather lost no time in setting *him* right, and you can believe me about that. Yes, we have names, and mine is Selsim—yes, we know who we are—yes, we have real conversations with each other—yes, we love, and we weep, and we laugh and suffer and endure as much as any bloody giants. He couldn't be sure if his impudence was making this giant angry, but he was too angry to care. Because he was telling him about *us*, about all of us, not just this one family. About all of us, at the top of his voice.

When he was through, or maybe when he just ran out of wind, the giant Dudrilashashek kept squatting there, still three, four feet taller than he was, staring at him and very slowly beginning to smile. Your grandfather used to say that all the giants had really beautiful white teeth, when you could see them through the tangly, greasy hair. Didn't smile much, though, none of them, but when they did smile, you noticed it. That's what I've heard, anyway.

"There," the giant said, "I was right, I *knew* I was right. Who would have thought you little ones had anything inside you but blind insect energy? Absolutely amazing. Oh, I knew I was right to insist on keeping you with us. Amazing."

"Keep me?" asked your Grandfather Selsim. "What are you talking about?" And now, now he was frightened as he hadn't been before, not when he was looking right into the rock-*targ*'s maw, not even when he knew the giants were quarrelling about whether he should live or die. "Why keep me? What for?"

"Why, to study, of course," Dudrilashashek answered him. "For we are a thoughtful folk, and pay all the attention we can to everything that crosses our lives—rock-*targs* or the tiniest waterbugs, it is all one to us. It is what we were put here for, we Qu'alo—to study, to consider, to turn over logs and stones and ideas equally, to learn what lies underneath. For that, and that alone, we were made."

What? That was what they called themselves, the Qu'alo. Means "The Proper People," if I remember it right. They never thought they were giants, by the way. They just thought humans were stunted.

Well now, between one thing and another, your Grandfather Selsim had had a really bad day. He put his hands on his hips, and he leaned back and shouted up into that giant's face, "You've made the wrong choice, big one! You can kill me, but you can't keep me here to be bloody *studied*! If I'm a bug, very well then—you just try guarding a bug every single minute of the day and night. This bug will be through your fat, clumsy fingers, down the road and long gone before you take your next bath. Which had better be pretty soon, by the way." Oh, he was definitely in a mood, and just getting warmed up, too.

But Dudrilashashek still didn't get angry. No, he kept on smiling that huge sweet smile, and he said back to your grandfather, "Please, little friend, if I seem callous, forgive me—it is merely that I am so *glad* of you. It is a lonely affair, being the only creatures in the world aware both of the world and of ourselves in it. Would you be offended now if I picked you up, just for a closer look? Being most careful, I promise."

Well, you can imagine Grandfather Selsim took his time over that one. He didn't think he was going to like being scooped up like a baby, like a pet, dangling between those immense hands, or flat on his back with his legs in the air, rocked in the curve of an elbow bigger than himself. Still, Dudrilashashek had asked very politely, considering he didn't have to, and your grandfather always appreciated politeness, especially from giants. So he said, "All right, but gently does it, then. And no upside-down business, understood?"

And Dudrilashashek answered him, "My word on it," and lifted him as carefully as he'd promised, one hand giving him a place to stand, the other steadying him with two fingers, so lightly your grandfather hardly felt the grip at all. The giant raised him up until their eyes were on a level and stared at him, just clucking with fascination, like your Aunt Kelya when she hasn't seen you for a while. "Look at that!" he kept saying, "you have fingernails almost like ours," and again, "Look at *that*—why, I think you could grow a beard like a real Qu'alo, if you fancied." Your Grandfather Selsim didn't know whether to fall down in his hand laughing, or to stand there and gape for realizing that everyone thinks they're the only Proper People in the world.

He didn't do either one. He kept his balance, and his dignity, pretty much, and he let Dudrilashashek sniff him all over without saying a word. Oh, there's another thing about giants, by the way—they heard better than they saw, what with all that hair, and they could smell another Qu'alo a mile away and know who he was, and what he'd had for breakfast, and how he was feeling right then. Of course, anyone else could smell *them* a good long way off, too, so much good it did them, hey? But your grandfather said he grew accustomed to the Qu'alo stink by and by—said he didn't even notice it after a time. And why not, hey? When you think what I've had to get used to with your mother's people.

What? No, I don't suppose he ever did know what *he* smelled like to them.

Well, when Dudrilashashek was done sniffing Grandfather Selsim, he said to him, "Now, if you don't mind, my brothers and sisters will do the same. Tedious for you, I'm sure, but the ritual has to be performed, if you are to stay with us. I'll bring you to them, shall I?"

"Indeed, you'll not," answered your grandfather—still a good bit cheekier than you or I would have spoken to a giant, I daresay. He said, "I'm quite tired, not to mention hungry and thirsty, and I hurt a good deal, and my left eye doesn't work. This is because I've recently been chewed on by a rock-*targ*. I'm very grateful to whichever of you saved my life, but I don't want to be smelled over anymore just now, and I'm not planning to stay a day longer than I have to. I want to lie down somewhere. If *you* wouldn't mind."

But Dudrilashashek replied, "I am sorry, this is more important, though I'm sure it can't seem so to you. The others must get your scent in their nostrils as soon as I do, in order that we may know you all in the same way, at the same time. For us, smell is so changeable, so easily affected by feelings, fears, health, age, diet, and endless other matters, that one of us might meet you only a few days from now and not know you at all. Which could be a very unhappy thing, for both of you. No, this *must* be done at once—forgive me, little friend."

And with that, he tightened his grip on your grandfather—oh, just slightly, but quite enough—and marched off into the woods calling for his friends and relations. They had a funny way of calling each other, a kind of hollow, hooty sound, not loud, but it seemed to carry forever. I've heard it said that when Grandfather Selsim was an old man, there were times when he would sit up in the middle of the night and swear he heard the Qu'alo calling to him, out on Torgry Mountain, so far away. They were all gone by then, and he knew it better than anyone, but even so. Wait, wait, you'll see.

Anyway. Nothing for it. Your grandfather had to stand in Dudrilashashek's vast palm for an hour or more, while the other Qu'alo came one at a time to touch and stare and smell him, just to be absolutely sure they'd know him again. Big foreheads, big cheekbones, small underslung chins, he said they all had, and the younger ones' hair was grayish-brownish, not really black. He was too weary to notice anything more then, or even to try telling the females from the males. When it was over at last, Dudrilashashek took him to a cave where they brought their sick ones, changed the bandage on his shoulder, fed him a soup of wild leeks and mushrooms out of a bowl he could have bathed in, and personally tucked him up in a sweet-smelling bed of green spring boughs. "There," he said, proud as proud. "Sleep now, and when you wake, I am sure much will look different to you."

Grandfather Selsim was already asleep, near enough, but he managed to mumble, "I'll not be staying long. As soon as I can travel decently, I'll be on my way. Rock-*targs* or no."

Old Dudrilashashek didn't contradict him, only nodded seriously and said, in that voice that always seemed to be coming right out of Grandfather Selsim's own insides, "When you are healed, we will talk of this. Sleep now."

"Giants or no," your grandfather whispered, and slept for two days.

Yes, indeed, he certainly did have to piss something terrible when he woke up, thank you very much, I'd have forgotten. *And* he had to have some more soup, *and* he had to wash himself, *and* he had to have his shoulder looked at and tended. Dudrilashashek said he was coming along very well, and lucky with it, because a rock-*targ* bite usually poisons up and kills you just as dead. But whatever the Qu'alo had put on it, the great ragged gash was already knitting as nicely as you please, not a sign of infection. He still couldn't see a thing out of his left eye, but it wasn't hurting him very much, and Dudrilashashek told him that in time he'd have at least some vision back. For now he was to rest and grow strong, and not think of anything else. Especially not about leaving.

Your Grandfather Selsim looked straight at that giant—as straight as he could with one eye gone, anyway—and he said firmly, "Three days. Three days, and maybe two. It's nothing to do with you and your tribe—I never stay anywhere any longer than that. I am a tinker and a traveler, and I must be getting along. That's what I do, get along."

But the giant shook his head, looking solemn and regretful, and answered him, "It cannot be, little friend. The others will not have it, and I can command them only so far. In return for your life, I have already promised that you would be kept with us always, for fear of your leading a swarm of your folk to bedevil us here. I myself believe you'd do no such thing, but they'll not hear of chancing it. Your pardon, Shelshim"—don't laugh, that was the only way the Qu'alo could ever say his name—"but I can see that you wish the truth. This is the truth."

"If I promised them," your grandfather said. "If I give my word. Where I come from, we set great store by keeping one's word. I could swear on anything you hold sacred." Dudrilashashek just looked sadder and sadder. Grandfather Selsim said, "I'll run away. You know that, too."

"Please," the old giant said, and they say he was that upset, his enormous face was rippling and trembling all over, just like that disgusting pink dessert your Aunt Kelya makes every Winter-Farewell feast. He said, "Please, Shelshim, don't, I beg you. We are so good at hunting and tracking, at smelling out on an entire mountainside the one plant we desire to eat—and we are so dreadfully clumsy with these fingers of ours, as you rightly point out. It would be terrible for us all, now that we know you, if you were accidentally harmed in being retaken. Or if the rock-*targs* found you before we did." *No*, they didn't call them that, of course not, they had their own word. No, I don't *know* what it was. Quiet.

Now your Grandfather Selsim never could abide being threatened, and he answered right off, "I'd rather die this minute with a rock-*targ* at my throat than live forever as the Qu'alo's pet human, with never a breath nor one single step to call my own. It won't do, Dudrilashashek. There's no one born who can keep me anywhere I don't want to be." And with that he turned painfully over and went back to sleep for another day. It's said that the giant watched over him all that time. Yes, I'm sure he had to go piss, too, at some point. Thank you.

So there's the way matters stood, and when your Grandfather Selsim woke again, it was time again for him to learn a great deal in a hurry. Tinkers are good at that, have to be. For one thing, he learned that the Qu'alo didn't have any one special place—a cave, or a clearing, or maybe a flat rock—where they lived together, or where they might be used to gathering, like the meeting hall in the village. Though if that's a hall, then our outhouse is a bloody palace, I'll say that. The Qu'alo roamed Torgry Mountain as they chose, alone or with one or two others, no more. They spent most of their days looking for food, because it's hard to keep that big of a body properly stoked when you don't eat meat, or even fish, no more than a *rishu* does. Well, grubs, they ate grubs and bugs sometimes. They nested wherever night found them, usually in a *sum'yadi* tree, because of those being the only ones big enough to hold them and thick-dark enough to hide them. And they could go days, weeks at a time without seeing another of their kind, never give a thought to it. But each one of them always knew where all the rest were, same way you know where your fingers or your toes are. Don't ever have to think about it, do you? Same with the Qu'alo, exactly.

What? Can't you listen for even one minute when I'm telling you something? No, he certainly *didn't* run off the first chance he got, as he'd sworn. It took him a good sight longer than he'd expected to get over his wounds—even after his shoulder had healed and he was starting to notice a few things out of the side of that left eye, he still ached where he hadn't been wounded, still moved timidly, looking behind him every other step he took. It'll do that to you, a rock-*targ* attack, people say. You know you're really dead, even if nobody else knows. You keep expecting the thing to come back and claim you.

Dudrilashashek looked after him for a while, showing him how to find the wild berries and roots and such stuff that the Qu'alo lived on, and where the best streams were, and the safe caves to sleep in. Very considerate giant, that one—he knew a human couldn't sleep the way the giants did, practically tying the *sum'yadi* branches in knots to make a bed. Your grandfather paid attention, not like some of us. He paid more attention to the way the Qu'alo did things than he ever had to anything before. Because his life depended on it right then, and he knew that, if he didn't know much else yet.

Mind you, it took him the longest while to tell one of them from another, except for Dudrilashashek. All of them huge, all of them covered with hair, all of them stinking to shame a *churfa* . . . it wasn't until after Dudrilashashek had left him on his own, more or less, that he began to know some of the other Qu'alo. And that was only because he was still afraid of being by himself, afraid of some rock-*targ* finding him alone. If those giants wanted to study him like a book or a bug, that was all right, that was fine—just so they bore him company and didn't leave him where the rock-*targs* could get him. Did he get over it? Being afraid, you mean? Oh, in time, in a way, but he never got back to the person he'd been a minute before it happened. Nobody ever does.

Gods, *that* wasn't belching, that *was* her, I know it! Seen her through enough birthings, I ought to know by now. Bloody spiteful animal—wait, wait, now she's stopped, not a sound out of her. I ought to go down there, but I won't, she's playing with me. They'll do that, remember that about *jejebhais*, they'll play with you like that, once they get to know you. Go in for *rishus*, boy, when I'm gone. *Rishus* are nice and stupid, that's what you want, believe me. *Rishus* don't play with you.

Well, just while we're waiting. But it might be any minute, you understand that. Now, the Qu'alo. Two or three, he never heard speak a word, not ever. You looked in those black eyes, your Grandfather Selsim said—like undersea caves, they were, once you looked past all the black hair—and you knew the Qu'alo really were a thoughtful people, they thought about things all the time.

Only they weren't like your Uncle Tavdal—they didn't think talking was the same as thinking, you understand? Just got in the way, more than likely. That's how they were, mostly.

Not all of them, though. There were a pair of brothers named something like Calijostylakomo and Galijosty-lakomo—and not a word out of you, those were their *names*, and that's all there is to that. Your grandfather called them Cali and Gali, and he could always tell those two apart because Cali never could grow a beard as thick as the other giants' beards, and it bothered him. Or maybe that was Gali, I couldn't say. Anyway, they were young, which is maybe why they talked a bit more than the others, and they were—I guess you'd say *mischievous*—at least for giants. They liked to wrestle—Grandfather Selsim used to climb a tree to stay out of the way, and even that was risky. And sometimes, instead of bedding down at sunset like the other Qu'alo, they'd go off together and spend the whole night hunting rock-*targs*. Used to bait them out of their lairs and roll boulders down on them. Used to invite your grandfather to come along—what? No. No, I'm sure he never did. Because none of *us* is that kind of a fool, not even your Uncle Tavdal. We're a different kind.

There was another one he was friendly with, a woman of the Qu'alo—her name was Yriadvele, more or less. Now they were even shyer than the rest of the giants, the women were, and the only reason Grandfather Selsim ever exchanged two words with her is that he once fell into a trap, a pit that Cali and Gali had dug to catch rock-*targs* in, and he was just lucky that they were young and too lazy to bother with putting poisoned stakes at the bottom. This Yri-advele heard his cries, and she came and scooped him out of there, quick as that. And afterward he somehow had a claim on her, the way it can happen. She'd pop him up on her shoulder and off they'd go for a long walk in the forest, or out on the open mountainside, toward evening, with no chance of travelers seeing them. I used to carry you like that, you remember?

Your grandfather didn't talk much about her for years, not until he was really getting on, that's what I was told. He said he could always tell Yriadvele from the others because she had a grayish sort of mantle up around her shoulders. The hair, I mean, that's because she was still young. Anyway, they'd talk for hours on end, your Grandfather Selsim and this enormous woman-creature who was *so* hairy and *so* stinking that after a time he didn't notice any of that at all. Truth of it is, he came to think she was pretty, in a way, with her huge black eyes and really delicate little ears—and he said she was graceful, too, moving that body silently among the trees. Like the rest of them, if she didn't want you to see her, you didn't see her. But when she was there, she was *there*, the trees and the mountain boulders all faded into air around her. Now that's exactly what your grandfather said, word for word, just the way I had it from my own grandfather.

What did they talk about? Well, she'd ask him how human beings lived, what they ate, where they slept, and what they did when they were sick, and about clothes, and about how they felt about being such small creatures in such a big world. And games, playing games, she never did understand about that. The Qu'alo didn't play, you see, they didn't have a notion of what the word meant. She asked him to tell her about the games over and over.

She didn't talk at all like Dudrilashashek. No, I don't know why, and your grandfather never did either. He used to wonder sometimes if she was maybe simple, but how do you tell with a giant? Once she said, slow and halting, sometimes a minute or two between the words, "When we sleep, sometimes we see a story, we are in the story. You?"

"Dreams," your grandfather said. "Yes, we dream, we see stories, too. Like you, just the same."

But Yriadvele turned her great head slowly to look straight into his eyes, and her own so dark you couldn't see yourself in them, nor the sky behind you, nor a green leaf or a bit of sun. She said, "With us, the same story every night. Always. The rock-*targs*. Our brothers."

Your grandfather must have just stared at her. She said, "Made at the same time, rock-*targs* and we Qu'alo. Looked the same once, lived together, the same people. But we changed, slowly, slowly, left them, lost them. So now, every night we live, the dream, every night, how it was once. The gods punish us for changing."

No, what do you think, of course I don't know if that's true or not. It's what the Qu'alo believed, that's all. Your Grandfather Selsim never said whether *he* believed it, but he did say it sounded just like the gods.

Do you know what she thought was the funniest thing in the world? Telling jokes—I mean the *idea* of telling jokes. It took a while for her to believe that humans would spend time making up stories and repeating them to each other just to make each other laugh. But once she did take hold of it—why, then it became hers, her own joke, and she might start giggling to herself at the thought of it, any time at all, the way you hear thunder back of the hills on a hot night. He'd find her that way sometimes, your grandfather, playing with her special joke. And sometimes she'd start in *really* laughing, no warning. He said the ground would tremble, blossoms and leaves would be coming down everywhere, birds would pop right off their nests, and your bones would buzz for an hour afterward. That's what it was like when the Qu'alo laughed.

One time he asked if the giants had families, the way humans do. He hardly ever saw more than two Qu'alo together, couldn't be sure how many of them there were on Torgry Mountain, and he certainly couldn't even guess which ones might be children. She didn't answer him, she didn't speak at all until the next day. Just about the time he'd forgotten his question, she said, "Not. Once, now not." Her voice was so soft he couldn't feel it in his body, the way he always did. She said it three times. "Once. Once. Once."

He didn't try to escape until he'd been with the Qu'alo two months, or maybe three, and by then he'd almost forgotten he was supposed to be their prisoner. They never caged or fenced or tethered him; he never saw them following him, watching him, not like that, nothing like that. He could wander any place he liked, stay out of sight of any Qu'alo as long as he felt like it. But the night he walked off through the deepest woods, not going near the trail he'd been traveling when the rock-*targ* jumped him, but veering, angling, first this way, then that, sidling toward the summit—do you know, he hadn't gone more than a mile when it was old Dudrilashashek filling his path, saying gently, "No, no, little one, I am sorry. Come, I will take you back, come now." Just as though he were no older than you, and walking in his sleep.

That was how it was every time he tried to slip away from the Qu'alo, to turn back to his interrupted journey, back into his own ordinary tinker's life. Never a reproach, never a threat, but always some huge creature suddenly *there* in front of him without a sound. Now and then it would be Yriadvele herself, and *she'd* simply pick him up and carry him, holding him straight out between her two hands, not on her shoulder, the way she did when they were off somewhere. That was how it was for eighteen years.

Eighteen years, that's right, that's how long he lived with the Qu'alo. Eating what they ate, sleeping when they slept, browsing in the shadows the day long, same as they did. Sounds like the most boring life you ever heard of, doesn't it? Well, it likely would have been just that for you or me, but it was something different for your Grandfather Selsim. Because after a time, might have been a few years, they say he started to think the thoughts of the Qu'alo, do you understand what I'm saying to you? Big thoughts, old thoughts, turning in his mind, the way you see a big fish come up in the evening and heave over at the surface with the sunset on his silver belly, and just slide away back down again. Long, strange, slow thoughts, take even a Qu'alo forever to get them right. Maybe you have to live that way to think that way. After a while, maybe that's all you want to do in the world. No, you don't understand, boy, and I don't either. What I *know* is, your Grandfather

Selsim spent eighteen years of his life with those stinking giants, and after the first three years, four years, he stopped trying to escape. He'd have stayed with them the rest of his life, if he could, and you wouldn't be here, nor me either. You think about that a little bit.

The winters? Yes, the mountain winters were hard, but Dudrilashashek taught him the Qu'alo trick for that. Do you know what they used to do when the leaves fell, when the streams all froze, when everything they ate was under two feet of snow? Do you know what the Qu'alo did? Why, they went to sleep, there's what they did. They'd find empty rock-*targ* caves—well, maybe they weren't always empty when they found them, but pretty soon after—and they'd pile together, two or three or four of them, and just sleep it out like that. And if it turned warm for a little, they might get up and wander around, dig under the snow for a nibble, then go back to sleep. People can do that, too, if they learn the trick. Your grandfather did. I think you should try it sometime.

Why couldn't he stay with them? Well, that's the story, isn't it? That's what we're getting to now.

Yriadvele it was who came for him when that first giant died. It was late on a summer afternoon, getting on for sundown. She just said, "Dead. With me," so he went with her, sitting on her shoulder like always. She wouldn't say who it was, nor even tell him his age—he was afraid a rock-*targ* might finally have gotten Cali or Gali. Well, and what was it he died of, then? That was when she looked sideways at him and said, "Qu'alo. Being Qu'alo." And what *that* meant, he had no idea.

They were in a clearing, all of them, gathered around the dead one. They had him laid out on a sort of scaffold thing—you know the way the Nounouris put their dead people up high in the trees? The Qu'alo did something like that except this platform wasn't any higher than about so, about my chest, and the body was mostly covered with fresh-cut branches that smelled sweet. He couldn't see the face, but he could see every one of the giants he knew to talk to, so he felt better. We can't help that, that's the way we are. As long as it's no one we know.

That was when he noticed how few of them there really were—no more than fifteen or sixteen, counting the children. And only about three of those, there's another thing. Now you're a farmer's son, you imagine they're *rishus* or *jejebhais* and work it out in your head, go on. Right—you can't keep up a herd of anything breeding at that rate, not a chance in the world. The Qu'alo were dying off; they were already doomed, almost on purpose. The way I've seen it happen sometimes.

Well, I have, and so have you, if you'll think about it. You remember that time when that whole flock of *makhyahs* over at the Jutt place, when he was going to get rich off those thousands and thousands of bright-red eggs they were going to lay—you remember when they all died, every one of them, almost overnight, and Bala Jutt came weeping for me to come look at the bodies and tell him what could have gone wrong. You were small, but you remember? Right, well, those *makhyahs* died because they didn't like Bala Jutt, and they didn't like the way he kept them, and they decided that living like that simply wasn't worth it. I don't mean they held a meeting and took a vote. I mean they just *decided*. Same with the Qu'alo. Not just the same, but the same.

Why? Well, if your Grandfather Selsim never knew, I certainly don't, and maybe the Qu'alo didn't know either, not in words. I don't think they ever put anything important into words, even to themselves. Just hush and listen.

Anyway, your Grandfather Selsim was most likely thinking about things like that when Yriadvele started to dance. He heard the heavy double thump behind him, and when he whirled around he saw her, stepping hard and slow, back and forth, one foot to the other. Then she was stamping, faster, making the platform with the body on it tremble, and then her arms began to lift away from her sides, as though she were getting ready to fly. Her eyes weren't looking at him or at anything, and her face was just as dark and hidden as always.

Then the others started in. Fifteen giants, stamping the ground all together. So now it was the trees shaking, and the ground *bouncing* like the skin on a drum, and people say the setting sun was bouncing, too, in the sky. I don't suppose it was what we'd call dancing—most of them just kept jumping up and down and waving their big arms around—but your grandfather said Yriadvele was turning and swaying, bending to touch the earth, kneeling, straightening, reaching out like for something nobody else could see. He said she was dancing, that one. He said he could still see her.

The way he told it, the frightening part was the *quiet*, not the noise. Underneath the noise, those tremendous feet booming on the ground, underneath it was still as could be, silent all the way down. And when they suddenly stopped, all of them together—oh, *that* quiet was too much for him, he backed away until he bumped into a tree, and then he hid behind it. But they weren't looking at him, not Yriadvele, none of them. They were looking at the dead Qu'alo on the scaffold thing.

This is what they did

I was just thinking, I don't know if I should be telling you this. If you start having nightmares, your mother will—what? Ah, don't tell me that—you had one just last week, woke me up yelling about *shukris* all over you, chewing you to bits. You don't remember, no, of course not. Your mother does. I think maybe you ought to go to sleep now.

All right, all right, just quiet *down*! Couldn't hear the *jejebhai* having triplets with you carrying on like that. Be quiet, I'll tell you the rest of it. Only if you do have a bad dream, I don't want to know anything about it. Me or anyone, that's agreed? Gods, how did I get *into* this?

So. This is what they did, then. They walked by him one at a time, the dead one, and each of them bowed his head and sniffed at him, really deeply, the same way they'd smelled your grandfather over, so carefully. It took a long time, because they were saying good-bye, not hello, and it was full dark when they all sat down to eat him.

You heard me. They ate him. They'd already cleaned him, same way you would with a fish, and now they built a big fire to see by—that was the first time your grandfather knew they could do that, they never had before—and they sat down together and ate that dead Qu'alo all gone. Only time he ever saw them eat meat, too. Don't make those silly faces—I'm telling you, that's what they did. It took them till dawn.

Listen to me, stop making those *faces*. Do you know what your Grandfather Selsim said about it? He said it was beautiful, somehow it was the most beautiful thing he ever saw. They sat around that scaffold in the dark, those huge creatures, and they talked, their voices not just low but soft, sad, gentle, a way he'd never heard them. He couldn't make out a word, even sitting close, but he knew they were talking about their friend. And at the same time they were eating him, they were praising him and honoring him and loving him, you understand? It wasn't like people gobbling and grunting over their dinner—it was different, it was beautiful. That's exactly what your grandfather said.

It took all night, I told you that. And at the end of it, with the morning rolling up over the trees, there wasn't a thing left on the platform but these long, clean bones shining there. Yes, sure, the skull too, what do you think? Nothing but giant bones, and they buried those in a special place, your grandfather never would say where. And that was what the Qu'alo did when a Qu'alo died.

The way old Dudrilashashek explained to your grandfather, they did it for two reasons. "First, the rock-*targs*," he said. "We have taught them fear, who would never have known such a thing but for us. They are almost, almost intelligent, but not quite, and they think there are thousands of us, they think we never die. If they dug up a body, if they realized how few we are, and how mortal, we would never know peace again. Then there is another thing." He didn't say anything for some while, but your grandfather just sat and waited. Being some better at that than he used to be.

And finally Dudrilashashek told him, "It is our way of keeping the one who dies with us forever. The flesh is unimportant, and passes through us, but what remains— our lives, our thoughts, our memories, our time in the world—the very last of the Qu'alo will contain all that, contain us all, every one ever. And when that last one is gone ..." Your Grandfather Selsim said he shrugged so slowly, so heavily that it was like watching a whole mountain range being born and dying, all in one motion. Dudrilashashek said, "Well," and nothing more.

Eighteen years, then. Eighteen years, your Grandfather Selsim lived on Torgry Mountain with the Qu'alo, and one by one he watched them go. Never a wound or an injury, never a sickness that he could see—they just died, one or two a year. Young ones, old, he didn't ever learn to tell much difference, except for the few he'd become a little friendly with. Jalayakudrilak, who could tell you weeks ahead what the weather was going to be; Tudoguraj, who loved to sing, imagine a giant chirping and twittering away like a tree full of hatchlings; and there was one called Rumirideyol, the only Qu'alo who refused to kill rock-*targs* if she could avoid it, and wept afterward when she couldn't. Cali and Gali went together—your grandfather was glad of that. He was the one who found them, lying side by side, one brother's head on the other's shoulder, and not a mark on them. One by one.

Mind now, this is going to sound really silly, and I don't want one solitary snicker out of you. Mind me. When you're down to just a handful of giants, it gets hard to do what you have to do with your dead. Are you laughing? You'd better not be laughing. The Qu'alo managed all right, but it was harder and sadder for them each time they came to sit around that brush-covered ceremonial platform. When Dudrilashashek went, your grandfather cried. He liked that old windbag of a giant, he missed him till the day he died himself. He even wanted to take part in the—you know, what they did—but Yriadvele wouldn't let him. She said it wasn't right, not while one Qu'alo lived, so that was that. But she let him dance with them, his little hops and thumps like the ghost of the dead one's dance. And he always helped to bury the great, shining bones.

Couldn't he have escaped, with so few giants to watch him? Well, of course, he could have, they were a long way past caring about that. But he didn't want to—by then he belonged with them, can you understand that? He didn't want to leave them, they were his family by then, some way. That's all I know, that's all I can tell you.

And finally there wasn't a Qu'alo left but Yriadvele. After eighteen years. They stayed very close together now, the giant woman and your grandfather—he said they even slept together, with him under her arm like a baby bird. She didn't seem likely to die any minute, but neither had the others, so he wasn't going to take chances. That winter, in the cave they'd been using for so long, he slept dreaming that spring had come and she wouldn't wake, he dreamed that over and over, waking himself up each time to make sure she was still breathing. Then he'd go back to sleep and dream it again. Like you when you're waiting for your birthday.

And it came true, that dream, near as makes no difference. Oh, she woke when it was time, but not completely, never all the way. She couldn't walk at all the first day or two, and your Grandfather Selsim had to forage for her. Well, there's no chance you can find enough food to fill a twelve-foot giant, especially one who hasn't eaten all winter. Maybe it would have been all right if she'd been able to feed herself, I don't know. He said even when she could walk she hardly ate a thing, but she was thirsty all the time and mostly stayed by a stream which had just wakened up itself. Her eyes were the color of cobwebs, not black as they should be, and her coat had that flat, staring, sticky look to it you don't ever want to see on a *rishu*, a *jejebhai* even a miserable *dhrushindi*. She didn't say a word, and your grandfather didn't know what to do except stay with her.

And finally she said to him, "You take me there."

"No," he said. "No, there's no need, there's nothing wrong with you, you're just still sleepy. You need to eat more, that's all."

But she put her hands on him in a way she never had done before. She touched his shoulders, and his face, and she took his head between those hands that could have crushed it like a rotten old *chouka* nut. Her poor streaked eyes were looking straight into his, and whatever she saw there, it made her smile a little. He'd never seen her smile at him just like that before, not in eighteen years.

"Time, Shelshim," she said. "Time, friend."

He said it took all day to get where they were going. She wasn't walking very well, and he couldn't support her, and he couldn't do much for her when she fell. Must have been like a tree going down, except a tree doesn't make a sound when it's hurt, and it can't clutch and scrabble and claw itself back up again. Once she tumbled into a ravine and lay there so long without moving he thought she really was dead, but when he climbed down to her, she opened her eyes, grabbed out to catch a root or a branch and started over. Come sundown, they were standing by that rickety scaffold where all her people before had rested one last time. She was staring down at it, holding herself as straight as she could, but her head was rolling on her neck, and she smelled wrong. The last day or so, that good Qu'alo stink had all faded, just thinned out and blown away. Now she just smelled like any old animal.

He said, "I can't do it, you know I can't. Even if I could make myself do it, I'm a human, I'm too small. It'd take me forever." He laughed a little, saying it, hoping she'd laugh, too.

"Bones, Shelshim," she said. Her voice was such a whisper that he couldn't feel it in his body anymore; she actually had to pick him up one last time, bring him close to hear. "*Bones*, Shelshim. Cover me, leave me, you come back sometime. Please, Shelshim."

He didn't understand. He said, "To bury your bones. Of course I'll do that for you. I can do that."

She shook him then—not hard, nothing like the way they did with the rock-*targs*, but his head still jolted back and forth and his arms flapped around, weak as she was. "Eat," she said. "The bones, eat. Not gone, so, not gone. Keep us, Shelshim."

And those were the last words Yriadvele ever spoke to him. She lay down on the platform, and your grandfather covered her with the softest new boughs and twigs and leaves he could find, and she just nodded when he had it right, and closed her eyes. He sat by her all that day and night, but he couldn't tell when she died.

He would have buried her right then, if he could have, to keep the rock-*targs* from finding her body and learning that the Qu'alo were mortal and gone. But there wasn't anything he could do, not for her, not for them, so he went away and he waited, the way she told him to. I can't tell you how long—how long does it take insects, little animals to strip away the rotting flesh from a twelve-foot giant? All I know is, as long as it took, your Grandfather Selsim lived alone in the woods, same way he'd lived for eighteen years. Except now he slept in the giants' old nests for the comfort of the smell, and he said he talked a lot to imaginary human beings, because he needed the practice after such a time of thinking Qu'alo thoughts in Qu'alo silence. And he thought about the world he almost remembered, and about what Yriadvele had asked of him, and whenever it was that he finally went back to the scaffold and pulled away the dead branches, there were the bones, and he knew what to do with them. You're making faces again, stop it.

No, there hadn't been any rock-*targs* there, he could tell. They wouldn't come anywhere near the smell of the Qu'alo, as they still won't, all these years later. Your grandfather took Yriadvele's bones, one by one, and he ground them up as fine as he could, stone against flat stone, and he ate them. No, I don't know how long it took him, what they tasted like. I don't know if he just ate them or drank them in water, or sprinkled them over some nice *kami* leaves. All I'm sure of is that he ate Yriadvele's bones, all of them, and then he stood up from there and he walked back to the trail over Torgry Mountain, and on down the other side, and he kept walking. And in time he came to this flat, hazy country where we live today, and settled to farming, and married and started our family, all that time ago. And that's the end of the story, and I'm in the barn, and you're asleep, good night.

What? Well, I told you, that's why we're all tall, that's why I know you'll be tall soon enough. *Now* do you understand me? We're whatever's left of the Qu'alo, you and me and the rest of our family—they're in *our* bones now, because of your Grandfather Selsim and his giant friend. Mind, we just got a bit of their height that's all; we didn't get the hairiness or the stink—the gods do get something right once in a while. And if any of us got any of those great, slow, wonderful thoughts, I surely haven't noticed it. But maybe those are inside you, who knows? Who knows what a little boy who can't keep his eyes open to ask any more questions is thinking, hey? Good night, then, good night.

What? In ten bloody years, that's when I'll have the strength to tell you another story. Most exhausting work I ever did. I swear I don't know how your mother manages every night. And that bloody *jejebhai*'s going to wait till I'm finally asleep, I know that much for certain. Good night, boy. Let go of my hand. Good *night*.

Peter S. Beagle is the bestselling author of such highly acclaimed fantasy classics as *The Last Unicorn*, *A Fine and Private Place*, and *The Innkeeper's Song*. He and his wife, the Indian writer-photographer Padma Hejmadi, live in Davis, California.